D1806498

CHERUBS 2

—A Josh Haman Novel—

CHERUBS 2

—A Josh Haman Novel—

by Marc Liebman

Cherubs 2 by Marc Liebman

Copyright © 2015 Marc Liebman

All rights reserved. No part of this book may be used or reproduced by any means without the written permission of the publisher except in the case of brief quotation embodied in critical articles and reviews.
This is a work of historical fiction. While based upon historical events, any similarity to any person, circumstance or event is purely coincidental and related to the efforts of the author to portray the characters in historically accurate representations.

ISBN-978-1-61179-355-0   (Paperback)
ISBN 978-1-61179-356-7   (e-book)

BISAC Subject Headings:
FIC014000FICTION / Historical
FIC032000FICTION / War and Military
FIC0012000FICTION / Action

Address all correspondence to:
Fireship Press, LLC
P.O. Box 68412
Tucson, AZ 85737
Or visit our website at:
www.FireshipPress.com

Table of Contents

The Vietnam Theater of Operations: Cherubs and Angels

In military aviation, cherubs and angels are **not** esoteric references to mythical beings. They're terms used to indicate altitude of an aircraft or helicopter. In U.S. Navy parlance, 'angels' refer to altitude units of 1,000 feet, and 'cherubs' refer to altitude units of 100 feet. If a naval aviator says he is at "Angels 8" he is telling everyone listening on the frequency that his aircraft is at 8,000 feet. If he reports his altitude as "Cherubs 2," those listening would know that his aircraft or helicopter is at 200 feet.

At sea, day or night, en route altitudes for helicopters are 500 feet or less, unless there is a reason to fly higher.

Radio communications is an area that appears to be repetitive, but there's a reason for this. The structure was designed to ensure understanding, and by repeating what he or she is told, an aviator is signaling that the directions are understood.

Then there are call signs and numbers which can be spoken in a variety of ways. The "official" way to speak the number 500 is "five zero zero." However, "five oh oh" and "five double zero" are often used. I've even heard "five double donuts," which was further shortened to "five double nuts"!

During a combat rescue, there are four main elements: the survivor, the helicopter or helicopters tasked to pick up the survivor, the airplanes flying close air support, and the individual coordinating the rescue effort. So there are a lot of people transmitting on the radio, and keeping track of who is speaking to whom, about what, and who is supposed to do what, can get very confusing. Maintaining situational awareness is a key and often difficult task. In the book, I have tried to give readers a taste of what it is like, without putting in all the radio transmissions and acknowledgements.

Author's Note

On the continuum of personal action in combat: at one end is the range of reckless behavior which, depending on the outcome, some call insane, others call courageous. Activities at this end of the continuum are easy to identify and are often immortalized in movies, medals and legends.

Moving toward the other end of the continuum, there is the more cautious, or, some might say, more rational behavior, that avoids risk and danger whenever possible. It is at this end that we find a very fine line between caution and outright cowardice.

Most members of the military hope that no matter what we do, the "C" word—coward—is never associated with any action that we take. I dare say many of us would rather die than be called a coward. We take pride in the shared knowledge that we didn't let our fellow servicemen down; we came to their aid when they were in trouble and, most importantly, didn't leave them behind when they were injured or dead.

Marc Liebman
November, 2014

Prologue

Derek Van der Jagt had not seen the outside of a jail cell in over a month, not since he had been arrested for his part in a liquor store robbery. Today he had been allowed to take a shower, even though it was not "his" day, because he was appearing in court. In the overcrowded jail, inmates were allowed a five-minute shower every third day. The showers weren't bad, if you didn't mind being watched by a guard and soaping down with five others. The worst part was the smell, a mix of moldy shower curtain and harsh disinfectant. Now Derek was sitting with his back to the wall, eyes closed, wondering what would come next. He was wearing an orange jumpsuit and ill-fitting sneakers; he was handcuffed, and a chain ran from the cuffs to a set of manacles around his ankles.

In June, Van der Jagt had graduated from high school. In July, he was in jail. He felt as if he was on a conveyor belt to prison with no chance of getting off.

"Van der Jagt. Your turn. Let's go!" The words and the metallic sound of the holding cell gate being unlocked brought him this feet.

He shuffled into the courtroom to the defendant's table and sat beside his attorney, a middle-aged man named John Bristol, a trial lawyer who occasionally did public defender's work pro bono. Bristol was resplendent in a three piece, charcoal grey, pin-stripe suit. The 22-carat gold cuff links on his white shirt were visible when he sat down.

Derek looked around the room and didn't see any friendly faces. Neither of his parents were there, but he didn't expect them to show. They were working.

When Judge Eisemann looked up, he focused his attention on Derek. "Before we begin this pre-trial hearing, I would like to have a short, on the record conversation with Mr. Van der Jagt. The results may change this young man's life and save the State of New

York the cost of a trial and possible incarceration. Mr. Van der Jagt, please stand."

After Derek struggled to his feet and made eye contact, Judge Eisemann continued.

"Derek Van der Jagt, you have been indicted as an accessory to second degree manslaughter in which the owner of a liquor store was killed. The only reason I am taking this step is that you did not pull the trigger. In fact, you were not in the store when the murder took place, because you were sitting at the wheel of the getaway car. Both of your accomplices have stated that."

The judge leaned forward. "Assuming that you are found guilty as an accomplice, I would be required by the New York Penal Code Section 125.25 to sentence you to a prison term of between fifteen and twenty-five years. That's a long time, even for an eighteen year old. Do you understand the seriousness of the charge and the length of the possible sentence?"

Van der Jagt spoke clearly, trying not to let his fear show.

"Yes, sir. I do."

Bristol had told him to keep his answers short and to the point.

"Good. I see that you graduated in the top ten percent of your high school class. Looking at your transcript, your grades could have gotten you into college. Why didn't you apply?"

"Money. I didn't have a job, and my parents couldn't afford to send me to college."

"Is this your first run-in with the law?"

"No, sir. I was arrested when I was sixteen for beating up a guy. He was pushing a boy around, so I got between them. He started the fight, and I finished it when I broke his jaw and knocked him out. The cops showed up and arrested me. There were a lot of witnesses who backed me up. I was later cleared in juvenile court, sir."

Judge Eisemann pursed his lips and took a deep breath. He'd talked to the school principal and two teachers. His mind raced back to 1940, when *he'd* stood before a judge for breaking and entering and attempted robbery. He had been told, "Army, Navy, Marine Corps, or jail—pick one." He'd spent the next five years on a destroyer in the

Pacific and had seen action in every major campaign, from Guadalcanal to dodging kamikazes off Okinawa. He'd started as a seaman and finished as a Chief Gunner's Mate. After the war, he'd used the new G.I. Bill to go to college and law school. The military had saved his life, and he wanted to give others the same chance.

"Young man, I am going to give you a choice that will, if you accept it, give you a second chance. If you accept it and meet the requirements, after a period of time, the court and police records of your arrest will be sealed and not available to anyone for the rest of your life. It will be as if all this never happened. Are you interested?"

Van der Jagt didn't hesitate. He'd had enough of jail. He responded with an emphatic "Yes, sir."

Eisemann thought that lack of hesitation in the kid's voice was a positive sign. "Good. Here is the deal. If you agree to serve in the U.S. Armed Forces for six years, AND during your enlistment you do not have any, repeat, *any* disciplinary problems, then when the proper documentation is certified by the service, this court will expunge the records. In other words, go serve your country, do it honorably, and all this will go away. Are you with me so far?"

Van der Jagt nodded. "Yes, sir."

The judge continued. "Sitting behind you in the courtroom is Petty Officer First Class James Bellamy, a recruiter from the Navy. When you leave this courtroom, the restraints will be removed. Petty Officer Bellamy will prepare and you will sign the enlistment papers for a six year term. You'll also sign a document that will go into your service record and into the court records that outline the conditions under which you have been released. You will get your civilian clothes back and be given a plane ticket and explicit instructions on how to get to boot camp. If you do not report on time, a warrant for your arrest will be issued immediately; you will be brought back to this courtroom and tried. Assuming you are found guilty, you will get the maximum I can give you. So it is up to you." Judge Eisemann's gaze held the young man. "Do I make myself clear?"

Van der Jagt responded with another firm "Yes, sir."

"Excellent." Eisemann made a note and then looked back at the eighteen year old. "Once at boot camp, you will join the next class and you are on your way. When your enlistment is up, you'll bring or send by certified mail to this court a certified original of your separation papers, which must, and I repeat *must*, include an honorable discharge; or, if you decide to stay in the Navy, your re-enlistment papers. At that point, the court will begin the process and provide certification to you that the records have in fact been expunged. If, at the end of your enlistment, you need help, please call the clerk of this court. Are you willing to accept these terms?"

"Yes, sir. Absolutely."

"Excellent. Let the record show that Derek Van der Jagt has decided to enlist in the United States Navy, and the matter of the State of New York versus Derek Van der Jagt has been put on hold pending completion of his first enlistment."

Map of Vietnam

Chapter 1 – THE CENTRE

Monday, August 24th, 1970,
2246 Local Time, Moscow

The high-wing Antonov-12 cargo transport plane shut its engines off on Khodinka Airport's vacant and unlit west ramp in front of a large, dull gray building known by those who worked there as "The Centre".

Western intelligence officers on the other side of the Iron Curtain referred to the concrete structure by its initials, GRU. Glavnoye Razvedyvatel'noye Upravleniye was the headquarters of the Soviet military intelligence agency.

As the turbo prop engines wound down, Major Pavel Mironov drove a small truck to the back of the airplane to meet its only passenger and the all-important cargo.

"Good evening, Maxim. How was your flight?"

"Much too long. But we got here. I was able to sleep much of the way because of this."

Captain Maxim Goncharov, a computer engineer in the operational technical directorate of the GRU, pulled out the plug of an olive drab air mattress, which began to deflate with a sustained hiss.

"It is American made; I got it in Hanoi. Along with earplugs, it makes long distance air travel on a military transport bearable."

Pavel Mironov had graduated college as a mechanical engineer. After impressing his first boss in the GRU, he had been sent off to get an advanced degree in electrical engineering. He had been examining Western electrical equipment for over ten years when he was tapped for this assignment.

"Let's get our new toy off to the lab," Mironov said, as he hopped onto the airplane's cargo ramp. "So what exactly *is* this...and is it intact?"

"This, my friend, is the KY-7 American encryption device. Our Vietnamese comrades assured me that they included all the attachments and cables that go with it. I have the manual on how to operate it in my briefcase. When I was not sleeping on the plane, I read it." The two men slid the crate onto the back of the truck.

"Maxim, how did the Vietnamese get this?"

"They overran the headquarters of a South Vietnamese army division, and it was sitting on a table in their command center. The North Vietnamese were smart enough not to blow it up. I was told that it took three months to bring it up the trail to Hanoi. And they considered that a fast trip!"

"Three months? But it's only 800 kilometers!"

"Yeah. At first it was carried by four men on a pallet through the jungle. Then the case was strapped to the back of a bicycle, and the rider walked along the edge of the Ho Chi Minh trail. Once they got the KY-7 north of the demilitarized zone, they put it on a truck. A senior officer realized what they had and assigned a squad of soldiers and two intelligence officers to get it to Hanoi. They were bombed several times along the way, but, lucky for us, they arrived with the KY-7 undamaged. It is in the original shipping case the Americans provided. Our own embassy built this wooden crate to conceal the markings. Once we get it out of the box, the handles will make the KY-7 easy to move around."

Goncharov tossed his briefcase into the cab and got into the passenger seat.

"And the Vietnamese sold it to us?" Mironov assumed their allies didn't just give it to the GRU out of the goodness of their hearts.

"*Sold* may not be the right word; *traded* might be better," Maxim replied as Pavel drove toward The Center's entrance. "Anyway, we have it now. An embassy colonel by the name of Rokossovsky told me that in the greater scheme of things, the machine didn't cost that much, but the Vietnamese did extract a stiff price. He was pretty sure that the Vietnamese talked to the North Koreans, who told them of our trip to Wonsan to examine the encryption equipment on the American spy ship, the *Pueblo.* That conversation probably increased the price."

"Maxim, tell me the most important thing: does it work?"

"Yes. I hooked it up and ran it while I was in Hanoi. I fed in one of the key cards I brought with me, along with information from one of the tapes we recorded from American radio transmissions before we agreed to take it. So, yes, it does work."

"Good. The head of the Operational Technical Directorate will be pleased. All of a sudden, we're very popular. I've had inquiries from several officers in the Fifth Directorate anxious to know if we can provide timely, operational intelligence. While you were gone, the admiral who runs the Fleet Intelligence Directorate wanted to know how long we thought it might take to test the machine and start producing decrypted messages. And, of course, we have our fellow officers in the Ninth Directorate who want to understand western technology and examine our little machine. I wanted to tell them all to fuck off, but instead I told them that we have to test it out, make sure it works, try a few messages, and then run small batches before we can report."

As Pavel spoke, the two men hoisted the crate and struggled down the corridor towards their work space.

"And let me guess, they all want results now, and the more senior the officer is, the less patience he has."

"Maxim, there is hope for you. You understand our problem."

"So the pressure is on. What else is new? At least it didn't come with threats."

"Well, threats were implied but not stated. They can send us to the Gulag at any time." Mironov chocked open the door to their lab. "Sometime later this week, we are supposed to get a series of recorded messages that we are to run through the machine. In that package, there will be a series of code keys that we match to the dates on the messages that were recorded. If they match, we'll get lots of good information. If not, we have to figure out why not. We can start testing in the morning."

Tuesday, August 25th, 1970,
0700 Local Time, Moscow

When Pavel Gronchov entered his five-digit code in the cipher lock to the lab, he was surprised to see Major Mironov sitting next to the machine with the manual open. "Maxim, how long have you been here?"

"About an hour. Just long enough to brew some tea and unpack the machine. It came with a small printer. Just as well; the big teletype printer that we are supposed to get still has not arrived."

"I'm not surprised."

"Maxim, go get some tea and then let's start with the check-out procedure. The manual is quite detailed on what we need to do. We can use the keys you brought with you to Hanoi to check it out."

When the first batch of taped messages and code keys arrived that afternoon, a day early, Pavel signed for the box and turned to his comrade. "Ah, Maxim, I often marvel at the efficiency of our Socialist economy! We get the material provided by an American spy before we get the printer our procurement people promised months ago. I was told it would be here today. The Ninth Directorate has been telling me that for a week. Still, no machine!"

"Never mind. Are you ready to see if we go to the Gulag, or become Heroes of the Soviet Union?" Maxim Gronchov was used to Pavel's gallows humor, and not-so-politically-correct opinions, which he shared privately, not publicly. Such remarks could be dangerous. However, he was sure their supervisors didn't want to send such a talented engineer to Siberia.

"I am. Let's do it. The cover letter says this was one day's worth of messages from Commander, Pacific Fleet to the Commander, U.S. Naval Forces Vietnam."

Thirty minutes later, the small printer stopped.

"This is too easy!" Gronchov looked at the pile of decrypted messages. My God, this is gold. We would never be able to decode these messages with our own computers. The GRU must have an American traitor giving them the code keys. "I wonder how fast they can get us the information. These messages are from May."

Gronchov wondered if they contained any information that would still be useful after three months.

Chapter 2 – FIRST MISSION

"Mac" MacIntosh sat in what had been the navigator's seat of the twin engine Douglas B-66, before the former bomber converted to an electronic warfare aircraft, designated an EB-66.

From his seat, he could look forward over the pilot's right shoulder. Next to him was the senior electronic warfare officer and behind him, there were two more electronic warfare officers sitting next to each other. These men sat in downward firing ejection seats in a windowless, pressurized compartment dimly lit by red dome lights.

General Lester MacIntosh, the new commander of the Thirteenth Air Force, was forbidden to fly over North Vietnam, but he wanted to see what his aircrews were facing, so he'd hitched a ride. Supposedly the airplane would be over Laos and not enter North Vietnamese airspace, but there were no signposts and the only navigational aids were back in Thailand, more than 150 miles to their rear.

He'd flown his last combat mission in F-84 fighter-bombers during the Korean War. He wanted to see if electronic warfare had changed the fundamentals of tactical airpower. His gut told him that EW—as it was often called—had not affected the basics.

As the EB-66 flew in its prescribed racetrack pattern, he could see the green, tree-covered mountains of northwestern North Vietnam. He was thinking that he'd spent way too many years in billets that were "good for his career." It may have helped him get promoted to general, but they'd kept him away from flying with front line Air Force squadrons.

"Where's the strike package?" asked MacIntosh.

He was trying to recall details from the briefing. He couldn't even remember the pilot's name. He was struggling to keep up and he was uneasy, because his brain and combat experience were telling him that a lack of situational awareness was usually fatal.

The pilot turned his head slightly as he keyed his mike. "General, North Vietnam is about twenty miles at our ten o'clock and we're about to turn east. That's when the fun starts."

MacIntosh was unfamiliar with the equipment in front of him. "Any gook radars up yet?"

"No, sir. They're pretty cagey. They won't turn them on until the Thuds, I mean the F-105s and the F-4s, get in range. We'll see the missile radars first because our gear is more sensitive and often the radars emit signals in their warm-up mode. Once they start looking for targets, the guys in the back get pretty busy."

"Do they ever shoot missiles at us?"

"All the time. We even get the occasional burst of flak, particularly when orbiting the trail. They only shoot the SA-2s at us when we venture deeper into North Vietnam to get our transmitters closer to the radar to improve the effectiveness of our jamming."

MacIntosh knew "the trail" was the North Vietnamese's logistics supply line. The U.S. referred to as the Ho Chi Minh Trail, which was actually a misnomer. In reality, it was a network of asphalt-surfaced roads and wide trails mostly on the Laotian side of the border that allowed the North Vietnamese to keep its army in South Vietnam well supplied.

"They told me when I said I wanted to go flying with you that these were always milk runs."

"Sir, whoever told you that lied. If you wanted a milk run, you should have flown with the EC-121s or the tankers, but even they get shot at every so often. I've brought back two birds with engine failures and dodged missiles on almost every mission. The EB-66 is pretty heavy and doesn't like to fly on one engine, so if an engine does fail it is a long, extended glide back. If we're lucky, we'll make it. If not, we get to punch out. A least we have ejection seats, unlike the Navy versions. The guys in the back go down and those of us in front go up!"

The pilot held up his hand while he listened to chatter on the radio. The navigator was halfway through answering when MacIntosh heard an unfamiliar screeching in the headset.

"This is ECMO 1. We're targeted. Fan Son radar strobe at six o'clock. Launch confirmed." The calm voice came from the most senior electronic warfare officer sitting in the ejection seat next to MacIntosh. He was known as ECMO-1.

"Rattlesnake 76, Jingo 55, multiple missile launches at your six. Break hard right now. We're rolling in on the launch site now." Jingo 55 was the flight leader of four F-105F Wild Weasel aircraft accompanying the EB-66, whose call sign for this mission was Rattlesnake 76.

"Everyone, make sure you're harnesses are locked. Rolling and turning now." The pilot rolled the twin engine jet into a sixty degree bank and shoved the throttles forward to the stops as he pulled two g's. MacIntosh was pushed down in the seat and felt his cheeks sag under the oxygen mask.

"Pilot, ECMO 1, jamming now." The speaker's voice sounded strained; the crew members in the first row of seats experienced about a half a g more than the pilot did, while the back row was pulling a full g more.

The radar warning system showed two strobes. "Jingo 55, we're showing two missiles coming up at us. Any more?"

"This is Jingo 55, I saw three going up at Rattlesnake."

Shit, MacIntosh thought, *where are they? Why do we only show two and they see three?* MacIntosh's feet came off the floor as the pilot shoved the nose down and rolled the aircraft. "Crew, I can see one... now two missiles going stupid. Are there any more?"

"Pilot, ECMO 1, if there are, we don't show them. We jammed their telemetry pretty bad and they could never lock on us after launch. I think the tapes will show that they shot four missiles at us."

"Shit."

The pilot pulled the nose up and the EB-66 climbed back to its assigned racetrack pattern altitude of 33,000 feet.

* * * * *

Two-and-a-half hours later, the general left the crew of Rattlesnake 76 in the debriefing room and headed to the office occupied by Colonel Wilson, Thirteenth Air Force's intelligence officer.

The full-bird colonel came to attention when the lieutenant general walked into his office with oxygen mask lines around his face. "Sir, how did your flight go?"

The general ignored the question.

"Colonel Wilson, you need to figure out how the North Vietnamese get so many fucking missiles. If I didn't know better, I'd say they were expecting us and knew our route as well as we did. They fired four just at my plane, and at times there were so many missiles incoming, it looked like a Fourth of July fireworks show!"

"Sir, the Soviets ship them in by the boatload. Literally. The Navy takes pictures of the ships and the docks every day and counts the crates containing the missiles. Next, we count them as they are trucked to the launch site. Our guess is that we see about 70 or 80 per cent of them on the road. We bomb those that we find, count what we think we destroy, and then adjust the inventory. It's been the best way we've come up with to determine how many they have on hand. But it's not perfect and we really don't know what they are holding in reserve," explained Wilson.

"Well, they fired a whole boatload at us today. If that's the rate of expenditure, they have to have another source."

"Sir, there is a rail line that comes down from Mengzi and crosses the border here." Wilson pointed to a thin cross-hatched line on the chart on his wall.

"Then about ten miles south, there is a marshaling yard at Ha Giang. Our rules of engagement don't allow us to attack it. Imagery shows the yard is always full on the Vietnamese side of the border. Then there is another rail line that comes down from Nanning and crosses into North Vietnam about 50 miles northwest of Hanoi."

"Show me." MacIntosh had arrived in Europe in mid-1944, had flown P-47s, and was one of many pilots who'd shut down the German rail transportation system by shooting up locomotives and any rolling stock they could find.

Wilson pulled a folder out of the bottom drawer of his four-drawer safe. "Sir, these were taken by either drones or RF-101s. You can see that the Ha Giang yard is full of all kinds of rolling stock— box cars, flat beds and even some tank cars. The flat beds often have artillery pieces of various types on them that they get from the Chinese, but we haven't a clue what is in the box cars."

"Find out."

"Yes, sir. I'll try."

"If you can't, let's find someone who can."

Same Day, 2046 Local Time, on the U.S.S. Sterett

The clammy, humid smell of the Gulf of Tonkin was the first thing to hit Lieutenant Junior Grade Josh Haman in the face when he walked down the cargo ramp.

The acrid combination of rotting vegetation, salty sea air, warm cooking grease from the base operations canteen, and burnt jet fuel assaulted his sense of smell. Then the heat and humidity condensed on his Ray-Ban sunglasses, making it impossible to see until it was wiped off. It also turned his starched khakis to soft, damp, wrinkled cotton.

Josh's mind and senses were still reeling. A week ago, after returning from a two week jungle survival school, he had been told he was *not* going to fly the HH-3A in which he was trained. After that bit of information, he had been rushed through a ten flight, twenty hour familiarization course in the HH-2C, which weighed just over 12,000 pounds on take off and had a rotor diameter of only forty feet, compared to the HH-3A's design take off weight of 19,000 pounds and rotor diameter of fifty-five feet.

Half of the twenty flight hours Josh flew in the H-2 were focused on using the three-barreled mini-gun, installed by the squadron with help from technical representatives from Kaman, the helicopter's manufacturer, and GE, the maker of the gun.

The rest of the time had been spent in the Cubi Point Naval Air Station traffic pattern doing approaches to a hover and in a hover, sliding the HH-2C left and right and forward and back around a square at ten feet off the ground.

Eight hours ago, with his logbook showing he had a whopping three hundred and twenty-one hours of flight time in the Navy, he'd boarded a Grumman C-2 cargo plane in the Philippines that brought him to Cam Ranh Bay in South Vietnam.

Four hours later, after depositing his gear and a hurried meal in the officers' mess, he was standing on the helicopter deck of the 8,000-ton guided missile destroyer, pre-flighting a helicopter with a flashlight for his first mission. Night flying in the H-2 was not included in the 20 hours training he'd gotten in Cubi. Between the training command and the H-3 syllabus, his logbook showed that he had 75 hours of night time.

On the flight deck, Josh enjoyed the fresh smell of the gulf and a gentle warm breeze made by the ship moving through the water at an economical twelve knots. It was different from the characteristic odor of a ship he remembered from his cruises as a Navy ROTC midshipman. That aroma, composed of sea water used for flushing, urine, and chlorine, along with food and machinery smells, was instantly recognizable.

All ships have the same ingredients, but the recipe is different, so each ship has its own scent. As soon as you leave the ship, it is gone; but when you enter the first hatch, it hits you with an immediacy that tells you that you are back.

Josh was stuffing the flashlight back into his helmet bag that was lying on the co-pilot's seat when he heard a voice behind him.

"Ready to go?" It was the helicopter aircraft commander and Helicopter Combat Support Squadron Detachment 104 officer-in-charge, Lieutenant Steve Higgins. Annapolis graduate, class of 1966 and don't you forget it. "How many chains?"

"Yes, sir. Four chains, two on each main mount. The helicopter is up. I didn't find anything on the preflight," Josh replied calmly enough, but internally his mind gibbered. Shit, who knows what I missed? I've completed all of 15 pre-flights of an HH-2C in my life, all of which were in daylight. The squadron commanding officer signed a letter waiving the minimum number of hours needed to qualify me as a co-pilot. I had just 20, and the NATOPS manual says you need at least 30. So what the fuck do I know? Shit, two weeks ago, I learned that those in the know referred to helicopter detachments on board ships were known as dets and supposedly, one only used the full word in official correspondence. Yet, people in the squadron used the words det and detachment in the same sentence. So, that's what I'll do.

"Where are the air crewmen?"

"Sitting on the other side of the helo's cabin, sir."

"Good, let's mount up."

Josh tracked the checklist items as they worked their way to engine start.

"I'll let the ship know that we're ready." Higgins keyed the radio, "Battle Torch, this is Clementine 26, ready to start engines," then rotated the mike switch up to the intercom position. "They'll either respond by radio or announce it on the loudspeaker. If they do that, the plane captain will hear it and give us the signal to start by pointing his wand at the number one engine and waving his wand in a tight circle."

Josh nodded his head enough to be seen, rather than touching the cyclic to use the intercom. He remembered that Higgins had told him Battle Torch was the call sign of the *Sterett.*

"Clementine, this is Battle Torch, you are cleared to start engines. Report when ready for take off."

"O.K., here goes." Higgins engaged the starter motor as he spoke. "Starting number one." He pointed in the general direction of the gauge that showed the percent engine rpm. "Gas generator is at eighteen percent."

Josh watched as the oil pressure and exhaust gas temperature gauges showed a normal start. "Gauges are good and the engine is at eighty-eight percent," he reported.

"Starting number two." Higgins didn't wait for the plane captain to move with his hand-held fire extinguisher from the right side to the left before starting the second engine.

In seconds, Josh saw the needles on the gauges of both engines aligned, indicating that everything was good to go for rotor engagement. "Temps and pressures are normal. Ready to engage. Engines are in the fly position."

Higgins stuck his hand out the door and twirled it in a circle. The enlisted man with the fire extinguisher responded by waving his light wand in a circle over his head. "Engaging." Higgins reached up and released the rotor brake and the HH-2C rocked back and forth as the rotor blades picked up speed.

Seconds later Josh reported, "Rotor RPM is at one hundred and two percent."

"Take off check list."

Josh read off the six items that were on a placard on the instrument panel. "Take off checklist complete, except for removing the chocks and chains. We're ready to go. Do you want to let the ship know?"

"You do it," Lieutenant Higgins replied shortly. "Your job is communication, navigation, and shooting the gun. I'll fly."

Josh keyed the mike. "Battle Torch, Clementine 26 is ready for take off."

"Clementine 26, this is Battle Torch, you are cleared for take off. Wind is 30 degrees port at one-five. Altimeter is 29.94. Contact Red Crown on 315.3 when able."

"Battle Torch, this is Clementine 26, roger. Good night," Josh replied.

"Give the signal to pull the chocks and chains. Remember to count the tie-down chains. I don't want to have to try to lift the ship out of the water. It'll ruin all our day."

Josh winced at Higgins's reference to what happens when one or more of the tie-downs are not removed and the helicopter tries to take off. The videos he'd seen in San Diego made his stomach churn because they were horribly graphic. Failure to remove a tie-down before attempting a take off usually resulted in a crash of some sort, followed by a violent explosion as the helicopter came apart. The chances of survival were not good.

He watched as the plane captain and his assistant each held up two chains; they handed the red-flagged pins from the landing gear to one of the air crewman. "I've got four tie-down chains, and the two pins are aboard."

The plane captain swung his flashlight wand over his head in a circle and then pointed to the port side of the ship.

"Good. We got a green light. That's the light on top of the hangar, if you didn't know. They can either turn it on or tell us by radio or both. In any case, we're cleared to take off. Lifting now."

The dull red deck lighting that flooded the cockpit gave way to total darkness outside as the HH-2C pulled up and away from the Sterett. Once they got to two hundred feet and the gear was up, Josh pulled the chart from its position between his armored seat and the center console. "Sir, we should head about 220 to get to our assigned orbit. I'll switch the radio to the strike frequency."

"Heading two-two-zero, level at two hundred feet so we will stay under the North Vietnamese radar. Call Red Crown."

Higgins's head was focused on the instruments as he rolled the helicopter out on the new heading and added enough power so the helicopter accelerated to the best range cruising speed of ninety knots.

Josh clicked the mike twice. "Red Crown, this is Clementine 26, level cherubs 2, en route to assigned orbit, over."

"Roger, Clementine 26, this is Red Crown. Hammer 703 has control if we need your services and is on this frequency. Ident."

Josh pushed the button on the control box of the device known as the *Identification, friend or foe*, or IFF for short. The official nomenclature was the AN/APX-76 transponder. Josh saw a yellow light flash, which meant that the system was being interrogated.

"Clementine 26, this is Hammer 703, radar contact about five miles south southwest of Battle Torch."

Josh rogered the call. He looked down at the chart and noted that their assigned orbit was four miles off the coast and ten miles north of the North Vietnamese port of Vinh. A feeling of pride flashed through his mind as he thought that the radio exchange had sounded cool and professional, as if he knew what he was doing! The nervousness he'd felt before the flight had dissipated as he focused on trying to do his job.

"So what the fuck is in the bags you brought on board the *Sterett*?" Higgins's tone was more curious than accusatory.

"My B-4 bag had all my uniforms and civilian clothes, and the parachute bag had my survival vest, spare flight suits and shoes. Why?"

"You had over a hundred pounds of stuff. Who told you to bring all that shit?"

"The squadron admin officer in Cubi."

"That's bullshit. All you need out here are working khakis and at least three flight suits. We don't pull into any ports other than Cubi, so you don't need any civilian clothes. It is okay to have some civvies with you, just in case, but most of the time, you really don't need them."

"I'll know next time."

Neither spoke until Josh looked at the clock. They'd flown almost twenty minutes in silence at ninety knots. "Steve, we're entering the area where we need to orbit."

"Good. Let Red Crown know and I'll start a north-south orbit with three minute legs and right turns, which will keep us well off the coast. It will also keep us out of sight and mind of the North Vietnamese gunners on the coast, who tend to be very trigger happy."

Josh clicked the intercom twice and looked down at the transponder to make sure that the right codes were still set; the yellow light blinked several times, telling them that at least one friendly radar was interrogating their IFF equipment. "Red Crown, Clementine 26, on station, one hour to bingo, over."

"Clementine 26, Hammer 703, roger, radar contact. Copy sixty minutes of playtime."

"Now we wait and hope that no one gets bagged," said Higgins.

A flash off in the distance to his left caught Josh's eye. Higgins swore.

"Those are SA-2 Guideline surface-to-air missiles. You may see the flashes of the shells from the 85 millimeter anti-aircraft guns, and if the planes are below 10,000 feet, you'll see the streams of tracer from the 57s and maybe the 37 millimeter guns as well. Get much closer and it gets really evil in a hurry. What you don't see are the 23 millimeter guns and the 12.7s, which are the real danger to us."

Josh watched as a dozen more SA-2s headed skyward. Every so often, he would see a bright flash high up in the sky, and he wondered if the missile was exploding on command from the ground or near an airplane.

"We only have the one UHF radio and can listen to only one frequency. Some guys like to listen to the strike frequency. I prefer to stay on the channel given to us by the airborne controller. It's quieter, and if they need us, they'll call," Higgins commented.

Josh thought, *Wouldn't you want to know what's happening so you can anticipate things by breaking out of the orbit and heading toward the guy in the parachute? You don't need to wait for a beeper that tells you someone has punched out before you start closing the distance. The HH-3A instructors drilled into our heads that the faster you got to the survivor, the greater the chance you can pick him up. The longer he's on the ground, the greater the chance he'll be captured. I think I'd listen to the strike frequency, but you're the aircraft commander and this is my first mission. What do I know? I need to listen and learn. Some day I may have my own crew, and it will be my decision.*

As if sensing his thoughts, Higgins asked, "How much training time did they give you in the Charlie?"

Josh knew Higgins was referring to their helicopter's official designation, HH-2C. "Just over twenty hours. I took all three NATOPs tests and managed to pass them on the first try with scores I am not proud of, but I passed. I got about ten hours in the helicopter and proved that I could take off, land, hover over a spot and fly it on instruments. The rest of the time, I played with the mini-gun."

"How'd that go?"

"I got pretty good with the gun. The trick is to fire short, two or three second bursts, and walk the tracers into the target. This way you don't have to worry too much about lead and lag or overheating the barrel. Everything I was shooting at was stationary and it was all daylight. I got zero night hours, and never fired the gun at night."

"I'd prefer that we never have to use it." Higgins rolled the helicopter into a fifteen degree bank and held it for one hundred and eighty degrees of turn before rolling out on a southerly heading. "How long were you waiting at Cam Ranh Bay?"

"Five hours. I got there about ten. The guy in the passenger terminal had no idea that you were coming to pick me up and wanted to send me to the transient BOQ. The guys in Cubi said you'd be there between twelve and one."

"I knew you were coming, but not the day or time. We've been restricted to daylight logistics operations until you got here, since we can't fly at night with just one pilot. We can do rescues during the day, but it is dicey for one guy."

"Det 1 at Cubi gave me a copy of the message that was sent out two days ago saying when I would arrive. Didn't you get it?"

"I never saw it. I flew in to get the mail for the *Sterett*, which is sorted by around two, and you were there."

Josh didn't say anything. Somehow, he didn't believe Higgins. How could the detachment officer-in-charge not know when his one and only co-pilot would arrive, the one who would enable them to fly missions day and night? Something didn't add up.

"Did you sample the cuisine at the greasy spoon in the terminal building?" Higgins asked as he started his next turn.

"Yup. I've had worse." Josh looked at the instrument panel. "We're down to fifteen hundred pounds of fuel. We need five hundred to get home, plus two hundred for a reserve, which means as of this moment we can fly about ten, fifteen minutes to a survivor and hover for about five before we have to head back to the *Sterett*."

"Tell them we had ten minutes left. We won't have enough fuel to go get someone unless he lands right by us. I don't like to trundle around out here with my low fuel warning light on."

Josh used two clicks of the mike to acknowledge his aircraft commander's wish and spoke into the radio before asking, "So what happened to my predecessor? All I was told was that he fell and broke his leg. I don't even know his name."

"Jim Vickers had been out here for six months. I was going to recommend that we make him a HAC, but he tripped and fell down a ladder on the *Sterett*. It was a spiral fracture and the ship's doc sent him to the Marine hospital in Quang Tri. They put some screws in his shin and sent him back to the States."

"Ouch."

"So rather than find someone who was already qualified as a 2P in the H-2, I'm guessing they decided to train you as his replacement."

"It was a complete surprise," Josh explained. "I had just come back from my one-week vacation in the jungle, followed by a five-day stay in the Navy's version of a North Vietnamese POW camp, when they told me I was going to learn to fly the H-2 and was leaving in a week. With that, the ops officer tossed a NATOPS manual on the table and said, "Start studying, your first hop is right after lunch.""

"So now you are a happy member of Det 104."

The radio cut in. "Clementine 26, Hammer 703. You're cleared to return to Battle Torch."

"Hammer, Clementine 26, roger."

The radio call saved Josh from answering.

Tuesday, October 6th, 1970,
0737 Local Time, on the U.S.S. Sterett

ADJC (Aviation Jet Engine Mechanic) Chief Petty Officer Slaughter refilled his bright white coffee mug, the one with the *Sterett*'s crest emblazoned on one side, before he pulled a folded, hand-addressed, business-size envelope from the shirt pocket of his grease-stained khakis. No amount of washing would ever remove the embedded grease; it only made the splotches lighter.

He was sitting on the only stool in the maintenance and administrative space. The stool's position on the side of the compartment let him lean back against the bulkhead. An IBM Selectric typewriter was pushed off to the side and covered with a rag to keep dirt and dust out of its innards. Two metal racks welded to the bulkheads held a row of six inch wide binders containing the HH-2C's maintenance manuals. One, on the lower shelf, was the helicopter's log book. It was propped against an olive drab can on which black paint indicated that at one time it had contained an altimeter. Smaller lettering below denoted the specific type, serial number, contract under which it was procured, date it was delivered to the Navy, and other data useful to those in contract administration and the supply system.

Using a pocket knife, Chief Slaughter slit open the envelope that bore the words *For Official Use Only* in the upper left corner. His fingers left grease smudges on the brown paper. The address read *Private, hand deliver to ADJC James Slaughter*. He had been given the envelope last night with the terse comment, "Chief, I found this in one of the packages we got in the mail today from the Det 1 guys."

He recognized the handwriting of Chuck Zweibel, the squadron's most senior enlisted man at Cubi who, as a Master Chief Petty officer, was two pay grades his senior. He took a sip of his coffee as he started to read.

10/3/1970

Jim,

I wanted to write you a quick note about the new pilot the squadron just sent you, by the name of Haman. He's got the makings of a very good officer. The enlisted aircrew who went to jungle survival school with him said he is a leader who knows how to take care of his people. They saw it in spades during the evasion portion and in the POW camp.

He asks a lot of good questions and then listens. One night he helped one of the AOs disassemble a mini-gun and then put it back together so he knew how it operated.

You've got the chance to help him along and do what chiefs do best, which is to train young junior officers. Bring Bennington along on this, because word from the admin chief is that Bennington should make chief on the next board.

The squadron gave Haman a raw deal in that they transitioned him to the HH-2 in a week. He never complained, just got down to work. The scuttlebutt on Haman is that they are going to send him off to Det 110 to fly H-3s after a couple of line periods in the H-2. The H-3 RAG chief in ops who was over here for a few days said Haman's a first class stick. By the time he finished training, the chief air crewman said he could fly the H-3 better than most of the instructors.

See you when you get back.

Chuck

Slaughter folded the letter away and shook his head. The *Sterett*, he mused, might not have been the best place to send a brand new co-pilot.

Same Day, 1230 Local Time, on the U.S.S. Sterett

The rubber-lined canvas hose bucked and twitched when Josh closed the nozzle of the four-foot-long adjustable wand, shutting off the stream of water. The sharp smell of chlorine dissipated. He was waiting for the aircrew men to finish soaping down the right side of helicopter's fuselage. Once they were done, he planned to rinse the soap and salt off that side.

"What are you doing?"

Josh turned around, surprised to see Lieutenant Higgins standing behind him in the military position known as parade rest and wearing a highly starched set of fresh khakis.

"Helping the guys give the helicopter a bath. We cleaned the rotor head with high-pressure steam to get all the excess grease off, and are now washing the rest of the helicopter to minimize corrosion."

"Why are *you* here?"

"I wanted to help."

"The enlisted guys can give the helo a bath without you. Go get cleaned up; we've got a run to the heavy cruiser *Newport News* to pick up some mail and then take it to the carrier *America*. Take off is in thirty minutes. If all goes well, we'll be back for dinner and won't have to fly a mission tonight."

Josh glanced down at the wet shorts, t-shirt, and shower shoes he was wearing. "Yes, sir." Before he thought about not asking the question, the words came out of his mouth. "I thought there was a strike package going out tonight and we were supposed to be on station."

"When we get down to the *Newport News* I am going to see if the guys in Det 103 want to fly our mission. The planned orbit is near the DMZ, well within their range. It is called spreading the wealth. They've not had a lot to do in the last few weeks and may be bored, so we'll see if they want our mission."

Josh was watching Higgins leave the helo deck when Petty Officer Third Class Derek Van der Jagt put his hand on the steel spraying wand. "I'll take it from here sir, you go change. I'll get the head greased before we take off."

Josh shook his head. "I'll finish hosing it down, Van der Jagt. The fresh water wash down is more important and I can change into a flight suit in a couple of minutes."

* * * * *

When they were still thirty minutes out from the *Newport News*, Higgins keyed the mike. "You fly for a while."

They were the first words Higgins had said other than the required communications about where Josh thought they were and their fuel state.

As soon as Josh had the controls, Higgins asked, "Ever land on a cruiser before?"

"No, sir."

"Then today you'll make your first." Higgins picked up the diagram of the *Newport News* helicopter deck.

"When the heavy cruiser was first built, there were two catapults for seaplanes on the fantail. Beneath the cruiser's armored deck is a hangar for storing the aircraft and performing maintenance. The deck is laid out like the *Sterett*'s, but about three times as large. They'll have their bird pulled forward alongside the aft eight-inch gun turret, which will give us plenty of room. They don't have to pull it up that far, but it makes it safer." Higgins used his finger to show Josh where the other helo would be.

"Approach the ship from the starboard side at about a thirty degree angle to the direction the ship is steaming. Just keep coming down the centerline of the deck and, as you get close, focus on your position relative to the circle and the centerline. There will be a noticeable burble from the aft eight-inch gun turret that, depending on the wind, will start thirty to fifty yards from the hull of the ship. Their helo will be visible in your peripheral vision as you cross the deck edge, but don't let it distract you."

"Got it."

"The key is that you want to be about sixty to eighty feet off the water, about one hundred yards out and below forty knots, which means you'll be overtaking the ship, which will be doing fifteen at most. When you feel the burble you may need some power, but don't add too much. You want to keep a positive but decreasing closure rate, so that as you cross the deck edge you just have to ease back on the cyclic to come to a hover. What you don't want is to come to a stop with the helo just short of the ship, or half over the deck and half off, because one end will be in ground effect and the other won't. Or if you're too fast, you'll have to haul the nose up to do a quick stop."

Josh clicked the mike twice to acknowledge just as the numbers on the distance indicator on the TACAN spun down as they closed on the cruiser. The remote magnetic indicator combined heading, bearing to a ground station, and distance; he kept the number 2 needle centered on the top of the dial to follow the most direct course to the ship.

"I'll take over as soon as they get the chocks and tie-downs in," Higgins said. "Then we'll shut down, stretch our legs and fill up with gas. It'll also give us time to socialize with our squadron mates. We'll pick up the ship's mail and take any passengers on to the *America*."

The ninety-five degree temperature and relative humidity of seventy percent created a haze that kept horizontal visibility to less than three miles. With the doors open and a 100-knot cruising speed, the inside of the cabin was warm but pleasant.

Josh saw the wake of the heavy cruiser before he saw the ship and followed it as he eased the HH-2C around the aft end to approach from the starboard side. After the helicopter descended, he glanced at the outside air temperature gauge and noticed that it was five degrees hotter at sea level than at their cruising altitude of 1,000 feet.

"Clementine 26, Thunder. Wind is thirty degrees port at fifteen knots. You have a green deck," came the call. A green deck meant they were cleared to land.

Higgins acknowledged the radio call as Josh passed behind the ship in what he believed was close to a textbook approach.

"You'll have lots of power, Josh. Keep it going, you're looking good. At our weight, and with the wind you'll have, you should have plenty of tail rotor authority and the burble from the turret shouldn't be too bad."

Higgins had his right hand out the door to signal to the enlisted man holding the wands that he was not flying. Seeing this, the man moved to his left to make it easier for Josh to see him.

Josh eased the cyclic back a fraction of inch as the HH-2C slid over the deck, which was covered with black, textured non-skid paint, and the helo stopped almost in the center in a ten foot hover. With the helicopter now going as fast as the ship, he waited until Van der Jagt called from the back, "Tail wheel is clear" over the intercom before lowering the collective. The HH-2C settled on its landing gear.

"Nicely done," Higgins said. "Chocks and chains are in. I've got it. Shut down check list."

Josh took a deep breath as he read off the items on his kneeboard card and flexed his fingers to relieve some of the tension.

The landing on the *America*, two and a half hours later, was easier. All he had to do was pull into a stable position ninety feet above the water matching the speed of the carrier, and then ease forward, landing on the space at the forward end of the angled deck where the tracks of the number three and four catapults converged.

Compared to the deck of the *Newport News*, the six acres of *America's* flight deck was huge.

An hour later, they took off on the last leg of their triangular tour of the Gulf of Tonkin. About 30 miles out from the *Sterett*, Josh was still flying when Higgins said, "Get us aboard the *Sterett*. Let's see how much you've learned today."

It took a few seconds for Josh to find good reference points to maintain a hover and get the HH-2C stable over the center of the smaller cruiser deck as it steamed at fifteen knots in a dead calm sea. The burble, coming over the large destroyer's superstructure, bounced him around for a few seconds. He could taste the stack gas as it flowed through the cockpit, causing his eyes to water. Josh had to force himself not to accelerate through the gas plume, which would have forced him to raise the nose in a quick stop and lose sight of the landing area.

After he shut down the engines, Higgins unstrapped, but before they shut off the battery he keyed the mike, "Good work. Take care of the post flight and the maintenance logs; I've got a message to send telling the Commander of Task Force 77 that we need crew rest and the helicopter requires some maintenance, so we can't fly tonight. Then they'll task the guys on the *Newport News*. I'll see you at dinner in the mess."

Josh waited until the helicopter had two tie-down chains running from the tail pylon to the pad-eyes deck along with the two on each main mount before he grabbed his helmet.

"Sir," Petty Officer First Class Bennington spoke up, "there's nothing wrong with the helo. We'll need to grease the head and tail rotor while we fuel it, but it's a full up bird." At six-foot-five, Bennington was almost a head taller than Josh. He hadn't said anything during the flight, other than what was needed to tell the pilots what was going on in the H-2's cabin. Van der Jagt was taking longer than needed to pull the grease gun from its bag under the cabin's passenger seat.

"I know that, Bennington." Josh sensed he was being tested. "When I get down to the maintenance space, I intend to fill out the yellow sheets so they reflect the true operational status of the helicopter." In the back of his mind, Josh wondered why would Higgins send out a message with information that wasn't true?

Wednesday, October 7th, 1970, 1037 Local Time, on the U.S.S. Sterett

Josh came into the wardroom to get a glass of apple juice to take back to the stateroom he shared with the ship's assistant operations and gunnery officer. When not flying, the uniform of the day for officers and chief petty officers was known as "wash khakis", which made a distinct, dull tearing sound as one stuffed a limb down a heavily starched pant leg or sleeve. Even in the interior of the destroyer, where it was kept a comfortable 72 degrees Fahrenheit, by noon most of the stiffness from the starch was gone, and by the end of the day they were wrinkled and ready for the laundry.

Josh didn't pay attention to the officer reading a piece of paper at the other end of the wardroom as he filled a glass with what was *supposed* to be apple juice. He was taking a sip of the overly sweet, golden liquid when a voice from behind him called out.

"Haman, take a seat."

Josh looked up and realized it was Higgins sitting at the end of the long table reserved, at meal times, for the destroyer's executive officer. The white table cloth and thin foam pad were folded forward, exposing the polished steel top. Higgins had several neat piles of paper and folders arrayed in front of him. Josh wondered why Higgins preferred to work in the wardroom rather than his own stateroom. It could have been that it allowed him to spread the paperwork out, which was always in nice, neat piles aligned along their edges. At meal times, Higgins always took the same seat when the executive officer wasn't present. Josh pulled out a steel chair and did as he was told.

"Tell me about yourself."

Josh took this more as an order than conversation. Since his arrival, he'd shared the cockpit with his detachment officer-in-charge for over a dozen hours, but all his own attempts at starting conversation had been greeted by monosyllabic answers. So now Higgins wanted to talk. *O.K. by me. It'll be a break in the monotony. He hasn't given me anything important to do, so I've been hanging out with the enlisted men, learning what they do and studying my NATOPS manual.*

"What do you want to know?"

"Let's start with where you went to school. What did you major in? Where were you born? Where did you grow up? You know, the basics."

At Cubi, Josh had been able to learn very little about Lieutenant Steve Higgins. He'd thought it strange that no one would talk much about an officer who had been with the squadron for more than a year. Each time he asked someone, they changed the subject. At first it had puzzled him, and then he'd decided to stop asking, figuring he would find out later. Maybe now he would.

"O.K. I got a mechanical engineering degree from Norwich University in Vermont. I was born in Burlington, Vermont and I grew up in central Germany because my dad was in the Air Force."

"Never heard of Norwich." Higgins made the statement sound like a question.

"It was founded in 1812 and is the oldest private military college in the U.S. It was created to provide engineers to the military. It has a small corps of about nine hundred cadets as well as a civilian school with about three hundred students."

"Why didn't you go to one of the service academies?"

"We were living overseas and my parents didn't have any connections with a congressman or a senator. We tried, but couldn't get an appointment, so I got a ROTC scholarship. I also wanted to go to a school where there were girls!"

Higgins raised his eyebrows. "Was your dad a pilot?"

"Yup. He did two tours during World War II and one in Korea. Right now, he is at the end of his tour as a Thud driver based at Korat." Josh let a little pride sneak into his tone because his father was his role model and he was proud of his accomplishments. Josh took a sip of his apple juice before he asked a question.

"So besides going to the Academy, where'd you grow up?"

Higgins answered, "Madison, Wisconsin. Until I left for Annapolis, I never spent much time outside the state. My father was a city planner and my mother was a social worker. They took me to DC one summer, but most of the time we went out to our lake house on weekends."

Higgins clasped his hands and rested them on top of the folder he just closed. "You play any sports?"

"At Norwich?"

"Yeah, were you a jock?"

His tone tells me he doesn't like jocks. Was Higgins jealous or was he never any good at sports?

"I don't consider myself a jock, but I was on the varsity school's ski team. We got pretty far in the NCAA tournament because several of us were good enough to be considered for the Olympic ski team." Josh left out that he also played on the varsity soccer and baseball teams.

"Were you one of them?"

"I was."

"Interesting. So you could have been in Grenoble a couple of years back?"

"Yes, but I didn't get picked. I was on the National B team and only the guys and girls on the A teams went to Grenoble."

"What was your best event?"

"Downhill and giant slalom."

"Oh. You liked to go fast?"

"Yup. It's a rush." Several times in downhill races, Josh had clocked in the upper seventies. He was both fast and consistent and it gnawed at him that he hadn't been picked for the A team; he was faster and better than some who were. It was a matter of team politics. He had been an unknown, someone who grew up in Europe and didn't go to one of the big name universities that attracted the best American skiers, even though he beat many of them regularly.

Higgins looked down as he toyed with his coffee mug and then looked at Josh. "I played trumpet and was good enough to hold first chair in high school and play in the marching band. But that was about it. They forced me to play intramural sports at the Academy and I spent four years trying to make sure I didn't hurt myself or anyone else in the process." Higgins studied one of the papers in front of him and then let it float back to its pile before he made sure the edges were aligned with those already there. "How'd you wind up as a helo pilot?"

"Not by choice. I wanted to fly A-1s, but they shut that pipeline down just after I started in the training command. So, I was hoping to get into fighters, but when I finished my carrier quals they sent twenty-five of us to Ellyson to learn to fly helicopters. I had a choice—quit or become a helo driver." Josh paused and then asked what he thought was the obvious question. "How'd *you* wind up as a helicopter pilot?"

"During my senior year, we were told we had four choices: aviation, special warfare, submarines or surface warfare. And if you chose surface warfare there was a 70 percent chance you would get sent to the Brown Water Navy to drive Swift boats around the Mekong Delta. The powers that be thought that a little combat was good for your career. I didn't want any part of that."

"So why did you pick aviation?"

"Simple. The thought of being cooped up in a submarine for ninety days at a time would drive me nuts. After the week we spent on them during my summer cruise, I knew I didn't want to be a SEAL or a surface warfare officer. So that left aviation."

"Do you like flying?"

"Yeah, it's O.K. It gives you something to do that's different and we don't have to stand watches like the black shoes."

"Why did you pick helos?"

"I wanted them from the beginning. On my dream sheet, I listed east coast vertical replenishment and anti-submarine squadrons as my first and second choices so I could stay as far away from this godforsaken war as I could. When I got my orders, they were to HC-7. When I asked why, they told me that as an Annapolis graduate it was good for my career, assuming I wanted to stay in the Navy. So here I am, and H-2s were all we had. I flew the single engine Bs for a year or so before I transitioned to the HH-2C, which is a much better helicopter."

Higgins picked up another folder, opened it and started reading. Josh took that to mean that he was dismissed.

Thursday, October 8ᵗʰ, 1970,
1232 Local Time, Gulf of Tonkin Orbit

To save weight and provide more airflow through the interior of the helicopter, the detachment had removed all the doors. Even so, as they flew a racetrack pattern at 200 feet above the gulf about ten miles east of the DMZ, everyone on board was sweating. All the 90-knot breeze flowing through the cockpit and cabin did was circulated the 90 percent humidity contained in the 98-degrees air.

Because they were off the DMZ, Higgins let Josh orbit closer to land so they could see the green, tree-covered hills in the distance. The closest point of approach was about a mile from the coast. They'd been on station for just over 45 minutes and the numbers on the fuel totalizer were saying that it was almost time to fly back to the *Sterett*. By now, Josh's t-shirt and the cotton flight-deck jersey under his flight suit was soaking wet from the heat and humidity.

The Nomex fabric used to make their flight suits was designed to prevent liquids, particularly jet fuel and aviation gas, from seeping through to the skin. In the event of a fire it formed a barrier that would, for about thirty seconds, keep the wearer from burning. In short, it gave the wearer time to get out of the fire. It didn't sound like much, but it was enough time to escape.

The bad news about Nomex was that the very features that kept one from becoming a crispy critter were the same ones that didn't allow the fabric to breathe. In hot and humid conditions, it became a mini-hot box despite the tiny holes surrounded by plastic grommets. They simply were not enough, and after a few hours, the wearer's undershirt was soaked with sweat and the tangy, pungent smell of body odor began to make itself known.

Josh looked down at the blue-green water as he rolled the helicopter into a 30-degree bank and saw pale yellow-green squiggles in the water.

"Steve, are those sea snakes?"

Higgins, who was resting his helmet on the back of the armor-plated seat, sat up and looked down. "Yeah. You don't want to land amongst those mothers. A couple of bites and you are dead. They're pretty placid unless you stir them up. When you see them, my advice is move your orbit away as soon as you can. They're more dangerous than sharks."

"Got it. I'll orbit farther to the north. When we get down to nine hundred pounds of gas I'll let Hunter 704 know, and we'll head back to the *Sterett*. We should arrive with about three hundred pounds."

"That's not enough gas. We need to leave now." Higgins looked at the clock on his side of the instrument panel.

When the helicopter got on station off North Vietnam, Josh noticed that Higgins moved the clock's indicator needle so that it pointed to a time which was before, according to the air tasking order, the end of their on-station period. According to Josh's clock, they had another 15 minutes to go.

"As you come around just head north, back to the ship. If you want, climb up to a thousand feet or so and see if we can pick up the ship's TACAN sooner. That will give us heading to shorten the time en route so we'll burn a little less gas. Or, if you want, you can stay down here at two hundred feet—your choice."

"Will do; I'll climb to one thousand feet and think zero-one-five will get us back to the *Sterett*," answered Josh.

"You're assuming the *Sterett* is..." The sound of a beeper transmitting on the UHF international distress frequency when a pilot ejected from his aircraft interrupted Higgins. "Head home, NOW!" he yelled.

The urgency in Higgins' voice suggested strongly that this was an order. Josh turned the helicopter almost 160 degrees to get to 015 while they listened to Hunter 704 direct other aircraft in support of the rescue.

"I'll fly," Higgins said.

Josh held up his hands to signal that they were off the controls. After he listened to the transmissions between Hunter 704 and other aircraft, he picked up the chart he'd looked at least a dozen times during the flight. Then, using his fingers, Josh drew imaginary lines to fix the position of the downed pilot who, based on the radio calls, was in the water just off the coast of North Vietnam. "We can zip over there and get him. It's a quick twenty mile detour. We've got plenty of gas and, if we run short, Hunter 704 can direct the *Sterett* to head toward us at flank speed. We can bring him to the *Sterett*, get gas, and take him back to his carrier."

"If they want us to help, then we will have a decision to make based on how much gas we have and whether or not I think we can rescue the pilot. Right now, we're heading home."

"Steve, based on the radio chatter, Red Crown is sending in an Air Force seaplane, which is a riskier option than a helo pick-up. Plus, we can be there in fifteen minutes or less. The seaplane won't be there for at least thirty. You know as well as I do, in a rescue time is of the essence."

"Again, if they want us, they'll call. The controllers know where we are and where the *Sterett* is located. The TACAN shows we have fifty-eight nautical miles to go. That's about thirty minutes, which means we land with seven hundred pounds of gas."

"If we make the detour, I'll bet we'd land with at worst two to three hundred pounds. That's twenty minutes. The low fuel lights will have just come on, if at all." Josh wasn't going to give up on the idea of attempting the rescue.

"Don't be so anxious to make a pick-up. You'll get your chances. Again, if they need us, they can call. They know we're out here. Meanwhile, we're going back to the *Sterett*." Higgins's voice was flat.

* * * * *

As soon as they shut down the rotors and engines, Higgins unstrapped and headed toward the cool, air-conditioned interior of the ship, leaving Josh to conduct the post flight. Josh moved to the left side and checked the left engine, transmission and combining gearbox for leaks. Petty Officer Bennington was on the other side; he leaned over the centerline of the helo so he could speak softly.

"Sir, I agree with you, we could have and should have gone to get that pilot today."

"It was Lieutenant Higgins' decision as the aircraft commander to make," Josh replied. The words didn't represent his feelings, but as an officer he *had* to defend Higgins.

"Sir, our mission is to go get downed pilots. Not going is affecting the morale of the men in this det." Bennington's voice was hushed, but it tone conveyed both hardness and disappointment. It was clear that he was speaking for all twelve enlisted men assigned to the detachment.

He's telling me, without saying it, that none of them liked Higgins's decision and this was not the first time it happened. Josh knew it was a matter pride to make rescues, or at least attempt them. When Bennington and the others in the detachment were with their fellow enlisted men, either in the bunk rooms on the *Sterett* or ashore with squadron mates, they wanted to compare experiences. These men, Higgins's men, *his* men, weren't completing missions. *How the hell do I answer?*

"I'll talk to Mr. Higgins."

"Thank-you, sir," Bennington said quietly.

* * * * *

Three hours later, Josh had showered and changed into a fresh set of khakis. He knew he'd been pushing the limits with Higgins, but he agreed with Bennington, they should have been the ones to make the rescue today, not an Air Force seaplane.

Summing up his courage, he knocked on Higgins' stateroom door.

"Come in."

Josh opened the door and was glad to see Higgins alone, but surprised to see him lying down. It was clear that he was about to take a nap, or, as his roommate put it, check his eyelids for light leaks. Dinner was still over two hours away. "May I have a word with you, sir?"

"Come in, Haman. What's on your mind?" Higgins sounded

relaxed, almost genial.

Josh couldn't remember any time that Higgins had addressed him by his first name.

"Sir, could you explain to me why you didn't want to go get that pilot today? I still don't understand."

Higgins' demeanor turned icy, and from his supine position on the bunk he glared his co-pilot. "Haman, as the officer-in-charge, I don't have to justify my actions or decisions to you or anyone else who is a member of this detachment. Am I clear on that point?"

"Yes, sir." Josh was surprised by his aircraft commander's belligerent, even defensive reaction. He was hoping that Higgins would be willing to explain his decision.

"As the aircraft commander, I am responsible and accountable for the safe, and I repeat the word, *safe* conduct of the flight and the mission. We didn't have enough fuel to go look for a downed pilot, hover for ten minutes to pick him up, and return to the *Sterett* with sufficient reserves."

"Sir, we landed with nine hundred pounds of gas. It would only have taken us one-fifty to two hundred to get to where the guy was. Hovering for ten minutes would have eaten up another two to three hundred; the trip back would have taken another two hundred at most. That would have left us with two to three hundred pounds, which means the low fuel lights wouldn't even have come on yet."

"What if the *Sterett* wasn't where we thought it was?" demanded Higgins.

"We could have asked Hunter 704 for radar vectors and asked the *Sterett* to close the distance while we headed towards the pilot. I'd bet the ship would have done that to help a rescue." He was about to explain that his roommate had said the captain would gladly head toward a helo at flank speed and provide radar guidance if they needed gas for any reason, but he noticed that Higgins's hand was now clutching the blanket. He knew enough about body language to know Higgins was pissed and controlling his anger.

"Haman, you don't know that. We don't task the *Sterett*. Hunter

704 does not task the *Sterett*. The Commander, Task Force 77 does. By the time the request went up the chain of command and down, we could be out of gas and ditching. The rescued pilot, who may have been hurt, would be getting wet for a second time and possibly injured even more." Higgins's eyes held Josh's, and he spoke coldly. "I am not going to discuss, much less argue with you about my decision. The matter is closed."

"Sir, I think you should consider the men's morale. They're out here to make rescues." Josh suspected he'd just crossed a line. "That's our mission…"

Higgins cut Josh off by slashing his hand across his through as a gesture to suggest to Josh to stop speaking. As he stood up, Higgins took a step forward so that his face was less than a foot from Josh's.

There was fire in his eyes and his face was turning redder by the second.

"My job as the detachment officer in charge is to bring all, repeat ALL of the men in this detachment home to their mothers, wives and girlfriends alive, in one piece, and without extra holes in their bodies. I am *not* going to risk their lives, or mine for that matter, unnecessarily. If they don't like it, when we get back to Cubi they can ask to be transferred to another detachment. This is not a popularity contest, Haman. I am not interested in making friends, just in getting us all home alive.

"One more thing." Higgins was hissing as he spoke. "You are one short step away from being insubordinate, so I suggest you watch your tongue. And if any member of this detachment voices concerns or criticizes my decisions publicly, I will take strong disciplinary actions against them. So if I were you, I would tell them to watch their mouths or they will incur my wrath, which will be backed by the Commanding Officer of this squadron. Good day, Mister Haman."

Same Day, 1330 Local Time, Washington D. C.

Colonel Anthony Macaluso sat on one of the steel chairs with Air Force Blue cushions in the outer office of the Air Force Chief of Staff. On the walls hung original paintings by well-known aviation artists. Underneath each painting was a small brass plaque that provided a brief history of the scene. Each time the intelligence officer saw these, he marveled at their level of detail and realism.

"Colonel, the general will see you now." The woman who stuck her head around the door had been the administrative assistant for many Air Force Chiefs of Staff. "Please go into the conference room and have a seat."

Macaluso waited until the secretary closed the door behind herself before he advanced to the large desk in the middle of the room and unrolled the chart he'd brought with him. He used four crystal coasters with the Air Force crest to weigh down the corners before he unlocked his briefcase. In it was a sealed envelope stamped *Top Secret, Specially Compartmented Information.*

The sharp edge of his folding pocket knife made short work of the brown paper and he dumped out six eight-by-ten black and white prints he'd signed for when he left the National Reconnaissance Office. Along with the photos was the chain-of-custody document with his name and signature denoting that he was their "owner." If he were asked to leave them, he would have the general sign the form confirming that he'd taken custody of the satellite photos. Macaluso would then give the form with the general's signature to the duty officer in the National Reconnaissance Office responsible for tracking custody of the photos, so they would know who now had the pictures.

"Macaluso, what do you have to show me?" The booming voice of the top general in the U.S. Air Force carried as if he were shouting when, in reality, he was not.

Right behind the general, Macaluso recognized the officer who would have, if one were looking at an organization chart of the U.S. Air Force, the designation A-3, Operations. Macaluso worked for the lieutenant general designated A-2 for Intelligence, who was in Hawaii getting briefed on the latest intelligence from Vietnam.

"Sir, it is what I don't have that is important."

"Explain yourself."

"General, these pictures were taken of a rail yard in southern China ten miles south of the city of Honghe. Another one was taken farther down the road at Mengzi, and there are several from a rail yard south of Nanning."

Macaluso pointed at the chart. The location of each yard was circled.

"The rail line goes straight from Kaiyuan southeast through Mengzi to the North Vietnamese border called Lao Cai. That's a run of about one hundred miles. From Lao Cai, the trains go down the Red River to Hanoi and Haiphong. The route from Nanning is much shorter and trains cross the border at Lang Son, one hundred and twenty or so miles from Hanoi."

"Got the geography," said the General. "Go on, Colonel."

"Yes, sir. These pictures were taken about a week ago by one of our satellites. This is the third pass this month over each of the yards. What we don't see, if you look at these pictures, are any missiles." Macaluso spread out the prints. "If you look, you'll see 57- and 85-millimeter guns, but no SA-2s. The Air Force photo interpreters think there is a possibility that there are missiles in the box cars, because the SA-2 is shipped in two parts, the booster and the missile itself."

"That would explain how they get so many missiles into North Vietnam."

"Yes, sir, it would."

"Yet the Navy says they are all coming in by ship and, as a result, they want to take out the docks and even the ships."

"Sir, that may be what the North Vietnamese want us to think while they bring most of the missiles in by rail."

"Well, how do we prove or disprove either theory?" The general was not about to go head-to-head with the Chief of Naval Operations; that would be a political disaster.

"Sir, we can do one of two things. Option one would be to use a U-2 or an SR-71 so we can vary the overhead times and take pictures more often. We are pretty sure the Soviets and the Chinese know the overhead times of our satellites and can move trains to keep them out of sight. Option two is much riskier. To execute it, we have to would send in a recon team to look in the boxcars."

The general scoped up the photos and signed the custody form.

"Keep digging and keep taking photos. I'll think about what we want to recommend."

Friday, October 9th, 1970,
0746 Local time, on the U.S.S. Sterett

Josh was watching one of the detachment's two plane captains complete his daily check. As the jar with the fuel sample was filled from each tank, Petty Officer Third Class Van der Jagt, who accompanied the plane captain, searched for impurities and bubbles of water floating around in the golden-colored liquid. After several inspections, he spoke up.

"Sir, the *Sterett* has some of the cleanest fuel in the fleet. I've been on ships where we've pull fuel samples that are full of all kinds of junk."

"I've heard that some of the ships have some kind of bacteria growing in their jet fuel tanks," said Josh.

"Yes, sir, they do. They are supposed to use the pumps to keep the fuel mixed and then test it daily for water, but if they don't have a helo on board, they get a bit lax and the stuff grows."

"Now hear this, now hear this, this is the captain speaking."

All work on deck stopped as the loudspeaker blared.

"The Sterett *is getting a great deal. We are being pulled off the line and sent down to Singapore to show the flag. We will be in port for three days, after which we go to sea with the Singaporean Navy for three, then back into port for another four days. We should arrive Sunday night in time for chow and evening liberty. Only the top-performing ships get these kind of invitations and the* Sterett *is one of the best. Congratulations, crew! Well done. Captain out."*

All around Josh, crewmen erupted into cheers and whoops.

Chapter 3 – SINGAPORE

The open area aft of the five-inch gun turret was a quiet and peaceful place to read a prayer book while the ship cruised south at twelve knots. Josh was sitting on a stanchion just inside the wire safety lines, enjoying the gentle, if humid, breeze, when a shadow fell across the page.

"Mr. Haman, sorry to disturb you, sir, but Lieutenant Higgins would like to see you in his stateroom."

Josh squinted as he looked up. The enlisted man was standing up-sun. "Koslowski, did he say want he wants?"

"No, sir, he just passed the word to Chief Slaughter that he wanted to see you as soon as possible. We saw you sitting out here on the after deck."

As he made his way below decks, Josh wondered what Higgins might want. The lieutenant hadn't said a word to him since their conversation the day before and had walked right past him twice in the passageway without even acknowledging his presence. At Higgins' stateroom door, he rapped twice on the door frame.

"Enter."

Josh decided to be formal. "Sir, I'm reporting as ordered. You wanted to see me."

"I did." Higgins picked up a piece of paper that was sitting in the center of his rack and looked down at the typewritten sheet.

"Since you like hanging around our helicopter so much with the air crewman, I'm going to give you a good deal. Next Tuesday morning, you get to give our Singaporean friends a tour of the helicopter. And since you seem to be so keen to make rescues, afterwards you get to give them a formal briefing on how we do it. Then you can answer all their questions."

"Yes, sir, no problem."

"I want an outline of the sequence of the tour your recommend and of your briefing to review before lunch today."

Josh cocked his head slightly. "I was hoping I wouldn't have to work today, since it is Yom Kippur. I can write the outline after chow tonight and have it for you before I go to bed. We can talk about any changes in the morning."

"No. I want it by noon. The war stops for no man."

"This is not for war, this is for a training exercise," Josh pointed out in as reasonable a tone as he could manage.

"Today, by noon. Understood?"

"Yes, sir."

"While we are at sea playing with the Singaporean Navy during the port visit, I am going to take one of their officers on a flight or two, and you get to stay behind. He can use your equipment, unless you can find a spare set."

"Yes, sir."

"And one more thing." Higgins started to smile. "Tuesday night there will be a formal reception, and the captain has asked that our detachment be represented. I am assigning you as the official HC-7 Detachment 104 contingent. You'll need a set of summer whites, which I believe you brought with you."

"I did, and I'll be happy to go." By being eager and unfazed, he hoped to maintain at least a professional, if not cordial relationship with his aircraft commander and detachment officer-in-charge. "Is that all, sir?"

"It is, Haman. Dismissed."

Tuesday, October 13th, 1446 Local Time, on the U.S.S. Sterett

Josh was standing on the forward end of the helicopter deck watching the crew fold the helicopter's blades. To do so, the head was rotated so that the blades were forty-five degrees off the nose and then a pin was pulled to unlock the blade. After that, a crewman walked the tip aft until it was put into a boot that was tied to one of the tie down loops on the aft fuselage. The first two blades were in place when Josh heard a voice behind him.

"Lieutenant Haman." Josh turned around and was surprised to see the ship's captain, a soft-spoken southerner by the name of Brian Danforth, standing behind him with his hands clasped behind his back.

"Yes, sir?"

"That was an outstanding brief and tour of the helicopter this morning," said Danforth. "The Singaporean admiral and his staff were most impressed. I do have a question, though. Why did you let Petty Officer Bennington and Chief Slaughter conduct much of the briefing?

"Sir, I divided the presentation into what I thought were logical parts. Chief Slaughter is responsible for the maintenance of the helicopter, and Petty Officer Bennington is the senior air crewman, so he can talk about what we do in the back during a rescue. I thought it would be best if the Singaporeans heard from the experts. They're a little rough, but they know their stuff. I'm just the pilot who takes the air crewmen to where they do all the hard, dangerous work."

"It was impressive for three reasons. One, you had enough confidence in your enlisted me to let them brief an admiral. Two, someone, and I believe it was you, helped them prepare so that everything went smoothly. And three, I think you wanted to let your men shine. I'll let HC-7's CO know how well you and your men did. Oh, by the way, where is Lieutenant Higgins? He wasn't at the helicopter tour or the brief."

Josh hesitated for a second, realizing the truth may toss his det OinC under the bus but he figured the ship's captain already knew that. "Ashore, sir, "

"One would think that he would take enough pride in his detachment to be on hand. I saw your name on the guest list but not his for the reception tonight, so I'll see you there. I gather he is skipping that as well."

"Yes, sir, he is, but I'll be there."

* * * * *

Josh came into the wardroom a few minutes before it stopped serving lunch, looked at the menu and ordered a grilled cheese sandwich with bacon and jalapeño peppers. Only one officer—Jeffrey Gainesville, United States Naval Academy, class of 1962—was still at the table. Gainesville was Josh's room-mate and the ship's officer responsible for guns and missiles. He was also the combat information center officer, and his battle station was the nerve center of the ship. Furthermore, now that the *Sterett* had a helicopter on board, he was also the air operations officer. Gainesville's four on, eight off work schedule and Josh's flying left them little time to socialize.

"Roomie, have you ever been to Singapore?" Gainesville inquired as Josh sat down across from him.

"Nope."

"Well, between my two years on the *Sterett* and my first tour on the *Hoel*, this is my sixth stop in Singapore, and it's a great place to spend a few days. It's clean and has lots of great restaurants and shopping. Prices are not as good as Hong Kong, but almost. And we tie up to a pier, so you can walk ashore and not worry about the liberty boats shutting down at one in the morning."

"Jeff, have you ever been to the Raffles Hotel?"

"Yes indeed. Last time we were here I got a room there for four days. It's a first-class hotel, supposed to be one of the best in the city. Plus the two-legged scenery is always spectacular. A lot of ex-pats from all over the world hang out at Raffles, most of them with families that include eligible daughters. What's even better is that many of them are single, and they're used to sailors who want company, conversation, dinner, and then hopefully more." The tall, former basketball player smiled. "You could say it's a target-rich environment!"

Josh laughed. "Cool. Very cool."

"You got everything you need for a set of whites? The ship's store is pretty well picked over."

"I do. I brought with me all the summer uniforms I had. That's why my locker is stuffed. It was overkill."

"No, it was smart because you never know what you'll need. Be happy we don't have to wear chokers tonight; if we did, we'd be miserable in the heat and humidity. Tell you what, since it's your first time, we'll head over together."

Josh was happy to go along with this plan.

Same Day, 1815 Local Time, Raffles Hotel, Singapore

The evening air was twenty degrees cooler than in the daytime, but still humid. As the bus left the causeway, the smell of sewage-tainted sea water, mixed with the dank odor of wet hemp and pungent fuel oil gave way to the smells of an oriental city. Pleasant food fragrances wafting through the open windows competed with exhaust fumes.

Raffles had been built in 1887 and had survived Japanese occupation and World War II. Now, besides being a luxury hotel, it was a national monument with its own museum. As the two officers walked under the portico, Josh realized that his roommate hadn't been wrong. Beyond the receiving line was sumptuous décor, an open bar, and a buffet fit for a king.

Both officers joined the line in front of a well-stocked bar. After receiving and taking a long swig of the local Tiger Beer, Josh looked around and said, "A reconnaissance of the buffet is in order. I'm hungry."

"Go ahead and eat, I'm going to look around and see if there is anyone interesting." Gainesville was scanning the room for women. At six foot seven, he had no trouble seeing over heads.

On the long buffet table, small white card tents with precise penmanship denoted the Chinese dishes that were intermingled with American ones. Josh carried a plate piled high with samples to one of the chest-high tables off in a corner where an older man and a young woman were standing. It was the only table with two occupants. The rest had four of five.

"May I join you?"

"Certainly." The man nodded and spoke with what Josh thought was a French accent.

Rather than making a mistake by assuming he was French, he replied in English. "I am Josh Haman."

Josh held out his hand and the older man gave it a vigorous pump. It was the way many Europeans shook hands. "Ah, an officer from the American ship that just arrived."

"Yes, sir, I am from the U.S.S. *Sterett.*"

"Allow me to introduce myself. I am Jacques Debenard, and this is my daughter, Danielle."

"*Si vous préférez, nous pourrion parler français,*" Josh responded. He had grown up speaking French and German and this was a chance to practice.

"You speak French?" The young woman had dark, coffee-colored skin and stood at just over five feet, nearly a foot shorter than Josh. Her white teeth flashed as she spoke.

"*Mais oui.*"

"Where did you learn to speak French?" Danielle continued in English that had a strange, lilting accent that wasn't French. Her black, almond-shaped eyes had an intensity that caught Josh a bit off guard.

"I grew up in central Germany. My parents were multi-lingual and they wanted us kids to speak more than one language. Several nights a week, the only language spoken in the house was French or German, so learning both was a necessity."

"You must be one of the ship's helicopter pilots?" Danielle had noticed the gold wings above his three ribbons. One was the National Defense Medal known as the "Alive in 65" medal that began to be awarded 1965 to anyone who had served at least 90 consecutive days on active duty. The other two were Navy blue with thin white stripes with the silver metal "E" that indicated he qualified as an expert shot. He hadn't been in theater long enough to earn any Vietnam campaign ribbons.

"I am." Josh waited for a second, then turned to Jacques. "Sir, pardon me for asking, are you from the French Embassy, and if so, what do you do?"

"Are you asking me why I am here?"

"I guess so. I was just curious." Josh had been told that the Navy invited members of the diplomatic community as well as American businesses.

"I am not from the Embassy. I am, or was, depending on whether or not the Pathet Lao control the area, a rubber plantation manager, as well as the country manager for Michelin in Laos. I am here visiting our company offices and fly back tomorrow to Vientiane. Danielle invited me to come to this event."

Josh turned to Danielle, enjoying the woman's beauty and her shoulder length, jet black hair that cascaded over a sleeveless emerald-green cocktail dress that shimmered in the light.

He didn't have to ask the obvious question, for she smiled and said, "I work for the French diplomatic service as a translator and interpreter. I am based here in Singapore and travel around to our embassies and consulates all over what used to be French Indochina. I also do administrative tasks to learn how embassies work. I hope to stay in the Corps Diplomatique."

"How many languages do you speak?"

"Seven. I am fluent in French, English, Vietnamese, Russian, Mandarin and Cambodian as well as Laotian."

"I'm impressed."

"Don't be. Southeast Asia is a lot like Europe. It has many small countries, each with their different cultures and languages. Vietnamese, Cambodian and Laotian are all very similar. A lot like French, Spanish and Italian. You learn one, the others are easy."

"Where did you learn Russian?" Josh asked in that language and enjoyed the surprise on Danielle's face.

"The Sorbonne. That is where I went to university. Being able to read, write and speak Russian helped me get into the Corps Diplomatique. Where and what did you study?"

"I went to Norwich University and have a degree in mechanical engineering."

"Where is that?"

"In the state of Vermont."

"Ahhh."

"I see your glass is empty. What are you drinking?" Josh enquired.

"They have an excellent Pouilly Fuisse. I could use a refill." Danielle handed him her glass. "You should try a Singapore Sling. It was invented here in 1915 by a bartender named Ngiam Tong Boon, who was originally from the island of Hainan."

When Josh came back, bearing a glass and a plate of delicacies to share, Danielle had moved two bar stools to the table and was sitting alone. He placed the drink on the table before her and asked, "Where is your father?"

"Talking to one of his friends. I am supposed to be working, but someone from the embassy will find me if they need help. I don't think they will. Most speak English fluently. It is Chinese and Malay that they struggle with." She made a classic Gaelic frown. "Tonight, I don't think they will need either Chinese or Malay."

"How long have you been in the Corps Diplomatique?"

"Two years. Singapore is my first assignment. How long have you been in the Navy?"

"Almost two and half years."

"And you have been to Vietnam?"

"Yes. This is my first deployment." He didn't think it was necessary to say he'd been in the Gulf less than a month.

"What do you think of Singapore?"

"I don't have an opinion yet. I just got here."

"Are you married?"

"No."

"Do you have a girlfriend back in the U.S.?"

"No. Most of the ones I went to school with didn't want to get involved with someone who might get killed in the war. How about you?"

"No amour. Most of the men around here don't like strong-willed, independent women who want to have a career for a few years before becoming a mother. They see me as a threat. Being half French and having a father who was a Legionnaire is both a blessing and a curse."

Josh didn't know what to make of that, so he decided to ask about her father. "Your father was in the French Foreign Legion?"

"Yes. He retired as a colonel and fought for France during the Second World War. He was *not* Vichy." Danielle spat out the last word as if it were dirt. "After the war he was sent to what is now Laos, where he met and married my mother. Then he was sent to what is now Vietnam to fight the communists. When his countrymen left, he retired and stayed behind and went to work for Michelin." She sipped her wine and looked over the top of the glass. "How long is your ship going to be here?"

"Two more days, then we go to sea for three and back here for four before we head north again. Tomorrow I plan to look around the city. Like I said, I've never been here before. I am a military history buff and there are places I want to see."

"What does 'buff' mean?" asked Danielle.

"Oh, sorry. It means that I am very interested in it."

"I see." Danielle looked at Josh as she took a delicate bite out of an egg roll. "Do you have a guide?"

"No. Are you volunteering?" Josh grinned as he spoke.

"Not yet, but I am thinking about it." The almond-shaped black eyes sparkled.

"While you are thinking, how about we go to one of the more quiet, private places in the hotel and talk? I've been told there are several. I just don't know where they are."

"We can do that. Or, we can go someplace else. But I can't leave until the function is officially over at eight-thirty."

"Then we can sit here and talk."

"*D'accord.*"

Wednesday, October 14th, 1970,
0750 Local Time, on the U.S.S. **Sterett**

"Good morning, welcome back. I gather you had a successful night." Gainesville's voice startled Josh, who was in the midst of removing the shoulder boards from his uniform.

His roommate, fresh from the shower, had a towel wrapped around his waist and was carrying a plastic box containing a bar of soap. His flip-flops left wet spots on the steel deck.

Josh balled up the shirt and stuffed it into the net laundry bag. "I had a good time."

"With the chick in the green dress?"

"That's the one."

"And today?"

"Going to spend some time with the guys to make sure that we have a full-up helo for the exercise, then I'm going ashore to look around."

"Before or after lunch?"

"As soon as we get done, which should be before lunch." Josh was now pulling on a set of wash khaki pants that were starched heavily so they looked like a pair of boards.

"Do you have a guide?"

"Yes, Lieutenant Gainesville, I do."

"And does the guide have long black hair and, on the scale of one to ten, is she at least a nine plus?"

"Yup, and her name is Danielle."

"Any other gory details you want to share?"

"Just that she works for the French diplomatic corps as a translator and interpreter and speaks seven, count 'em, seven languages. Her father is a retired Legionnaire and runs rubber plantations in Laos for Michelin."

"Very interesting." Gainesville paused while he pulled a white V-neck undershirt over his head. "Just remember, we get underway at 0600 Thursday morning to rendezvous with the Singaporeans, and the gangway is pulled around 0430. I wouldn't want you to miss our departure. I've got the bridge watch and get to take the *Sterett* to sea. I'll leave the detailed exercise plan on your desk. You guys are going to spend about four to six hours a day in the air."

"Are you sure? Higgins didn't say anything about that."

"Yeah, most of the flights will going up and down the outer edges of the channel in the Strait of Malacca looking for signs of pirates. Piracy, if you don't know, is a big business in the strait. Also, they added a firing exercise where you get to demonstrate how well the mini-gun on the helo works. In the debrief after his tour of your helo and the *Sterett*, the Singaporean admiral made it a point to request that a demo of the gun be included in the exercise."

"What are we going to use as a target?"

"I don't know. It is up to you guys."

"Can we get a small boat we can toss over the side and then sink?" Josh asked.

"I don't know. But I have a meeting with the Singaporean exercise officer in about an hour and I'll ask. It's better than shooting up a special smoke flare that floats in the water. So just what has Higgins told you about the exercise?"

"Not much, other than that he is going to take a couple of Singaporean helicopter pilots on several flights."

"You two don't get along, I gather."

"Let's just say our relationship is cordial at best. Strained would be a good word. I'll probably get to go on the flight in which we shoot the gun."

"Just between you and me, Higgins is an asshole. I know guys who were his classmates at the Academy. They've told me he was a jerk then, and nothing has changed."

Higgins is a sanctimonious jackass who likes to bully people, Josh thought, but he kept quiet.

"You don't have to say anything. I know, and every officer on the ship knows, he is ducking rescues. Higgins always has a good excuse, but the *Sterett*'s job in the gulf is to support combat SAR, provide naval gunfire support and act, when needed, as shipboard air traffic controller. We hear most if not all of the transmissions. It makes me sick."

"Try being in the cockpit."

"It can't be fun."

"No, it's not." Josh paused as he opened the door and turned to face his room-mate. "Jeff, thanks for the heads up. I'll be back well before 0400."

Gainesville checked his uniform to make sure that everything was in place and picked up his notebook. "Enjoy. I expect a full report when I get back."

Josh laughed. "Gentlemen don't tell tales out of school. Anyway, what Danielle and I will be doing is highly classified and on a need-to-know basis."

Sunday, October 18th, 1970,
1346 Local Time, Singapore

Josh looked across their table and watched the gentle sea breeze rustle Danielle's hair. The small restaurant was right on the beach, but a big yellow and orange umbrella gave them lots of shade. Josh had pulled on a tee-shirt to keep from getting sunburnt and she was wearing a thin white shirt over her two-piece pink bathing suit. Under the shirt, you could see the suit's flower pattern. The remains of chicken and shrimp satays were piled off to the side. "You've been very pensive this morning. What's on your mind?" he asked.

"I am worried about my father, mother and younger sister."

"Why?"

"They won't leave the plantation. The Pathet Lao have raided it several times and forced many of the adult men to join their army. My father is afraid they will come back and take the rest, along with the teenage boys. Some of the older workers have fled, either into Vientiane or the refugee camps. The plantation is all but shut down because there aren't enough people to run it. My father and a couple of other Frenchmen are doing what they can to preserve it, so they can resume production after the war."

"You would think that the Pathet Lao would want the plantation to run as a source of revenue and jobs."

"Papa is convinced that they see it as a holdover from colonial rule and will destroy it if they take control."

"So why doesn't your family leave? They're French citizens and can go back to France."

"That is the problem. My mother won't leave Laos. It is her home. But the Pathet Lao know my father is a former Legionnaire and will either kill him or send him to a re-education camp if they take over the country. I am afraid my parents will try to defend their home and get killed."

"How close is the fighting now?"

"It comes and goes. Right now, most of the fighting is still two to three hundred kilometers away, up north on the Plain of Jars. But it gets closer every day. The plantation is in the southern end of Laos, only eighty kilometers from the border with Vietnam."

Josh took her hand. "I am so sorry. I wish there was something I could do."

"I just wish this war would end. It has been going on since the Japanese invaded in 1940. Then the French left, and now the Vietnamese Communists want to rule all of what used to be Indochina and won't stop until they do. It is just a matter of time. I don't think you Americans have the stomach to fight the North Vietnamese for as long as it takes or do what is necessary to win."

"You sound as if you know everyone in your family will all die soon."

"No matter what I do, I cannot get the thought out of my mind. It may be karma. I don't want them to die prematurely because they were too stubborn to leave Laos, especially when they could be safe in Thailand or here in Singapore."

Monday, October 19th, 1970,
1330 Local Time, the Pentagon

The Chairman of the Joint Chiefs of Staff looked more grim than usual. The war in Vietnam was eating at him and he'd just come from another frustrating meeting with the President and the Secretary of Defense. By virtue of his position he was the most senior member of the military on active duty. The admiral, a combat veteran of World War II, looked around the room at the four other flag officers of equivalent rank, one from each branch of the service, and said two words. "Seats, gentlemen."

"How'd the meeting go with the President?" The Chief of Staff of the U.S. Army sounded grim. His men were bearing the brunt of the fighting and incurring the most casualties.

"Short answer: not good. It's the same story. They don't want to fight to *win* the war. Instead, he and Laird want to keep things *contained*—that's the buzz word of the day—by using restrictive rules of engagement and dictating both strategy and tactics. We're fighting with one hand tied behind our backs. We have the wrong strategy, because they're trying to fight a war that is not the war we have. It is if they are living in another world. Then they wonder why we are taking heavy casualties. Good God, it's frustrating. You would think that a President who was a Naval officer during World War II would know better. Oh, I forgot, he never saw any action..."

Shit. The Chairman realized he never should have said that. He looked down at the one-page agenda in front of him to make it clear he didn't want to talk about the meeting with the President. "Air Force, what's bugging you? Just pile it on. This seems to be the day for it."

"Sir, our biggest concern is still the surface-to-air missiles that the North Vietnamese have. My intelligence folks think they are bringing them in by trains that are transiting the People's Republic of China via two routes. One from Nanning crosses the border near Lang Son, so near Hanoi. The other entry point is in the northwest part of North Vietnam at Lang Song."

The Chairman put his hand on his chin and his elbow on the table. "What do you want me to recommend to the President?"

The Air Force Chief of Staff responded instantly. "More reconnaissance. We need to overfly southeastern China with SR-71s or U-2s. One way or another we have to find out if there are missiles on those trains."

"I'll get the National Reconnaissance Office to see if they can get more satellite passes over the southeastern China. I don't think that, based on the current mood in the White House, we can get them to approve over flights. They would view that as an escalation and contrary to the desire to *contain* the war!"

"Sir, we could mine Haiphong harbor," the Chief of Naval Operations interjected. "That would slow, if not stop, the ships coming into the harbor, and we'd find out if they have a second source very soon. If they keep shooting, then we know they have a second source."

"That's too logical. Neither the Secretary of Defense nor the President would agree to it. Again, they would see it as an escalation, never mind that it's an easy way to slow down the arms shipments and cut off their oil supply. My goodness, it might endanger neutral shipping! Sorry if I sound sarcastic as well as pessimistic, but I don't think the President would sign off on mining."

"Can we bring it up at another time?"

"Sure, maybe someday things will change." The chairman looked down at the piece of paper. "Let's get through the items on the agenda."

Thursday, October 22nd, 1970,
1446 Local Time, Gulf of Tonkin

Three miles off the coast and two hundred feet above the gray-green waters of the Gulf of Tonkin below a clear blue sky, Higgins rolled into the first turn of the orbit and keyed the mike. "Haman, based on our fuel, how much time do you think we have left on station?"

"Boss, we have about twenty-one hundred pounds left, enough for an easy hour and a half."

"If Hammer or Red Crown asks, tell them we have less than sixty minutes left. We will leave this orbit when we get down to one thousand pounds. Clear."

Josh started to say something, then bit his tongue. After their last conversation, he didn't want to challenge Higgins again, particularly in the presence of two enlisted men. Instead, he clicked his mike twice.

Neither man said anything for a few minutes until Higgins keyed the intercom. "Captain Danforth told me that the Singaporeans thought the exercise was very productive. They're going to see if they can schedule more exercises. They really like the mini-gun. "

"It can be effective."

"He also said that they Singaporeans were impressed by your brief. I'm sure getting the outline to me by noon and having the extra half-day to prepare was helpful. Well done."

Josh wasn't sure what to say. The indirect reference to interrupting his time off for Yom Kippur made him grit his teeth.

"I understand you had a good time in Singapore."

"I did." Josh didn't want to give anything away that Higgins might use against him.

"I heard your roommate say you scored with a lovely young Chinese lady. Is that true?"

"I will neither confirm or deny the rumor. The lady in question works for the embassy as an interpreter. And she is not Chinese, she's Laotian."

"So are you going to be one of those sailors who has a girl in every port?"

"I don't know." He didn't want to tell Higgins anything.

Higgins flew the racetrack pattern for about ten minutes before turning the helicopter over to Josh. Flying three minutes at 90 knots and then rolling into a thirty degree bank and flying the opposite direction for 180 seconds was boring. Josh was keeping an eye on the second hand of the clock when Higgins spoke again.

"Keep us at cherubs two. I don't want the North Vietnamese to be able to see us with binoculars or on their radar. We're about halfway between Vinh and Haiphong so if you see a fishing boat, we move our orbit because I don't want the bad guys to know where we are. If you see any big sharks, let me know, and I'll let you play with the mini-gun. We haven't fired it in a while and it will be nice to see if it works."

Asshole, we haven't needed to use it because you keep avoiding having to make a rescue. Josh was finishing his third orbit when the sound of a beeper filled their headsets. It meant just one thing: a pilot had punched out. He turned the knob on the ultra-high frequency radio to let it home in on the beeper. As soon as it stabilized and pointed in the direction of the transmitter, he rolled the helicopter onto the heading that would take them to the beeper's source.

"Where are you going?" Higgins demanded.

"Towards the beeper. Someone has been shot down and we need to see if we can pick them up."

"Stay in the orbit until they call us. If they want our help, they'll call," ordered Higgins.

"The sooner we get there, the better the chance we have of picking him up."

"That's someone else's theory, not mine."

Before Josh could think of a reply, the radio crackled:

"Clementine 26, this is Hammer 700. Vector three-four-zero, about three-zero miles, buster. We have a pilot in his parachute. Two A-7s are orbiting and have ordnance to support a rescue. Say estimated time of arrival."

The term "buster" meant 'fly as fast as the helicopter will go', so Josh accelerated the HH-2C to 110 knots.

"Clementine 26 copies," Higgins said into the radio. "ETA 15 minutes." Then he rotated the mike switch to the intercom position. "I've got it. Get the gun armed, Haman. Bennington, rig for possible rescue."

"Aye aye, sir," Petty Officer Bennington responded from the cabin, and Josh heard him moving around the ammunition tray for the mini-gun. Bennington was so tall he had to go on his hands and knees, so he wore a set of foam kneepads.

Josh could feel his heart racing as he went through the checklist to arm and ready the gun. He rested his hand on his knees for a second to make sure they weren't shaking, not sure if he was more scared or excited. This would be his first combat rescue!

To make sure he did everything right, he went through the checklist a second time. He saw the familiar aiming circle in the gun sight's reticle. As he moved the handles, he could hear and feel the gun track. He squeezed off a short burst. The tracers arced out and stitched into the water well over a thousand yards ahead.

"Gun's ready." Josh pulled out the chart he'd used to plot their orbit and drew a line with his finger to where he thought the downed pilot might be.

"Clementine 26, Hammer 700. Pilot is reported in the water a little over a half mile off the beach. Call sign is Power House 310. His wingman, Power House 307 and Saddleback 406 and 408 all have a visual on the pilot as well as radio communication with him on two-four-three point zero. Surf is driving the raft toward the beach, copy?" Hammer 700 was the call sign of a twin turboprop E-2 Hawkeye circling the gulf at 25,000 feet, communicating with the Saddleback A-7s that were orbiting the survivor.

Josh activated the mike button, taking care not to put pressure on the cyclic. "Clementine 26 copies."

"Clementine, this is Hammer 700, fly three-three-five for just over twenty. Buster. Say ETA?"

Josh looked down at the airspeed indicator. Higgins had the H-2 up to 120 knots. "Estimate on scene in less than one-zero mikes." He was getting salty. "Mikes" was another word for minutes.

Josh felt the helicopter slow. He checked and saw their speed was now down to 90 knots. Puzzled, he glanced over at Higgins. *Should I tell him? What the fuck is going on in his head?*

"Clementine 26, switch to UHF frequency two-niner-five point six. You can coordinate with Saddleback 406 who is on the frequency and is the search and rescue combat air patrol and on scene commander They reported seeing mortar shells exploding near the raft and there is a welcoming party gathering on the beach. Copy?"

"Clementine 26 copies and is switching." Josh twirled the knobs on the UHF radio and heard the distinctive side tone before he keyed the mike. "Saddleback 406, Clementine 26 is up."

"Clementine 26, this is Saddleback 406. We each have twelve Mark 82 bombs plus twenty millimeter and are down to less than twenty minutes of play time. Say intentions. Over."

Josh looked at Higgins, whose face was frozen as he stared straight ahead. He waited about five seconds before he keyed the intercom for private conversation. "Suggestions? Steve, what do I tell them?"

"I'm thinking," blurted Higgins.

"We're about five minutes out and the A-7s don't have much fuel left."

"Neither do we."

"We've got plenty of fuel," said Josh. "We can get in, pick the pilot up and still make it back with plenty of gas. That's not our problem. Bad guys on the beach are. What do you want to do? We'll be there in about three minutes."

Silence.

Higgins' head didn't move.

OK, I've been thinking about what I would do if I were the HAC, so if you're not going to tell them what we need, I'll give them instructions. Josh keyed the mike. "Saddleback 406, Clementine 26, can you see the bad guys and the mortar positions?"

"Affirmative. There's about twenty or more soldiers on the beach shooting at Power House 310. We can see the mortars in a clearing about one hundred yards inland."

Josh looked at Higgins. "What now?"

Higgins turned to face him and his wide open eyes told Josh he was scared. His sarcasm was conveyed in a high pitched voice that trembled with fear. "O.K., genius co-pilot, I gather you've got a plan. Tell them what it is."

Dammit, Higgins, you're the aircraft commander and you SHOULD have a plan. Pressing down his own fear, Josh keyed the mike. "Saddlebacks, Clementine 26. As soon as we start to hover, lay your eggs along the tree line to take out the mortars, then come back around for a strafing pass to get what you missed. We'll try to make the pick-up while their heads are down."

"Clementine, we have enough for one pass. Two more A-7s, Power House 301 and 311, are en route. ETA plus ten."

Bennington spoke up from the cabin. "Sir, I've got the horse collar rigged. We can let the pilot hook onto it and drag him seaward to get out of range of the mortars and the small arms fire before we haul him up. We've done it before and it is easy to do."

"Good idea." Josh thought about asking Higgins if he wanted him to fly but decided against it. "What do we do, slow to a hover and toss it to him?"

"A slow three to five knot creep gives him a chance to grab the horse collar, but we don't have to hover. All he has to do is grab hold of it and hang on. He doesn't have to get into the horse collar until we are ready to hoist him up."

Josh turned to Higgins.

"You O.K. with that, Steve?"

No answer. The aircraft commander's face was a blank mask with his eye frozen as he stared straight ahead. Josh could see his face was white and drained of all color. He wasn't sure if it was panic or fear that had taken hold, but he knew some pilots froze at the controls when confronted by enemy fire or serious emergencies. The results were usually fatal. He was determined not to let that happen to him.

"One more thing, Mr. Haman," Bennington called out, "Van der Jagt can jump into the water and help if needed. He's ready to go."

Josh turned around and could see Van der Jagt sitting on the doorway, his feet in swim fins resting on the external fuel tank. The grinning young airman turned around to gave a thumbs up.

Questions raced through Josh's mind. *Higgins, what are you thinking? Don't freeze up now! Should I take over flying the helicopter? Would you let me? If I did take over, who would fire the gun if they needed it?*

The radio crackled. "Saddlebacks have a tally on Clementine 26. Rolling in hot."

Josh didn't see the A-7s but did see their work. For the first time he saw the orange flashes of exploding 500 pound bombs, followed by a ragged row of black clouds. Even from where he was, he saw the splashes along the water's edge from the debris thrown up by the bombs and felt the concussion.

"Roger, Clementine is switching to guard." Josh twirled the knob so that now the radio was tuned to the international ultra-high frequency emergency channel. "Power House 310, this is Clementine 26, do you copy?"

"Roger, Clementine."

"Here's the plan. We're going to toss you the horse collar and then tow you out of range of the mortars. Copy?"

"You'd better hurry, because I'm just 500 yards from the beach and about to go into the water. I'm taking all kinds of small arms fire."

"Copy. Don't pop a smoke. We'll find you."

"Roger."

"Clementine 26 has a tally on Power House 310." Josh could now see the yellow raft and the rows of splashes that, even though he'd never seen them before, looked like what he would expect from a machine gun. The raft jumped and when it settled, it was deflating rapidly.

"I'll keep the bad guys heads down while we make the rescue." He grabbed the two handles that extended from the sight, flipped the red switch cover that allowed him to change the electronically powered gun from safe to on, and put the reticle on the place in the tree line where he saw a series of flashes. Without thinking he squeezed the trigger, and the sand in front of the trees erupted. He raised his aim point and squeezed the trigger again and saw chunks fly off the palm trees. Satisfied, he fired a series of bursts where he thought the machine gun positions were. The winking along the tree line stopped. It was then that he noticed out of the corner of his eye that they were passing over the raft and the helicopter wasn't slowing or turning. Sunlight glinted off the reflective tape of the helmet of the pilot of Power House 310. Where the hell was Higgins going?

"What are you doing? We're supposed to slow down and drop the horse collar and tow the pilot out of here."

"That was your plan, not mine."

"Then what are you going to do?" Josh looked into the cockpit and Higgins had the HH-2C up to 120 knots headed out to sea. "Answer me. We're supposed to pick him up."

"Too much enemy fire. It is way too dangerous to slow down."

"You're going leave him behind?"

"Yes, unless the next two guys can guarantee they can stop the ground fire, I am *not* going back in there."

"Steve, they can't do that!!! We can keep their heads down with the mini-gun and bombs from the A-7."

Before Higgins could answer, an agitated voice filled the head set. "Clementine 26, this is Hammer 700, what just happened? Power House 310 said you flew over him and didn't stop."

Higgins keyed the mike. "Hammer, Clementine 26. Too much... ahhhhhh, too much ground fire. That makes it much too dangerous for us. Need Power House and his playmate to suppress the automatic weapons before we go back in."

Josh looked at his aircraft commander as he rolled the helicopter in an orbit a mile out to sea. He could see the North Vietnamese launching two rubber boats into the surf. Behind him, Van der Jagt was back inside the helicopter with his fins off and was pulling on his flight suit.

"Steve, if we don't go back in now, Power House 310 is going to get captured."

"If we go back in, there's a risk that the gooks will get four more prisoners. It is not worth it."

Bullshit. We could have gotten him on the first pass and everyone in this helicopter as well as the guy in the water knows it. If were that pilot and I survived my time in the Hanoi Hilton, I would come looking for pilots who didn't get me when they had the chance and beat the shit out of them.

The radio crackled again. "Hammer, Clementine, this is Power House 310. Tell my wife I love her. The gooks are about to get to me."

Same Day, 1531 Local Time, on the U.S.S. Sterett

There was none of the usual bantering that went along with the work of putting the helicopter to bed for the night. The grim faces of the detachment's enlisted men matched Josh's dark mood. After noting a minor discrepancy on the yellow sheets of the helicopter's maintenance log, he hung up his helmet bag and survival vest on the rack in the little storage room next to the maintenance office. Josh left without saying a word to either Chief Slaughter or the two air crewman.

Although the ship's captain preferred that officers not eat in the wardroom in their flight suits, they were allowed to get a cup of coffee or something else to drink from the mess. After downing a Coke, Josh grabbed a second one and headed down the passageway and banged on the stateroom door that was two down from his.

"Enter."

Higgins was already showered and changing into a set of khakis.

"What the fuck to do you want, Haman?"

"Sir, we left a man behind out there we could have rescued."

"In my judgment, it was too dangerous."

"In what way?" demanded Josh.

"We were taking heavy machine gun fire. And, besides we didn't have enough fuel."

"The enemy fire stopped when I hammered the tree line. The other A-7s could have made strafing passes. And we had enough fuel to stay in the area for the better part of an hour. So that excuse, sir, is…" Josh paused, then decided to use the word that was on the tip of his tongue. "…bullshit."

"Watch your tongue, Haman! Your mouth may cross a line your brain knows it shouldn't. You don't know that your mini-gun or the A-7s could have suppressed the enemy fire. The gun could have jammed, which it has a habit of doing, then what would you have done?"

"Still tried to pick the guy up. I am confident we would have succeeded. We had plenty of time and gas. We could have saved a man from going to the Hanoi Hilton and we didn't."

"That's his problem, not mine. He knew the risks when he climbed in that A-7. It comes with the job. I wasn't going to hang around long enough for the gooks to figure out how to shoot us down."

"We are here to pick pilots up who are shot down. That is our job and we didn't do it when we could have. Aren't you worried that this detachment will get a reputation as one that won't rescue pilots?"

"No. I'm not worried at all as long as I don't get shot up or go home in a body bag." Higgins stood up and jabbed his finger into Josh's chest. "I have grown weary of your desire to be a hero and in the process get me shot or killed. You've been out here a little over a month and don't know shit from shinola about what we do or how we do it." Higgins turned his back on Josh as he went to his bunk bed.

"Sir, on the contrary, I know what my job is and what our squadron's mission is. I even have an idea of how to do it. And I will try to accomplish it to the best of my ability. Today we had a good plan and it would have worked. If it didn't, then we would have tried something else. He bit back his next thought: *From you, I'm learning how* not *to do this job.* "If it requires getting shot at, so be it. If I get killed in the process, tough shit. At least people around me can say I tried." *Which is more than they can say about you.*

Higgins turned and took two strides across his stateroom. His forefinger stabbed into Josh's chest again, his face, less than a foot from Josh's, was beet red.

"Let me make this clear. I don't give a shit about making rescues, accomplishing the squadron's mission, or this goddamn war. What I give a shit about is getting home in one piece. And if that means I don't take risks and avoid being shot at, so be it. I didn't ask to be assigned to this goddamn squadron, I don't support this fucking war, and if some other poor bastard gets wounded, killed or captured, then it is too bad for him. I just want to survive."

Josh reached up and gently removed the finger that had been tapping on his chest. *I am not going to hit the son-of-a-bitch, no matter how much I want to, but I am not backing down!*

"Sir, I suggest you have someone else come out here and relieve you as the officer-in-charge and that you request an immediate transfer out of HC-7. This will let the rest of us do the job we are trained and assigned to do. I'm not going to leave another man behind."

"Get the fuck out of my stateroom before I put you on report for insubordination!" Higgins snarled.

"With all due respect, Lieutenant Higgins, sir, that would be an interesting discussion. What do you think Power House 310, his squadron mate, and the pilots in the A-7s who were overhead and saw what happened would say at my court martial?"

"What are you now, a fucking sea lawyer?"

"No, sir, but you and I both know I'm right." Josh took a deep breath and twisted the door handle. "Sir, as the administrative officer of this detachment, I'll have your letter requesting a transfer ready for you to sign after chow tonight."

Higgins got squarely in front of him. "You will do NOTHING, repeat *NOTHING* of the sort. That is an order."

Josh leaned back a bit so the spittle spraying from Higgins' mouth didn't land on him. "Sir, if you don't sign it, I will get someone else to endorse it and send it up the chain of command." Josh opened the door and left. When he closed it, he leaned his forehead on the cool metal bulkhead. *This bastard is going to give me a reputation that will ruin my career just as it starts. What a fucking mess!*

"That was interesting."

Josh spun around and saw his roommate. Gainesville pointed towards the aft end of the ship and started walking. He waited until they reached the open main deck by the five-inch gun mount before he spoke.

"I heard most of what was said," stated Gainesville. "Josh, the combat information center is full of enlisted guys who know what went on because they heard the transmissions. I am sure things are being said in the enlisted messes and berthing spaces that don't make your guys happy. Anyway, the captain has the search and rescue frequency piped into the bridge, so he knows what is happening. Captain Danforth heard what went on today and Higgins is making him look bad too. To put it mildly, he doesn't like it. I am sure that he'll do more than endorse the transfer letter. If needed, I think he'll have the ship's admin officer write it. This way, you won't need Higgins's signature. Believe me, if Higgins or anyone from your detachment showed up on the *Oriskany* today or tomorrow, he might get beat up or killed."

"Thanks for the help. I almost called Higgins a coward."

"He is, and he's a disgrace to the Academy and the Navy. There's a fine line between cautious and cowardice and he's on the wrong side. You don't have to sugar-coat it."

"Shit! This is not what I envisioned for my first tour. *Nothing* I learned in school or the training command prepared me for this." Josh looked down at the can of Coke in his hand and took a sip.

"War is hell," sighed Gainsville. "Sometimes the enemy is one of us. I've been in your shoes. When we get to Subic, let's have a beer and I'll tell you about the division officer on my first ship. He was another martinet like Higgins and the captain got him transferred to the Swift boats. On almost every mission, his boat had some kind of problem and he had to return to base. The commanding officer wrote him a bad fitness report and forced him out of the Navy, which I think is what he wanted. What he didn't want was the general discharge with no GI Bill or VA benefits. But that's what he finally got."

Josh swallowed the rest of his Coke and crushed the can. "In the meantime, I have to live and work with the bastard."

"Yes, you do."

Friday, October 23rd, 1970, 0822 Local Time, on the U.S.S. Sterett

Josh was sitting on a makeshift chair made from two of the olive drab cans used to ship parts. They were stacked one on top of the other, and to keep the dirt and grease from staining his khakis he'd folded a piece of two-inch thick packing foam over the top one. He'd just finished proofreading a summary of hours flown and maintenance squawks on their H-2 when Higgins walked into the maintenance space wearing his flight suit and carrying his survival vest and helmet bag.

"Go change, Haman. Our presence has been requested on the *America*. Then go see if the Chief has any mail or stuff they want to send over. We're leaving in ten minutes."

As they were settling in to their seats and strapping in, Higgins leaned across the center console and hissed, "You, *asshole,* will read check lists and do exactly what you are told, nothing more and nothing less. I will handle everything else. Understand?"

Josh nodded.

At one hundred knots, Clementine 26 covered the ninety-five miles to the *America* in less than an hour. Higgins slid the helicopter to a landing on a spot at the forward edge of the angled deck. Waiting for them was Lieutenant Commander Montemayor, the officer-in-charge of Det 110, which had three HH-3As and almost fifty officers and men. Technically, he wasn't in their chain of command, but he was the most senior man in the squadron in the Gulf and acted as the local problem solver for the single plane HH-2C detachments.

As soon as they shut down, Montemayor spoke. "Higgins, you come with me. Haman, you and the crew go down to Ready Room Seven and wait for me." Montemayor, who was half Apache and half Mexican and a very large man, was not smiling.

When Josh and the crew got to the ready room, Van der Jagt and Bennington were summoned by Det 110's Senior Chief. That left Josh sitting by himself, wondering. With nothing to do and no one to talk with, Josh pulled his NATOPS manual out of his helmet bag. As soon as he opened it, a handwritten note on a yellow government phone message form fell out.

> MR. HAMAN,
>
> WHEN WE GET TO THE AMERICA, THE SHIT MAY HIT THE FAN. YOU DID THE RIGHT THING BY TAKING ON HIGGINS. WE'RE AS PISSED AS YOU ARE THAT WE DIDN'T PICK UP POWER HOUSE 310 AND WILL LET EVERYONE KNOW.
>
> BENNINGTON

How the fuck did Bennington know about my conversation with Higgins? Josh wondered. *Shit, it must be all over the ship.*

"Mr. Haman." Josh looked up at a young enlisted man. "The boss wants to see you on the hangar deck by the H-3 at the number one elevator. I'll take you down there."

They wound down a maze of ladders and passageways. On the hangar deck, Josh was careful to step over the tie-down chains as he followed the sailor between the packed planes to where Montemayor waited. He was sitting on one of the yellow tractors used to move planes, one leg up on the tractor and the other on the deck. He gestured for Josh to sit alongside. "Mr. Haman, I want to hear your version of what happened yesterday."

After mounting the tractor, Josh's legs dangled loosely over the side. It took him nearly ten minutes to recount the details of the mission. Montemayor let him finish before asking, "Do you think you could have made the rescue?"

"Yes, sir, without a doubt. The guy wasn't hurt. We could have towed him out through the surf or just picked him up. We had plenty of air cover to support us."

"Well, for what it is worth, everyone on board the helicopter except Higgins agrees with you." Montemayor stopped and took a deep breath before continuing, "Look, this stays between us. Higgins is a problem: to you, to the detachment, to the squadron and to the Navy. But you're going to have to live with him until we get a replacement out here. CTF 77 sent a personal message to our squadron commanding officer demanding that Higgins be relieved. It was so hot that it's still smoking. The H-2s are being phased out, and Higgins is one of the last H-2 aircraft commanders in the squadron. I've got the first HH-3As in Det 110 and more of them are coming. But until they get here, we've got to keep the H-2s at sea. So, Haman, you are stuck in a shitty situation. I had a heart-to-heart with Higgins a few minutes ago that was one part ass chewing and one part trying to encourage him. I also told him to give you as much stick time as possible. I don't know what effect it will have on him, but hopefully he won't teach you any bad habits. Oh, and Higgins doesn't know about CTF-77's message. The commanding officer of the *Sterett* does. So everyone in the chain-of-command is aware of the problem."

"Sir, what am I supposed to do? I don't want my career tarred and feathered by this guy."

"Live with him until we make the change. That will be when the *Sterett* comes into Subic in about two to three weeks. Bennington will brief Chief Slaughter so the enlisted guys don't get hurt with the flak from this. You're doing what you are supposed to do. Keep it up. I know it is hard dealing with Higgins. Everyone—enlisted, me, and the squadron chain of command—has got your back. You'll come out of this okay from a fitness report perspective, and you just have to trust me on that."

"What if he refuses to make another rescue?"

"Figure something out. We *can't* leave another guy behind."

Chapter 4 – STAND DOWN AND CEASE FIRE

Saturday, October 24th, 1970,

0825 Local Time, on the U.S.S. Sterett

Josh waited patiently while the Filipino steward put down the white china plate on the wardroom table. The plate had a thin navy-blue band around the rim of the dish, and the two fried eggs on the center of the plate looked up at him like two large eyeballs.

This morning he'd waited to eat until his roommate came in after finishing the midnight-to-six a.m. Combat Information Center watch. With the food served, coffee and juice cups filled, the stewards retreated to the pantry and left the two officers alone.

"Sorry we didn't get a chance to talk before you left. The captain showed me a draft of his message to CTF 77 and asked me if he had the facts straight." Gainesville slid a sheet across the table. "This is a copy of what was in the log."

"So you know what's about to happen?"

"Yeah, sort of. Hopefully, it will be done quietly. The Navy doesn't like it when an Academy graduate doesn't perform. We're supposed to be the best, the brightest and the bravest, but like everyplace else, there are occasional bad apples in the barrel."

"Do you know when we're heading back to Subic?"

"Unless the ship's schedule changes, we arrive on November 13th. That's a Friday, so if you are superstitious, it's significant."

"I'm not."

"Neither am I. We're in the middle of a bombing halt, so things are going to slow way down until we start up again. You may be lucky; it may be quiet and boring and you won't have to make a rescue."

Higgins stuck his head into the wardroom. "Haman, suit up. We're going flying. Launch in about 30 minutes. Meet me on the flight deck."

Gainesville looked at Josh, who was as surprised as his

roommate. Before either man could say anything, the bridge announced that the *Sterett* was going to flight quarters.

Josh was buckling the crotch straps to his survival vest when Higgins came around the front of the helicopter.

"Get in the right seat. You're going to be the HAC today and do most of the flying. Montemayor told me to get you as much flight time in the right seat as possible, so we're starting today with a few approaches and landings on the *Sterett*. Then we're going to get the ship's mail at Cam Ranh; by then it'll be dark and the *Sterett* will use its fire control radar to provide a controlled approach to the deck, on which you will try to land. If all goes well, you'll get about eight hours in the right seat and a bunch of landings. If it is not dark when we get back, we'll take a break, get something to eat, then fly around at night and get you some instrument approaches to the ship."

"Yes, sir."

* * * * *

It was almost ten at night and Josh was dog-tired after almost nine hours of flight time. The adrenaline from six night approaches to the ship was still flowing through his body more than an hour after his last landing on the *Sterett*'s helo deck.

The night was dark and moonless and the wind calm. With the *Sterett* steaming at 15 knots, it provided the only wind over the deck. On his first pass, the strength of the burble from the ship's superstructure surprised him, and they'd wallowed around before he got the helicopter stable enough to land.

He was still damp from a mixture of sweat and a recent shower as he typed a letter to Danielle, sitting at the desk that folded down from the chest of drawers bolted to the stateroom's bulkhead. Next to him, his flight suit was drying out on the door of the closet. He'd already put his rank insignia and wings on a fresh set of wash khakis that were laid out on the top bunk.

"How'd it go?" Gainesville tossed his notebook on his cluttered desk and began to undress.

"Great. Higgins made me fly approaches from all kinds of angles to show me what a good approach looked like and a bad one. To be honest, mine weren't unsafe but they weren't pretty. I need a lot more practice before I'll be able to do it well."

"How was Higgins?"

"Very professional. Not very talkative, but a good instructor. He's not like some of the screamers I had in the training command."

"What's a screamer?" Gainesville leaned forward as he pulled off his black steel-toed boots and tossed them into the corner next to his rack.

"There are some instructors who like to create stress and pressure on their students, so as soon as you get strapped in they start screaming instructions non-stop and nothing you do is right. Hence the name screamers."

"Why does the Navy allow these guys to teach?"

"They do it to test students and see how they perform under duress in a hostile environment."

"What do you do when you get a screamer?"

"Well, you can't ignore them because they're strapped into the same airplane, so you try to just filter out the noise from the instructions and try not to get a down on the flight. I'd turn the volume on the intercom down as low as I could."

"How often did you come across them?"

"I had one in primary for two flights. He was a Marine captain who started out the hop brief by telling me that he thought that the Navy was letting too many students get their wings and it was his sacred duty to weed more out so they don't kill his fellow Marines. It went downhill from there."

"What happened?" Gainesville sipped from a glass of cherry-flavored drink that he'd brought from the wardroom. The sweet flavor helped mask the taste of chlorine added to the water that came out of the ship's desalinization plant.

"On the first hop I had with him, not much. He ranted and raved while I did my level best and hit all the check points in my maneuvers. I think it pissed him off that he wasn't rattling me. I knew my procedures and maneuvers cold so I could focus on doing them well and, like I said, I ignored the noise coming from the back seat."

Josh closed the notebook that contained his notes and his diary. "Then, about a week later, I had him for another flight. He started out by saying that he thought my last flight was a fluke and he was going to give me a down for the flight. He said I was just an average stick and average wasn't good enough. I knew that my grades, even from him, were really good, so I didn't react. Then, when we got airborne, we were practicing emergency landing patterns as the last item on the flight, and one of the things we do is open the canopy of the T-34. Apparently I opened it before he was ready, so he threw his knee board at me. It clanged off my helmet and down onto the side console. I looked at it and said over the intercom, 'Captain Moon'—that was his name—'a large piece of debris just landed in my cockpit and I am going to dispose of it.' Then I tossed it out of the plane! We were five thousand feet over Perdido Bay, so I knew it wouldn't hit anyone. He didn't say a word other than 'Take me home.' In the debrief, all he did was smile and say, 'You'll do fine.' He gave me all above averages on the grades for the flight! I found out later that he did that to all the students to see what happened. He'd get kneeboards that were damaged and fill them up with useless stuff. I was the first who tossed it out of the airplane."

Gainesville chuckled. "I want to hear more of these stories. You're the first aviator I've roomed with. Tomorrow looks to be a slow day, but you never know what they'll lay on us in the wee hours. You can stay up, but I am going to go to sleep."

"Me too, I'm bushed."

The light over Gainesville's pillow went out. Josh looked at his watch. It was almost midnight. He put the khakis on a hanger, climbed into the top rack and turned out the reading light.

Sunday, November 1st, 1970,
0826 Local Time, on the U.S.S. Sterett

In the maintenance shack, the black phone jangled.

Chief Slaughter, when he was not out by the helicopter or down in the machine shop, was the primary occupant. He unhooked the dial phone from the cradle and put it to his ear without looking up from the manual he was reading. "Helo det."

He listened for a few seconds. "Yes, sir. I'll let Mr. Haman know. He's out by the helo."

Slaughter put down the phone and called over the aviation ordnance man. "Koslowski, tell Mr. Haman that Lieutenant Gainesville asked him to come to CIC. While you're out there, make sure that Van der Jagt gives you the preflight card so you can sign off on the gun. It should be fully loaded and ready to go. And make sure that the cover on the gun's power switch has shear wire on it to keep it closed."

* * * * *

CIC was a warren of grease pencil displays and scopes for radar and sonar, as well as status boards for every one of the ship's sensors, weapons, radars and communications and navigation equipment. It was located just aft of the bridge and petty officer opened the cipher-locked door after Josh knocked. He was ushered him to a swivel chair by one of the communications consoles.

"Haman," Gainesville said, "we've going to be the controller of a three-plane reconnaissance flight off the *Oriskany*. A photo bird with the call sign Cork Tip 602 is going to go feet dry south of Haiphong and then travel down the coast and exit south of Vinh. Two fighters, call sign Hell Cat 106 and 109, will be providing escort. Sometimes the North Vietnamese Air Force try to bounce the photo birds, particularly if we are snooping around something they don't want us to see. The E-1s on the *Oriskany* are all down with some sort of maintenance problem, so we've been assigned as the controller. The board over there shows the squadrons and the call signs. *Oriskany* has two F-8s—Red Flash 200 and 207—and two A-7s—Saddleback 403 and 405—on two minute alert, so sit back and watch the show. My call sign is Battle Torch and the *Oriskany's* is Sea Lord. Now, you get to see *me* work for a change!"

Josh gave his roommate a thumbs up and sat back on the chair. In a corner of the room, an enlisted man began drawing the track of the three-plane formation on a giant plotting board.

Jeff leaned across the console between the two chairs. "Bullseye

—that's the imaginary reference point we set up for all missions– is that star about ten miles off the coast. All the direction calls will be made noting the bearing and distance to that point unless it is a bogey call and we start vectoring the fighters."

"Boss, this is Radar. We've got six bogeys heading south toward two F-8s, the Hell Cats. We're notifying them now."

Josh could see the lines with arrowheads showing the six possible MiGs moving down from the north, and in the background he could hear the muffled voices of the flight leader acknowledging the calls. Even though the two flights were almost one hundred miles apart, at a closing speed in excess of nine hundred knots it wouldn't be long before the dogfight started, assuming the North Vietnamese pilots wished to engage.

Gainesville picked up the closest of two handsets. "Sea Lord, this is Battle Torch. Recommend you launch the alert fighters. Six bogeys closing in on the Hell Cats. Copy."

"Battle Torch, Sea Lord. Launching Red Flash 200 and playmate 207 now. They will check in with you on channel 19 for vectors."

Gainesville turned to Josh. "Did you understand what just happened?"

"Yup. And, it's only about 50 miles from where we are."

"Correct, and we are heading north at about 12 knots."

"I see the board says Det 110 on the *America* is on alert for SAR. They don't have anyone airborne. If you believe the board, they're 140 miles east of us. That means an hour and half flight time to get to the action, even if the helo det is on two minute alert and has a H-3 pre-flighted and ready to go. Who made that call?"

Gainesville just looked at Josh and rolled his eyes.

"Oh fuck. No one wants us to be on alert because they don't think we'll do our job!"

"Josh, I didn't say that."

"You didn't have too."

The tracks showing the MiGs now looked like fishhooks as the MiGs headed north, refusing to engage the pursing F-8s, who were now trailed by the two fighters just launched from the *Oriksany*. "Jeff, how long can the F-8s stay up there? Shouldn't they be turning for home by now?"

"They can stay up a few more minutes before they have to turn home."

"Mr. Gainesville, we have a problem."

"Put it on the speaker." Gainesville reached up and twirled the volume knob on the red-painted speaker housing in an overhead rack.

"Battle Torch, this is Red Flash 207. My playmate Red Flash 200 has an engine problem and is going to ride it down as far as he can. We've got about 30 miles to go before we go feet wet. He's a sitting duck for their AAA."

"Jeff, what's his position from the *Sterett*?" Josh demanded. He was half out of his chair.

"Bearing is three-five-oh at about 60 miles."

"Mayday, mayday, Red Flash 200 has flamed out. Restart failed. Ejecting now."

"Jeff, call Higgins and the maintenance shack and tell Chief Slaughter that we're going to get Red Flash 200. We'll launch as soon as we can and get vectors from you as soon as we're airborne." Josh was walking backwards toward the door as he spoke. He slid down the ladders to the O-1 level and then sprinted to the helo deck.

By the time he got to there, Van Der Jagt and Bennington had already removed the blade tie downs and were donning their survival vests, while others had removed the tie-down chains by the tail wheel.

"Where the fuck are you going?" Higgins pulled Josh around by the shoulder so they were face to face.

"To get a pilot of an F-8 who just punched out."

"No you're not. No one authorized this mission. We have not been tasked or assigned this mission."

"Lieutenant Higgins, I just came from CIC and it will be authorized by the time we're airborne. We're going with you or without you. Your choice." Josh started to climb into the right seat.

"You're not a HAC. You're not qualified to go." Higgins grabbed

Josh's arm and yanked.

"Let go of my arm." Josh tried to keep his voice calm and level. "Either get in the other seat or go back to your stateroom. Either way, we're going to go try to make a rescue. Make a fucking decision."

Higgins pulled Josh off the main mount. As soon as he regained his balance, Josh shoved Higgins in the chest. He staggered backward and fell. Enraged, he charged, tackling Josh and slamming him into the side of the helicopter. Chief Slaughter and two other enlisted men pulled Higgins away from his co-pilot.

"Sir, we've got him and know what to do!" the chief shouted. "Get the helo started and get going."

"Haman! I will have your fucking ass for this!" Higgins screamed as he flailed at the three enlisted men who were carrying him into the hangar. "I'll make sure that all of you are fucking court-martialed for this! This is mutiny!"

"No, it's not!" Josh yelled back. "Mutiny is when men *refuse* to do their duty. We're going to *do* our duty."

"Need a co-pilot?" Van der Jagt was smiling as he strapped into the left seat of the helicopter.

"How often have you flown as a co-pilot?"

"How many times have you flown as the HAC?"

"Point made." Josh tossed him the checklist. "Read it and let's get the show on the road."

Once airborne and headed north, Josh keyed the mike. "Battle Torch, this is Clementine 26. We're cherubs two, heading three-five-zero. Say pigeons."

"Clementine 26, head three-four-five for forty-five." Gainesville's voice came over the radio. "Have notified all concerned that you are on your way. Battle Torch Zero Zero Actual approved launch and the mission. Good luck. Copy?"

"Clementine 26 copies and thanks." Josh knew that when Gainesville used Zero Zero Actual the commanding officer of the Sterett had authorized the mission. At least for the time being, his ass was covered.

"Sir, what was that about?"

"The skipper of the ship approved our launch. Lieutenant Gainesville has told the *Oriskany* that we are en route and will make or at least attempt to make the rescue. Or we'll die trying! But let's not be too reckless about this!"

"Yes, sir. It's about time we started out wanting to make the rescue, instead of trying to find an excuse not to."

"Van der Jagt, who's in the back? I never did look."

"It is me, sir, Bennington, and Koslowski is the swimmer," a voice called out.

"Welcome aboard. You all know that by being on this helo, you may have ended your careers."

"I doubt that, sir." Bennington, as a petty officer, first class, was the senior air crewman in the helicopter. "But if we make the rescue and they throw us out of the Navy, we'll know we've done the right thing. If we get killed, at least we tried."

"O.K. Just wanted to let you know there is no turning back. Next subject, Van der Jagt, have you ever fired the mini-gun?"

"No, sir. But I have spent a lot of time shooting from a helo with an M-60."

"It is really simple. Just turn it on and look through the reticle. Use short bursts and walk the tracers into the target. It will shoot 1,200 rounds a minute in the low mode, which is all you really need."

"Got it."

"Bennington, when we get there, tell me what you want me to do with the helicopter and I'll figure out how to get it done. If we're lucky, the pilot will be out in the water."

"Clementine 26, Red Flash 200 is in the water about three to four hundred yards off the beach. He says he is taking small arms fire from the tree line. Saddlebacks are in an orbit at angels 12 when you need them."

"Clementine 26 copies."

"Clementine 26, this is Saddleback 403. Are you really going to do this?"

"Saddleback, this is Clementine 26. Affirmative or die trying."

Josh kept the HH-2C at a steady 120 knots at 200 feet and marveled at how smooth the ride was. They were just below the speed at which the helo started vibrating from the blades going too fast through the air in an aerodynamic condition known as blade stall. His mind raced.

* * * * *

Five minutes after the HH-2C lifted off the *Sterett*, the phone rang in the detachment's maintenance office. "Chief Slaughter."

"Chief, this is Captain Danforth. I have been told that Lieutenant Higgins is being confined in the helo det's storage compartment back by the helicopter deck. Is that true?"

"Yes, sir, it is. We had to pull him off Lieutenant Haman."

"That's what I heard. I want to speak with him."

"Yes, sir. I'll get him, sir. Please stand by."

Slaughter stuck his head around the corner where three of the enlisted men had a frustrated, angry Higgins boxed into a corner. He was screaming invectives and had made several attempts to break out of his virtual prison. Each time, the enlisted men kept their hands clasped behind their backs as they maintained a solid wall of human flesh between Higgins and the open hangar.

"Mr. Higgins, Captain Danforth wants to speak with you on the phone."

The three men were joined by three others, and all six escorted Higgins to the phone.

Chief Slaughter handed him the black handset and sat back on the chair.

Higgins was red-faced and his eyes shot darts at everyone in the room. He took a deep breath and put the phone to his ear.

"Lieutenant Higgins here, sir. Captain Danforth, I need to report a mutiny by Lieutenant Junior Grade Haman and three enlisted who took off without my authorization on an unauthorized rescue mission after assaulting me, their detachment officer-in-charge and a superior officer. If they return, they need to be arrested, thrown in the brig and brought up on formal charges. Furthermore, Haman is totally unqualified to fly such a mission. We'll be lucky if he doesn't get shot down and the crew killed or captured. They wouldn't listen to me even though I gave them the order to stand down. They stole my, I mean, the detachment's helicopter. Haman and the three crewman need to be hauled in front of a courts martial. The charges will start with theft of government property, assault and mutiny. Chief Slaughter and three others whose names I will give you in a minute also need to be arrested and charged with assault. As soon as the men confining me to the hangar are ordered by you to let me go, I will write a formal report and outline the charges to be brought against these men."

Higgins took another deep breath as he stared daggers at the enlisted men keeping him boxed in the little office. He shifted impatiently on his feet as he waited for a voice on the other end of the line to respond.

Danforth's voice was firm. His Southern drawl made it sound comforting. "Lieutenant Higgins, thank you for your report." Higgins began to smile as he listened to the calm, soft voice.

"However, the purpose of this call is to inform you that I am relieving you of your command. You will be escorted to your stateroom by the two Marines who are headed aft right now. Once in your stateroom, you will remain there until the *Sterett* returns to Subic Bay. A steward will take your meal orders by phone and you will be escorted to go to the head as needed. You will talk to no one without my express permission. You will get an hour a day to exercise on the foredeck, during which time you will be watched by a member of the Marine detachment. Any violation of my instructions will result in your immediate confinement in the brig. Do I make myself clear?"

Higgins' head rocked back. "But sir, Haman led a mutiny! Chief Slaughter and three other men attacked me! Haman stole the helicopter and took off on an unauthorized mission that he is unqualified to fly…"

"Lieutenant Higgins, I am not going to debate this with you. By the time they lifted off, I had approved the mission. Just so you know, the reason you are being relieved as the detachment officer-in-charge is based on your actions on previous missions as well as this one. That is all. Put Chief Slaughter back on the phone."

* * * * *

At cherubs one, Josh watched the jungle transition from a line on the horizon to a green blur to distinguishable trees less than a mile from shore. Between the water and the trees was a thin strip of sand. The radio crackled to life.

"Clementine 26, you're about five miles from Red Flash 200. Two boats are trying to get through the surf, and two more boats are north of the survivor, but they haven't gotten into the water yet. Red Flash 207 went to the tanker and should be back in about ten mikes. Bad news. We're all you're gonna get for awhile. Sea Lord has a catapult problem and cannot launch aircraft. Estimated time to repair is at least another thirty mikes. Over."

"Clementine 26 copies. On our run in, we'll make the call as to when and where we need you to suppress enemy fire."

Josh keyed the intercom. "Van der Jagt, get the mini gun ready. Once you go through the checklist, I want you to test a one-to-two second burst. We only have two thousand rounds, and it will go through them in a hurry if you keep the trigger down. As soon as we see the boats, I want you to take them out. My guess is that their guns will be along the tree line waiting for us to show up. Shoot at anyone who is shooting at us."

"Got it."

As Josh checked the chart, he heard the humming of the mini-gun.

"I like this thing!!! I fired two bursts and fired about fifty rounds each time, according to the counter on the armament panel. It sure spits out a lot of lead in a hurry."

"We should see the boats any minute now. As soon as they are in range, which is anything under one thousand yards, let them have it. But save some ammo for the rescue."

"Yes, sir."

"Boats at 1030, sir," called Bennington, kneeling in the doorway with his M-16 in hand and his head peering around the cabin frame.

He turned back just in time to see a row of water spouts erupt just short of the first target. The second burst walked across the mid-section the 18 foot boat. The third group of bullets sent the man by the outboard engine over the side in a pink haze, and the man in the front slumped forward in a shower of splinters.

"Second boat has a machine gun in the bow. Engaging now." Van der Jagt's voice was calm and very measured as his first burst found the range. On the second, he held the trigger down for three seconds as he hosed the boat from bow to stern and turned it into matchsticks. "I don't think either one will bother us anymore."

As the helo passed the sinking boats, Josh looked at the water around them, red with blood. "I agree."

Josh rotated the mike switch from radio to intercom. "Bennington, if we have to, we'll drag the pilot out to sea and then hover to pick him up. Van der Jagt, you engage anything on the shore that shoots at us. Koslowski, you don't go in the water unless the pilot can't get into the horse collar. Everybody got it?" Josh looked back in the cabin and got two thumbs up.

"Sir, you fly, I'll shoot." Van der Jagt had a grim smile on his face.

Josh rolled the HH-2C into a 60 degree bank. As he did, a series of large spouts started 50 yards in front of the helicopter and passed under it.

"Sir, I see muzzle flashes. Am returning fire."

"Where?"

"Two o'clock."

Josh saw tracers flash overhead and tried to ignore them.

"Sir, there's a second one over there at ten." The mini-gun hummed. The water spouts stopped.

Josh keyed the radio. "Saddlebacks, Clementine 26 is taking heavy machine gun fire from the tree line from my ten and two o'clock. Can one of you knock them out?"

"Already on the way down. Pull out if you start taking hits."

"Roger that."

"I've got the horse collar ready to toss, sir. About fifty feet to go,"

Bennington reported, his head out the door.

"I see him." A row of green tracers zipped past the cockpit, others set off water spouts right by the raft. The mini-gun hummed and Josh could hear the clanking of empty brass shell casings as they struck the bottom of the turret just below his feet.

Ping! Ping! Bang! Ping! Ping!

"What the fuck was that?"

"Sir, the helo is taking hits." Bennington kept his head out the door as he spoke. "Pings are bullets going through the airframe. S*mack* means a bullet hit something solid."

"Where?" Josh's eyes flew to the instruments. No caution lights were lit and all of the gauges were normal. So far, the damage wasn't serious.

ZZZZZZiiiippppp. Thwack. Josh felt the heat of something that went past his face and smelled burned gunpowder. He looked to his right and saw Van der Jagt gazing through the reticle of the mini-gun, pumping out bursts. Just above his left hand, there was a big dent in the side of the gun sight handle.

"Easy. Try to maintain forty feet, sir."

Josh realized that he had yanked up on the collective on the bang and eased it back down to 40 feet. The helicopter suddenly rocked and shuddered from the concussion of a string of bombs that turned trees into matchsticks.

"Horse collar in the water!"

Thwack!

"Survivor is getting into the collar."

Ping ping, thwack, ping, ping, ping.

"Survivor is in the horse collar and coming up. Let's get the fuck out of here."

The HH-2C shuddered and groaned as the main rotor blades bit into the humid air and the nose started rotating to the right despite the fact that Josh was applying full left rudder. By the time he realized he'd lost rudder control because he'd added way too much power to quickly, the helicopter was skidding as it climbed and accelerated. Josh glanced down at the two needles of the torque gauge. They were just below the maximum limit. Going over it for more than a few seconds would mean they would have to replace the transmission. The helo was past 60 knots by the time he got it back into balanced flight.

"Sir, we have the survivor in the cabin. He's O.K."

"Great work, Bennington."

Josh activated the radio. "Saddlebacks, Clementine 26, we have Red Flash 200 on board. Say pigeons to your home plate?"

"Clementine 26, great work. Pigeons to Sea Lord are one-one-zero at seventy-five. Do you have enough gas?"

"Roger. See you there."

Josh began a slow climb to 1,000 feet. Once level, with the HH-2C trimmed and at a comfortable 90 knots, he dialed in the *Oriskany's* TACAN channel; his hand was shaking visibly and his feet were jittering against the floor. He forced his feet flat.

"Van der Jagt, follow the check list to make sure the gun is in the safe position and the power is off. Then dial in channel forty-seven on the TACAN so we can find the *Oriskany*. Meanwhile, I will check in with the *Sterett*. Break break. Bennington, how's our new passenger?"

"Wet, but no worse for wear. He said he wrenched his neck on the ejection but I don't think he did any major damage and he doesn't have any numbness. He should be fine."

"Great. Thanks for all the help."

"Sir, you do know we took some hits. As loud as they were, I think all they hit was the armor plate. No leaks back here and we can't smell jet fuel."

"If we can, I want to go back to the *Sterett*. When we land, take a good look at the rotor head and rotor blades and check for leaks." Josh keyed the mike. "Battle Torch, Clementine 26, over?"

"Clementine 26, this is Battle Torch. Understand mission successful. Well done! We'll celebrate when you get back. Battle Torch out."

Same Day, 1306 Local Time, on the U.S.S. Sterett

As he pulled into a hover over the deck of the *Sterett*, Josh saw his roommate standing off to one side of the hangar. As they landed, he keyed the mike. "Van der Jagt, start the post flight and I'll join you in the maintenance shack as soon as I talk to Mister Gainesville. Hopefully, we won't be airlifted to Leavenworth."

"Sir, I kind of doubt that will happen. You did what was needed to be done and I'll tell that to anybody who will listen."

"That goes for Koslowski and me," Bennington added.

"Thanks guys." Josh pulled off his helmet and tossed it on the seat. He felt as if someone had drained all the energy out of his body.

Josh greeted the smiling men of Det 104 as they looked over the helicopter and offered their congratulations. "Josh, that was out-fucking-standing. The skipper is proud of you." Gainesville held out his hand.

"Thanks." Josh shook his roommate' hand. "Where's Higgins?"

"He's confined to his room until we get to Subic. The skipper relieved him after you took off and fired off a message to CTF 77 outlining his actions."

"So I'm not going to jail?"

"Not yet. There are some that may disapprove, but there are nothing but cheers around here—and on the *Oriskany*."

"Jeff, do you know how many rules I just broke?"

"No, but you are going to tell us while the ship's yeoman records your statement, as well as one from each member of your crew. We've already got statements from the men in the det. As far as breaking the rules go, look, a pilot went down, you saved him before he was captured. Everything else is secondary. You may get your hand slapped, but not by this ship's CO. He authorized the mission and that is in the ship's log."

Jeff pointed toward the passageway. "There are special cakes being baked for dinner tonight. Higgins has been on this ship for almost a year and this is the first time a helicopter that launched from the *Sterett* ever picked anybody up."

Chapter 5 – SHIPBOARD CASUALTY

Thursday, November 12th, 1970,
1224 Local Time, Beijing

The empty wicker baskets that had contained steamed dumplings were cleared away. A Soviet Army officer, stocky and dark of hair, wearing the shoulder boards of a colonel and the colored collar tabs of the GRU, pulled out an envelope from the breast pocket of his tunic.

"Brigadier Chia," the Soviet officer said in his deep voice as he straightened out three folded sheets of paper, "my government would like to give you a gift. I think the People's Liberation Army will find these messages very interesting reading."

The Chinese officer didn't look at the papers. "Before I read them, I would like to know why you are giving them to my country?"

Colonel Vassily Raiskov, a twenty year veteran of the GRU and one of its experts on the Chinese military, leaned forward. "Consider it a gesture of my country's good will and friendship."

"What is their source?" As a member of the Second Department of the General Staff of the People's Liberation Army, the general was a trained intelligence officer who had also spent time in the Third Department, which specialized in electronic intelligence gathering.

Raiskov put his hands back in his lap and continued in a voice that was just above a whisper. "We have the ability to decode American electronic messages sent by radio. We run about two months behind, so it is of no use on a battlefield, but we can learn what they are planning and what they have learned."

"How do I know that this is not some kind of disinformation? Or that this Soviet capability is real?"

"If you read them and closely follow events, you will find they are very, very real. I know we do not know each other well, but I assure you, General Chia, these are not fakes." Raiskov gestured with his hand as if to say, *read.*

When he had been directed to contact Chia, Raiskov hadn't known what the man's rank really was, since all ranks had been abolished in the Cultural Revolution of 1965 to further promote the egalitarian organization that Mao had led to victory in 1948. His superiors had simply given Raiskov a name and a phone number, and ordered him to use these messages as a way to build a relationship. *Cultivate him,* his superiors had said, *and see where it leads.*

Raiskov had started studying the People's Republic of China right after graduating from the academy. He was promoted to colonel after he predicted that Mao would do something to return to power after the Great Leap Forward failed to turn the country into an industrialized nation and created the Great Chinese Famine. Raiskov was right in saying that Mao would exact revenge on those he thought were members of the bourgeoisie and not true communists.

He also predicted that the Chinese might attack across the Amur River. They did so in a series of bloody skirmishes in March of 1969 that brought both countries to the brink of war that had a chance of going nuclear. What Raiskov's analysis failed to predict was how bloody the socio-political convulsion would be or that now, in 1970, four years after it started, it was still going on and affecting Sino-Soviet relations.

Nonetheless, his analysis had impressed the lieutenant general who led the GRU's Third Directorate. So now he was assigned to Beijing with the sole purpose of trying to figure out what was going on. Building a relationship with Chia was just one of the many initiatives he'd either started or been handed.

Succeed and Raiskov knew that he would be promoted again. Fail, or be perceived to fail, and he would wind up at a desk with nothing to do—or wind up in the Gulag, or shot. Many of the GRU officers joked that they didn't know which was worse, a bullet to the back of the head at an early age or spending the rest of your live in some godforsaken prison in Siberia being worked to death. The consensus was a bullet was better.

Chia scanned the first sheet and then the second before he

returned to the first and read it carefully.

Raiskov wanted to make sure that the Chinese officer understood the implications of what he just read. He wasn't sure how good the man's English was and this was a test. "The messages say the American Air Force wants to send either U-2 spy planes or high speed SR-71s to photograph trains in yards near Nanning and Mengzi to see if there are SA-2 missiles hidden in the box cars."

"I understand that. The message is very clear."

"As a result of this information, we shot down one of the U-2s over Russia and another over Cuba."

Chia sat back in his chair. "I remember. Eventually you traded Gary Powers for a Soviet spy." The Chinese officer put the messages down. "Colonel Raiskov, the information in these messages can't be true. There is no reason to photograph the trains because there are no missiles on them."

"You know that, General, and I know that, but apparently the Americans do not," Raiskov said smoothly. "We decoded other messages and the Americans have done just what they say they are going to do. That is why we are confident that this is not a hoax." Raiskov looked at the Chinese general, trying to see if there was a glimmer of emotion. The man's face was impassive.

"I need to see much more before I take this to my superiors."

"You will, because my government has asked me to share them with you. It is a gesture of friendship between our fraternal, socialist countries." *What bullshit!!! Mao didn't trust Stalin and Stalin didn't trust Mao. Now Mao doesn't trust Brezhnev, and we're confused as to why anyone would create something as bad as the Great Cultural Revolution. It has everyone in Moscow scratching their heads.*

Anyway, you're hooked, you bastard. You won't take it forward because you are afraid of losing face if they contain disinformation. You need more, so I give you enough to let you verify it. Then you'll use it to become a hero. That's O.K. by me. I'm just doing what I am told.

"Ah, our duck dish is here. Let us eat."

Same Day, 1426 Local Time, on the U.S.S. Sterett

The *Sterett* pitched and rolled in the swells caused by the thunderstorms that had been pelting the ship for the past week. Josh wondered if he should start building an ark.

Working on the helicopter in the hangar was difficult. There was barely enough room to walk by on either side. Salt water and magnesium alloys liked each other and the corrosion that followed their mating happened quickly. It found minute cracks in the paint and, over time, turned the alloy into a fine white powder. The detachment's only defense was to wash the helo and check everywhere for bubbles in the paint, under which one often found corrosion.

Josh was reading the draft of the daily aircraft status message prepared by Chief Slaughter when the phone rang.

"Helo, det." The chief listened for about ten seconds. 'Yes, sir, I'll tell him and we'll get ready."

"Get ready for what, Chief?"

"We've got a sailor that needs to be evacuated and the skipper wants you to fly him to one of the carriers as soon as the doc gets him ready. Lieutenant Gainesville wants you to meet him in CIC."

"Tell him I'm on my way."

Josh knocked on the CIC door and was directed to the back. It took about 30 seconds to wind through the warren of consoles and plotting boards to reach Gainesville.

"Jeff, what's up?"

"Bad news. Both the primary and secondary surface and air search radars are out. We know the motor on one is the culprit, and the only place we can get it fixed is at Subic Bay. We're not sure about the other, yet. But in the process of troubleshooting, the technician got badly burned in an electrical flash fire. He's in sick bay and the doc says he may lose both arms if we don't get him to a hospital quickly. So Captain Danforth asked me to ask if you would fly the young sailor to the *America* as soon as possible. The captain knows you are not supposed to fly without a HAC, so he said he'll put whatever you want in writing to cover you. Before you got here, Higgins told him it was legal to fly the H-2 with a single pilot under visual flight rules."

"Higgins is correct, but the single pilot has to be a designated HAC. I'm not." Josh looked at his friend and roommate. "Tell the skipper I'll go, and a written order would be nice to cover my ass, but not necessary. I'm probably in such hot water anyway that I'll be lucky if they don't send me to Leavenworth."

"Ye roommate of little faith, I keep telling you that Captain Danforth has your back, along with the men in your det. He'll be glad you can do this. So how do you want to transport the kid?"

"I'd like to have one of my crewmen in the back along with a corpsman and the patient strapped to a Stokes litter. This will make it easier to get him in and out of the helicopter. I'll go get the helo cranked up. As soon as they're all set in the back, we'll take off."

"Got it." Gainesville referred to the chart. "We're seventy-five nautical miles southwest of the *America,* based on her position two hours ago. That's the closest ship with a decent hospital. The carrier knows you are coming. My guess is that it'll take you about forty-five minutes to get there and about thirty back."

"What's the weather forecast?"

"Shitty. Rain."

"Is the *Sterett's* TACAN working?"

"Honest answer is not sure. We don't think it was hurt by the power surge because it was working before we shut it down to check everything out. The captain doesn't want to use the search radars until we find out what caused the flash fire. If needed, I'll crank up our fire control radars to guide you if you get lost. Give us a shout when you are on your way back."

"Got it." Josh mulled the mission over in his mind as he left the combat information center. Take off from the *Sterett* with a badly burned sailor; find the *America,* whose last known position was 75 miles away, but knowing how carriers operate, she isn't there anymore. Then, after unloading the sailor, take off and find the *Sterett,* which is steaming east toward the Philippines. And, oh, by the way, do it without your final destination having any viable radar capabilities in weather that requires serious instrument flying. And don't forget, you have less than 80 hours in the HH-2C and you are not a qualified HAC.

On his way to the helo, Josh stopped at his stateroom and pulled the Mark 1 plotting board out of its hiding place at the bottom of one of his drawers. It took him three minutes to plot the relative positions of the two ships and likely their tracks.

As Josh approached the helo, Van der Jagt tapped him on the shoulder. "Sir, I drew the short straw and will be, because of my vast experience, your co-pilot."

"Good, glad to have one of my future Leavenworth cell mates sitting next to me."

"Sir, even at Leavenworth, they separate the officers from the enlisted." With that Van der Jagt smiled. "I'll preflight the left side, if you'll get the right. Then we'll push the helo out of the hangar."

* * * * *

An hour and a half later, after seeing the bandaged petty officer carefully unloaded and transferred to the shipboard hospital of the *America*, Josh got pelted with rain as he did his walk around. The matte dark charcoal gray HH-2C sat chocked and chained on the front end of the angled flight deck.

Soaking wet, he looked up into a darkening sky. When they'd left the *Sterett*, the base of the cloud deck had been around 5,000; but now he guessed it was 2,000 and dropping.

Van der Jagt was pulling the shoulder harness down and hooking it into the three-inch-wide lap belt. "It's getting ugly out there, sir."

"Yes it is. Now is the time to use the Ouija board. I've got the *Sterett's* relative motion plotted as a back-up in case our TACAN isn't working yet."

"Yes, sir. It sure is fun flying with you."

"Why?"

"Because we get to do neat stuff. Higgins would never have said yes to this flight. He'd have found an excuse not to do it, like the weather was too bad."

"I guess we're all young and stupid." Josh was smiling when he handed the pocket check list to Van der Jagt. "Co-pilot, read the engine start check list, please."

* * * * *

The HH-2C dodged in and out of the cloud bases at 2,000 feet. All the while, the windscreen was pelted by such heavy rain that Josh turned off the wipers because they were unable to keep the windscreen clear. He had just started to notice a drip of rainwater on his right shoulder when the radio crackled with a message from *America*.

"Clementine 26, this is Courage tower. Radar contact is lost at two-four nautical from Courage. Pigeons to Battle Torch are two-two-five at forty based on its last reported position. Good afternoon."

Josh rogered the call and addressed Van der Jagt. "Van, here's where it gets interesting. *Sterett's* radars are hard down. If she is steaming on the course we were given, we should intercept her in fifteen to twenty minutes, assuming the wind isn't blowing us way off course. Switch to the *Sterett*'s TACAN channel, which is twenty-seven, and if that's working we can maybe pick it up. That will make our life easier." *I have to sound like I know what I am doing. Our lives depend on it. One step at a time and hopefully, I don't fly us into an early grave.*

"And if the TACAN isn't working, sir?"

"We go to plan B."

"And what is Plan B?" The words no sooner came out of Van der Jagt's mouth when the cyclic jumped and the air crewman flinched. "What the fuck was that, sir?"

Josh looked at the hydraulic pressure gauge. The needle was in the middle of the white band that indicated normal pressure. When cyclic thumped again, Josh recognized it as an errant kick and turned the automatic stabilization equipment off. "Guys, I think we have problems with the ASE. I am going to leave it off for a few minutes and then turn it back on."

No one answered and Josh waited until the clock wound around a full minute. "Van, turn the ASE back on."

The cyclic was calm for about 30 seconds, but then started to move erratically; Josh felt the rudder pedals move against his feet.

"O.K., everyone listen up. I am going to descend five hundred feet. I don't want to fly the helicopter on instruments with no ASE."

"What can we do to help?" Petty officer Bennington stuck his head forward.

"Right now, nothing other than to offer moral support." Josh scanned the instrument panel.

"Shit, I think we have more problems." His attitude gyro showed that they were in a 60 degree bank, which he knew, from looking at the rainy horizon, was not true. "Attitude and directional gyros have died, so let's shut everything down except the transponder and the radio. Hopefully, those are still working."

"No, sir, they're not. The lights are out on the transponder and I don't get a side tone on the radio." Van der Jagt was looking at the center console.

"Great..." Josh took a deep breath and forced himself to be calm even though he no longer had any navigation or flight instruments that worked. The radio was dead, so he had no lifeline to call for help.

Shit, piss and corruption!!! *The only things I have are the needle and ball, altimeter, vertical speed indicator and a wet compass. So, ace of the base, figure it out. You can fly partial panel and were good at it in the training command. That's why they pay you the big bucks and put gold wings on your chest. The good news is that the engines are turning and burning, you're pretty sure the data on the plotting board is good, and you're not being shot at.*

"Sir," Bennington spoke up, "this is not an uncommon problem in the H-2. You know how the nose splits open so we can get to the avionics compartment. Well, the rubber seals have a history of not working well in heavy rain. Rain gets into the wiring and fuses, and circuit breakers start popping. There's nothing we can do to fix it now, but my guess is that's what happened."

"Makes sense, Bennington." Josh said. "Van der Jagt, find the total electrical failure tab in the pocket checklist and call out each item as you follow it. This way we have everything off that we should. Meanwhile, let's hope the *Sterett* is someplace out in front of us. Keep a sharp look-out. We'll continue on this heading for another fifteen minutes. If we don't find the *Sterett*, we turn east for fifteen minutes and then we head back to the *America*."

Josh smiled when he thought of something his father once told him: Good pilots are never lost, they are just temporarily unsure of their exact geographic location.

"Sir, the checklist is complete."

"Good. We still have about an hour and a half of gas. Again, look for a wake or the ship."

Josh was busy keeping the helicopter straight and level. When he'd gone through the RAG in San Diego, one instructor had said that trying to fly a helicopter on instruments without the stabilization equipment was like trying to stand on a large, rapidly rotating greased ball. He wasn't on instruments all the time, but he was close as he descended another 500 feet to stay under the cloud base. They were now one thousand feet above the gray-green water that was being beaten up by the heavy rain.

"Sir, this is Bennington. I've got a wake on the starboard side about four o'clock."

Josh rolled the helicopter so he could see it. *It's going in the general direction of the Sterett's course back to the Philippines. Hopefully, whatever it is has a flight deck.*

"Guys, I'm going to follow it."

A minute later, the gray shape of a large guided missile destroyer loomed out of the pouring rain. "Van der Jagt, turn the radio back on and switch to channel one."

Josh keyed the mike. No side tone. "We're going to wake up the bridge. I am going to fly up the starboard side with the landing gear down and then approach to land. If it is not the *Sterett*, we'll land anyway and sort out what we'll do next once we're on the deck."

"I'll get the landing checklist."

"When you are done, turn off the radio. It's useless."

* * * * *

"Josh, how bad was it?" Jeff Gainesville walked into their stateroom as Josh was pulling off his wet flight suit.

"Which part, the flying or the navigating?"

"Both."

"Actually, until we lost our radios and navigation equipment, it wasn't bad. I'll tell you, I breathed a lot easier when we saw the wake of the *Sterett*. That's when I realized the wind out of the east was much stronger that I thought, and it had blown us a few miles farther west. I've made a mental note to learn how to gauge wind direction and speed better. That's what will keep me awake at night, because if Bennington hadn't found the wake, we could be sitting in a raft right about now!"

"Well, we're glad you're back. We got a message from the *America* that Petty Officer Jackson is on his way to Subic Bay." Gainesville slid into the chair in front of the gray fold down desk. He was grinning from ear to ear. "I got another piece of paper today."

"Which is?"

"My date of rank for lieutenant commander. The skipper is going to pin them on tonight at quarters. He thinks that I should receive my orders any day now, and hopefully they'll be to the Naval War College in Newport, Rhode Island."

"So now I have to call you sir?"

"Of course, and you have to salute as well."

"When you make admiral, I can say I knew Jeff Gainesville back when he was a lowly lieutenant."

"You can even say you went with me on liberty and got the good-looking girl and I went home empty handed. Speaking of girls, have you heard from Danielle?"

"I got a letter from her the other day. I'm going to Singapore in the near future."

"That's serious."

"It beats hanging around the bars in Olangapo or hustling someone's wife at the Cubi or Subic O'Club."

"True." Gainesville closed the desktop and put his feet on his lower bunk. "So, speaking of dating, you had started to tell me about the NAS Whiting's CO's daughter the other day and never finished the story."

"You really want to hear it?"

"Sure. Dinner's not for an hour or so and I don't have to go on watch until oh four hundred."

"Where was I?"

"You'd just met the captain when you stopped to help him change a flat. Apparently, his spare was flat as well, so you drove him to a gas station where you filled the spare tire and helped him put it on."

"Ahhh, yes. So, after he thanked me, he asked me if I would, being an officer and a gentleman, take his daughter, who was a freshman in college and home for the summer, out to dinner on Saturday night. The implication was that if I tried to get into her pants, he would have my ass."

"That sounds like a smart father, using sound professional and parental judgment. Knowing Naval Aviators as I do both by reputation and in person, the implied threat was appropriate. So, was she easy on the eyes?"

"On the official Naval Aviator scale she was at least an eight plus, and she was going to Vanderbilt, so she was no dummy."

"Good to know. I like them smart. That way you can talk between bouts of sex."

"True, very true. Soooooo, I took her to a nice steak place in Pensacola near the San Carlos hotel and had a great dinner and conversation. As a Navy brat, she knew more about the Navy than I did, but this was the first time her dad had been back in Pensacola since he went through the training command. So, as we were eating dessert, she says to me, 'What's there to do that's fun in Pensacola? I've heard all kinds of stories."

"I sort of hemmed and hawed, so she said to me, she'd heard that Trader Joe's was a hopping place. I gulped and said it wasn't a place that I thought I should take her to, and she laughed and asked why. I said, 'It's a noisy bar with strippers.' So she–her name was Caroline– picked up her purse and said, 'I've never been to a strip joint. Let's go check it out.'

"So what did you do?"

"I took her. My orders were to take Caroline out to dinner, show her a good time, and bring her back safely." Josh started to laugh. "She was ogled by a couple of the men in the bar, but we were left alone. We had a few beers and I got her home around midnight. I never laid a hand on her, so to speak."

"Anything happen?"

"Oh yeah... I had a 6:30 launch on Monday, which is too early for most commanding officers, but when I landed, this petty officer came up to me and said, 'Sir, Captain Craig would like me to drive you to his office immediately.' And he said it loud enough so that everyone in the room just looked at me."

"Sounds like a major embarrassment."

"Yeah, it was. Anyway, the yeoman leads me to the Captain's office and points to a closed door. He doesn't open it, he just points. So I pound the pine twice and there is a very official 'Enter.'"

Josh leaned forward, remembering. "I came to attention in front of Captain Craig's desk and said, 'Ensign Haman reporting as ordered.' The captain gave me that look that means he is about to rip you a new asshole but just can't figure out where to start. I stared at the wall above his head, convinced my brief Navy career was about to end."

Josh grinned as he remembered standing there at his best version of attention. "Then Captain Craig says, 'Ensign, did you or did you not take my 19 year old daughter to Trader Joe's Saturday night?' I said, 'Yes, sir, she wanted to go; my mission was to make sure she had a good time and ensure that nothing happened to her. I believe, based on the feedback I got from your daughter Caroline when I dropped her off at your house, that I accomplished that mission. And, sir, I did so in the best traditions of the Naval Service.'"

"O.K., I'll play the straight man." Jeff was smiling. "What did Captain Craig say?"

"Well, I could see out of the corner of my eyes that he was struggling to keep himself from laughing. He didn't say anything for a few seconds and then said, 'Ensign Haman, you'll make a fine Naval Aviator. Now get the fuck out of my office!"

Same Day, 1845 Local Time, Moscow

Pavel Mironov was in a bar in downtown Moscow, waiting for his GRU counterpart to return from the bathroom. He stood with his back to the counter so he could examine the women as they came and went. The direct view was better than watching them in the rows of mirrors behind the bar. The two GRU officers had picked this particular watering hole for its loud music and crowds, which made conversation impossible for any listening device to record or overhear.

"I ordered you another drink." Mironov slid the glass of beer, which left a trail of moisture on the polished wooden bar, so that it was in front of the junior officer.

"Thanks." Goncharov, who was still single, looked around. "I like this place. The scenery is very nice. Some of these ladies might even be willing to sleep with a humble servant of our socialist state."

"Maxim, stop thinking with your crotch! We have something serious to discuss."

"Ahhh, but I do my best work after satisfying a fine example of Soviet womanhood. Sex stimulates my brain, and breeding is good for the state. As a hand-picked member of the GRU, my seed will create better citizens for our socialist paradise. I think that is what they call genetic engineering!"

"You're impossible, Maxim."

"No, just horny."

"Will you be serious for a moment, please!"

"I am very serious. Sex is good for my mind and my body." Maxim Goncharov, whose blond hair, blue eyes and good looks made women swoon, took a long swig of his beer.

"So, what, Comrade Major Mironov, do you want to talk about? If it is about the impossible task given to us by our masters today, can it wait until tomorrow? You do remember that in a socialist wonderland such as ours, the government is always watching out for our best interests and nothing, other than arrests, happen at night."

"Do you think we can do it?"

"Sometimes a hangover helps. I am not sure whether I do my best work hung over or after a night of great sex or both. That's why I am always testing my theory."

"Be serious, Maxim."

"I am."

Goncharov leaned closer to his supervisor. "Pavel, the decrypts are like a powerful, addictive drug to our superiors, and they want more. This makes us like Mafya drug dealers. Unfortunately, we can't charge money or we would be very rich and very capitalistic young men. Women are attracted to men with both money and power. What do you think?"

Mironov leaned over to make sure his friend heard him. "If we don't produce, they could make us disappear into the Gulag."

"You left out that they can shoot us. They can do either any time, Comrade Major, and you and I both know that they don't need a reason."

"That's a given in our socialist paradise. So now, my good friend, answer my question." Mironov was not going to give up.

"O.K., Comrade Major. Here is your answer." Goncharov finished his beer and plunked the empty glass down on the bar and signaled for another. "First, we need a second machine, because we don't want to risk breaking the one we have. So, let's assume either our North Vietnamese friends or the clever procurement people in the Ninth Directorate can furnish another working machine. If they can't, can we build one? To do that, you need to tell me the answers to five very important questions." He hiccuped.

"Question one: Do we have to rely only on Soviet parts to build the reverse-engineered machine?

"Question two: Can we get component parts from American manufacturers?

"Question three has three parts... Part A—Who will be assigned to help us? Part B—Do they know how to write software the way the Americans do? And part C—Will they be dedicated to the project?

"Question four: How much time do we have?

"And last, question five: How much political interference are we going to get that will waste our time and resources? Tell me the answers to these questions and I will answer yours."

Mironov just shook his head and took a long drink from his beer.

Friday, November 13th, 1970,
0917 Local Time, on the U.S.S. Sterett

When Josh walked out on the helo deck he saw Chief Slaughter supervising a technician who was blowing hot air into the avionics compartment of the HH-2C. The odor of hot wires wafted out alarming him.

"Chief, what are you doing?"

"Getting the moisture out. The hair dryer works really well. It's not an official piece of equipment, but it does the job. As soon as we finish, we'll hook up power and see what works. Then, sir, if you don't mind, I'd like you to start the engines and engage the rotors and check out the avionics. I want to do this before we get to Cubi Point. This way we can sign off on all the gripes and not have to replace everything."

"Is there any water damage?"

"Sir, we don't think so. We found water in some of the canon plugs, which is usually the trouble when the H-2 flies through heavy rain and has the problems you had. We replaced the fuses and reset all the circuit breakers, so if this works, we'll be back up. If not, then they're going to have to replace wiring bundles back at Cubi, and that will take forever. I don't want to ruin my reputation and have this bird craned off a ship. It has never happened in the past and it won't happen with this one."

"Mr. Haman."

Josh turned around to see a sailor who was not in the detachment standing behind him. "That's me. What can I do for you?"

"Sir, Captain Danforth wants to see you in his at-sea cabin. He asked me to take you there."

The captain's at-sea cabin was just aft of the bridge on the sixth deck, and Josh was directed to wait inside. The stateroom was cluttered with papers and files. The steward was making the bed and had stacked the remains of the captain's breakfast on a tray. As

Captain Danforth entered, the steward exited.

"Lieutenant, thank you for taking Petty Officer Jackson to the *America*. He's in the hospital in Subic and they think they can save his arms. I'm going to visit him when we get in."

"You're welcome, sir. It was the least Det 104 could do."

"You could have turned the mission down because you are not a designated aircraft commander. The weather was bad and the forecast was worse. I would have understood."

"Sir, he was in very serious condition and time was important," Josh said in his usual calm manner.

"That's what Mr. Gainesville said you would say. Anyway, the reason I asked you to come up here is that I want to give you copies of messages about what happened on November 1st. The first one is a recommendation from me that you be designated a helicopter aircraft commander as soon as you meet the requirements and be given your own detachment, if they are still deploying single plane detachments. You've earned it. I know you don't have enough flight time, but you have already shown the leadership and skill that this Navy needs. It will be up to HC-7's commanding officer when that happens, but I think the recommendation of a black shoe captain may hold some weight."

"Thank you, sir."

"This stack, and you can read them later, are copies of the P Fors that describe the incident with Lieutenant Higgins, my relieving him of his duties, and my recommendations. There are also copies of those between the Commander of Carrier Air Wing 19 on the *Oriskany* and me." The captain slid the pile toward Josh. "You need to read them; they are in order with the oldest on top."

"Yes, sir."

The captain took a deep breath and said in a serious voice, "This last message is the one that notifies you that you will be ordered to report to a Field Naval Aviation Evaluation Board that will be investigating the incident. It has the members, as well as a list of those who will be asked to appear. All of Det 104 is on the list, along with Lieutenant Commander Gainesville and myself. Also on the list is the Commander of Air Wing 19. The board has the option of deciding who they will interview."

"Sir, pilot disposition boards are held to determine the fitness of a Naval Aviator to continue to fly and even remain in the Navy." Josh tried to keep the worry out of his voice but knew he was not succeeding.

When he was in the training command, evaluations were called "Speedy" boards, for the acronym Student Pilot Disposition Board. Students who appeared before them rarely finished flight training. Regular officers, unless they volunteered for Swift boats, were shunted off into some meaningless, career-ending billet. Reserve officers were discharged from the Navy.

"Lieutenant, the only thing you did wrong was take off on a rescue mission without a piece of paper that said you were an aircraft commander. Were you qualified to do it? Yes. The men who flew with you said yes, and more importantly, they said they would fly with you any time. If you didn't notice, when you took off yesterday, you didn't have trouble finding a crew. The board should see it that way. Trust an old black shoe who knows a fellow warrior when he sees one."

"Thank you, sir."

"One more thing, Lieutenant. You are a natural leader who instinctively does the right thing. Sailors will go to hell and back for you. I see a bright future for you in this man's Navy and I, for one, will not let the bureaucracy fuck it up. Do I make myself clear?"

"Yes, sir."

"Good. So, assuming your helicopter is up, you'll fly to Cubi Point. Please don't bend the helicopter or do anything else stupid and make me look bad."

Sunday, November 15th, 1970,
0746 Local Time, Naval Air Station, Cubi Point

Josh had just finished signing off the helicopter's maintenance log when a young petty officer came up to him.

"Sir, we've got everybody's bags in the van and we are ready to take you to the BOQ and the crewmen to the BEQ."

"Is there anything else I need to do?"

"No, sir, once you sign off, the bird is ours. We'll get a dump from Chief Slaughter on what needs to be done. Knowing him, I doubt there's much to do on this bird."

* * * * *

Thirty minutes later, after a long shower in water that did not come through a desalinization plant and didn't have the heavy fuel oil smell, Josh sat down on the Bachelor Officer Quarters bed in his assigned suite. This was a small apartment with a bedroom, bathroom and a sitting room that had, along one wall, a stove, refrigerator, and cabinets with enough dishes for a serving for four. The sitting room had a couch, a TV, and a table with two chairs. It wasn't much, but it was free.

After he hung up his uniforms and put away his clothes in the dresser, he went back into the living room where, on the way in, he had dropped the envelope on the table. Using the switchblade he carried in the inner thigh pocket of his flight suit, he slit it open and dumped out the contents.

On the top was a set of original orders that officially informed him that he was no longer assigned to Det 104. Another set informed him that he was to report to the legal officer of the Naval Air Station, Cubi Point, at 0730 on Monday, November 16th, 1970, for a briefing on the pilot disposition board proceedings and his appearance before said board.

The orders noted that the uniform for officers was summer white, which sent him to the closet. He pulled his three sets down and examined them. These were the ones he'd been issued as a midshipman, and while they were good enough for everyday use, he decided to buy three new sets.

Monday, November 16th, 1970,
0715 Local Time, NAS Cubi Point

The base administration building was surrounded by lush, green, manicured grass and sidewalks bordered by white painted bricks. In front, there was a row of palm trees that were taller than the three story building.

Josh stopped momentarily inside the lobby to find out that the legal office was on third floor. By its number, he noted, it was not far down the hall from the base commander's. He climbed the stairs and walked down the quiet hall to his destination. The door was open.

"Good morning, I am Lieutenant Junior Grade Haman."

A yeoman in working dungaree blues was making a pot of coffee and looked up.

"Good morning, sir. Lieutenant Nash has been assigned to help you and he should be here any minute. Can I make you some coffee, sir?"

"No thanks." Josh stood there awkwardly, not quite knowing what to do.

"Good morning, Petty Officer Winters." A booming voice filled the room. "And you must be Lieutenant Joshua Haman."

Josh turned around to see one of the biggest men he'd ever seen in his life, bigger than Montemayor. He was also very bald and very black. "Yes, sir, I am."

Nash pointed to a room off to the side. "Good, Josh. Or is it Joshua?"

"I prefer Josh." *Only my parents used Joshua and that was when they were angry at something I did or didn't do.*

"Well then. We have lots to talk about. Petty Officer Winters, bring this man some coffee. Josh, how do you take it?"

"I don't drink coffee, sir."

"I don't know how you survive in this man's Navy without coffee. It's the blood of the sailor. What do you want?"

"Water or hot chocolate, if you have it."

"I know we have water." Nash held out a hand and Josh's was swallowed up in a palm that could have contained both his hands. "Gary Nash."

"Josh Haman."

As they entered his office, Nash grabbed one thick and one thin folder and put them on the table. He pointed to one of the chairs, which Josh took, and settled his massive frame in the other.

Winters placed a bottle of water next to Josh and then closed the door as he left.

"So, Lieutenant, How long have you been in the Navy?"

"Just over two years. I'm a service brat. My dad was in the Air Force and we lived all over, but mostly in Germany. Why?"

"Just curious. I grew up in Bridgeport, Connecticut. Never left the States until the Navy sent me here." Nash toyed with the thinner of the two folders and then reached back and pulled a pad of yellow paper off his desk. "How'd you get your commission?"

"ROTC." Eventually, he'd find out why Nash was asking these questions.

"I'm ROTC too. Went to Notre Dame because I knew I wasn't good enough to play pro football and it didn't cost the school one of their precious NCAA scholarships. I was too big to fit into a plane or a submarine, and in the pool I sink like a stone so I couldn't be a SEAL, so I asked if the Navy would send me to law school. Much to my surprise, they did!"

Josh didn't say anything.

Nash crossed both hands on top of the folders. "Ever been to a pilot disposition board?"

Josh shook his head.

"I didn't think so. My job is to brief you on the process and answer any questions you might have. And, if you ask, I can help you prepare."

"Great, I need all the help I can get," said Josh with a small smile.

"Before we begin, I just want to let you know that I will be advising the board members on legal matters. If you think that is a conflict of interest, we have half a dozen lawyers here at the air station and at the naval base that can help you prepare. Down the hall, Lieutenant Higgins has his own lawyer who will be advising him."

"Is this the same as a court martial?"

"No. In this case, the board's sole purpose is ask questions about the incident, determine what the facts are and make a recommendation based on those facts." Lieutenant Nash then spent five minutes explaining how a board operates, what kind of documents they can review, and how they interview participants before they compile a formal report. Nash then explained the review process and described possible outcomes.

Nash flipped open a copy of the instructions governing pilot disposition boards. "I'll give you a copy of this instruction later so you can read it. But let me summarize. A Type A decision means at most they slap you on the wrist and let you finish your tour with HC-7. Or they can conclude you did nothing wrong. In other words, a Type A decision is not punitive."

The attorney looked at Josh, who was staring at him intently. "Do you follow me?"

"Yes, sir, I do." *A Type A decision means I could be cleared from any wrong doing.*

"Good. In a Type B decision, they can recommend a letter of reprimand or a bad fitness report. Or, if they believe the Navy should take stronger action, such as yanking your wings or holding a court martial, the recommendation goes up the chain of command. If the recommendation is a court martial, the Commander of the Pacific Fleet makes that decision. He, or his designee, will determine who will attend and where the proceeding will be held. Any questions?"

"No, none so far."

"Good."

"Lieutenant Nash, may I say something before we begin?"

"Sure, go ahead. But please, call me Gary."

"I know what I did and would do it again if it meant keeping one of my fellow aviators from being captured. If they yank my wings or toss me out of the Navy for that, so be it. I can live with any punishment because I'll be able to look in the mirror and not want to slit my throat."

"Based on what I've read, and I've read all, I mean *ALL* the message traffic and reports, what you said sums it up pretty well."

Josh liked the frankness and easy-going manner of the former football player. "I'm good with you helping me."

"Okay. I'll make a note of that so we can enter it into the official record." Nash scribbled something on a piece of paper. "I'll have Petty Officer Winters draft up the standard letter that says that you are not requesting special counsel and have asked me to help you prepare. It'll be ready for you to sign after lunch."

Josh nodded but didn't say anything.

"Let me begin by telling you that this is not a legal proceeding per se, although you may think you are in a court room at times. It is a fact-finding event and the board will probably be in session for two or three days. It could go longer, but I doubt this one will. The official title is Field Naval Aviator Evaluation Board, which is authorized in section 1610-10 of the Bureau of Naval Personnel military personal manual."

Nash took a sip from his mug and grimaced at the strength of the brew. "The board must be made up of three officers senior to you who, to quote the instruction, are thoroughly versed in the type of flight operations involved. That means helo pilots with combat search and rescue experience. There will also be a flight surgeon who will evaluate the Naval Aviators' mental fitness to continue their careers. If needed, the flight surgeon can recommend the board have either or both of you interviewed by a psychiatrist. You still with me?"

"Yup, it all makes sense."

"Good. Once the board has interviewed everyone on its list, it will adjourn to review documents, determine what its recommendations will be, and write its final report. I'm probably going to be the editor. Before they finish the actual report, they will bring all the participants back into the room and tell you what they have decided. At that time, you can, if you wish, appeal or ask for a court martial. Those requests, if any, will be in the final report."

"I understand."

"Good. As I said before, I have read all the message traffic; and Lieutenant, in my opinion, and I've been the legal officer on many of these boards, I don't think you have anything to worry about."

"I hope you're right."

Nash looked at the young man sitting opposite him. He didn't look frightened, but he was clearly nervous. He looked out of his element, which was probably what was eating at him. Underneath, he'd bet there was a ton of confidence that has been sorely tested.

"Let's begin with who's on the board. The president, Captain Drysdale, was a commanding officer of an attack squadron that came through here. He had an officer with some ugly legal issues that we helped resolve. Now, let's move to who the board will question."

Nash opened the thinner folder and took out a single sheet of paper. It was on the naval air station's letterhead. Under the control number was a list of every member of HC-7 Detachment 104, including Lieutenant, now Lieutenant Commander Gainesville, and Captain Danforth.

Josh looked at the piece of paper that Nash slid across the table. "Who is Commander David Bristow?"

Nash consulted his notes. "He is... Commander, Carrier Air Wing 19, which is on the *Oriskany*."

Chapter 6 – SPEEDY BOARD

Tuesday, November 17th, 1970,
0715 Local Time, NAS Cubi Point

Josh got to the room at 0700; he was the first to arrive. He sat in one of the chairs in the front row, opposite a table covered with a soft green felt cloth. The air smelled fresh, with the slight smell of furniture polish. The names of each of the five board members were in front of their assigned chairs, and the board's recorder had a small table off to the side. *So, this is what they mean when they talk about the long green table*, he thought. A smaller table with two chairs, where the person being interviewed would sit, stood apart in an open space. It did not have the green cloth, but it glistened from a recent polishing.

Here was a bit of private time for him to gather his thoughts. The only noise was when he sat down and the chair scraped against the wooden floor. He wondered if this stillness was the proverbial quiet before the storm.

Yesterday afternoon, Nash had spent almost two hours tossing questions at him, one right after another. After each answer, Josh would hear the words *good, great*, or would get some coaching on a better way to provide the requested information. The lawyer said he was trying to prepare Josh for the type of questions he would get, rather than giving him time to rehearse an answer.

Spontaneous answers were good, Nash had emphasized. Rehearsed answers were bad. If you don't understand the question, ask the board member to clarify, but don't do it too often, or the board will think you are trying to be evasive. If you don't know, say so. But again, too many 'I don't knows' or 'I don't remembers' will not go down well with the board.

Nash had a list of questions he'd written down on a pad, but based on Josh's answers, he changed some and added more. Just before the three hour mark, Nash had tossed his pen onto the table.

"I'm out of questions. Josh, believe me, you'll do fine. Now, if this was the business world I would say, let's go out to dinner and I'll pick up the tab. Unfortunately, this is the Navy and as a board member, I can't socialize with you. However, when this is all over, I'll buy you dinner."

"You're on." When Josh stood up, he held out his hand. "Thanks, Gary. I appreciate the coaching."

"It was my pleasure, and it was my job. Spend some time relaxing tonight. I know it'll be hard, but take a break. You know what you did and why you did it, and you believe what you did was right. Now, it's up to you to convince the board of that. Good luck tomorrow."

Walking back to the BOQ, Josh was surprised by how tired he was. It had to be the stress.

During training command, several of his instructors had said many pilots would rather violate the rules of engagement and face the long green table, than not hit the target or let one of their fellow aviators die.

He'd also heard stories of Naval Academy graduates who would roll their class rings upside down and tap the wooden top of the table, reminding members of the board or court martial that they were graduates of "Canoe U" in Annapolis. Hence the term "ring knockers." He was sure Higgins would play that card.

Why am I so calm and at peace, though? Because, dummy, he said to himself, *you did what was right. This is just a process to clear the air and, as Nash said, provide a basis for whatever steps will come later. But what will Higgins do or say?*

Higgins was forbidden to communicate with any member of Det 104 or the crew, except as authorized by the captain. He was, in effect, a prisoner. *Gainesville told me that Higgins asked for the ship's copies of the Judge Advocate General's and the Bureau of Naval Personnel manuals, a typewriter and paper. Lots of paper.*

"Mr. Haman."

Josh's head snapped round to see Petty Officer Winters, wearing what enlisted men referred to as "Crackerjack whites" in reference to the image on boxes of caramel-coated popcorn candy, standing behind him.

"I'm sorry to disturb you, sir, but would you like a pitcher of ice water on your table?"

"Yes, Petty Officer Winters, thank you."

"Attention on deck."

Josh stood at attention and stared straight ahead as men filed into the room. Captain David Drysdale, the president of the board, was the last to enter, and he stood behind the chair in the center. He looked left and right before saying, "Seats, gentlemen."

As Drysdale sat down, Josh turned around and, for the first time, noticed that the room had filled up with members of Detachment 104. He had been so intent on his thoughts he hadn't heard then enter. Sitting two rows behind him, Jeff Gainesville showed him a thumbs-up from his lap.

From his seat on the front row on the other side of the aisle, Steve Higgins glowered at him before looking to the front. Next to Higgins was a lieutenant commander; by the insignia on his shoulder boards, Josh could tell he was a lawyer.

Drysdale cleared his throat. "The Field Naval Aviator Evaluation Board is now in session concerning the incident on November 1, 1970. At that time, Lieutenant Joshua Haman took off as the sole pilot from the U.S.S. *Sterett* to make a rescue after Lieutenant Higgins, the detachment officer-in-charge, attempted to stop him."

Josh could feel the seriousness in the room and hear it in Drysdale's tone. "Lieutenants, each of you have been given a list of the witnesses in the order in which they will be interviewed. As part of our preparation, the members of the board have already read your statements and other related documents. The proceedings of this board are classified as Secret, no foreign dissemination. Each witness is ordered not to discuss the questions we ask or your answers with anyone. Once the board has released you, you are ordered to report back to your respective units and resume your normal duties. You are further ordered not to discuss the events of this board until and if you are cleared to do so."

Drysdale made eye contact with both lieutenants. "Only the board members and the individual who is being interviewed and his attorney will also be allowed in room during questioning. Any questions or comments?"

"Captain Drysdale, sir." Higgins stood up and assumed the position of attention. "I would like to ask that the board be suspended and in its place, I respectfully request a general court martial be convened to try Lieutenant Junior Grade Joshua Jonathan Haman under Article 90 for assaulting a superior officer, Article 94 for mutiny and sedition, and Article 97 for unlawful detention of the Uniform Code of Military Justice. There are other serious charges noted in the paperwork I submitted to the board which I can recite if needed. All of them, but these three in particular, led to a breach of the good order and discipline of HC-7 Detachment One Zero Four. In addition, I respectfully request that similar charges be filed against other member of the detachment and court martials be scheduled for them as well. I have prepared a full list of the charges for each of the names on the list." Higgins held up a folder.

"Duly noted, Lieutenant Higgins. You may sit down." Drysdale waited until Higgins was seated. "Did you determine which charges you thought were appropriate or did you have help?"

"Captain," Higgins leaned forward and smiled with pride, "I came up with them while studying the Uniform Code of Military Justice. From November 1st after the mutiny took place until Sunday, November 16th, I was kept in unlawful solitary confinement on board the *Sterett*. Yesterday, I reviewed them with my counsel, Lieutenant Commander Noah Klein, who concurred with my recommendations."

Captain Drysdale nodded his head. "Thank you, Lieutenant Higgins. Your comments are now on record. Whether or not you were confined to your stateroom in an unlawful manner is, at this time, undetermined. I am sure that Captain Danforth had his reasons." The president of the board let a good 15 seconds go by before he spoke again. "I do want to remind you that this board was convened as authorized by the Commander, United States Pacific Fleet. As the president of the board, I was instructed to make recommendations that will be contained in a report signed by all the board members. The Commander United States Pacific Fleet will review it. If they decide, upon reviewing our report, to take further action, they will do so. Therefore, Lieutenant, we will proceed as authorized."

Josh forced himself not to smile. *Smooth move, Higgins. You pissed off the board's president with the first words out of your mouth.*

Drysdale looked to the other side of the aisle. "Lieutenant Haman, are you ready?"

He stood at attention and was glad he'd bought new sets of whites and had them heavily starched. "Yes, sir."

"Lieutenant Haman, please take a seat at the table and we will begin. Everyone else, please clear the room."

The time it took for the men in the room to file out gave Josh a chance to review, for the umpteenth time, the three folders he'd brought with him, which he put in a row on the table. One had his notes, another the information that Captain Danforth had given him, and the third held the papers Nash had provided. A fourth folder with the bios and other information stayed in his BOQ room. He'd committed the backgrounds of each member to memory.

"Lieutenant, we have read Captain Danforth's report of the incident as well as all the statements and messages that have been provided to the board. However, before we get into our questions, we would like get some other information into the record. Lieutenant Commander D'Angelo, I'll turn it over to you for the first questions of Lieutenant Haman."

"Yes, sir. Thank you."

According to the biographical notes Josh had studied the night before, Lieutenant Commander D'Angelo had been a Helicopter Attack Squadron pilot who'd crash-landed a Huey gunship in the Mekong Delta and, despite a crushed ankle, pulled his air crewman and co-pilot out of the smoldering wreckage before it blew up.

"Lieutenant Haman, how many total flight hours do you have?"

"Sir, I have, according to my log book, 462.8 hours."

"When you arrived at Cubi Point, what helicopter were you supposed to fly?"

That was an interesting question, one Nash hadn't asked. "The HH-3A, sir. I went through the RAG at HS-10 on an abbreviated syllabus that cut out the anti-submarine warfare portion. All I got was the familiarization, day and night hovering, approaches to night hovers, and water landing flights. That was it. I was told I would learn SAR tactics when I got to Subic Bay. Most of the students get about a hundred hours, I got about sixty."

"How did HC-7 transition you to the H-2?"

"The day after I got back from the two week jungle escape and survival training school, the HC-7 Detachment One ops officer informed me that they needed a co-pilot for an H-2 detachment, as soon as possible. So they gave me twenty hours of flight time in the HH-2C over five days and sent me on my way. I passed the open and closed book as well as the oral NATOPS exams on the HH-2C before they gave me a check ride the day I left for Vietnam."

"And you passed with what grades?"

"Sir, my lowest grade was 3.8 out of four on the closed book exam."

"We saw the scores in your training jacket. I'd like the record to show that Lieutenant Haman earned 4.0s on the open book test and oral exam, a 3.8 on the closed book test and a 3.9 on the flight check. These are excellent scores." D'Angelo paused to let the recorder catch up. "When you took off on November first, how many hours did you have in the HH-2C?"

"Sir, I didn't know it at the time, but in preparation for my appearance at this board, I totaled it up. I had 70.7 hours in the HH-2C."

"And yet, you took off without hesitation to attempt to rescue the F-8 pilot."

"Yes, sir."

"Were you worried that you didn't have enough flight time or, more important, experience?"

"To be honest, sir, it never entered my mind." Josh stopped, not for effect, but to decide what he was going to say next. "It was broad daylight and the downed pilot was less than thirty minutes of flying time away. It seemed pretty straightforward. Take off, go pick-up the pilot before he was captured and bring him back to either the *Sterett* or the *Oriskany*."

Lieutenant Commander d'Angelo looked at the recorder. "For the record, the official requirements for a helicopter aircraft commander in the H-2 series are as follows. NATOPS states the Naval Aviator must be recommended by his squadron's commanding or detachment officer in charge, have a minimum of five hundred hours total flight time and at least a hundred hours in the specific model, and pass a flight check. Lieutenant Haman, when he took off on the rescue, met none of these requirements."

D'Angelo tapped the table with his forefinger as he made each point.

"Even though Lieutenant Haman passed his exams and flight check with flying colors, he did not meet the minimum flight time standard for an H-2 co-pilot. In sending Lieutenant Haman off to Det 104 when it did, HC-7 and its Detachment One violated NATOPS. I understand the needs of the Navy and we're at war, but I thought that this information should be in the board's record."

He looked down at his notes and continued. "I would also like to have included in the board's record that by his performance on this mission, Lieutenant Haman showed leadership, initiative and what it takes to be a combat search and rescue helicopter commander, and this flight was his flight check." D'angelo nodded to the lieutenant commander on his right.

"Why'd you go by yourself?" The speaker was Lieutenant Commander Manfred Groener. *I read some of your rescue reports while I was in the RAG. You spent two years in HC-7 right after it was formed. Your rescues are the stuff legends are made from.*

"Sir, we'd had several aborted rescue attempts where I was sure we could have picked up the pilot with minimal risk of getting shot down. I wasn't going to let that happen again."

"Explain that, Lieutenant."

Shit... "Sir, one of the reasons HC-7 is in business is to make combat rescues. That is our job and our mission. Whenever someone is shot down, it is up to us to try to rescue them if at all possible. If that means getting shot at in the process, so be it. If we get bagged, then we died trying. It is also our job to make sure we do it in the fastest, least risky way. Getting to the pilot as soon as possible is one of those tactics."

"While you were a member of Det 104, how many times did Lieutenant Higgins abort, as you said, a possible rescue?"

"While I was a member of the detachment, there are two that I know about, and that doesn't account for the times we left our station early, when he swapped days as the ready rescue det to make log, excuse me, logistic and mail runs."

"Lieutenant, I don't remember see a mention of those in your statement." Captain Drysdale tapped a thick folder that was in front of him. "Can you elaborate?"

"Yes, sir. The first one was on a night mission, and we could see the missiles. When we heard a beeper, Higgins wouldn't let me call Red Crown and tell them we were on our way. He said we didn't have enough fuel."

"Did you note the fuel levels at the time?"

"Sir, I thought we had enough if we didn't have to search or hover for more than ten minutes once we got near the survivor. We would have landed with the low fuel lights on, but we would have had enough. Plus, Red Crown could have ordered the *Sterett* to head towards us at flank speed to close the distance."

"Can you give us another example?"

"Yes, sir, on October 22nd, we were called to attempt a rescue of a pilot who was in his raft just outside the breakers. We got to him before the North Vietnamese made it through the surf. We didn't have much in the way of air support and were taking fire from the beach, which was about four hundred yards away. We could have made the rescue, but Higgins was flying and we passed right over the pilot and kept going out to sea. He said we were taking too much fire." Josh stopped for a second. "It made me sick to my stomach." *And, dummy, don't tell the board that you vowed you would not let that happen again.*

There was at least 30 seconds of silence that ended when Commander Stewart Macleod, who'd earned a Silver Star while he was with an anti-submarine warfare squadron that was pressed into flying search and rescue missions early in the war, asked a question. "Were you taking heavy fire?"

"No, sir, not in my judgment."

"Did your air crewman hear Lieutenant Higgins say that?"

"Yes, sir. Petty Officers Bennington and Van der Jagt were on board that day. I believe they will tell you that they were as surprised as I was."

"Did they hear the conversations during the other instances where Lieutenant Higgins was, and I will be polite, *reluctant* to attempt, much less make a rescue?" MacLeod leaned forward to hear the answer.

"Yes, sir, he used the intercom, and I think if you ask any of the three air crewmen, Kowalski, Van der Jagt or Bennington, they would tell you the same thing."

"In the other incidents, what did Higgins say?"

How far do I want to bury this guy? Just tell the truth. "If there was an opportunity to make a rescue, he would tell me we didn't have, in his experience, enough fuel to get to the survivor, find him, hover to pick him up and get back to the *Sterett*. In one instance, he had me tell Red Crown that our play time on station was half of what it was, because we could tell from the radio traffic that a plane was struggling to get feet wet and we might have to go get him."

"Were you asked by Red Crown to attempt the rescue?"

"No, sir we were not."

"Do you know why?" MacLeod fired the question at Josh.

"No, sir."

"Can you give us your opinion?"

"Sir, I believe Higgins had me tell them we were low on fuel to preclude us from being asked to attempt the rescue." *These guys aren't surprised. Someone has provided them with a lot of background information.*

D'Angelo waited about ten seconds before he spoke. "Captain Drysdale, sir, if I may, I would like to go back to Lieutenant Haman's training?"

"Please do."

"Who was your primary instructor at Helicopter Training Squadron Eight?"

"Lieutenant Ernie Zrybek." *That's an interesting question. So I'll give them the full answer.* "Sir, he is the reason I volunteered for HC-7. Lieutenant Zrybek had just completed a tour in HAL-3 and convinced me that it would be an interesting and challenging assignment. He said there would be times when it was downright dangerous, but the satisfaction of saving our fellow Naval Aviators from capture and possibly death was worth the risk. So I volunteered." *I'll bet they already know that Zyrbek won a Navy Cross and a Silver Star during his tour with HC-7.*

"I'd like to go back to the situation on the flight deck before you took off on November first." Commander MacCleod spoke up. "What did you say to Lieutenant Higgins?"

"Sir, when I first arrived on the *Sterett,* he told me that if we ever had to launch in a hurry, then the first person who got to the helo should get it started and the other would fly co-pilot. I was just climbing into the right seat to get the engines started when he showed up. That's when he told me that we were not authorized to go. Lieutenant Commander Gainesville had already told me we would be cleared to launch as soon as we were ready to take off. He also said Captain Danforth was talking to the Commander, Task Force 77 to let him know we were launching. If we weren't supposed to go, they could have easily told us on the radio and we would have returned to the *Sterett.*"

Josh stopped to make sure he had the sequence correct. His hands remained clasped with his forearms resting on the edge of the table. He thought he would have sweaty palms by now, to go along with all the adrenaline in his system, but they were dry.

"Then I told Lieutenant Higgins that he could either go with me or he could stay on the *Sterett*. It was his choice. He kept screaming that it wasn't an authorized mission and I wasn't qualified to fly the helicopter alone."

"Did you strike or hit him?"

"No, sir."

"He claims you hit him repeatedly in the shoulder and the face."

"I shoved him away when he tried to prevent me from getting into the aircraft commander's the seat and he fell down. I know I pushed both his shoulders, but I didn't hit him. Chief Slaughter and two of the other members of the det—Petty Officers Jenkins and Hazelton— helped pull him away from me." *Gainesville told me that the ship's doc saw no bruising when he examined him that night. By that time, any bruises or black and blue marks would have had a chance to show.*

"Did Lieutenant Higgins hit you?"

"He grabbed me around the chest and slammed me into the side of the helo. I don't know if that means he hit me, sir.

MacLeod didn't say anything as he consulted his notes. "Did you see what Chief Slaughter and the two enlisted men did after they pulled Lieutenant Higgins away?"

"Not everything, sir. By then I was going through the checklist. What I saw was that the chief and Petty Officer Hazelton tried to move him off the deck. Higgins was fighting and kicking them; that's when Jenkins grabbed both of the lieutenant's feet and they carried him off the helo deck. That's the last time I saw Lieutenant Higgins until this morning."

"Did you see any of the enlisted men punch or strike Lieutenant Higgins in any way?"

"No, sir. It was a wrestling match, if you will. I didn't see any punches thrown by either of the enlisted men. By then, my attention was focused on getting the helicopter started."

"When did Petty Officer Van der Jagt get in the co-pilot's seat?"

"Right after they dragged Lieutenant Higgins away. Petty Officer Kowalski got in the back with Petty Officer Bennington and we took off. Chief Slaughter told me that he would take care of Lieutenant Higgins. At that point, I didn't know what he meant or would do because I was focused on getting on with the rescue. I was confident that Chief Slaughter wouldn't harm Lieutenant Higgins in any way."

"Lieutenant, are you familiar with the term mutiny?"

"Yes, sir I am." Josh took a breath and sat back, letting his hands drop into his lap. "Sir, historically mutineers are either refusing to carry out their orders or are rebelling against their commanders and their authority by taking over a ship. We, and by we, I mean the members of the crew and the detachment, were trying to carry out our orders to save a downed pilot. At the risk of sounding like a sea lawyer, Captain Drysdale, I wouldn't call that a rebellion, sir." *Watch what you say... That part about 'taking over a ship' has sharp teeth...*

"Are you challenging Lieutenant Higgins assessment of your actions that day?" Drysdale frowned.

"No, sir, not at all." *I shouldn't have said that...* "Just that this flight and rescue was not a mutiny. This was a crew wanting to do what it was tasked and trained to do. If we were rebelling in any way, it was against Lieutenant Higgins, who was reluctant to attempt rescues."

"Lieutenant, let me take this in a different direction for a moment." Captain Drysdale rested his forearms on the table. "Let's assume that this board sends you back to HC-7 with a clean bill of health. Do you think that every commanding officer for the rest of your career will wonder if you are going to pull something like this again?"

"Sir, that is a very good question. The honest answer is that I don't know. I did what I did because I thought it was the right thing to do. It would have taken at least ninety minutes for another helicopter to get to Red Flash 200, and by that time he would have been, at best, a POW. We got there in twenty minutes, picked him up, and brought him back to safety. I couldn't be sure Higgins would make the pick-up. Lieutenant Higgins's refusal to take off without someone telling him to do so would have led to a delay in launching, and as a result of that delay, we might have gotten there too late to make the rescue. I suppose in the back of my mind, I doubted that Higgins would have made the rescue if we were fired upon." *Oh shit,*

I just called Higgins a coward without using the word.

Drysdale jumped in when Josh paused. "Is that all, Lieutenant?"

"No, sir. My experience with Lieutenant Higgins during several earlier missions told me that there was a very high probability that he would have waved this one off as well. I couldn't in good conscience let that happen again. If the Navy yanks my wings and kicks me out, I can live with that because I did what was right." Josh stopped and made eye contact with every member of the board and then with its president for about fifteen seconds. "I'm sorry, Captain, but I don't think I answered your question very well."

"I disagree, Lieutenant." Captain Drysdale looked to his left and right. "Anyone else have any further questions?"

No one at the long green table spoke.

"Lieutenant Haman, you are free to leave this room. Please make sure that Petty Officer Winters knows where to reach you so that you can be here in fifteen to twenty minutes after being notified."

"Yes, sir."

As he opened the door, Lieutenant Higgins was standing just outside and hissed as Josh walked by. "I'm going to fry your ass. Get the fuck out of my way!"

* * * * *

"Lieutenant Higgins," Captain Drysdale waited until both Higgins and his lawyer finished arranging their files on the table.

"Before you begin answering our questions, I want the record to note that it is well within Lieutenant Higgins' rights to have legal counsel present and that this board will not allow the fact that Lieutenant Noah Klein, a judge advocate general officer, is present and assisting him, to affect their recommendations in any way."

Captain Drysdale looked at the recorder to make sure that he had caught up. "Lieutenant Higgins, just out of curiosity, why do you think you need an attorney present?"

"Three reasons, sir," stated Higgins calmly. "I wanted to make sure that the board understands the seriousness of the actions taken by Lieutenant Junior Grade Haman and other members of the detachment during their mutiny and physical assault on me, as well as Captain Danforth's unlawful order to confine me to my quarters without due process.

"I also want to make sure that my rights as the victim are respected in this mutiny against my authority as the detachment officer-in-charge as well as in the assault by both Lieutenant Junior Grade Haman and three enlisted men on me.

"And finally, I want to make sure the board understands that I am requesting a general court martial to clear my name and bring justice to the members of HC-7 Detachment 104 who mutinied and attacked me on November 1, 1970. Lieutenant Commander Klein is here to guide me and make sure that there are no legal impediments to either the Navy or me filing charges against Lieutenant Junior Grade Haman, Chief Slaughter, Petty Officer Bennington and the rest of the detachment. Each of them should be tried by a general court martial."

Captain Drysdale stared coldly at each of the two men before him, then spoke.

"Lieutenant Higgins, it is the role of Lieutenant Nash to guide the board on the legal aspects of the conduct of this board, not you nor Lieutenant Commander Klein. Your attorney knows he has to restrict his recommendations and activities to advising you and you alone. I am sure Lieutenant Commander Klein has made that clear to you."

Drysdale tapped his pad as he made his next point.

"First, your request for a general court martial has been duly noted. This board does not have the authority to convene a court martial of any kind. It can recommend to the convening authority that it consider one. This is the second time you have made that request and you need not do it again. It will be in the record. I must warn you to be careful what you ask for because the Navy may grant you that wish, but it might not be in the manner you desire."

Drysdale waited a few seconds, before speaking again.

"Ultimately, the Commander Pacific Fleet will decide whether or not to court martial Lieutenant Haman or anyone else, not you."

"It is for this board, not you," continued Drysdale, tapping the pad again, "to determine whether or not you were attacked or if there was a mutiny, or if you were confined improperly."

The board president let a few seconds elapse. "Are we clear on that?"

"Yes, sir, " answered Higgins.

"Good. Then we will begin our questioning." The captain looked to his right. "Who would like to go first?"

"I would." Lieutenant Commander Gruener raised his hand, waited for the president to nod approval, and began.

"Lieutenant Higgins, when did you check into HC-7?"

"March, 1969, sir."

"So your tour is almost up?" asked Gruener.

"Yes, sir, this was supposed to be my last series of line periods. The HH-2C is being phased out, so I am told, and I have too little time left in the squadron to warrant the time and expense of transitioning to the H-3."

"How long have you been an aircraft commander?"

"I made it about eight months into my tour, first in the B model and then the Charlie."

"About how many hours do you have?" Gruener asked.

"I just passed one thousand hours."

"How would you rate Lieutenant Haman's skill as an aviator?"

Higgins took a deep breath. "First, I would like to make sure the board knows that Haman is only a lieutenant junior grade and is, for all intents and purposes, a nugget on his first cruise. Having said that, he learns fast and I think he will be, one day, if he is allowed to stay in the Navy, a good helicopter pilot. On the other hand, he is in my professional judgment much too aggressive and reckless. He's a bit of a cowboy and if he is not controlled, he will get people killed. I believe I am the person most qualified to make that assessment because I have flown more with Lieutenant Junior Grade Haman than any other helicopter pilot."

Gruener checked off one his questions. "Lieutenant Higgins, just so you know, we know Mr. Haman's rank and the board has decided to refer to him as a lieutenant, and we are well aware what a nugget is a newly designated Naval Aviator on his first deployment because, at one time, we have all been one." Gruener paused and looked back at his pad. "In your twenty months in HC-7, how many rescues have you made as an aircraft commander?"

Higgins didn't say anything.

Gruener stared at him. "Come on, Lieutenant. You must know. It is something that those of us who are SAR pilots take pride in knowing. One, two, maybe three. More?"

Higgins glared.

"Captain Drysdale," Gruener said calmly, "I would like the record to note that statistically, in a two-year tour, an aviator in HC-7 would be involved in between four and six combat rescues either as an aircraft commander or as a co-pilot. During my tour in HC-7, I was involved in five, three as co-pilot and two as the aircraft commander. So Lieutenant Higgins, as a co-pilot, how many rescues did you make?"

"Two."

"How many did you make as an aircraft commander?"

Higgins just stared at the lieutenant commander. His mouth did not move.

"I'll rephrase the question. As the detachment officer-in-charge and as its sole aircraft commander, how many opportunities did you have to attempt to make a rescue but decided for whatever reason, not to attempt one?" Gruener had been well briefed.

"Only one. It was too dangerous to hover because we were taking heavy weapons fire from the beach and the survivor was only a couple hundred yards from the tree line." Higgins had a grim face.

"How far from the beach were you?"

"Three, maybe four hundred yards."

"On that mission, did you attempt to hover?"

"No, we did not. It was much too dangerous. The gooks would have blown us out of the sky."

"Where there fixed wing aircraft available to suppress that gunfire?"

"Yes, but not enough."

"Were there more available?"

"I am not sure. We didn't have much fuel left when we got there."

"What happened to the pilot you were sent to rescue?" Gruener didn't want to use the word *attempt*, because there hadn't been any. He'd read the report from the Commander, Air Wing 19 and the crew of Clementine 26 on that day.

"I don't know."

Gruener turned to the captain. "I would like to enter into the record that according to the Commander of Carrier Air Wing 19, the pilot was seen being taken prisoner. May I?"

"Please do, Mr. Gruener. Recorder, please make sure that is in the record of this interview. Also, please note that the letter to the board from the Commander, Air Wing 19 on that incident will be a part of the record of this board. Please continue with your questions.

"Thank you, sir." Gruener looked at Higgins, "Were the shooters in range of the mini-gun?"

"I'm not sure."

"What's the effective range of the mini-gun?"

"Seven or eight hundred yards."

"You were within five hundred yards of the beach, so the North Vietnamese gunners were within range?"

"I'm not sure. I never saw them."

"How did you know you were under fire?"

"Because I saw the splashes in the water and the tracers that went past the helicopter."

"Did your co-pilot ever fire the mini-gun?"

"No. Well, he may have gotten off a burst or two."

"Did it have any effect?"

"I don't know."

"Did your co-pilot on this mission ever practice with the mini-gun?"

"Yes, my co-pilot did several times." Higgins stopped for a few seconds. "He kept bugging me for permission to use it so he could get better at it. I didn't think he needed the practice because he always chewed up the smoke. In my judgment, practicing every day or every other day was just a waste of ammunition and required extra maintenance by the detachment to clean the gun and reload the ammo chute."

"What is the name of this co-pilot?"

Higgins didn't answer.

"I didn't hear you, Lieutenant? Do I need to repeat the question?"

Higgins had his hands clasped tightly on the table. "No, sir."

"Then please, tell the board his name. If you would like, either Captain Drysdale or I can make it an order."

No answer.

"Lieutenant Higgins, let me phrase the question in a different way. Was your co-pilot on this mission Lieutenant Haman?"

Higgins mouth moved slightly.

"I couldn't hear you. Was that a yes?"

Higgins nodded his head.

Gruener turned to the recorder. "Please let the record show that Lieutenant Higgins agreed by nodding his head in the affirmative that Lieutenant Haman was the co-pilot in question."

"Lieutenant, I'd like to ask you about the incident that took place before Lieutenant Haman took off on November first. Can you describe to the board what happened?"

"I certainly can." Higgins leaned forward eagerly. "I was in my stateroom keeping up with my paperwork when the ship announced it was going to flight quarters for an emergency launch of the helicopter. It was a total surprise. Normally, they would call my stateroom to let me know. So, as the detachment officer-in-charge, I headed back to the hangar and helo deck to see what was going on. When I got there, Lieutenant Junior Grade Haman was already climbing into the right or aircraft commander's seat."

Higgins took a deep breath. "I asked him what was he doing and he said, 'We're going to make a rescue.' I then told him that he was not authorized to fly this mission as an aircraft commander, and he then said, and I am quoting, 'We're been told by the ship to launch because there is an F-8 in trouble.' I ordered him to get out of the aircraft because I wanted to get properly briefed so we knew what we were up against. He then said, and again I am quoting, 'We'll get briefed en route. We need to hurry.' I then repeated my order to get out of helicopter down, but he refused and said 'Higgins, I'm going now with or without you.' At that point I tried to pull him out of the aircraft. I didn't want him to go because he was unqualified, repeat, *unqualified* to fly the mission. He simply didn't have the time in the H-2, experience in rescues or the designation to fly as a helicopter aircraft commander.

"That's when," Higgins worked his jaw, "he resisted and punched me first in the chest and then in the face. I kept ordering him not to go but he knocked me down and got back in the helicopter. After that, I was overpowered by two of the enlisted men and dragged away. When I ordered them to stop, they ignored me and shoved me into the room they use to store parts and tools. After dumping me on the floor, Chief Slaughter told me to stay there. By then, Haman and all three of the detachment's air crewmen—that's Petty Officer First Class Bennington and Petty Officer Second Class Van der Jagt and Airman Koslowski—had taken off."

"So, excuse me for interrupting, Lieutenant, but did you ever say, "Wait for me, I'll get in the co-pilot's seat?"

Higgins didn't say a word.

"Did you or did you not tell Lieutenant Haman that you would go?"

"I don't remember."

"You said Chief Slaughter told you to stay there… Was the Chief ordering you or advising you?"

"Ordering me. He had several enlisted men block the doorway so I couldn't escape."

"So, you, as the detachment officer-in-charge allowed a chief petty officer to order you to stay where you were?"

"Yes, that is correct. I was physically coerced as well. I was carried off the flight deck and pushed into the corner of a storeroom and told to sit on the floor, which, despite the efforts of my men, is dirty because we store parts and some of them are oily and greasy. Petty Officers Hazelton and Jenkins just stood there blocking the door despite my repeated orders to move and let me out. I yelled at Chief Slaughter, who was the senior man, to let me call Captain Danforth. Hazelton, if you have not met him, is as big as a damn house and there was no way I was going to be able to fight my way free and report to the captain of the *Sterett* that a mutiny had occurred."

"Lieutenant, I would be careful with your words." Lieutenant Commander MacLeod put his hand in front of Gruener to signal that he wanted to say something. "This is the second time you used the word mutiny, and this board will render an opinion on whether one happened, not you. We understand your point of view, but be careful how you use that word. So far, none of the criteria for a mutiny—which is that there is a planned conspiracy to oppose, change or overthrow a proper military authority—have been met. Lieutenant Higgins, please continue with your narrative."

"Sir, I believe they were planning this type of action for some time, and sir, they *did* oppose my authority as the detachment officer-in-charge. They *did* disobey my order not to take off until we were fully briefed."

Higgins took a deep breath. "As I was saying, I was forced to stay in this room until Chief Slaughter stuck his head in the room and said Captain Danforth, the *Sterett's* captain, wanted to speak to me."

"What did Captain Danforth say to you?"

"He told me that Lieutenant Haman had taken off with his knowledge and authorization. I told him that I needed to report a mutiny in which I was assaulted and struck by Haman and three enlisted men and unlawfully detained and that Haman was not qualified to fly this mission. If told him I believed that Lieutenant Gainesville, the ship's assistant operations and gunnery officer, and Lieutenant Haman had planned this… this…" Higgins struggled for a word. "…*event* for several weeks."

"What was his reaction?" inquired Gruener.

"He told me that I was relieved of my duties as the detachment officer-in-charge and that I was to report to my stateroom and be confined there for the remainder of the line period. I then requested Captain's mast, which is a formal way to request that the captain of the ship take formal action. Captain Danforth said I was... was incompetent and unfit to lead my, I mean, Detachment 104."

"Are those the words that Captain Danforth used or are you paraphrasing?"

"I am not sure of his *exact* words. I was too upset and angry. I didn't think I deserved to be treated this way."

"Lieutenant, we'll ask Captain Danforth what he remembers he said, but he put in his official report to the Commander, Task Force 77 that you were relieved of your duties because, and I quote..." Drysdale looked at the report in front of him on which he had highlighted several sentences. "...unfit to be a detachment officer in charge. As the commanding officer of the U.S.S. *Sterett*, I came to that conclusion by watching Lieutenant Higgins' performance or lack of it over a period of several months during which time when tasked to make several rescues, he failed to even attempt a single rescue... Unquote. That's pretty damming, wouldn't you say, Lieutenant Higgins."

"Sir," Higgins said stiffly, "if that is the captain's position, so be it. But he is not a Naval Aviator and may not know what is required to run a helicopter detachment. It does not change the fact that I was unlawfully held as a prisoner in my stateroom. This confinement for attempting to use my authority to prevent a very junior officer from taking off on a risky, unauthorized mission is unwarranted. I was not allowed to speak to anyone on the ship's crew except to order meals. The captain said I was allowed on deck under an armed Marine guard. It was, in effect, solitary confinement without any due process or authorization."

"Lieutenant," Captain Drysdale replied, "Captain Danforth was well within his rights as the captain of the ship to order this and, I might add, he could have put you in the brig if he wanted to."

"Sir, with all due respect, I think his actions were unnecessary and inappropriate. He let an inexperienced co-pilot take off on an impossible combat rescue, putting the safety of the three air crewmen in danger. And, we could have lost a valuable helicopter. That should never have happened."

"Lieutenant Higgins, you bring up an excellent point."

Captain Drysdale put his pen down on his yellow pad and sat back in his chair. "So, let's say you took off with Mr. Haman. Would you have made the rescue?"

"Captain Drysdale, sir, I can't say because I wasn't there. But I can assure you that I would have evaluated the situation, determined if it was safe to make the rescue and then done so if possible."

"Even if the helicopter was taking hits and under fire?"

Higgins didn't answer for a few seconds. "Again, I would have evaluated the risk and then made a decision based on what I thought was prudent to do."

"Would that decision have been similar to the ones you made on the other occasions when you waved off without attempting a pick-up because you were under fire?"

"On those occasions, we could have been shot down if we tried to pick up those men. That would have made four more people POWs or added to the list of those killed in action."

"You don't know that, Lieutenant." Gruener blurted out. "Sorry for interrupting, Captain. Lieutenant Higgins, it was your mission, *your job* to try to pick up your fellow Naval Aviators who were shot down. Sometimes the rescuers get shot up in the process. It is unfortunate that some people get killed and captured in a war, but your job was to prevent the capture of Naval and Marine Corps Aviators and Air Force pilots who were shot down. That was why the Navy trained you, and that's one of the reasons the *Sterett* was where it was. And according to the information provided to this board, despite several opportunities, you failed to attempt a pick-up. I think that is why you were relieved. Captain Danforth was probably embarrassed."

"Lieutenant Commander Gruener, please refrain from expressing your opinions until we have finished our interviews and are ready to present our recommendations." Captain Drysdale leaned across the table so he could look at the petty officer who was acting as the board's recorder. "Recorder, please strike from the record Mr. Gruener's last statement."

"Yes, sir." The petty officer pecked away at the keys and when he was finished he looked up, signaling that he was ready to continue.

"Captain, may I ask a few questions?" Lieutenant Commander Stanley Roland was a member of the Navy's Medical Corps; he had the wings of a qualified flight surgeon above his ribbons on his left pocket. After two cruises on the U.S.S. *Constellation*, he was now assigned to the Subic Naval Base hospital as its head of internal medicine.

"Please go ahead."

"Thank you." Roland tented his hands tented under his chin. "Lieutenant Higgins, when Captain Danforth relieved you, were you surprised?"

"Yes, sir, I was."

"What was your reaction, lieutenant?"

"I thought the wrong person was put in solitary confinement."

"That's a pretty strong statement, Lieutenant. If I am not mistaken, you were restricted to your stateroom and allowed two hours a day to go outside for exercise. You were allowed to order meals from the wardroom. That's a far cry from the brig, but I understand your intent." Dr. Roland lowered his hands to the table. "So what did you do?"

"I read and I prepared."

"Read what and prepared for what?"

"This board, and for my testimony at Lieutenant Junior Grade Haman's court martial."

"What did you read?"

"The Uniform Code of Military Justice. I read it several times, along with the examples that were available in the ship's library from the ship's legal officer. From it I made a list of charges that I recommend be filed against Lieutenant Junior Grade Haman and each of the other members of the..." he searched for the word, "...the confrontation. The details are in this folder which I am happy to give to the board."

"What else did you read?"

"The pertinent parts of the Navy's military personnel manual so I knew precisely what process to follow, how long it should take, who in the chain-of-command would be involved, who had the authority to do what. I mapped out each step in a flow chart that lists, by title, who does what and how long they have to make decisions."

"How long did you spend reading this material?"

"Fourteen to sixteen hours a day. I made notes and cross-checked them to make sure I knew where the critical paths were and what my rights were."

"How many days did you do this?"

Roland, observing that Higgins kept toying with the file folders and re-stacking them to make sure they were aligned in a neat pile, was making tick marks to see how many times Higgins did this.

"I started that night after I calmed down. So that makes twelve days. I spent most of yesterday going over my notes with Lieutenant Commander Klein to make sure I didn't miss anything and to prepare for this board."

"Did you ever take Captain Danforth up on his offer for exercise and fresh air?"

"No, sir, I didn't want to take the time away from my research."

"What do you think is a fair outcome of this board?"

Dr. Roland's question caused Captain Drysdale to raise his eyebrows.

"Several things," Higgins replied quickly. "First, the board recommends that a general court martial be convened to try Lieutenant Junior Grade Haman and others in the detachment for the charges that I have prepared. If needed, I can help the Navy prosecutor prepare the charges." Higgins had turned his Academy ring upside down and was tapping the table lightly as he made his points. "Second, re-instate me as the officer-in-charge of Detachment 104. Three, let me appear at Lieutenant Junior Grade Haman's trial as a witness for the prosecution. Then, after Lieutenant Junior Grade Haman is convicted, as I am sure he will be, then I would like a letter put in my jacket exonerating me and noting that Captain Danforth erred in relieving me."

Gruener sat back in his chair. His body language screamed *You've got to be kidding me!!!*

No one on the board said anything for at least 30 seconds before Captain Drysdale spoke. "Does anyone have any more questions?"

"Captain, sir, I do." Lieutenant Gruener spoke up. "Lieutenant Higgins, how many attempted rescues in which you were the aircraft commander were either aborted because of enemy fire, or the pilot was already captured, or you couldn't find him?"

"I don't keep count of them."

"Well, the board knows of two just from Lieutenant Haman, plus other instances in which you communicated to Red Crown that you were low on fuel when, according to documented fuel levels, you were not. So, again, Lieutenant, how many?"

"*I don't know.*" Higgins glared at the pilot, who was wearing ribbons that showed he had a Silver Star and two Distinguished Flying Crosses. Roland made another tick mark.

Captain Drysdale let the air clear for a few seconds. As the only Naval Academy graduate on the board, he thought he would toss a fellow graduate a softball.

"Why did you pick aviation coming out of Annapolis?"

"I didn't like the confinement of submarines, didn't want to be a ship driver, so I thought I would try flying. It looked like fun, and it is."

"How did you wind up in the helicopter community?"

"It wasn't my first choice. I was hoping to get into P-3s, but after we did the carrier qualification, I was told that the Navy wanted more academy graduates in the helo community, so they sent me to Ellyson Field."

"Did you volunteer for HC-7?"

"No, sir, I didn't. When I was finishing up at Ellyson, the operations officer told me that it would be good for my career as an academy graduate if I volunteered for HC-7. He made it sound like an order. I didn't think I had a choice."

"What was your first choice?"

"I wanted an East coast vertical replenishment squadron flying H-46s. That looked like fun, and their helos are new. Or anti-submarine warfare."

"Captain Drysdale, I have a couple more questions I would like to ask before we excuse Lieutenant Higgins." The speaker was Lieutenant Commander D'Angelo, who still used a cane to help him walk as he recovered from his own helicopter crash a year earlier. A nod from the president of the board told him to continue.

"Lieutenant, how do you, on a scale of one to four, rate yourself as a Naval Aviator?"

"I'm not 4.0, Commander d'Angelo, but I would give myself a solid 3.8 or 3.9. I think I am a very good pilot and aircraft commander. I know my procedures and all the systems of the helicopter cold."

"If you were objectively grading your performance as a detachment officer-in-charge for your annual fitness report, what would be the overall grade that you would give yourself?"

"Sir, I would be in the top five percent, no question. Not only do I get the paperwork done properly, but we had ninety-one percent availability for the helo, which is very good for an H-2, particularly when you don't have a full parts bin handy."

Lieutenant Commander MacLeod had to turn his head. Lieutenant Commander Roland made another tick mark. He was up to twenty-one.

"Do you consider yourself an effective combat leader?"

"What do you mean by that?"

"Precisely what I asked, lieutenant. When the bullets start flying, how good are you under fire? How would you rate yourself?"

Higgins leaned forward. "I'm as good as anyone in this room."

Captain Drysdale forced himself not to shake his head as he counted to 30 in his mind. Hearing no further questions, he looked at his watch. "I think we have covered enough ground today. We'll reconvene tomorrow at 0830."

Same Day, 1326 Local Time,
Office of Naval Intelligence, Washington, D.C.

Lieutenant Randy Westbrook stepped back from the pad on which he was making notes in the photo interpretation center. Stacked on the light tables around him in neat piles were six months of photos of Haiphong Harbor, annotated by ship and date. For the past two weeks, he and three photo interpreters had been poring over the photos, attempting to count the missiles.

"Attention on deck." One of the petty officers had noticed their captain, accompanied by an officer with one very wide band and one narrow band around the sleeve of his blues, signifying a rear admiral.

Westbrook's move to the position of attention was automatic, but he was shocked. *Senior officers never come down here! We go to them. Apparently, this is a big deal.*

"As you were." The admiral came up to his desk. "Lieutenant, any progress?"

"Yes, sir, but, Admiral, I don't think you'll like the answer."

"Try me, Lieutenant."

"Sir, we've gone back through the imagery of Haiphong taken by airplanes, satellites, U-2s, SR-71 and even drones for the past twelve months. We've blown up the images of the docks and any ship that has an open hold. And yes, we've been able to estimate the number of crates on each ship by knowing its dimensions and the probable size of its hold. We have a very accurate estimate of the dimension of the SA-2 shipping crates. We can see they stacked missile crates on the piers, took them to one or two warehouses for assembly, where they then emerge on trailers to be towed to the launch sites."

"And?"

"I still come up with a number that is within ten percent of what we have been telling the Commander of the Pacific Command and everyone else who asks. They are unloading about two hundred and fifty missiles every week. It may vary by plus or minus ten percent, but that's the number."

"And are you sure you didn't miss any ships?"

"Yes, sir. Despite several days of cloud cover, we could identify each ship either as it was making its way to the piers or after it left. It takes at least a day or two to unload one and they work day and night."

"When will you have your report?"

"Tomorrow. I'll send it over with a sample of the photos. One of which will show the missile in an open crate."

"Excellent. Keep up the good work."

Same Day, 1855 Local Time, Subic Bay Naval Base

Josh was reading a book at the end of the bar of the Naval Base's Officer's Club. As long as the board was in session, he was a pariah at HC-7. He was not allowed go to the squadron spaces or talk to any of its personnel, and he felt very alone.

The exchange on the Naval Base was much better than the one on the Air Station. After the board adjourned for the day, he spent an hour shopping at the Naval Base's exchange before deciding on a Pioneer 5000 amplifier and tuner to go along with the Wharfedale speakers he'd already picked out. The boxes were now sitting in his room in the Bachelor Officer Quarters on the Naval Air Station. Another fifty cent cab ride brought him back to the black shoe club, which was much quieter than the one at the Naval Air Station.

"Buy you another beer, rotor head."

Josh turned around to see the tall figure of Jeff Gainesville standing next to him. "Sit down and I'll take you up on it."

"How about if we had dinner at a table where we get served? You look like you need to talk to someone."

Josh folded down the corner on of the page in his paperback and tossed two quarters onto the bar, giving the bartender a 100 per cent tip. "I do. Let's go get a table."

"Here. I've got something better for you to read." Gainesville handed him two letters on flimsy light blue air mail stationery that had Singapore stamps on them. "I was going to take these over to the BOQ after dinner tonight and slide them under your door. Seeing you here saved me a couple of cab rides."

"Thanks." Josh folded them gently and slid them into his back pocket.

After they ordered and a waiter delivered their beers, they clinked glasses. Gainesville said, "Captain Danforth had me go back through all the CIC logs and dig up each time Higgins was available for a rescue and didn't go or, when he got there, reported it was too dangerous or that he had less fuel than he actually had. We also copied all the notations in the ship's log when he informed me the HH-2C was down, or they needed crew rest. I pulled all the radio transmission tapes and have them in a stack of cassettes all cued up for the board to hear. The guys in CIC worked on it for days as a way of venting their frustration with Higgins. Danforth is pissed because Higgins's behavior affected the crew's morale, and he is worried that it affected his own performance rating. This would be the only blemish on his record until Petty Officer Jackson got hurt. Danforth is eligible for the flag board this coming year and doesn't want this mess reflected on his ranking."

"I guess it isn't just my career that asshole is fucking up, then."

"Your career will survive this. *You're* not a prisoner in the Hanoi Hilton right now. That's the real, irrevocable damage."

Josh shook his head angrily, and silently raised a glass to the pilot they'd left behind.

Wednesday, November 18th, 1970,
0930 Local Time, NAS Cubi Point

Commander Bristow had been waiting at the small table for a few minutes while the board sat down in the same chairs as the day before.

Captain Drysdale looked at the officer and asked, "Commander Bristow, are you ready to begin?"

"I am."

"Excellent. I would like the record to reflect that Commander Bristow, commander of Air Wing 19 based on the U.S.S. *Oriskany,* offered to be interviewed for two reasons. First, two pilots from his air wing are missing in action and are presumed to be prisoners of war after a HC-7 Detachment 104 helicopter arrived on scene and failed to even attempt a rescue. The helicopter aircraft commander on both those occasions was Lieutenant Higgins, and on one occasion the co-pilot was Lieutenant Haman. Second, on November first, Captain Bristow's wingman ejected and was rescued by the helicopter flown solely by Lieutenant Haman and his crew."

Captain Drysdale folded his hands and leaned forward. "Commander Bristow, tell us what you know about the rescue on November 1st."

"Lieutenant Commander Ogelthorpe in Red Flash 200 barely made it past the beach when he punched out after his engine quit. We circled and saw him land in the water and get into his raft about four to five hundred yards off the beach. The surf was carrying him toward the beach, which made time of the essence. We could see North Vietnamese gathering on the beach and pointing at him. We were already marshaling aircraft to provide close air support for a rescue. I heard that Clementine 26 was on its way and my heart sank. And I think all the other guys orbiting felt uneasy about what was about to happen to Ogelthorpe."

"Why?"

"Well, I've heard the expression 'Clementine 26 means no picks' in the ready rooms on the *Oriskany*. It means that if Clementine 26 is sent to rescue you, you are not going to get picked up. Regarding the October 22nd mission in which one of his pilots was captured, the on-scene commander wrote that the fire coming from the beach could have easily been suppressed, and the helicopter was far enough off the beach to make it hard to hit. In fact, based on the radio transmissions, someone in the helicopter knew what he was doing. He was clearly telling us what support was needed and the timing of a planned pick-up. Then something changed and the helicopter passed over the survivor and flew out to sea. Based on what I know now, Lieutenant Haman was attempting to coordinate a rescue that his aircraft commander refused to carry out."

"Commander Bristow, would you please tell us about the rescue on November first."

"No problem." The air wing commander took a breath. "I was mentally writing the letter I was going to have to send to Ogelthorpe's wife when Clementine 26 came on the air, coordinating cover to suppress ground fire. I thought it sounded like the same guy from October 22nd. He sounded as if he was really pumped up, but also like he had a plan, even after we told him that we didn't have much help on scene and it would be a while before the cavalry arrived. Anyway, the North Vietnamese were launching boats from the beach and the helo used its gun to chew them up. From my position at 10,000 feet I could see tracers going out from the mini-gun. The helo was taking far more fire than they got on October 22nd, because Ogelthorpe was a lot closer to the beach. Still, Clementine 26 hovered long enough to pick-up Ogelthorpe and get out of there."

Commander Bristow sat up straighter. "When Clementine 26 arrived on the *Oriksany* with Ogelthorpe, I walked over and shook Lieutenant Haman's hand. Later that evening, I talked to Ogelthorpe, who told me how much ground fire the helo took. He said it was hit repeatedly. That's when I drafted a recommendation for Haman and his crew to be awarded medals. A few days later I found out what was going on and offered to appear in front of the board. If I may, I want the board to note that I want Haman on station as the aircraft commander anytime we cross the beach. The man knows what he is doing."

Captain Drysdale looked left and right. "Any questions for Commander Bristow?"

The other four members of the panel, who had been listening intently, shook their heads.

"Thank you, Commander Bristow." Captain Drysdale dismissed the commander and asked Lieutenant Nash to see if Captain Danforth had arrived.

The board members used the interval to refill their cups of coffee while Captain Danforth entered, carrying three folders and a cardboard box of cassettes. He stood and waited for the board members to take their seats before he sat down.

"Good morning, Captain Danforth. I am glad that you could take time from you duties as Captain of the *Sterett* to appear before us."

"Thank you, Captain Drysdale, it is my pleasure and duty to appear."

After making the necessary introductions, Drysdale got straight to the point. "I would like to start with a simple question, Captain Danforth. How did you find out about what happened on the helo deck on November 1st?"

"On the *Sterett*, we monitor the strike frequencies on the bridge, and I heard that Red Flash 200 was in trouble. Lieutenant Commander Gainesville called the bridge and asked if we could scramble the helicopter in case the pilot ejected, since we were the closest ship with a helo that could make the rescue. I approved and ordered the ship to launch the helicopter for a possible rescue as soon as we could. I found out later that at the time I gave the order, Lieutenant Haman was sitting next to Mr. Gainesville in CIC. It was not uncommon for Lieutenant Haman to sit in CIC even when we were not on alert. He liked to do this to familiarize himself with how the ships and air wings operated in the gulf. Gainesville plotted the location of the downed pilot on a chart and ran to the helo deck to give it to Haman before they took off."

"Captain, our records show a Lieutenant Gainesville on our list of interviewees, so I presume he has been promoted?"

"Yes, Captain, he has. I pinned on his oak leaves a few days ago."

"Excellent. Captain, prior to the events of November first, did you have any concerns regarding the performance of either helicopter pilot?"

The captain said slowly, "It was well known on the ship that our helicopter det had not made a single rescue despite many opportunities."

"Did you discuss the failed rescue on October 22nd with Lieutenant Higgins?" Captain Drysdale asked.

"Captain, I did, and his excuse was that there was far too much hostile fire and they didn't have enough fuel. He was there, I wasn't; so I had to take the word of a fellow naval officer. But I had my doubts, because there was not a bullet hole in the helicopter. That's when I had my operations officer go through the ship's log to identify all the times since Higgins arrived on board that the helicopter was launched because an airplane went down within its range or time and station. I also had him identify the times when the helicopter actually went to make a rescue. Once we had those, I had them make copies of the tapes from those days so you can listen to radio transmissions that we monitored. In the six months since Det 104 was on board with Lieutenant Higgins as the officer in charge, there were eight times he launched and, for one reason or the other, didn't make the rescue. To be honest, I had thought it was only two or three; I was surprised to find it was eight." Danforth tapped the top of the box. "The board can, if they wish, review the cassettes. The relevant transmissions are all cued up. They're pretty damning."

"We would like to have the tapes. Recorder, please note."

Captain Drysdale turned back to Captain Danforth.

"Back to November first. Did you ask the Senior Chief why they dragged Mr. Higgins away?"

"I did. He said everyone on the det was tired of Mr. Higgins not even attempting rescues. It was causing trouble for them when they met with other detachments in HC-7 and with their fellow enlisted men on my ship. Several of them had called the aircrew yellow."

"What happened when you first spoke with Lieutenant Higgins over the phone?"

"He started telling at me that his det had mutinied, that they needed to be arrested, and that 'that Jew bastard Haman' took off on an unauthorized mission. After listening, I thought that Mr. Higgins had lost control. That is when I told him that he was relieved of his command and that he was confined to his quarters. I ordered him to report to me when he calmed down. He then informed me that I couldn't do that, at which point I told him that I could and, if I needed to, I would send armed Marines to throw him in the brig."

"What did Higgins say then?"

"He insisted that the det had mutinied and that he was being assaulted by enlisted men. I repeated what I said and hung up. Lieutenant Commander Gainesville was in the passageway and could see Mr. Higgins. He was not being restrained, but the det did have two big strong sailors between him and the door."

"Was Lieutenant Higgins physically harmed in any way?"

"I had the ship's doctor examine him in his stateroom, and other than being disheveled from the scuffle, he was fine. The ship's doctor's report has been submitted to this board."

"Then what happened?"

"We monitored the strike radio frequencies on the bridge. When Lieutenant Haman reported that he had the survivor on board and was headed toward the *Oriskany*, the men on the bridge cheered. I had the tapes of the rescue played over the ship so my entire crew could hear it.

"After Lieutenant Haman returned safely, I had our ship's administrative and legal officer separately interview both officers, as well as other members of the helo crew and detachment. Then I asked each of them a few questions." Danforth reached into his service dress breast pocket and pulled out two cassette tapes. "These are the originals interviews. These will let you hear their tones of voice."

"Why did you relieve Lieutenant Higgins?"

"I think he is incompetent," Captain Danforth said bluntly. "He may be a good pilot, but he is an ineffective leader. His actions adversely affected the morale and combat effectiveness of my ship and, as the commanding officer of a warship, that is something I could not tolerate. If you listen to the interviews, it is clear that his enlisted men do not respect him and all but call him a coward. If you want my personal opinion, Higgins should be asked to resign, and if he doesn't, the Navy should shove him out the door. I wasn't there, but after listening to his air crewman and Lieutenant Haman's description of what happened on the aborted October 22nd rescue, he should be charged with cowardice in the face of the enemy. Lieutenant Higgins is a disgrace to the Naval Academy, our Navy and the nation we serve. I know those are strong words, but the facts back up my opinion."

No one said a word. The air was so thick it could have been cut with a knife when Captain Drysdale looked at his fellow board members. "Does anyone have any questions for Captain Danforth?"

The four men shook their heads.

"Captain Drysdale, may I add something about Lieutenant Haman?"

"Please do, Captain."

"Two incidents bear reporting to this board. I've spent a lot of time with Lieutenant Haman over the last few weeks and have seen him in several difficult situations. The first one was in Singapore where we participated in an exercise with the Singaporean Navy. Lieutenant Higgins delegated an assignment to him to brief our guests, and Lieutenant Haman did so superbly. He showed he had confidence in the enlisted men who worked for him. He had Petty Officer Bennington describe to a Singaporean admiral how they executed a pick-up, while he answered questions about the helicopter. I found out later that he'd peppered Bennington, who knew his business, with questions that he thought a foreign admiral would ask. I was impressed, but more importantly, so was the Singaporean admiral, who thought it unusual that the U.S. Navy would have a senior enlisted man brief a flag officer and do it well. That's one."

Danforth looked down and moved one folder on top of the other. "The second occurred just a few days ago when a sailor got second and third degree burns from a flash fire, and I asked Lieutenant Commander Gainesville to see if Mr. Haman would fly the injured sailor to the *America*, where they could treat him or fly him here. Higgins was still confined to his stateroom. The weather, as I found out later, was much worse than forecast, but Lieutenant Haman didn't hesitate to say yes. Two of the helo det crew members volunteered to go along with him. The result is that while the sailor is horribly burned, he will recover, and getting him to the *America* as fast as we did probably saved the man from having both hands or arms amputated."

The surface warfare officer met the gaze of each officer on the board in turn. "I have to tell you that I am very, very impressed with Lieutenant Haman. That doesn't happen very often. Lieutenant Haman is a natural leader and the word on the mess decks, according to my chief petty officers, is that the men in his det would follow him through the gates of hell. I can't judge what kind of aviator he is, but I can tell you that if the Navy screws him over in this process, it will be doing itself a tremendous disservice and the aviation community will ultimately lose one fine officer for doing what is right. Thank you."

Petty officer Winters held the door open for Captain Danforth. As soon as he left, Chief Slaughter and Petty Officer Bennington filed in and stood at parade rest behind the seats at the small table.

"Please sit down." Captain Drysdale waited as they did so. "Before we ask our questions, I would like to make clear that this is not a court martial or a legal hearing. Nor is it about the behavior of either of you. As far as I know, no charges have been filed against either one of you. This board has been convened to determine what exactly happened on the helo deck of the *Sterett* and make recommendations to the Navy on what actions, if any, it should take regarding Lieutenants Haman and Higgins. Do you have any questions?"

The two senior enlisted men, who represented over 35 years combined experience in the Navy, looked at each other. Chief Slaughter, as the senior of the two, turned to the board. "No, sir, we're good to go."

"Good. One more point for the record. In the interest of time, the board has decided to interview both of you in the same session rather than one at a time. We've interviewed both lieutenants as well as Captain Danforth and Commander Bristow. We are pretty sure of what happened, so we don't have to rehash that again."

Captain Drysdale was using a soft, gentle tone. "Petty Officer Bennington, what do you think of Lieutenant Higgins and Lieutenant Haman? If the question makes you uncomfortable, I'll withdraw it. But I think you are in a very good position to evaluate the capabilities of the two officers."

As a young man, Bennington had enlisted before he graduated high school; the day he got his diploma, he'd boarded a bus in south Philadelphia for boot camp at the Great Lakes Naval Station. Other than to bury his parents, he'd rarely gone back. He'd found a home in the Navy and loved everything about the service, warts and all. Bennington planned to stay in the service until they forced him to retire.

"Sir, I've seen Mr. Higgins in action on many missions. Mr.

Higgins is not overly cautious. He is a coward, pure and simple. The air crewmen think Lieutenant Haman is an outstanding officer and pilot, and all three of us will volunteer to be on his crew any time. I've flown with a lot of pilots in my ten years in the Navy and he is already one of the best."

"Chief Slaughter, do you have anything to add?"

"No, sir. Petty officer Bennington summed up my feelings pretty well. I'll serve with Mr. Haman anywhere or anytime."

"Any more questions from the board?" Hearing none, the captain added. "Chief Slaughter and Petty Officer Bennington, thank you for your time. You may go."

Drysdale waited until the door was closed. "I think we have heard enough. We can ask more people to appear, but I think it will only get repetitive. My suggestion is that we adjourn, read our notes and the transcripts and reconvene tomorrow to discuss our recommendations. Any objections?"

There were none.

Same Day, 1525 Local Time, Subic Bay

The two letters from Danielle sat on his desk unanswered. Josh didn't know what to write. He had been hoping that she could fly to Manila for one of his one week in-port periods, but now he didn't know if or when the next one would be. Until the board reported out, he was in never-never land—a naval officer and aviator without an assignment. His detachment had been disbanded and he didn't know what his future would be.

The easy solution would have been to go out and get hammered, which at the Naval Air Station at Cubi Point was easy because the bar at the BOQ started serving drinks at six a.m.—after closing at four a.m. Or, he could have gone to the Cat Room in the O'Club, which started serving drinks at noon and also went until four in the morning. Going into Olangapo was out of the question because, while he was not officially confined, Gary Nash had asked that he remain on the base. But showing up with a major hangover when the board reported out didn't seem to be a smart idea.

So he ran six miles and worked out, then took a taxi to the main exchange complex at the Naval Base where he bought Leon Uris' latest novel–*QB VII*. He'd been reading for a few hours back in his room when the two letters from Danielle beckoned him. They were numbered five and six, so that he knew which to read in sequence. He read them at least a half dozen times. Finally he drafted a reply.

Sitting in front of the battered Smith Corona portable typewriter his parents had given him as a high school graduation present, he carefully scrolled in a piece of the thin, blue, fold-out air-mail stationery he'd gotten at the station's post office. Josh pecked away, copying the note he had written and edited by hand. The thin paper was unforgiving when it came to type-os.

He had typed the first full sentence when the black rotary phone on the desk rang, startling him out of his thought stream. The only call he was expecting was from the board. With a sense of trepidation he picked up the receiver.

"Good afternoon, Lieutenant, This is Commander Bristow, the air wing commander from the *Oriskany*. A couple of us would like to like to buy you a few beers and dinner tonight. Can you be at the Cubi O'Club at 1900? Meet us one of the private back rooms reserved in my name."

"Yes, sir, I'll be there." Josh knew an order when he heard one.

* * * * *

When Josh arrived, the maître d' led him to one of the private dining rooms that captains and commanders had first dibs at reserving. Each had a sliding glass door facing the stepped dining area and stage that provided a view of the Olympic-sized pool beyond. With a door open, you could hear the music from the band. With it closed and the curtains drawn, as they were now, they were quiet and private.

Captain David Drysdale was sitting at the table along with two other officers, one of whom rose to greet Josh with an extended hand. "Our honored guest has arrived! I'm Commander Glenn Bristow, and this is Lieutenant Commander Henry Ogelthorpe. He's buying your dinner and booze tonight as a cheap way of paying you back from keeping him from a crowded, dirty room and an extended stay in the Hanoi Hilton. Captain Danforth sends his respects, but cannot join because the *Sterett* is pulling out in a couple of hours. His stand-in is a lieutenant commander by the name of Gainesville, who, since he is a black shoe, is slow to arrive. Take a seat, lieutenant."

"Yes, sir." Josh quickly sat down and remained attentive.

"The rules of engagement for this evening are as follows. Assume we are all in a giant cockpit, so it is O.K. to use first names. Nothing we discuss in this room leaves this room. And last, we will not talk about the board. Understood?"

"Yes, sir."

"Good. You need to relax, and all of us need to start eating and drinking. And don't worry about the cost, Henry is buying!"

Thursday, November 19th, 1970, 1530 Local Time, NAS Cubi Point

"Sirs," Petty Officer Winters addressed the two lieutenants standing near the door to the conference room, "instead of a single table in front of the board, there are two. Mr. Haman, you are to go to the one on the right and Mr. Higgins, you are to go to the one on the left. Your attorney, Lieutenant Commander Klein, will not be allowed to be at your table and will have to sit in the chairs set aside for other individuals."

"Thank you, Petty Officer Winters," Josh said formally. Out of the corner of the eye, he could see Higgins glaring at him. He could feel the hatred emanating from the academy graduate.

The enlisted man opened the door and everyone who'd appeared before the board filed in and took seats. Josh looked around; Gainesville was smiling and mouthed, "Good luck."

Board members looked over the room as they stood behind their chairs, waiting for Captain Drysdale to come in. Once he was behind his chair, he looked around the room and said, "Seats, gentlemen."

After the scraping of chairs across the wooden floor ceased, the board president opened a blue folder.

"The board is now back in session. Recorder, please put in the appropriate words." Drysdale waited until the recorder stopped typing. "The purpose of this session is to share our recommendations that will be in our final report, which we will forward to the Commander, Pacific Fleet, with copies to the H-2 and H-3 type commanders at Commander, Naval Air Wings, Pacific. If either Lieutenant Haman or Lieutenant Higgins disagree, or want to challenge the recommendations or ask that additional comments be added, you are free to do so and we will include them. They have thirty days after receiving the report to submit their comments."

Drysdale used his notes to recite the review process. "First, the Commander, U.S. Pacific Fleet or his designee has seven days after receipt to review and endorse or take action as needed. Then the Commander, Naval Air Forces, Pacific or his designee has ten days after he receives the report to approve the recommendations or suggest further actions at which point the Navy will formally notify either officer of any further actions within ten days. All supporting documents and tapes will be available for use in any further legal action." After finishing, Drysdale put his note card down and looked at both officers. "Is that clear, gentlemen?"

"Yes, sir." Josh and Higgins responded with the same answer.

"Good." Captain Drysdale looked around the room. "I will first summarize our recommendations with regard to Lieutenant Joshua Jonathan Haman, as it was his actions that caused this board to be convened and presented the greatest challenge. There is no doubt in the mind of anyone on the board that Lieutenant Higgins gave Lieutenant Haman an order not to take off, which he repeated more than once. It is also clear that Lieutenant Haman was under the impression that by the time they were airborne, Captain Danforth would have given his approval for the mission. The interviews and logs show that his assumption was correct. Captain Danforth had the authority to issue the launch order and Lieutenant Commander Gainesville, as his CIC officer on duty, also had the necessary authority."

Josh was sitting at attention with his back as straight as he could make it. It was not touching the back of the seat and he felt it tense at the captain's first words. He felt a droplet of perspiration work its way down the small of his back despite the air conditioning that kept the room at a comfortable temperature.

"There is also no doubt that Lieutenant Higgins was carried against his will, maybe a better word is dragged, from the helicopter and the helo deck, and that he was confined against his will in a storeroom. Soon after, Lieutenant Haman and three enlisted members of the crew took off."

A small, satisfied smile flitted across Lieutenant Higgins' face.

The captain looked at his notes and crossed off a couple. Josh, sitting upright and with his hands in his lap, could feel cold sweat beginning to soak his undershirt. *I am about to get fucked. The guys were just trying to keep my morale up! Last night, in a manner of speaking, was my last supper!*

"For the record, my fellow helicopter aviators who fly combat rescue missions cannot find fault with how Lieutenant Haman and his crew executed the rescue, which was performed under heavy fire. Therefore, we had to separate the rescue from the events on the flight deck. This led us to carefully search for the answers to two questions. One, was Lieutenant Higgins' order legal if it countermanded the orders of a superior officer, Captain Danforth, who was the officer in tactical command? Two, was Lieutenant Higgins mentally prepared to attempt and carry out a combat rescue?"

Captain Drysdale continued to choose his words carefully as he spoke in an even, measured tone. "The board is unanimous in its belief that when Lieutenant Haman left the *Sterett's* combat information center, he was taking off on a mission duly authorized and ordered by the *Sterett's* assistant operations officer, Lieutenant Commander Gainesville in his capacity as the ship's CIC officer. The question in our minds was whether or not Higgins, had he been given the order to go pick up the downed pilot, would have made the pick-up. The reality is that the answer to this question, as far as the board is concerned, is moot because Lieutenant Higgins chose not to go on the mission. On the other hand, Lieutenant Haman, knowing that the H-2 could be flown by a single pilot, took off believing he could make the rescue. Any orders given by Lieutenant Higgins to the contrary of what Captain Danforth authorized are invalid. If you want to use stronger words, they could be deemed unlawful or illegal. It also put Lieutenant Higgins in the position of countermanding a lawful order by the officer in tactical command the moment it was given. This is a long way of saying the mission flown by Lieutenant Haman was legal."

Drysdale turned to Lieutenant Nash. "Counselor, did I get that right?"

"Yes, sir, you did."

Lieutenant Higgins shifted slightly in his seat and his eyes narrowed as his face flushed with anger. He glanced over at his lawyer, who was listening intently and making notes.

The president of the board looked straight at Josh. "Lieutenant Haman, the board spent most of its deliberations discussing what we would have done in your situation, and also what I would have done as a commanding officer when I found out what happened. I have been both a squadron and air wing commander. In those tours of duty, I have been faced with many difficult decisions on the best way to discipline Naval Aviators who, by their very nature, are confident in their abilities and aggressive, sometimes to a fault. Those attributes are also what makes us able to fly in the difficult maritime environment in almost any weather, day or night. The board was faced with a conundrum because, on one hand, we commend you for your initiative, skill and courage; while on the other we would chew your ass out, make you the permanent squadron duty officer for a couple of weeks, and probably ground you for a period of time. Consider the angst and preparation that you had to undergo to prepare for this board and appear before this board as an ass-chewing by your commanding officer. I'll get to the grounding part later."

Josh nodded his head because his tongue felt glued to the top of his dry mouth.

Captain Drysdale looked left and right and got subtle nods from the other board members. "So let me get to the board's conclusions and recommendations. First, the board was unanimous in its recommendation that no punitive action of any kind be taken against Lieutenant Haman. He did what any officer facing the challenge of combat should do, which is show initiative, physical and moral courage, the ability to improvise and the determination to succeed in carrying out his assigned mission. It is worth noting that Lieutenant Haman, as well as his three crew members, took off knowing that he was not a qualified aircraft commander and that all of them might be subject to disciplinary action when they returned."

Josh could feel the tension in the room but decided not to look left or right. Instead, he moved his head just enough to make eye contact with each member of the board.

"The board will not recommend disciplinary action against any member of Detachment 104 involved in the incident on the *Sterett*. Lieutenant Haman was faced with a very difficult decision, and to their credit neither he nor his crew hesitated to attempt and, if they could, make the rescue. We find that commendable and something we expect from naval officers and enlisted men. In fact, the board is strongly recommending that Lieutenant Haman be awarded at least the Distinguished Flying Cross and his air crewman all be awarded Bronze Stars with Combat Vs."

There was a visible reaction from the room. Captain Drysdale stared at the audience as if he were ordering them to become quiet. "The second part of our Type A recommendation is that Lieutenant Haman and his crew members be returned to HC-7 with evaluations and, in Lieutenant Haman's case, a fitness report signed by Captain Danforth, that detail their outstanding performance. They are to be returned to flight status, reporting the day after the board releases its report, which, I am led to believe, will be this Friday. If this is not possible, then the next official work day. As a practical matter, Lieutenant Haman has been grounded since he returned from the medical evacuation mission, and that is, in the view of the board, long enough.

"Lieutenant Haman, because the H-2 is designed to be flown by a single pilot and often is, we can overlook, to some extent, your taking over as the aircraft commander. My fellow Naval Aviators on the board, who are all helicopter pilots, have told me that a co-pilot of any helicopter would have done the same thing if Lieutenant Higgins were incapacitated during the mission. The aviation community is filled with stories of co-pilots and even crew members who have completed their assigned mission and flown airplanes back to their bases when the pilots have been either killed or wounded. However, the board cautions you not to make a habit of doing this."

Captain Drysdale looked down at his notes. "And, last, Lieutenant Haman, upon your return to HC-7, the board's recommendation to the squadron's commanding officer is to assign you to an H-3 detachment and get you the needed hours and proper NATOPS checks so you can be designated as a helicopter aircraft and mission commander as soon as practical. You certainly have proved to the helicopter pilots on this board who have flown in combat, that you have demonstrated the ability to be an aircraft and mission commander. The local detachment officer-in-charge has already been informed and fully supports this recommendation. From what I was told, Lieutenant Commander Jesus Montemayor, the officer in charge of HC-7 Detachment 110, is expecting you in his office no later than 0730 on Saturday morning. Good luck, Lieutenant, and Godspeed."

Josh didn't know if he should say anything, but he could feel the depression and worry evaporate from his body. He fought the urge to let his posture slump with relief.

"This brings us to our conclusions about the actions of Lieutenant Stephen Albert Higgins on November first. To be blunt, we would, if we were your superior officers, expect much more of you. You should have flown with Lieutenant Haman. As an academy graduate, you are supposed to be the best of the best and demonstrate the highest traditions of the naval service. In this board's view, as the officer-in-charge of Detachment 104 you did not. There is no way to sugar coat it."

Drysdale held up his hand because he could see Higgins' mouth open as if he was about to say something.

"The members of the board had to find a middle ground that we could all agree upon. I will not go into the options and scenarios that we discussed. However, let me assure you, it was not easy. Our recommendation is Type A and includes the following actions. One, you will remain on flight status as a Naval Aviator. Two, on Friday, you will receive orders detaching you from HC-7 and you will report to the commander, Naval Air Station Norfolk, for further assignment. You are entitled to take whatever leave you have accumulated before reporting. However, upon arriving in Norfolk, you will be required to undergo an evaluation by a qualified flight surgeon and by a psychiatrist to determine your fitness to continue as a Naval Aviator. The Bureau of Naval Personnel has already approved this transfer and the station's legal office should have message copies of your orders by Friday. You are not to return to HC-7's spaces. If you want to stop someplace for leave, please make that known to Petty Officer Winters, who will be processing your paperwork."

Captain Drysdale referred to his notes. "Second, the commander of the U.S.S. *Sterett* will be sending a letter to be included in your personnel file describing your performance as the detachment officer-in-charge. Based on his testimony, it will not be complementary and may affect your chances for promotion to lieutenant commander. Third, Captain Danforth and I will brief the commanding officer of HC-7 so that he will be able to write your detaching fitness report. It too may adversely affect your chances before a selection board. I will add, however, that others have started their careers on a sour note and risen quite high in this man's Navy, so it is possible. It all depends on you."

The captain nodded toward Higgins. "Do you understand the recommendations of the board?"

"Yes, sir, I do. With all due respect, sir, it is a complete screw job. This board has decided to ignore the fact that a mutiny took place on the U.S.S. *Sterett* and I was confined to my quarters without due process. I want that on the record!" Higgins banged the palm of his hand on the table. "And again, I demand a court martial to clear my name." He banged a fist on the table to further emphasize his demand.

"Lieutenant Higgins, you need to calm down. Your request is duly noted, and I can assure you that your request will be in our recommendation." Captain Drysdale turned to the yeoman sitting by himself off the side of the board's table. "Recorder, please stop taking notes because I am going to go off the record and give this young officer some fatherly advice."

Captain Drysdale waited until the recorder had his hands in his lap, then leaned forward. "Lieutenant Higgins, my strong recommendation is for you to take your medicine and learn from it. It may or may not be career ending. But the last thing you want to do is force the Navy to defend this board's recommendation during a court martial in which both Lieutenant Haman's actions and yours are debated and where the witnesses, many of them who are in this room, will appear. Based on my experience, you will come out second best and may not like what the court recommends as a sentence. Understood?"

"Yes, sir." Higgins stared coldly at the captain, who ignored his look.

"Good. Recorder, we are back on the record." The board's president waited a few seconds. "Lieutenant Haman, do you have any questions?"

"No, sir."

"Good. The formal work of the board is done. We have a report to finish. This evaluation board is adjourned."

Before he left the building, Josh stopped by Nash's office to thank him for his assistance, but he was not there. Instead, there was a commander looking through a pile of papers. He looked up, studying Josh for a few seconds.

"Ahhhhh. Lieutenant Haman, would you please step into my office?"

The tone of voice told Josh it wasn't a simple request. If he declined, saying he had something else to do, he was sure it would turn into an order. The commander took a seat behind his desk, leaving Josh to stand at a loose position of "at ease" in front of the Navy-issue, battleship-gray desk, onto which someone had grafted a veneer of teak or rosewood. The name tag, placed in the center of the desk, indicated he was meeting with Commander Ryerson.

"Lieutenant Haman…" The commander clasped his hands under his chin and rested it on his fingers before looking up. "I don't know if Lieutenant Nash told you this, but as the base's senior legal officer, I get to review the board's report from a legal perspective. I make comments on Lieutenant Nash's review and then forward it with my endorsement, favorable or unfavorable."

Josh thought it best to hold his tongue. *The board just cleared me. Where is this going?*

"What I understand from Lieutenant Nash's verbal debriefing is that the board is going to take your side of the story, and that Lieutenant Higgins, a fine officer from what I can tell, is going to be told that he needs to change his ways or his career in this man's Navy is over."

Another pause, and Ryerson rotated a college ring around his finger. "I find that troubling, and here's why... Having junior officers defy—and I think that is a good word—orders from their senior officers does not help maintain what is known as 'good order and discipline.' From what I understand, you pushed Lieutenant Higgins out of the way and took off despite his order not to go. In short, you went against your commanding officer's judgment who, I might add, is far more experienced at combat rescues than you are. In short, you disobeyed a direct order."

Ryerson kept playing with his ring. The light blue stone of the setting indicated he was a Naval Academy graduate. "So my endorsement will recommend that the Navy look into some type of disciplinary action against you, such as a court martial. I realize I am going against the recommendations of the board, but as a lawyer and a naval officer, we must learn to follow orders, no matter how unpleasant they may be or how much we disagree with them."

Josh waited to make sure that he was not going to interrupt Ryerson. "Sir, with all due respect, the board didn't see it that way. I was there to fly combat rescue missions. I don't think Mr. Higgins had the same..." Josh struggled for the right word because he didn't want to piss Ryerson off. "...dedication and focus. The board's conclusion was that the order to take off was legal and Mr. Higgins's order countermanding the one given by Captain Danforth wasn't, even if he didn't know or believe that at the time. I think you have the sequence of events out of order. In any case, Lieutenant Higgins wasn't willing to go, and the crew and I were. We went, made the rescue and brought everyone home. That was and is our mission."

"What are you saying, Lieutenant?"

"Only that I was, with the assistance of a crew that volunteered to go with me, willing to do our job. That is all."

"I thought you might be suggesting something more serious."

"No, sir. That's for someone more senior than me to decide."

"Dismissed," Ryerson said curtly.

As he walked down the echoing hallway towards the exit, Josh suspected that he'd be dealing with the repercussions of his actions for a very long time. *Now I am about to experience the Naval Academy Protective Society first hand. They're going to close ranks and protect Higgins as one of their own, even though he is a bad apple.*

Same Day, 1845 Local Time, Naval Air Station Cubi Point

The bartender left the two dollar bills on the wet bar because he wasn't sure how many drinks the young man in front of him was going to want. At 25 cents for each beer, the two dollars was good for six and a nice tip.

The bar ran about half the width of the terraced dining room, and the pool was clearly visible to patrons who stood with their back to the bar. Anyone standing there at the moment could watch the four young women in bikinis exchanging splashes with four equally fit young men who, by their haircuts and taut bodies and the carrier in port, were Naval Aviators.

Josh was enjoying the view and had a beer halfway to his mouth when someone shoved him roughly from behind. Only quick reflexes prevented him from splashing beer all over his clothes and the floor.

"Move over, asshole." The tone wasn't friendly.

Josh turned around. "Steve, I don't think a conversation between us a good idea."

"Fuck you, you goddamn Jew bastard. You fucked up my career!" Higgins voice was loud enough to be heard throughout the bar. Heads turned toward the two officers.

"Steve, I did nothing of the sort. You did it all by yourself." Josh put his beer on the bar and stepped back and away from his former aircraft commander. "Go away. Leave me alone, please."

Higgins took a step forward and jabbed a finger at his chest. "I won't stop until you are in a jail cell in Leavenworth. I can prove that the board was rigged against me. I saw you and Captain Bristow together the other night before the board reported out. You were in cahoots with the witnesses and determined to ruin my career. I was fucked by a conspiracy, probably set up by you and your friends." Higgins's loud voice stopped the conversation in the bar.

Higgins leaned forward. His breath reeked of beer and whiskey. Josh's hand shot out, grabbing the incoming arm around the wrist before it could reach his chest and twisted it out of the way. "Steve, you've had way too much to drink. I suggest you go away because it will only make things worse if you continue to come at me. Please don't do anything stupid!" He was struggled to keep his voice calm but was ready to defend himself. *Make the first move asshole. A punch from you will send you to Leavenworth and be worth the pain.*

"You goddamn kike bastard! You're all alike. Sucking blood like leaches and then getting everyone to cover for you. Haman, I will get you if it is the last thing I do. I promise you, I will find a way to fuck up your career just like you screwed up mine."

"Then why did you pick Noah Klein to help you?"

"Because everyone knows that you need a good Jew lawyer to help you."

"I heard that, Higgins. Now why don't you be a good boy and go back to your room and pack."

Josh turned to see Jeff Gainesville standing nearby.

Higgins turned and yelled, "Fuck you too, Mr. Gainesville, you Jew-loving bastard!" Heads in the bar were now focused on the confrontation, and more officers were coming to watch what might turn into a fight.

"One more word from you, Lieutenant Higgins, and I will have the Shore Patrol throw you in the brig and report your actions to the board, which has not finished its report. A night in the brig for conduct unbecoming of an officer might change what they write or recommend. It's your choice. Make a decision." Gainesville wanted to add "you coward" but didn't, because he was trying to calm Higgins rather than egg him on.

As Jeff finished speaking, he could see people in the bar opening a path for an officer in summer whites and two enlisted members of the shore patrol wearing arm bands. "The shore patrol is here, Higgins. Either move out and go back to your BOQ room, or you can spend the night in the brig. I am waiting. Make a fucking decision."

Higgins glared at Jeff Gainesville for a few seconds and dropped his arms. As he turned to leave, he looked at Josh. "I'm not done with you."

Chapter 7 – LIBERTY IN SUBIC BAY

Friday, November 20th, 1970,

0710 Local Time, Naval Air Station Cubi Point

The loud drumming of the heavy rain beating on the thin roof of the taxi that jerked to a stop at the street entrance to the HC-7 hangar. Josh pulled his canvas parachute bag containing his helmet, flight suits, boots and survival vest off the back seat and lugged the gear as fast as he could into the building.

No one was in the pilot's locker room, which gave him a chance to find an empty locker with a couple of wooden hangars to stow his equipment. He hung his soaking-wet fore and aft cap and his dripping dark blue plastic raincoat on one of the steel pegs on the door. The locker closed with a soft clunk and he slid a combination lock into place.

Josh took a deep breath and looked at his watch. It was 0725. *It is time to find out whether or not people will blame me for Higgins being sent home under a black cloud.*

The smell of freshly brewed coffee filled the passageway that ran the length of the hangar and connected the squadron's operations and administration offices with its maintenance shops. Josh stuck his head in the administrative office, hoping to see at least one familiar face, but no one was there. It was the same for the operations office. He hesitated for a few seconds before he let sound of voices draw him to the squadron's ready room.

It was a place for pre-and post-flight briefings and a general office for those who needed a place to work but didn't have an assigned desk. It was also the source of the freshly brewed coffee smell.

Josh stopped outside the doorway when he heard Lieutenant Commander Montemayor's voice. It was 0735 and he was holding the morning muster.

"I want to give all of you a heads up. Lieutenant Higgins is no longer with HC-7. He will be picking up his orders at 0900 this morning at the base legal office and then heading stateside. I want to remind those of you who appeared before the board that you are not to discuss your interviews or the board recommendations unless given permission to do so. That's an order. The rest of you, please don't make it harder on them by asking. Does every one understand?"

A murmur of "Yes, sir"s followed.

"Good. Lieutenant Haman, Petty Officers Bennington and Van der Jagt will be joining me on Det One Ten. Mr. Haman will be a 2P. As soon as he shows up we'll give him a few fam flights to re-introduce him to the H-3. I'd like to get six flights in with him, two today, two tomorrow and two on Sunday before we leave Monday morning. The rest of Det 104 will stay here in Cubi or be sent to one of the other remaining H-2 dets. The admin officer will post the new assignments by noon today. Questions?"

There were none.

"If Mr. Haman doesn't show up by 0900, Van der Jagt, your job is to find him. Take one of the jeeps over to the BOQ and bring him back here. I know he doesn't have to report until tomorrow, but there's a war on and I want to get him back in the saddle as soon as possible."

"No need to do that, sir." Josh stepped around the corner.

An hour and half later, Josh was standing on the fold-down cowling that allowed pilots to examine the transmission and rotor head of an H-3. He was going through a practice H-3 pre-flight for the first time since he left San Diego when he heard Van der Jagt's familiar voice. "Mr. Haman, Lieutenant Commander Montemayor wants to see you right away. It looks like we're going flying, sir."

"In this weather?"

"Yes, sir. Rumor has it that you are one hot-shit instrument pilot!"

"Oh bullshit." Josh climbed down the steps that were built into the side of the fuselage.

"Sir, just remember, I sat next to you in some pretty crappy weather when we lost all our avionics and flight instruments. I have faith."

"Thanks, I think. Where's Mr. Montemayor?"

"He is in the ready room. By the way, sir, it is good to have you back, and we can't wait until you get your own crew. Petty Officer First Class Bennington and I have already volunteered to fly with you. Kowalski will join us if he decides to re-enlist." Van der Jagt waited as Josh put his flashlight in a pocket. Then the two of them started towards the ready room.

"I appreciate your confidence. But becoming an aircraft commander with my own crew is a long way off. I have lots to learn."

"That's not what the board said, sir."

"Getting enough hours and being qualified are two different things."

"Sir, Bennington said that he's flown with a lot of guys who have more hours than you, and you're better than they are. Anyway, if you'll have Bennington and me, we'd love to fly with you."

"I'm honored by your confidence in me, Van der Jagt, but let's not put the cart before the horse. We'll see what happens out in the gulf." He entered the room followed by the young petty officer.

"Haman, are you ready to go flying?" The half-Mexican, half Apache Commander was almost twice as broad at the shoulder and a good head taller than Josh. His physical presence could be intimidating.

"Yes, sir. Where are we going?"

"Clark Air Force Base. Base ops just called and said their C-47s are scattered all over the Philippines and won't be back in time due to the weather. So the only way the guys at base ops can make their flights home is if we take them."

"Sir, how's the weather?"

"It is just supposed to be heavy rain. There are no reported thunderstorms in the area, so we can stay at about 3,000 feet and be O.K."

"When are we leaving?"

"As soon as you file the flight plan. We'll taxi over to base operations and while we're getting everyone on board, you can dash in and officially check the weather."

"How many passengers?"

"Ten plus a crew of four. Higgins is one of them, along with that black shoe friend of yours, Gainesville. The icy air between them will keep the cabin cool. I presume you will continue to act as a gentleman. That's more than I can say about Higgins."

What the fuck is that supposed to mean? "Of course I will. He has more of a problem with me than vice versa. Gainesville told me that he is going to the Pentagon for six months to work in the office of the CNO on special projects before he reports to the Naval War College in Newport, Rhode Island in August."

"I heard what happened in the O'Club. It's all over the base. Well, after today, he's gone. Out of sight, out of mind."

Josh hoped Montemayor was right.

Saturday, November 21st, 1970,
1922 Local Time, Olongapo, The Philippines

The three officers stopped momentarily on the bridge leading from the Subic Naval Base into Olongapo. On either side was a mesh fence, ten feet tall and topped with razor wire.

"Haman, ever been over this bridge in the daytime?" Montemayor's bulk forced the stream of people on the walkway to go around him.

"No, sir."

"Well, you can toss money off the bridge and there are kids sitting in banca boats who will dive in into and try to get it. The fence forces you to toss the coin high in the air and gives them time to see where it will land."

"Into the Shit River?" Josh didn't know what river's real name, so he used what everyone who'd been to Subic Bay called it. The water reeked of garbage, feces and lord only knew what else. The smell assaulted your nose and kept hammering away at your senses until you were several blocks away. Then it was replaced the smell of exhaust, sweaty bodies and food.

"Yup. Pretty sad. And I can relate because back on the reservation in New Mexico, you'd be surprised what we would do for a few coins when I was a boy."

They continued walking, dodging sailors going in and out of the bars along Rizal Avenue. At each intersection, they'd wait for a gap in the stream of the colorfully painted jeepneys, then dash across the narrow street. The vehicles were U.S. Army jeeps left over from World War II that had had their frames lengthened and could easily seat a dozen or more. There was no meter. One simply got on and off when it stopped and gave the driver a couple of coins before you stepped off.

At one intersection, Montemayor turned to the two officers with him. "Hopefully, when we get to Papagayo's we won't have to wait too long for a table. It is a pretty good restaurant that serves a combination of Mexican and Filipino foods. There are no bar girls, but it's just a block down from the East End Club if you are interested."

Bars lined both sides of the street, none of which had doors to impede access. As the three officers passed, lithe, attractive young girls waved at them to come inside, and Josh could see Americans in civilian clothes on bar stools with Filipino girls sitting on their laps. Male hawkers tried to entice them into one bar or another, because girls were forbidden by law to solicit on the street.

The maître d' of Papagayo's treated the lieutenant commander as a long lost friend. "Ahhh, Mr. Montemayor, it is so good to see you. I will find you a quiet table in the back."

Josh knew that this was Montemayor's second tour in South East Asia. He'd been with HC-1 when it was split into three squadrons, one of which was HC-7, which made him one of the squadron's plank owners.

The cold, dark brown bottles of San Miquel beer were already covered with condensation when the waiter set them down on the table. The third officer, Daryl Richardson, was Detachment 110's maintenance officer and, after Montemayor, the most experienced HAC. Richardson held up his bottle. "Josh, welcome to Det 110."

"Thank you."

"Have you ever been to Olangapo?"

"Not really. Right after I checked in, they packed me off to jungle survival and then, when I returned, I was assigned to Det 104 and had to learn a new helo. So I spent my evenings studying."

"Well, it is known as the Pearl of the Orient. If you like sex, and who doesn't, you can get all you can handle of any flavor and no one will say anything. Just walk down the street and walk into any bar that tickles your fancy." Richardson's Texas twang was pronounced.

Josh didn't say anything, just sipped his beer. He'd heard the enlisted crewmen talk about their experiences in the bars, but never did anything other than listen. Montemayor excused himself and headed for the bathroom.

"The East End Club caters to officers. The bar is open to anyone, but the whore house will only take officers. You have to show your ID card to go upstairs. I don't know if they are stuck up or not, but we're their target market."

"I gather you've been there." Josh noticed that Richardson wasn't wearing a wedding ring. He'd just met Richardson today as his newly appointed co-pilot for the maintenance check flights, and they hadn't talked about anything else but getting the H-3 ready to go. Richardson was about the same height as Josh, but much broader at the shoulders. He'd grown up on a ranch near Bonham, Texas, a football player who became the starting safety at A&M.

"I have sampled the wares available and they are mighty fine. One word of advice: even though the girls are required to undergo weekly medical exams by U.S. Navy and Filipino doctors, you don't know where they've been before you, so it is best to protect yourself, if you know what I mean."

"I do."

"One more thing. Many of your sailors will have what they call cribs here in town. What they do is pay for a room and a girl, so they have all the comforts of home. For an 18-year-old sailor, this place is paradise. All the sex and beer you could ever want. Some of the guys even marry the girls."

"Daryl, are you married?"

"Nope. I'm still looking, so I am free to sample the local merchandise. I'm just taking care to make sure I don't catch something that will cause my dick to fall off. There are guys who have been held in the base hospital well after their rotation date because the docs are trying to cure what they have. Sometimes it takes months, and that is a hard thing to explain to your girlfriend—or worse, your wife."

"So do you go to the East End Club?"

"Yessir, and another one called the Indian House whose décor tries to remind you of the American Southwest but doesn't quite make it. Something is missing, but I can't quite figure it out. It's quieter than the East End and has a smaller bar. The girls aren't as pushy and you get to look around and pick what you want. Or, if you have something special in mind, just tell Miss Lee and she'll arrange it. Indian House is a bit more expensive than the East End Club, but for five to ten bucks, you can have the time of your life and fulfill your wildest sexual fantasies."

"I gather you've done so."

"I have, but officers and gentlemen, as well as fellow graduates of Texas A&M, don't tell tales. Interested in a visit?"

"No thanks. I don't mind buying drinks and a dinner to get laid, but walking into a whorehouse and plunking down my money doesn't excite me. I guess I like the chase."

"Suit yourself. It's not for everybody. But you'll get really horny out here." Richardson finished his beer and set it down on the table. It was quickly replaced by another bottle. "Do you have a girl friend?"

"When I graduated college, no. But, I met someone I really like in Singapore. We're going to get together and see if there is something there."

Richardson grinned. "Hmmmmmm. From the dreamy look on your face, I think there probably is much more. Is she an American?"

"No, she's a French citizen and works in the French Embassy in Singapore."

"Is she good looking?"

Josh smiled broadly. "Oh yeah! On the scale of one to ten she's a nine plus, and that's not my grade, it's someone else's."

"Very impressive for a guy who just got here. How'd you meet her?"

"The *Sterett* pulled into Singapore for a week and I met her at a reception. We spent the next few days together."

"Doubly impressive." A second bottle of San Miguel appeared at each place setting.

Daryl tipped the top of his bottle in Josh's direction then drained it. "So, how'd you wind up in our fair squadron?"

"Do you want the long or the short version?"

"Let's start with the long one. The night is young and we have time. If I get bored, I'll tell you. By your class ring, I gather you are not a graduate of Canoe U."

"No, I graduated from Norwich University. It's up in Vermont."

"Sounds cold."

"It is in the winter, but the skiing is great."

"I prefer to live in climates where one doesn't need a snow shovel."

Josh laughed. "I went through the T-28 training pipeline because I wanted to fly A-1s. But they shut down the Spad pipeline and sent the whole class, except for two guys, to helos. I ranked number one, and I was told that the top guys in the class got what they wanted. But in this case, the admin officer said the needs of the Navy overruled class standing. So it was either helos or quit."

Richardson held up his hand. "Let me guess, the two guys had some stroke."

"You got it. One guy's father was a two star admiral who called the squadron and got his son and his buddy slots in Kingsville to fly jets. Anyway, when I got to Ellyson to learn to fly helicopters, my instructor in the second half was an ex-HAL-3 pilot by the name of Ernie Zyrbek. One day he asked me what I was going to put on my dream sheet. I told him that I'd go crazy doing vertical replenishment, and anti-submarine warfare looked boring. That left search and rescue or HAL-3. After we talked a bit, I volunteered for HC-7. So here I am."

"I went through the training command with Ernie; he and I are pretty good friends. Did he tell you about his last flight in Vietnam?"

"No, other than he got shot up a couple of times."

"What he didn't tell was that his feet got smashed when he rolled a UH-1 into a ball after getting shot up. He has pins in both feet and was in the hospital for months before he was sent to Ellyson."

"That explains a lot."

"Why?"

"He didn't like to stand. It probably was painful."

"Yeah. I just got a letter from him and he is leaving the Navy with a disability. He's going to try to get on with an airline or a helicopter operator. I know some guys at Petroleum Helicopters Incorporated and they fly back and forth to the rigs out in the gulf. I'm pretty sure I can get him an interview, and I hope they'll hire him. He's a good guy."

Montemayor arrived back at the table just as the food arrived. "We're having flan for desert. I just gave the chef my mother's recipe." He crossed himself before picking up his fork. "You guys talk about Higgins?"

"No." Josh spoke the work emphatically.

"Good. This will be the only discussion we will have on the topic. Darryl and I flew with Higgins a lot and he's a good stick and, at times, can be a good person. However, he was the wrong person in the wrong place at the wrong time. Josh, I'm sorry you had to go through what you did, but many of us thought it was inevitable. Darryl?"

"Agreed. Most of us recommended that Higgins be kept back at Cubi as the admin officer because he was really good at paper work. But the powers that be in Atsugi thought otherwise. They ignored our strong recommendations and sent him out as 104's detachment officer-in-charge. The rest is, as they say history."

Saturday, November 21st, 1970,
1848 Local Time, Washington, D.C.

The hotel for the Pentagon's Thanksgiving senior officer reception was just a few blocks south of the Pentagon and a few blocks north along U.S. Highway 1 from the growing number of office buildings where defense contractors had their offices. Also along Route 1, there were the annexes that housed Navy offices and the many apartment buildings that gave Crystal City its own unique skyline.

The Chairman of the Joint Chiefs hated these functions for at least two reasons. One, they took a chunk of what little private time he had. Second, the country was at war. The idea of having a reception paid for by the taxpayers to provide food and drink to selected and influential members of the press and defense contractors when American servicemen were fighting and dying in Southeast Asia just seemed wrong.

His wife referred to these events as "command performances." In this case it was the Secretary of Defense commanding.

Knowing his distaste for these types of events, his aide reminded had reminded him on Friday morning, and also when he departed Friday night. The third not-so-subtle reminder came when his aide had handed him the day's calendar at 0800 this morning. The reception was the last item of the day, highlighted in yellow.

As the Chairman of the Joint Chiefs, the admiral was required to wear his uniform. In November in D.C., you could wear the worsted wool uniform and it would keep you warm.

Service dress blue meant wearing Navy blue trousers, which were in reality black, white shirt, black tie, blouse with two rows of gold buttons, and ribbons, on top of which, if you asked the man, was the most important insignia—the gold wings of a Naval Aviator. On each sleeve, the wide gold band and three narrower ones told everyone that he was a four star admiral.

His career, which would come to an end when his tour as the Chairman of the Joint Chiefs ended, spanned three wars—World War II, Korea and now Vietnam. Unless pushed, he rarely talked about his combat experiences in World War II, which had earned him a Silver Star and a Distinguished Flying Cross. Yet those close to him knew the Alabama native had loved flying fabric covered biplanes off the original carriers—the U.S.S. *Enterprise, U.S.S. Yorktown and* U.S.S *Saratoga* when Naval Aviation was in its infancy in the 1930s.

As he walked in, he handed his aide his hat and waited for the colonel to get the two tokens from the woman in the coat room. Satisfied, he looked at his aide and took a deep breath and exhaled. "Here we go. Remember, if Laird is here, we stay until ten minutes after he leaves. If he doesn't show up, roughly one hour from now, please remind me that I have a call. Don't mention who it is or the topic. Just remind me. That way we can both go home and enjoy what's left of the evening!"

In the meantime, the chairman released his aide to float around the room and find out what people were talking about.

Like any good Naval Aviator, the first place the chairman stopped was the bar. Several civilians and officers junior to him got out of the way, but he waved them back. He was content to wait in line for the scotch he planned to sip for the next hour. He also knew that since the Office of the Secretary of Defense was, so to speak, buying, the hotel would have the top brands. Seeing one of his favorites on the bar, he ordered three fingers' worth of the golden liquid, neat. No ice, no water, and definitely no soda to dilute its taste.

The chairman held up the glass of the Laphrohaig 10-Year-Old "Cask Strength" Islay Single Malt Scotch toward the light and stepped away to take a sip. He studied the room as he swirled the scotch around his mouth so he could enjoy its smoky, almost sweet flavor and the hint of peat. Fortified, he headed out into the room, hoping to be inconspicuous.

He'd gotten about halfway across the room, and other than a few retired admirals who were now vice presidents or board members of defense contractors, no one said anything other than hello or to exchange updates on their families. It was another subtle reminder that being at the top of the military pyramid was a lonely place. The retired admirals, many of who he'd served with, knew better than to try to lobby him about one of their products or a pet idea.

After one admiral was hustled off by a compatriot to talk to a program officer, the chairman took a piece of bruschetta from a waiter. Seeing the black man holding the tray made him look around after finishing the finger food. All of the waiters were black, even the man behind the bar, just like it was when he grew up in Alabama. And the lady in the coat room was also black. They stood out among all the others in the room who were, almost without exception, white.

When he was growing up in Mount Willing, a small town in the south central part of the state, there were separate washrooms, dining areas and theaters for the Negroes. Much had changed since 1929 when the he left for the Naval Academy, but not enough.

Over the past few years, he's seen the press begin to change its lexicon from Negro to Black. He made a mental note to have a chat with the chief of naval operations and the chief of naval personnel to get an update on the progress of recruiting, training and promoting blacks. He also wanted to make sure that there were opportunities for them to get out of the steward rates. Progress was being made; he remembered seeing pictures of recent winging ceremonies with black faces in the group of newly designated Naval Aviators.

The chairman also decided that he would bring it up at the next meeting of the joint chiefs. It would be a break from the other administrative material they covered. His brain screamed that this was his duty, to promote real talent, ability, and patriotism regardless of color.

"Admiral…" The chairman turned around to see man standing behind him holding a glass of red wine. The face was familiar, but he couldn't connect it to a name to a topic.

The man held out his hand. "Jonathan Schell."

The chairman hesitated and then shifted his glass of scotch from his right hand to his left and shook hands. "That's right. Now I know who you are. I've even read some of your work in *The New Yorker* and your book, *The Village of Ben Suc.*"

"I'm surprised."

"Don't be. I read a lot of articles and books to get perspective."

"Is that a polite way of saying you don't agree with my reporting or my point of view?"

"No, not at all. Reading different viewpoints gives me exactly what I said, another perspective and angle. I find it stimulates the mind. Your book made me think."

"Interesting."

The chairman looked at the writer, who was known for his vocal and written condemnations of the U.S. involvement in Vietnam.

"Just because I wear a uniform doesn't mean I am a Neanderthal or a war monger."

"I never implied that. It is just that men in uniform want to play with toys, so you lobby to get into wars. In fact, you even misrepresented the data to get us into one."

"Mr. Schell, if you are referring to the incident with the U.S.S. *Maddox*, I think you have your facts wrong. The ship was attacked in international waters by three North Vietnamese torpedo boats. We have the technical data to support the fact that the *Maddox* was attacked. The incident with the destroyer *Turner Joy* was a bit different. Radar anomalies are very common in the Gulf of Tonkin. Its radar picture led it to believe that it was under attack from North Vietnamese torpedo boats. Keep in mind, this was a few days after the *Maddox* was attacked."

"Admiral, one could argue that data was deliberately skewed because the military wanted to increase our participation in what amounts to a civil war. We should let the Vietnamese people decide this for themselves. It is not our war."

"Mr. Schell, the data was not skewed or altered in any way. In fact, we admitted that the *Turner Joy* was not under attack. It is a matter of public record. Let me ask you this simple question. Would you let a sovereign nation whose independence is guaranteed by treaty and by the United States be invaded by another and do nothing?"

"Look, both you and I now that the Republic of South Vietnam was created as a fiction by the French to avoid recognizing Vietnam —all of it—as one sovereign nation."

"Mr. Schell, you didn't answer the question. And you are ignoring the will of the people of South Vietnam who didn't want to be ruled by the Communists."

"Admiral, like I said, if they want to fight the communists, then let them. My research says it was a group of wealthy families supported by their military who engineered the creation of South Vietnam against the will of their people. I believe most of the people in South Vietnam would be happy to be re-united with their countrymen in the north. We shouldn't be sending our people to die in a Vietnamese rice paddy for a corrupt government that oppresses its people."

"And, the North Vietnamese government is not corrupt or oppressive? Are you suggesting that the North Vietnamese government responds to the will of its people and its leaders are freely elected?"

Schell looked at the admiral but did not say anything, which gave the chairman an opening. "Mr. Schell, I am not going to debate whether or not we should be in Vietnam, because the president and the Congress commit us to war. The military doesn't. We get the mission and do our best to carry it out within the restrictions placed on us. That's point number one."

He took a sip of scotch while he looked into the reporter's eyes. Schell looked away. "Point number two. In June, 1933, I took an oath to defend the United States, and if that meant dying in the process, so be it. Since then, in one way or another, I have been involved in three major wars, none of which the United States started. Losing any one of them would have affected the freedom of this country and our way of life, to say nothing of that of our allies. We've managed to keep the peace more or less throughout the world and the Soviets out of Western Europe. Sometimes it hasn't been pretty, but it has worked. So, the lesson that you need to take to heart and tell your friends that in reality, peace is my profession. We—the United States and our Allies—defend the peace so we don't have fight World War III. If that means arming the Israelis or supporting our Vietnamese allies, so be it. I can live with that. The point I really want to make is that if we were standing in a reception like this one in the Soviet Union, or Cuba, or the People's Republic of China, or North Vietnam, and I was the head of their general staff, would we be having this conversation? I think not. You would be either in prison or dead for writing what you do. American men and women have been dying all over the world to protect your right to free speech. So, before you write your next anti-war article.

Think about that."

Out of the corner of his eye, he saw his aide coming in his direction. It was a good time to go. "Mr. Schell, please excuse me, I have work to do. It involves keeping this country free so you can attend receptions like this one and write what you want to write. Good night."

Monday, November 23rd, 1970, 1230 Local Time, the Pentagon

The Chairman of the Joint Chiefs came around his desk and warmly greeted the Chief of Staff of the Air Force. After thanking him for coming early, the chairman pointed his guest towards an overstuffed dark brown leather couch and took his place in the chair that had come with the original set sometime after the National Security Act of 1947 created his office. The leather was starting to show its age with tiny cracks around the edge of the cushions, but the Chairman was reluctant, as had been his predecessors, to have it replaced. Too many famous asses, the chairman once remarked to someone who pointed out that he could get a new one, had sat in that seat, and he was not going to throw out any of the wisdom that they left behind. Besides, it was comfortable.

Time was of the essence; his regularly scheduled staff meeting, in which sensitive topics could be discussed freely and openly, would convene in thirty minutes. The only record of what was said was the documented decisions based on his notes.

Now that the door was closed, The Chairman got right to the point. "John, I need to ask you for a favor."

The Air Force general shifted on the couch. They both knew they didn't see eye to eye on the conduct of the war in Vietnam. Their differences came from their backgrounds. The Air Force four star was a bomber guy who thought that all of the world's military problems could be solved by bombing the enemy to hell. He'd spent most of World War II in training and administrative billets, but also flown combat missions in the B-17 from bases in Italy.

The Chairman of the Joint Chiefs of Staff had got his first taste of combat when Pearl Harbor was bombed.

"What do you need, boss?"

"As a courtesy, I need to give you a heads up. The U-2 and SR-71 imagery of the rail yards at Mengzi and Nanning are inconclusive. They show trains, but after several missions, we don't see any signs of missiles on them. And CIA intelligence coming out of the People's Republic of China says none are coming from the Soviet Union by rail. Their analysis says that the Soviets are reluctant to let anything go through that country for fear of it being stolen. The Soviets and Chinese were on the brink of war in the summer and fall of 1969 and nothing much has changed since, other than their ambassadors returning to their posts."

"With all due respect, sir, Air Force intelligence disagrees. We are convinced we are undercounting the number of missiles getting into Vietnam by as much as half. We need to find the second source. If we need to take a peek on the ground, so be it. I believe the risk is worth it."

The Chairman had expected that answer. He glanced at the clock. "Look, I need you to get your guys to stop this inter-service bickering over money and programs. When we have a war to fight and new weapons to develop, it is very counter-productive and expensive. I've had the Chief of Naval Operations put the word out and he backed it up with action. One Navy captain got relieved and retired because he couldn't follow some flag guidance."

"The Air Force needs weapons that meets its own unique requirements."

"We both do, John, but your guys are going way over board. You want control over every major weapons program, including naval ones. That is not going to work."

"Why not? The Air Force has developed some fine airplanes. We can do that for the Navy as well."

"That's bullshit, John and you know it. Right now, Air Force squadrons in South East Asia are full of Navy airplanes. You've already bought F-4s, which are equipped with Navy developed Sparrow and Sidewinder missiles so they can shoot down enemy airplanes. The B-66 and all its variants are just Navy A-3s with different engines and ejection seats. You had to buy the A-7 because you didn't have an airplane that was good at close air support, which is why the Army put so much pressure on the Air force to buy the A-7. So don't give me a bullshit parochial answer."

Both men knew that the Air Force chafed at buying Navy airplanes, but they were better airplanes for the missions.

The chairman leaned forward and his forefinger pressed into the leather on the armrest on his side of the couch. "We cannot afford to have two separate development programs, nor have everything controlled by the Air Force."

The Air Force general pursed his lips rather than say anything. He knew that another four star stood between him becoming the Chairman when it was the Air Force's turn. A bad evaluation and he would have to retire at the end of his tour.

There was too much at stake. *Eventually this war will end just like the one in Korea did. After that, there will be a draw down.* The Air Force needed to win the coming budget battles. That was the war the Air Force general wanted to win.

To do so, the Air Force needed to control as many of the programs as possible, to cancel the ones it didn't want no matter which service needed them. *The trouble with this Navy guy is that he's too focused on winning the war, not what comes later. It is all about budgets and which service gets the biggest share of the defense budget.*

"John, the squabbles and misdirection have to stop, and stop now. I need your word on that."

"I'll think about it."

"Just so you know, I have the secretary's support on this. He and I went over a list of the most critical programs, and he will announce later today, which ones will be cut and which ones will continue."

The Air Force officer felt a wave of panic, just like when his B-17 took a lot of flak hits and engines had to be shut down over enemy territory. *When did that happen? Where were my friends in the Department of Defense? If this happens, heads will roll.* Then he remembered that the secretary was a Naval officer during World War II and was probably giving the edge to his old service.

"Do you have the list?"

"I do."

The bastard is going to force me to ask for it. "May I see it?"

"No, it has not been finalized."

The Air Force general leaned forward. "Then some changes could be made."

"To the list, no. Laird's boys are looking at this from a purely financial and development risk perspective. If the programs won't contribute to our fighting the war, they will be either shut down or given just enough funds to keep the program office alive, but no contracts will be signed." *Translation, the Navy is going to wind up with the lead on the most critical electronic warfare programs.*

The Chairman sat there waiting for an answer. Hearing none, he dropped the hammer. "John, you and I both know that it is the Air Force's turn to be the chairman after I retire. I know you want my job badly, but your reluctance to cooperate will color my recommendations to the President and the Secretary of Defense. My guess is that you won't get to sit in this chair."

Chapter 8 – FREQUENCY PROBLEMS

Monday, November 30th,

1130 Local Time, the Pentagon

Exactly seven days ago, Jeff Gainesville had touched down on U.S. soil on the way to a Thanksgiving dinner with his family in Lansing, Michigan. It had taken him two and a half days to get stateside from Subic Bay. Two days had been spent either in the air or hanging around airports, waiting.

The last leg had been the flight to Detroit, which got in near midnight. His parents had met him. After hugging him, his mother had asked what he wanted most. Jeff had said, "A long hot shower!"

Saturday, he'd left Detroit in the VW he'd been driving since he graduated from Annapolis. On the way to DC, he decided that he needed to celebrate becoming lieutenant commander and buy a newer, nicer car. He'd arrived on Sunday afternoon and rented a studio apartment in a suites hotel at their special, temporary duty rate for members of the military. At least he had a small kitchen, so he didn't have to eat out all the time. Now he was waiting at the security desk at the Pentagon.

"Lieutenant Commander Gainesville?" A voice interrupted his musings. Jeff looked up.

The speaker was a captain wearing wings on top of five rows of ribbons that showed he'd flown in both Vietnam and Korea. "I'm Captain Stan Grainger. Welcome."

"Sir, thank you, but I am a little behind. Just over a week ago my orders to the War College were modified to report for temporary additional duty to the Pentagon and the special projects office. Why the change in my orders? Not that I am complaining."

"You're here to work for the CNO as part of a small group of post command captains and commanders. We work directly for him on special projects. They range from simple research to solving problems. We're authorized to go anywhere, ask anyone in the Navy questions, and they have to give us the information we need. The unofficial name we've been given is CNO's Rat Pack. Does that answer your question?"

"Not exactly, sir. I'm not a commander or a captain. I just made lieutenant commander. So why am I here?"

"Three reasons. One, we pull promising young lieutenant commanders and lieutenants on their way to other assignments into the group as worker bees. You were available! Two, you were highly recommended by Captain Danforth who, if you haven't heard, was just selected for flag. And three, you're an expert on surface-to-air missiles and spent the past year on a cruiser off Vietnam. Our project is about missiles, Soviet surface-to-air missiles. Specifically, how they get into North Vietnam and how they are used."

Thursday, December 3rd, 1970,
1423 Local Time, Gulf of Tonkin

Josh awoke with a start as someone kicked his boot sole. "Mr. Haman, get up, sir. We're going flying."

When Josh had stretched out, trying to sneak in a nap, the prep for first launch of the day was not due to start for another two hours. He'd picked the H-3 as a place to take a nap because Darryl Richardson's crew was on five-minute alert. Rather than hang out in the ready room, he'd stretched out next to the tray that contained 4,000 rounds of 7.62mm ammunition that fed the mini-gun in the cargo door and fallen asleep. The padded horse collar rescue sling, when positioned under the back of his neck, made a perfect pillow.

Since getting to the *Ranger* on Monday, he'd flown in circles at 200 feet three miles off Vinh for two consecutive nights. The night before, they'd orbited off Haiphong for the better part of eight hours, landing on the deck of the *Oklahoma City* to take on fuel and go to the bathroom without shutting down, then returning to their station off Haiphong. That was after he had been the co-pilot on a morning log run to Cam Ranh Bay. Montemayor wasn't kidding when he said he was following the board's recommendation to get him the flight time to qualify as a HAC as soon as practical. Josh was flying his ass off, and he didn't want fatigue to degrade his performance.

"What's up, Van der Jagt?"

"Don't know sir, they just announced that the Alert Five SAR bird is being launched, and that's us."

"Got it." Josh climbed into the co-pilot's seat and had the number one engine running when Darryl Richardson climbed into the cockpit and plugged in his helmet.

"Keep going. I'll take over when it is time to engage the rotors."

Josh nodded and began the process of starting the number two engine. By the time it was running, Richardson was strapped into his seat.

Josh looped the hook on the shoulder straps into the buckle on the three-inch wide lap belt and pulled all of them tight. Richardson keyed the mike. "Tell the ship that we're ready to go. I'll do the take off check list."

"Gray Eagle tower, Big Mother 22 is ready for lift-off," Josh reported. Gray Eagle was the call sign for the *Ranger.*

"Big Mother 22 is cleared for take off. Contact Hunter 010 on 312.6 when airborne."

After checking in and getting a heading, Josh waited until Richardson had the H-3 level at 500 feet before he keyed the intercom. "Darryl, what's going on?"

"Big Mother 30 had some kind of mechanical problem and is heading back to the ship. We'll go pick up their orbit, and hopefully it'll be boring. I hope you're not mad that we interrupted your nap!"

Josh held up a balled fist with the middle finger extended. "I got a question for you."

"Shoot."

"In a situation like this, wouldn't it be helpful to stop by CIC and get a quick brief?"

"It's a great idea, but it won't work for two reasons." Darryl had the H-3 climbing and accelerating. "One, you'd never make the five minute launch window, and two, they may or may not be following what is happening. They only keep a full team in the center when we're the flag ship or if we've got planes in the air."

"Big Mother 22, Hunter 010, we have a fox 100 with battle damage trying to make it to the beach. Call sign is Tractor 61. Head three-four-oh and buster."

"Fox one hundred" was an Air Force F-100, the first Air Force fighter that could go supersonic in level flight. In Vietnam, they were used for close air support and forward air controllers. By 1970, they were being replaced by the Air Force's version of the A-7, which was newer and much more capable, but which could not go supersonic. Buster meant 'fly as fast as possible.'

At cherubs two, the green-blue waters of the Gulf rushed by noticeably faster. Josh saw the gentle swells did nothing to hide the very noticeable yellow, worm-like forms of sea snakes and the larger, gray-black shapes of sharks that came the surface to hunt and bask in the warm sun.

"We'll stay about a mile off the beach. If we make gentle ten-to-twenty degree bank turns, we're hard to spot visually or on radar. Or so the intelligence guys tell me." This was Darryl's way of planning and teaching at the same time.

Josh wiggled in his seat and pulled the lap belt and shoulder straps tighter. "How long—" The screech of a beeper stopped him, and a high-pitched warbling sound that came from a transmitter in the ejection seat told everyone monitoring the guard frequency that someone had just punched out.

"Big Mother 22, Hunter 010, Tractor 61 is down in a rice paddy about three miles inland. Tractor 66 is orbiting. No bad guys in sight, over."

"He's asking us if we want to attempt the rescue. Here's the rub: our rules of engagement say the Air Force has all the rescues over land and we get the guys who land in the gulf, but up to about fifteen miles inland is a gray area," Darryl explained. "We're the nearest rescue asset and it'll probably be hours before the Air Force can get there. How far away are we? Thirty, maybe thirty-five miles?"

"How about less than twenty."

"So, mister future HAC, do we go or do we pass?

"I say we go. The longer Tractor 61 is on the ground, the more likely he is going to get captured."

"Right answer. This is what is known in the rescue business as a judgment call. If we pick him up, we made the right call. If we die, well too bad, so sad. At least we tried. The worst would be we go in, get shot up and can't for whatever reason make the pick-up. That's when some rear echelon mother fucker decides that he can get a top one percent fitness report by screwing us over because we didn't follow the rules made by guys who don't do the actual work."

"Understand. Been there, done that AND I have the scars. They're still red." Josh activated the radio mike. "Hunter 010, Big Mother Double Deuce is en route. Say pigeons to Tractor 61 and what close air support assets are available." When he was finished transmitting, he pulled out a pencil to write down the bearing and distance to the survivor from his helicopter.

"Pigeons three-four-zero at 15. Tractor 61 now says he is taking small arms fire from the tree line. He's hunkered down behind one of the dikes in the rice paddies. Tractor 66 only has twenty mike-mike ammunition left, but four A-7s from Gray Eagle have an ETA of two-zero minutes. Call sign of the leader is Battle Cry 407. Say your ETA?"

"We should be there in less than ten mikes. Stand-by for instructions for Tractor 61."

"What's this double deuce shit? That's pretty salty."

"I can be more formal."

"No, it's cool. So mister future HAC, what's the plan? This is your rescue."

"We get there as fast as we can and position ourselves between Tractor 61 and the tree line. Petty Officer Bennington works his magic with the mini-gun, and if it is wide enough to land on the dike, we do it. If not, we put one wheel on and get him in through the passenger door. I think that will be faster than trying to hoist him up, and it gives him more cover. I'd hate to pull up a dead man."

"Sounds like a plan. Just remember, I'm co-pilot so you have to tell me what to say on the radio." Richardson raised his hands in the air and Josh put the chart on the console so his aircraft commander could use it.

"Crew, this is Mr. Haman, prepare for a ground pick-up, but just in case have the horse collar handy. You heard my brief to Mr. Richardson. Any questions?"

"No questions, sir. We're rigged and ready. Van der Jagt is ready to go get him if needed. Kowaski's got the M-60 ready."

Josh turned around and saw that Kowaski had swung the gun mount into place. They had removed the top half of the door, and the boron epoxy armor plate was in place as well.

"Darryl, tell Tractor 61 to pop a smoke when he sees us."

"You sure you want him to do that?"

"Yeah. The gooks already know where he is and it'll save us time finding him. It is not like we're going to sneak into the rice paddy."

"Agreed."

"Tell Hunter 010 that as soon as we cross into the rice patty, have the two A-7s drop their bombs along the tree line to—"

"Big Mother 22, Hunter 010. Tractor 66 reports two groups of twenty to thirty people advancing from two directions toward his playmate and one group is within one hundred yards. He is requesting instructions."

Josh keyed the intercom. "Tell Tractor 61 to strafe the closest bastards first and then get the others!"

As they raced toward the rice paddy, tracers lanced out at the helicopter. Josh started using uncoordinated movements of the cyclic, rudders and collective to make the HH-3A erratic and harder to hit as he dropped down to less than 50 feet above the trees. "Gunners, return fire as you see targets shooting at us."

"Will do!"

Josh was skimming the helicopter 40 feet above the muddy water of the rice paddy when a cloud of orange smoke billowed out from the middle. He could hear the humming of the mini-gun as he adjusted his track so that he could flare and skid the helicopter to a quick stop.

"Gear. Darryl, do the landing check."

"Gear going down. I was wondering when you were going to drop it."

The M-60 machine gun just behind his head began hammering out rounds at the rate of 600 per minute.

"Are you going to authenticate?"

Shit, I forgot to do that. "No, because his wingman has been on top of him the whole time. This one can't be a decoy." *I hope that is a good enough answer.*

"I would have had Hunter 010 verify for us on the way in. Too late now. I've dialed up full power. We're good to go. I'll back you up on the throttles if you need it."

Josh rolled the helicopter and reduced power. The HH-3A shuddered and groaned, acknowledging what he was trying to do with it, but telling him it was not the way the helicopter was designed to be flown. He fed enough control inputs in opposite direction to bring the helicopter into a slow creep ten feet off the ground.

"Am going to put the left main mount on the dike. Tell Tractor 61 to get moving toward the passenger door. I don't want to hang around here forever."

Just then, a spout of mud erupted 100 feet in front of the helicopter, followed by another ten feet closer.

"Mortars?" *What the fuck do I do about them?"*

Ping, ping, thwack.

"Survivor's running to the helo."

"He's on board."

More pings and thwacks and the controls jumped in Josh's hands as a black object flew across the cockpit and parts of the instrument panel disintegrated. Then he heard a sickening thud. He glanced to his right and saw Darryl's head slump down and blood spray all over the right side of the instrument panel.

Instinctively, he pulled up on the collective and dumped the nose with the cyclic to get the helicopter moving. It yawed sickeningly to the right because he hadn't pushed far enough on the left rudder pedal to compensate for the added torque. "Crew, Mr. Richardson is hit. Get him out of the seat and see what you can do for him."

"Yes, sir." The mini-gun hummed. Behind his head, Kowalski kept firing short bursts. Van der Jagt reached around the seat and unbuckled the aircraft commander's harness and unhooked the cord connecting his helmet to the helicopter radios before looping his hands under his armpits, lifting and dragging an unconscious Richardson out of the aircraft commander's seat.

Another thwack was followed by a loud bang. The H-3 shuddered. More mini-bangs. Then a louder BANG followed by the sound of a jet engine unwinding. Out of the corner of his eye, Josh saw the rpm for the number one right engine headed to zero. He shoved the emergency throttle for the left engine up to the stop and watched as the rotor rpm began to decay. *Shit, piss and corruption!!!* They were only going 60 knots, but at least they were slowly accelerating. Good.

"Sir, Mr. Richardson took a round that went through the seat and his right bicep before going into his chest. We're doing what we can back here, but he's in a bad way. We need to get him to a hospital."

"Got it." Getting them all back was up to him now. "Hunter 010, Big Mother 22. We've got Tractor 61 on board but took a lot of hits. Have one seriously wounded and we've shut down the right engine. Need vectors to nearest ship and ask them to close our position as fast as they can."

Seventy knots. *Do I climb so I have altitude and choices but become a big slow target, or do I stay low and make it harder for them to track the helo?*

"Sir, if you can keep the jinking to a minimum, we can work on getting the bleeding stopped and give Mr. Richardson some plasma to help replace the blood he lost."

They just told me that I have to fly straight and level or Darryl is going to die. "Let me know when I can turn again. We're about five minutes to feet wet."

Van der Jagt stuck his head between the pilot and co-pilot seats. "Bennington says Mr. Richardson is barely conscious. I did a security check and we've got lots of holes in the airframe, but no hydraulic leaks. There's jet fuel streaming down the side of the fuselage, which is probably why the engine shut down. None of the fuel lines inside the cabin were hit."

"Good. Climb up here and you can help me out."

Van der Jagt stepped up and sank into the pilot's seat. He looked around as Richardson's blood oozed out of the cushion around him. After plugging his helmet into the intercom, he waved his hands. "Sir, I hope you don't want me to fly this thing for you."

"What's wrong?"

"The top part of the cyclic has been shot off and the box at the end of the collective looks like it stopped a round. I'm using the foot switch to talk on the intercom."

Josh looked down and saw the handle to the pilot's cyclic stick lying on the Plexiglas of the bubble beneath his feet. *Those bastards were aiming at the cockpit and AT ME!*

"Sir, do you want me to close the fuel shut off valve to the right engine?"

Shit, I forgot to do the engine shut down check list. "Van der Jagt, here's the pocket check list. Under emergency procedures, find the single engine shut down checklist and read the items off to me."

"Yes, sir. It seems like I've done this before."

"Yeah, but let's not make it a habit." Josh started to say something else but held up his hand when he heard the beginning of a transmission.

"Big Mother 22, Hunter 010, we have you one-eight miles from Battle Torch. Fly one-six-zero. He is closing your position at two-five knots and will have a ready deck on arrival. Remain this frequency and we will notify Battle Torch when you are within five miles. Copy?"

"Big Mother 22 copies." *This is going to be a series of firsts. First landing on the back of a destroyer in a shot-up H-3! First single engine landing on the back of a destroyer that is not certified for an H-3! It is up to me to make sure that this is not my first crash! The only good news is I know the flight deck of the Sterett. There won't be much room to spare, as in only six feet between something solid and the tip of the H-3's rotor blades if I land on the center of the deck.*

The horizon was now filled with blue water. "Hunter 010, Big Mother 22 is going feet wet."

"Roger. Battle Torch is now twelve miles on your nose and closing. Medical team standing by. Big Mother, say angels."

"Big Mother is at cherubs two." Josh switched to the intercom.

"Bennington, how's Mr. Richardson doing?"

"He's breathing and I got the bleeding stopped. I gave him some morphine for the pain. If you don't crash on the *Sterett,* the doc there should be able to keep him alive."

"I'll do my best..."

Agonizing minutes later, Josh saw the familiar shape of the *Sterett* looming ahead. White water from the bow wave poured down the side of the ship. When the ship was steaming at flank speed, this was called "having a bone it its teeth." As the helo crossed the bow to get make its approach, Josh could see why. The white water looked like a big shank bone!

"Crew, let's get ready for landing. Once we touch down, I want you to get Mr. Richardson out as fast as you can, then we'll shut down. Van der Jagt, you'll need to watch the torque and the rotor RPM. If it drops below one hundred percent, let me know. I think we'll get some droop, but not too much. We're relatively light with only about a thousand pounds of fuel."

"Yes, sir, got it."

"Big Mother 22, Battle Torch. We have you in sight. Wind will be thirty degrees to port at two-zero knots. You have a ready deck."

As Josh approached the *Sterett*, he could see the water churned up by the ship's screws even as it was slowing down to just under twenty knots. He slowed the helicopter to a slow creep.

Fifty yards from the side of the ship, Josh could see the ship's doctor and two corpsmen standing in the hangar. Beside them, a wire-framed Stokes litter lay on the deck. At one end, a pole with two IV bags, one dark and one clear, was attached to the litter. Off to the right, the enlisted man assigned to guiding him aboard was waving him forward.

At 30 knots on the airspeed indicator and 40 feet over the water, the helicopter's relative closure rate to the ship was only ten knots. Josh stopped the forward motion when Kowalski, who had his head out the aft cargo door, called out, "Tail wheel is over the deck and clear."

Josh lowered the collective. The helo settled faster than he wanted and landed with a thump. He felt the helo settle on the deck and all the tension and fear left his body. Out of the corner of his eye, he saw four men carry the litter and one hold the pole with the head into the hangar. As soon as he heard the number two engine start to unwind, he pulled back on the rotor break.

Once the rotors stopped, Josh sat there numb, staring back and forth at the hangar deck and the blood-splattered, shot up instrument panel. The damage assessment would come later.

"Sir, the helo's tied down."

"Thanks." With that he unstrapped. Before he stepped down from the cockpit, Josh steadied himself on the seat, afraid his knees would buckle or that he would throw up.

* * * * *

Josh was still wearing his survival vest as he walked around the H-3, surveying the battle damage. On the right side were a series of holes in the fuselage just aft of Richardson's seat. Most of the incoming bullets had been stopped by the wing of the seat, leaving dents in the boron epoxy armor. One had penetrated the plate that protected the actuators and went on through the seat's side armor making a jagged, elongated hole. He was sure it was the bullet that had struck Richardson in the arm and then entered his chest.

"Sir, the captain of the ship would like to see you in his at sea cabin."

Josh turned to see Petty Officer Bennington standing next to him, a respectful distance away. "Any word on Mr. Richardson?"

"No, sir, other than he's in surgery."

"We took a lot of rounds."

"Yes, sir, we did. That was a great piece of flying, sir."

"Thank you, Bennington. Good work on Mr. Richardson. You

probably saved his life. Where's the rest of the crew?"

"Thank you, sir. We've been in sick bay. The corpsman gave each of us a couple of small bottles of brandy. We're going to be on the ship for a couple of days, so they're arranging some clean clothing. We can wash our flight suits then."

"Good. I'll go see what Captain Danforth has to say."

As he made his way to captain's at sea cabin just aft of the bridge, the vibration from the *Sterett* churning through the gulf lessened to a more normal thrum and hum as the ship slowed to cruising speed. A Marine in fatigues was sitting by the door with a .45 caliber pistol in an unbuttoned holster. Josh could see the brass jackets of the .45 rounds in the two magazines in a pouch on the web belt.

The Marine came to attention. "Mr. Haman, it is good to see you again. Captain Danforth is expecting you."

"Thank you, Sergeant Gittings. When did you get promoted?"

"The message came in last week, sir."

"Congratulations."

"Thank you, sir."

Josh tapped on the door, and after hearing "Come in," opened it.

Captain Danforth stood up and held out his hand. "Well done and welcome back. Close the door and have a seat." Josh did so, while the captain went to a table and picked up a glass, which he set in front of the helicopter pilot. Then he twirled the dial on the safe behind his desk, swung open the door and pulled out a bottle of Chivas Regal. Without saying a word, he poured four fingers into the glass, which had the ship's logo etched onto the side. "Drink this, you need it. You're not going flying for a while."

"Yes, sir." Josh took a sip and grimaced slightly as the alcohol burned his throat.

"Josh, you are *not* leaving this stateroom until that glass is empty. If you want another, just say so."

Josh nodded and took another sip, this time enjoying the taste and feeling the heat in his stomach.

"Lieutenant Richardson's will be out of surgery in about twenty minutes. The doc is stitching him up now and the word is he will probably live, but he's going to need more surgery. It'll be safe to move him in a few hours, so CIC is going to call the *Ranger*. They'll send over a helo with a medical team and take him to one of the hospital ships south of us. Kudos to your guys in the back for keeping him alive. "

Josh nodded, sipping scotch.

"My guess your helicopter is going to clutter up my deck for a few days."

"Yes, sir, it will need an engine change."

"How bad is it?"

"Sir, it is pretty ugly. If you look at the bullet holes, it is obvious that they were targeting the tail rotor, the cockpit, and the engines. It looks like they had a 12.7mm machine gun, because that's the round that went through the armor plate and hit Mr. Richardson. The plates protecting the engines took several rounds as well, one of which knocked out the fuel control of the right engine. A few inches above and it would have hit the combustion section, and who knows what would have happened then."

"Are you O.K?"

"I think so. This is the first time someone got hurt in my helicopter. I liked flying with Mr. Richardson." Josh took another sip. "I'll be alright. I'm still pretty pumped up."

"Let me give you some advice. It's normal to be scared and upset. Don't be afraid to talk about it with other pilots."

"Sir, you sound like my father."

"Why?"

"He told me the exact same thing, sir. My dad flew in World War II and Korea. He also told me that there is a randomness about death in war, and he often wondered why a burst of flak tore up the plane flying on his wing and not his. Or, why the German fighter choose to attack another plane in the formation and not his. His message to me was that you had to be fatalistic about it and do what you need to do to survive. He said never give up trying to stay alive, but if it is time for you to buy the farm, it's time and there is not a lot you can do about it."

"He sounds like a wise man." Captain Danforth paused, then said, "Just remember, this door is always open for you."

Same Day, 1238 Local Time, Beijing

Raiskov had been waiting for quite a while when he finally saw General Chia enter the restaurant, one chosen by the General himself for their meeting. A sealed, four-centimeter-thick envelope was on the seat beside Raiskov. He'd already consumed the basket of crusty Italian-style peasant bread and was, when Chia showed up, impatiently waiting for a refill.

The restaurant's location was in the small area where a few Western companies were allowed to conduct business with the People's Republic of China, and where employees were free to walk about without either an official or unofficial escort. Nevertheless, Raiskov simply assumed he was followed by both Chinese military and civilian intelligence officers every time he left the embassy. Sometimes he spotted the tail, other times he didn't. He was sure that by this time, the People's Republic of China's intelligence agency knew exactly where he was.

By the time the lunch was over, he figured most of the Western agencies would know as well. As long as they didn't know about the contents of the conversation, they could speculate however they wanted.

"I am sorry I am late." General Chia held out his hand as Raiskov stood up.

"Not a problem. I took the liberty of ordering us some sparkling water. Thank you for joining me." Raiskov spoke in Mandarin; despite years of study, he knew his accent was horrible.

As a Moldavian he'd learned Romanian from his parents. Russian was mandatory in grade school. As soon as he'd known he was accepted into the GRU, he'd started mastering English, figuring that he ought to speak the language of his country's main enemy. Mandarin had come later.

He'd spent six months at the Moscow Language Institute taking an immersion course in Chinese before leaving for his first of three four-year tours in Beijing. Unlike many of his counterparts, he enjoyed the challenge trying to use the language, even when he knew he was butchering the pronunciation of the words.

"Your Mandarin is getting better every day." Brigadier General Dao Chia gave him high marks for persistence and trying.

Vassily waved his hand in an sweeping gesture. "This is an interesting choice of restaurants," Raiskov commented, hoping to elicit an explanation. He's noticed that the indirect approach tended to get better results than blunt questions.

"I thought we would try Beijing's one and only Italian restaurant run by a good Italian communist. The man came here a few years after marrying a woman from Canton."

Raiskov thought, *This is not a country or place I would start a business. There has to be an intelligence-gathering reason he is allowed to run a restaurant.* "I have not been here before. How is the food?"

"I am not an expert, but I am told it is very good and reasonably priced."

Of course it is reasonably priced, the government probably tells him what to charge. "If it is good, I will have to tell my friends." *Which no doubt is exactly what General Dao Chia wants, so they can listen in on our conversations and record them.*

Chia waited until they were almost done with their second course. The owner came out and, in fluent Chinese, told them the pasta was homemade and that he used local ingredients for his mother's recipes.

"Did you know, Colonel Raiskov, that the explorer Marco Polo brought noodles back from China and introduced them into the Italian diet?" General Chia asked, after the owner had returned to the kitchen.

"I did not know that."

"Yes, it is a true story. The Italians changed how it is made and added many more shapes, but think about it. Every day Italians eat pasta, they are actually eating Chinese food!"

Raiskov laughed. "I don't think the Italians think of their food that way."

"No, I am sure they don't." Chia put his fork and spoon in the middle of the plate, signaling that he was finished eating and it was time to talk business. "So, what do you have for me today?"

The name Chia loosely translated as 'merchant' in Mandarin. Raiskov wondered if the man's ancestors had dealt with Marco Polo, or if their trade has always been information.

"More messages. The Americans are very interested in your trains, particularly those that enter the People's Republic from the Soviet Union and exit into North Vietnam in the south. They are taking pictures of the Amur River region with their satellites as well. Our guess is that they want to see if we really fought or if it was just propaganda."

Raiskov put the envelope on the table; Chia opened it and did a quick scan of their content before looking up. "The mothers of hundreds of dead People's Liberation Army soldiers would tell them it was not propaganda. The missiles you send us come by ship. Why are the Americans so obsessed with this?"

"They are trying to figure out how the North Vietnamese get so many missiles to shoot at their fighter-bombers. They can't believe that they are all coming into Haiphong by ship." Raiskov paused before he asked the key question. "We understand you are trying to build a new nuclear attack submarine. How is that project going?"

"I wouldn't know."

Raiskov didn't say anything in response. He had been told to ask the question and note the response.

"I have eaten too much. Why don't we take a walk to get some exercise before we go back to our offices? They are in the same general direction and the weather is not too cold."

"Excellent idea." Raiskov laid enough money on the table to pay for the meal and to provide a generous tip. *Chia just told me he has more to say but doesn't want to risk being overheard. So either he knows this place is bugged or doesn't want to take the chance.*

Chia waited until they were a block from the restaurant before he turned to Raiskov.

"We have learned much from operating the well-used nuclear submarine you sold us, but we are going to build one that is better suited to our needs. I have heard that we are having problems with both the hull and the reactor. Also, our Soviet comrades promised us material and technical assistance that was not provided. It is my understanding that your country has not been very helpful, and the head of our navy is not pleased." Chia stopped. "My good colonel, here is where we part company. Your office is a couple of blocks down that street and mine is this way. Let us have lunch again in a few weeks."

Raiskov stood there for a few seconds watching the Chinese officer cross the street before he turned into the icy wind. *My god, he used the familiar rather than the formal way to address. Was that a signal that he sees me as an ally, or contempt for a hireling? He was delivering a not so subtle second message that his government is not happy with my government because they are not delivering on their promises. But is that the truth? Was he briefed on the answer in case I asked, or did he really know?*

Same Day, 1640 Local Time, U.S.S. **Sterett**

Josh climbed into the co-pilot's seat and laid the pocket NATOPS manual on the center console, ready for use. Time to test the replaced engine. He was surprised that he couldn't smell JP-5, the Navy's version of jet fuel. Considering the mechanics had to disconnect and then reconnect the fuel lines and test them for leaks before they started, the lack of a smell from spilled fuel was a testament to the care and skill of those who changed the engine.

In the 20 some hours since he'd landed, his aircraft commander, Darryl Richardson, had been hoisted aloft in a Stokes litter for transfer to a hospital, and a maintenance team had been delivered, along with boxes of tools and parts and a hoist that enabled them to lift the damaged engine off the airframe. A CH-46 had brought a spare engine in a large, olive drab can. Josh had observed the maintenance crew as they maneuvered and installed the 55-inch long and 285-pound engine, replaced fuel lines, and secured mounting bolts and safety wires.

While they were at it, the rotor head, main and tail rotors and tail rotor drive shaft was visually inspected for damage. There was none that could be seen. It was a sobering realization that his life depended as much upon their workmanship on deck as his own abilities to handle the helicopter once it was airborne. Now a hovering HH-3A was preparing to deposit Lieutenant Commander Montemayor onto the crowded helo deck.

After shaking hands, Montemayor looked up at the helicopter. The engine access doors were still open. "Is the engine pre-flighted and are you ready to test this bird?"

"Yes, sir. We just finished."

"Great. My timing is perfect. I'll have a look and then we'll fire it up. Go get strapped in."

A few minutes later, the dark-skinned Montemayor climbed into the aircraft commander's seat.

"Here's the drill. We light off the engine and, assuming it doesn't blow up, let it run. Van der Jagt will be on the engine platform to check for leaks. If there are none after ten minutes, he'll button it up, and then we start the number two engine and sit here for a few minutes to see what else might be wrong. If nothing bad happens, we engage the rotors and do the same thing. After ten minutes of turning and burning, we take off and fly back to the *Ranger*. This can be hairy for two reasons. We don't know what other damage has been done to the helicopter that we can't see. Once we're airborne, the other helo will land, pick up everyone and their tools, and follow us back. Van der Jagt will be the only crewman on board with us. There are less men at risk that way. Understand the drill?"

"Yes, sir. What's the second reason?"

"Oh. Well, you're flying us back because there are no flight controls on this side of the cockpit that work." Montemayor looked the young pilot as if he was inspecting him. "Are you up for it? You can say no."

"Yes, sir. I'm good... I mean, I can do it."

"I figured you would be, but the flight surgeon said I had to ask and give you the chance to pass. We'll debrief the mission after we get back to the *Ranger*." Montemayor pointed to the instrument panel with its nine bullet holes, three from 12.7mm rounds and six from smaller, 7.62mm bullets. "How much of this stuff works?"

"Sir, I really don't know. The engine and rotor rpm and torque gauges on my side work, along with the RMI and attitude gyro, or we'd never have made it back. The fuel gauges are iffy. I don't think any of the caution lights work because the panel took a hit."

"Good. Let's start with the normal start checklist and go from there."

"Yes, sir. Circuit breakers are all in except for the ones that popped on the way back. I made a note of which ones I pushed back in so we'll see if they pop back out. Brakes?"

"Parking brake set.

"Battery on." Some of the electrical gauges came to life; lights on the caution panel flashed and then went out.

"External power." Josh signaled to plug the external power cable in.

"Battery off."

At this point in the check list they were supposed to start the number one engine, but Montemayor held up his hand. "Pretty much all the flight instruments on my side are fucked, along with the fuel gauges, caution panels and the fire warning system. The only thing that seems to be working normally over here is the clock." Montemayor turned to the mechanic standing between the seats. "Did you check the fire warning sensors and lines?"

"Yes, sir. They checked out. We didn't see any damage."

"O.K. For the moment, let's assume that the indicators are not damaged. You go ahead and start the engine."

Montemayor signaled the air crewman, who was standing on the deck with a fire extinguisher, by twirling his index finger in a circle. As soon as he did, Josh pressed the starter button; both pilots were glad to hear the whine of the starter. "Boss, we've got positive oil pressure."

"Good."

When the engine got to 19 percent, Josh slid the speed selector around to ground idle and both pilots heard a normal, soft whump as the engine lit off and settled down at idle. "Leave the fuel boost pumps on for a few minutes to make sure we have all the air out of the lines."

Josh looked over his shoulder and Bennington had his head out the cargo door, looking up at the number two air crewman. "Sirs, Van der Jagt says there are no leaks."

As they continued through the check list sequence, Montemayor said over the intercom. "Sometime today, they're flying Richardson to Cam Ranh Bay. One of the docs and a corpsman are going with him. Then he will be flown to either Subic or back to the States. They're going to have to open up his chest and take the remaining chunks of metal out. While they can do it on the *Ranger*, the medical officer would prefer it done in a regular hospital. They are more concerned about his arm because he may or may not regain much use of it. The nerves are pretty badly damaged."

"I hope they can save his arm."

"Well, if you'd left him in the seat, he would have died. Getting him out and letting Bennington and Van der Jagt work on him saved his life. We're going to be short one aircraft commander for a while, and we'll have to make do until we have a replacement. Any major lessons learned you want to share with me, or are you going to hold those back until you write your after-action report?"

"Only one major one, sir."

"Care to enlighten me?"

"It is obvious. Time is important, but so is close air support. If I had to do it again, I would have waited until the fixed wing guys had plastered the tree lines just before I got there. That way, we may not have taken as much ground fire as we did."

"And maybe if you waited, you're thinking Darryl wouldn't have been hit?"

"Yes, sir. I have been running scenarios through my mind about how to do it differently. So yes, it has crossed my mind."

"Look, as it turned out, the pilot was down about 17 miles inland, not the three that you were told. Our ROE says we are restricted to five miles. Some rear echelon mother fucker will point out the fact that you violated the ROE and got a helo and a crew member shot up. He will then try to make a federal case about it, but the fact remains, the pilot was down and you were the closest rescue asset."

"But sir, if we had waited until I had more close air support, we may not have gotten shot up so bad."

"Or the pilot could have been killed or captured. Remember, the rice paddy was crawling with bad guys." Montemayor twisted around to look back over his shoulder. Satisfied with what he saw, he keyed the intercom switch again. "Josh, don't beat yourself up. Don't go Higgins on me. Casualties are part of war. You got there in time to make the rescue. Richardson was the aircraft commander and if he wanted to do something different, he would have. This wasn't his first combat rescue. If you'd waited, then there was a chance the North Vietnamese soldiers would have gotten to the pilot first. So you were between the rock and the hard place. The good thing is that you guys had a plan and were flexible. The bad news is that you got shot up, but you saved an Air Force pilot from being captured or killed by the North Vietnamese."

Montemayor looked at the engine gauges and made a note on his knee board. "Ten minutes are up, so let's start the number two engine and engage the rotors."

They'd been sitting there for five minutes with both engines running and the rotors turning when Montemayor turned to Josh. "It is time to go flying." Montemayor read the items on the take off check list, then gave the "chocks out" signal. The enlisted man nodded, signaled to two other men standing by each of the main mounts, and they pulled the chocks away and took off the two remaining tie-down chains.

"Boss, we're ready in the back. Cabin is secured for take off," Van der Jagt reported.

"Here's what I want you to do. The book says we should pull into a hover for ten minutes. We're not going to do that. Instead, I want you to slide off to the side of the *Sterett* and fly in gentle circles around the ship at 70 knots while the other helo lands and picks everyone up.

Then head to the *Ranger.* This way, if we have a problem, we can put it in the water if we have to, or make another landing on the *Sterett.* If we have to land back on the *Sterett,* please avoid crashing on the ship's helo deck. It'll ruin too many people's day. As a stellar co-pilot, I will do a great job of navigating. When we get to the carrier, do a run on landing to avoid hovering. After we land, this helicopter will be hard down until we get it fixed. Questions?"

"No, sir." Josh grinned in appreciation of the commander's confidence in him.

Saturday, December 5th, 1970,
1646 Local Time, Laos

The two meter wide porch that went around the entire house gave anyone sitting or standing on it a clear view of the rows of rubber trees that started fifty meters from the house. For the first two or three hundred meters, the bases of the trees were whitewashed.

Danielle could tell that not much rubber harvesting was going on. From the porch, there wasn't a whiff of the pungent smell that she knew so well, a by-product of the coagulating sap known to the world as raw rubber.

Growing up, she had often watched the skilled workers make the cuts in the bark, tap a spout and attach a tin bowl that captured the dripping milky-white, sticky latex. After two or three hours, they would return and transfer the glob into a larger container for processing.

This time of night, it was peaceful in Champassak province in the southern tip of Laos. The nearest Laotian town of Prakse was only forty miles from the Thai city of Ubon on the west side of the Mekong. Vientiane was almost four hundred air miles to the north and west from the plantation.

The Vietnamese border was less than a hundred miles to the east, and it was common to hear American fighter jets screaming overhead as they pulled off their bombing runs or sped back at low altitude to their base at Ubon. On a quiet night, sometimes you could hear the distant crump of exploding bombs. If one didn't know better, the explosions could be mistaken for thunder.

There wasn't enough wind to cause the leaves on the thirty-meters-tall rubber trees to rustle. Chirping birds returning to their nests after a day of foraging broke the silence.

A series of half-meter diameter mahogany pilings sunk in the ground every three meters supported the house. Under the main floor, the neat rows were far enough apart to provide room for several cars to park. This allowed the driver and any passengers to park sheltered from the frequent rains and walk up the stairs directly into the house. Another stairway in the back led right to the covered veranda, which was five meters off the ground. The height allowed the breeze to flow under and around the house and keep it cool in the summer and dry during the monsoon. It also kept them above most of the flying insects that populated the jungle.

The frame of the house was made from sunda oak and was bolted to the pilings. The exterior walls were made from a local evergreen tree that often grew to over fifty meters in height, and from sunda oak, whose red veins provided natural decoration. Bamboo interspaced with sunda oak made up the internal walls, providing accents as well as practical structure. When it was first built, the house originally had a roof made from corrugated metal, but the noise from the monsoon rains proved unbearable, so it had been replaced with one made from plywood sheets nailed to the oak beams, over which asphalt shingles were laid.

The house had a large open area that served as a living and dining room. Three small bedrooms were off to one side and there were two bathrooms that drained into a septic tank, into which her father dumped lime and other chemicals. It was an unpleasant monthly chore that her brothers helped with, beginning at age ten. When the tank needed pumping, one of the fertilizer trucks was used to suck out the waste that was then used as fertilizer for the fields in which they, along with the families who worked on the plantation, grew much of their food.

Jacques Debenard had designed and built this house with the help of the plantation workers, rather than live in the official three story, thirty-room residence of the plantation owner. When he had taken over as the manager in 1954, shortly after Laos became independent in 1953, he'd turned the administration building into a series of apartments for the workers who had been displaced by the war. Then, as they built and moved into houses along the entrance road to the plantation, the administration building was returned to its original use, except for two rooms that shared a bathroom on the top floor which were kept for guests, and three rooms on the main floor that were used as a clinic and mini-hospital. The plantation now had a full time nurse who also taught in the local school that was about five kilometers away.

Between the houses, which looked much like smaller versions of the one Danielle grew up in, there were several sheds under which the tractors, trucks and other equipment that the plantation needed were parked to protect them from the rain and the sun. A smaller building was a combination machine shop and repair facility.

Danielle remembered moving into the house from Vientiane, which was where her mother and brothers had lived while Jacques was off with the Foreign Legion, fighting in Vietnam and Laos. After living in an apartment since they were married right after the end of World War II, her Laotian mother Dara (which translated loosely as 'evening star') wanted a more traditional Laotian house. What resulted was a compromise that they all loved.

To Danielle, living in the country's capital of Vientiane was a distant, foggy memory. She knew it now as an adult who worked there more than from her early childhood.

The plantation, with its neat rows of trees and the tins strapped to the trunks to catch the sap that would ultimately become rubber, was her home. It had been, until the war became a reality, a peaceful place and the source of many joyful memories.

So far, the plantation and its workers had not been directly affected by the war. A couple of times, her father saw Pathet Lao patrols moving through the rubber trees and the surrounding jungle.

When the patrols spotted her father, they quickly disappeared to the east toward the Laotian-Cambodian border where the North

Vietnamese had their bases inside Laos. Jacques was sure they were just monitoring production. The Frenchman believed the Pathet Lao were not going to do anything to affect rubber production, since it was one of the country's most lucrative exports. Michelin paid a healthy tax on each pound of raw rubber that it exported. And, the plantation kept almost two hundred men fully employed.

From the time they were planted, rubber trees took seven years before they were capable of producing economically viable amounts of rubber. They would produce for between twenty-five and thirty-five years, at which time the trees would be cut down and replaced with younger plants. The wood was used to build things on the plantation, or sold. Jacques Debenard always gave local farmers a chance to take what logs they needed before they were trucked off to market.

Danielle liked to walk or drive around the grounds, looking at the younger trees. She loved to monitor them through growth from young saplings to mature, productive trees.

She was sitting on the one of the wicker chairs on the west side, looking at the orange ball sitting above the horizon, sipping a glass of burgundy, when she turned to her father. "Papa, when are you and mother going to leave the plantation? You and I both know that it is only a matter of time before the Pathet Lao overrun this place. They will not like the fact that it is run by a Frenchman."

"Both your brothers and are forbidden to come back until this war is over. You are out and safe in Singapore as well, so there is only your sister Gabrielle, your mother and me here. Your mother does not want to leave, and I will not leave my workers."

"You can't protect them, nor can the government. The Communists when they take over will want to run everything. They will leave you alone for a while, and then—poof! They'll take Gabrielle, mama and you away and we'll never see you again!"

"Michelin has agreed to pay a special tax to the Pathet Lao. In return, they promised not destroy the plantations or take the foreign workers like me prisoners. We will see if they are true to their word." Her father gave a Gaelic shrug. "And if the Communists lose, then we continue on as if nothing happened."

"Papa, you know that the Pathet Lao will not stop until they take control of the country. Do you trust them?"

He shrugged his shoulders again as only a Frenchman can. "Officially, I must. Michelin made a deal, and I am here to make sure the company honors it by keeping the plantations running. The people who signed the papers are safe back in Michelin's headquarters in Cleremont-Ferrand." Jacques waved his hand. "What do they know? To them, it was just another contract. A couple of percentage points here and there won't affect their costs so to them, it is a minor matter."

Another shrug that Danielle knew he made when he was being philosophical. Her father nodded slightly and held up his glass of red Bordeaux and waved it horizontally. "My countrymen back in Cleremont-Ferrand are not living here. We are. And I do see the danger, Danielle. So, I have already officially requested that we, along with the families who work here, be evacuated. Their response was to instruct the office in Vientiane to provide Gabrielle, your mother and me, and any other of my immediate family members, with transportation. We can go back to France or choose another destination. I will have a job no matter where. When I asked about the rest of the workers, they said they would do the same for five families. I told them I was not Solomon. They told me to pick five, no more."

"So what did you tell Michelin in Clermont-Ferrand?"

"I have not responded. My silence is speaking for me and telling them what I think of their answer."

"Papa, I still I think you should leave. The Pathet Lao will not leave a retired French Legionnaire alone, particularly one who is a highly decorated colonel. They will kill you. Some people will wring their hands, and your family will mourn you, but nothing will be done and you will have thrown away your life. And what of mother and Gabrielle?"

"You have been reading too many newspapers and watching too much TV in Singapore."

"No, father, I have been reading intelligence reports that come into our embassy. They are very pessimistic. The Americans are doing better than France did in the early fifties, but they are losing public support for the war. President Nixon even made a campaign promise to pull the United States out of the war. And then, if they haven't already, the Pathet Lao will take over all of Laos. If you wait until that happens, it may be too late. You must leave in the next few months."

Danielle heard a soft but very firm female voice. "I am not leaving Laos. It is my home. If I am going to die here, then that is my karma." Her mother came around and held Danielle's hand before she pulled a chair close to the two of them, reach out with her other hand to hold her husband's. "I am a Laotian. I grew up in this country and I will die here. I have no desire to live anywhere else."

"But mama, what about Gabrielle? Staying here may be a death sentence for her as well as papa."

"It is not. Papa knows he is free to go at any time, and if he does I will insist he take Gabrielle. I will stay, alone if I must, and face my fate."

Danielle took a deep breath. East was now meeting west and she was caught in between. As a westerner, survival and a chance to live someplace else was the logical option. As an easterner, she understood her mother's feelings about fate and karma. Her mother had already accepted it and nothing would change her mind. She looked at her father; in the dying sunlight his look said, "I told you that would be the answer."

Chapter 9 – REPLACEMENT HAC

Monday, November 7th, 1300 Local Time, the Pentagon

The Chairman of the Joint Chiefs of Staff was sitting in his conference room scanning a report when the other Service Chiefs started arriving. After the greetings and small talk about the early snow storm threatening the nation's capital, he got down to business.

"Today is the 29th anniversary of Pearl Harbor. I presume that all of you have sent messages to your respective Services to commemorate that tragic day. I also expect you all to be visible at the ceremonies around town. I lived through that attack, and I still have vivid memories of what happened. I cannot and will not forget how we were caught by surprise. As the Chairman of the Joint Chiefs, I am determined never to let that happen again."

One of the generals sitting at the table nodded his head and said "Amen."

"With that said, I want to summarize the missile problem in Vietnam in one hundred words or less, and then move on to the real purpose of this meeting. First, the North Vietnamese are changing their tactics, and we may be facing a new version of the SA-2. Therefore, we need better equipment to detect, counter and destroy the missiles. I have been assured by the Secretary of Defense that this is one of his highest priorities and the department has several programs underway. Some programs have been canceled, and you have all been briefed on those which remain and which ones your Service is leading. Second, the Air Force still believes that there is a second source, so I am pursuing the overflight issue with the National Security Advisor and the President. Still no decision."

The chairman's didn't want to waste any more time on stale ground, so he moved on to the topic of the day, which he knew several people in this room, and many of their subordinates, would not like. "On the agenda there were only four words—*the Chairman's pet project*—which I am sure had your staffs scurrying about, trying to find out what that might be. My guess is they couldn't, because only two people know the answer—myself and my chief of staff. It has to do with the opportunity that the U.S. military can offer the men and women of this country."

The four-star admiral looked around the room and assessed the various levels of curiosity, interest, and guarded alarm before continuing. "I grew up in a very segregated south, where conditions were made worse by the Depression. While it has been documented in pictures and described in articles and books, no one can really know what it was like unless you lived it."

He addressed the Chief of Staff of the Army, "You grew up in South Carolina, and probably saw segregation up close and personal was well."

"Yes, sir, I did."

"Anyway, on Saturday evening, I had an epiphany at a reception because, as I looked around the room, all the attendees were lily white and all the people serving food and drink were black. That struck me as odd for 1970. Later in the week, I saw a class picture of a group of young Navy and Marine Corps officers who'd just got their wings. There were no black or Asian faces. The services have been officially desegregated since 1948 when President Truman signed the executive order, but we have not done enough. I know that there are men of every race and color dying in Vietnam, but I want us to take a deep look at the composition of our Armed Services from a racial and cultural perspective. We must, and I'll say it again, *must* have the same cross section of the society that we protect, or we will not be creditable. And the subtle sort of pre-screening that eliminates many qualified men from becoming officers needs to stop. You all know what I am talking about."

The chairman began tapping his pen on the table. The other flag officers in the room this as his way of emphasizing a point. It was how he said, *pay attention.*

"I want each service to take a hard look at the mix, rank by rank, of its people by occupational specialty and prepare a report. And don't pretend it can't be done. We have the data, and someone in your admin shops has it or knows where to get it. That's task one.

"Task two is to evaluate the promotion rates from E-1 to O-8, again by MOS and by race and religion over the past five years. I know for a fact that Jews are sometimes discriminated against. I've seen it in awards and in billet assignments, and I saw it happen on an officer promotion board about ten years ago. Several of us took that flag officer to task afterwards."

By this time, the other officers around the table were all taking notes. He smiled a bit grimly.

"You can stop taking notes because as you walk out of here, my chief of staff will be handing you a document that lays out how and what I want you to analyze, as well as the format to use." Several of the officers sat back, relieved that they wouldn't have to recite all this to their heads of personnel.

"Task three is to take a look at how and where we recruit our officers. I want you to look at your individual Service academies, ROTC, officer candidate programs, etc. I want to know where these young men and women come from. The time frame is the past five years.

"Task four, I want your recommendations on how we can broaden our appeal. I want specific, actionable ideas that we, the joint chiefs of staff, will discuss, vet, and then—as the Armed Forces of the United States of America—put into action. The Secretary of Defense has already been briefed and will fund this effort. He also told me that his office will provide any data that is needed. The protocol for any data requests is, however, to go through my chief of staff, who is the action officer.

"Task five, I am asking each service to contribute six individuals— three officers and three senior enlisted men—to form a joint team that evaluates the reams of data from the summary analysis. Make sure they are your best and brightest and can do the work. In the document you will get, there are details on the classification level, as well as funding and accounting information. I would encourage you to bring in men and women from outside the beltway to get a broader view."

The chairman waited a few seconds. "Questions?"

"Yes, sir. When do you want this information?"

"The evaluation team will report to us on Monday, February 1st, 1972. Block your calendars, gentlemen, because we will be in this room from 1300 until 1700. I will expect you to be familiar with the information from your respective service, but not how it compares to the others. I hate to add a threat to end my soliloquy, but if any of you or your staff give out any details of the analysis before it is ready, I will deal with you personally, and the results, I can assure you, will not be pleasant. Do I make myself clear?"

The four other heads in the room nodded, and three responded with crisp "Yes, sir"s The Chief of Naval Operations said, "Aye, aye, sir."

Tuesday, December 8th, 1970,
2015 Local Time, U.S.S. Ranger

Josh opened the front door to the ready room and selected a seat in the second row in front of the large screen. Crews scheduled to go flying got the front seats. He settled in, put his updated chart on his lap, and sniffed appreciatively. The reconnaissance squadron's popcorn popper was hard at work and the smell of fresh popcorn filled the air.

As soon as the mission briefing was over and the 2100 launch crews left the room, the movie would start. But no matter what was happening on screen, the movie was stopped during recovery and the deck-mounted, high resolution camera, which was aimed up the glide slope, relayed the incoming flights so everyone could see their squadron mate's approach on the black and white TV. The camera even had cross-hairs, so the viewer could see airplane relative to where it should be during its approach. As the plane got closer, viewers could see the wildly moving control surfaces as the pilot made last minute adjustments just before his plane slammed down onto the deck.

The primary crew came in right after Josh, followed a few minutes later by the back-up crew. Josh had just popped open a can of Coke when he heard his name.

"Haman, where have you been?"

Josh looked up to see Lieutenant Commander Montemayor towering over him. "Sir, I just got back from the intelligence center. I went over the strike package ingress and egress routes and updated my chart with all the triple-A positions. We'll be covering two launches from the *Ranger.* I wanted to be prepared with the latest info."

Montemayor took the chart and studied it for a few minutes. "This is very interesting. Who maintains this chart?"

"I do. Every day or so, I go down there and compare what is on this chart with what we've seen and what the intel guys have. I'm mostly worried about the twenty-three, thirty-seven and fifty-seven millimeter guns. The North Vietnamese move them around all the time. I want to minimize the chance of stumbling over one. If there are a lot of changes, I make a knew chart and put the old one in my safe."

"Do you share this with anyone?"

"Darryl used to look at it every time I updated it, but no one else has asked for it. I think the other guys just take what intel provides. Why?"

"This is outstanding, and it's something all our pilots should see; everyone should have a copy. Every crew ought to provide input so that we have the best possible intel. You never know when we'll be asked to make a rescue close to the beach or have to go inland. I want you to keep it updated and start briefing the other pilots in the detachment, as well as get their input. When we get back, I'll assign someone to work with you so we have back-up charts for the other crews."

"Yes, sir, no problem."

"On tonight's mission, you're flying in the right seat. Pretend I'm a newbie co-pilot and you have to explain everything. Just assume that I do know where all the switches and dials are and that I won't do anything malicious. If you want me to do something, you'll have to tell me, and I might ask for an explanation. If nothing else, it'll keep the guys in the back awake."

"Yes, sir. When do you want start this little exercise?"

"Right now." Montemayor stepped over Josh's outstretched legs and plopped into the seat next to him. "So, HAC, what's going on?" Montemayor changed his voice to a higher pitch so he sounded like an eager newbie.

Josh started to laugh. *O.K, I'll play this game, because what he is really doing is seeing what I know and how I'll act if I were in charge.* "Well, sir, I already stopped by the weather guesser's office on the island to look at their maps. We're about to get the official weather brief that will tell us what to expect in the target areas as well as over our alternates in South Vietnam. We'll also get the weather updates for Dixie and Yankee Stations. We're up here, in the northern part of the gulf on Yankee Station, and this area is supposed to get rain squalls for most of the night that will move through roughly west to east that could affect landing conditions. The other carrier, the *Oriskany,* may or may not be under the squalls. The only other alternative within our range is the *Oklahoma City,* which is not as good a place to land if the weather is really crappy."

"Where are we going?"

Josh indicated on the chart where he had penciled two ovals, one just off Haiphong Harbor and one south of the city. "We have two orbits. For the first strike package, four A-6s, eight A-7s and eight F-4s are supposed to hit a SAM site southeast of Hanoi and a missile storage area."

He moved his forefinger inland, pointing to the triangle of roads that connected Nam Dinh, a small city about fifteen miles from the gulf in the Red River delta, to Hanoi and the port city of Haiphong. "The second strike is about the same size, and we orbit a little farther south. The A-6s are going to keep going inland on a road reconnaissance along in this area.

"Both the 2200 and the 2345 launches are supposed to go feet dry about halfway between Nam Dinh and Haiphong and come out here, which is where we'll be orbiting. I'll keep us between one and three miles off the beach. This way, if we have to cross the beach to make a pick-up, we can minimize the time it takes to get there."

"What altitude are we going to be flying at?"

"En route, I think we'll climb to angels one until we're about twenty-five miles from the coast, then ease down to cherubs two for our orbit."

"Why not orbit at cherubs five?"

"Because I want to make us harder to find. The closer we are to the water, the less chance they can see us or pick us up on radar. Also, we'll orbit at seventy knots to save fuel so we can stay on site longer."

"It's safer at five hundred feet. We have more time to react if something goes wrong."

"Sir, are you asking me why I want to be lower, or telling me we have to fly at five hundred feet?"

"Asking."

"It is a trade-off between safety and risk. I think the greater risk is the gooks bagging us with a surprise burst from a fifty-seven millimeter gun because they can see us at five hundred feet two miles off the beach. I'd rather be down low in the weeds hiding, as close to the shoreline as possible to minimize the time it takes to get to a survivor who is between five miles inland and three miles offshore."

"What if the survivor is twelve miles inland?"

"We make sure we have the close air support assets." *That's one mistake I don't need to make again.* "If we're the closest helo and think we can get him, we go. If not, we go to plan B."

"What's plan B?"

"It is situation dependent. When we know what is happening around us, we create plan B and C at the same time." The clacking of the tele-printer stopped Josh from continuing. "Sir, the weather brief is about to start…"

Two hours later, Josh was flying the helicopter as they descended below five hundred feet on the way to two hundred. Montemayor, who had peppered him with questions for the first twenty minutes of the flight, had been silent for the past ten.

It was instrument flying at its purest, no external visual clues—no moon, no starlight, and no horizon. Josh constantly scanned the primary flight instruments in the order he'd been taught—attitude gyro, directional gyro, altimeter, needle and ball, vertical speed indicator. Every other cycle, he'd glance at the engine instruments and the rotor rpm and engine torque gauges. His eyeballs told his brain what the helicopter was doing and his brain told his limbs how to respond, which resulted in subtle, delicate control movements that kept the altimeter pinned at exactly two hundred feet, a.k.a. cherubs two.

Inside the cockpit, the dull red light from the instruments glinted off the white reflective tape on their helmets. Outside the cockpit windows there was nothing to see. Occasionally, they would fly over a fishing boat that was showing a white light on its mast, but other than that, it was if they were flying inside a milk bottle painted dull black.

Josh activated the intercom to address the crew. "Everyone in the back, get your heads out and watch for fishing boats. Some of them can get pretty aggressive."

Mike clicks acknowledged his instructions. It wasn't uncommon for junks to be armed with 12.7 millimeter machine guns and take pot shots at helos orbiting off their coast. Unless one attempted to prevent them from making a rescue, Josh told the crew that he didn't want to engage fishing boats. If one was under their orbit and fired on them, they would just shift the orbit.

The bigger threat were the North Vietnamese patrol and torpedo boats that mingled with the fishing fleets. These were there for three reasons. Job one was to protect the boats from the Chinese, who boarded them and forced the fishermen to pay a tax on their catch. Job two was to monitor them to make sure that they didn't head south and defect. These activities were of no concern to Josh. Job three affected their mission. The boat crews got a bonus if they picked up a downed airman.

"Tracers, four o'clock. Tracking..." Bennington's voice was so calm he sounded like he was bored. The last word meant that he'd seen at least a burst or two that indicated the gunner was tracking their flight path and lining up to intercept. "Break right, NOW!"

Josh didn't need any encouragement. He rolled the airplane into a thirty degree angle of bank. He had to take care that the helo didn't descend too far and dig a rotor tip into the water. He forced the thought of the consequences of *that* out of his mind. At this bank angle, the rotor blades were probably only 150 above the water, so he added a bit more power and the helicopter climbed a few feet. As he did so, a group of tracers floated under the nose of the HH-3A.

"Josh, turn left. There's at least two boats out here that ... Oh fuck, that was a torpedo boat." Montemayor twisted in his seat. "Josh increase your rate of turn."

A group of tracers passed over the helicopter. Then there was another. As soon as he saw it coming, he increased power to keep the helicopter climbing, then he reversed his turn. The next burst when right through his old path of flight.

Josh keyed the intercom. "Bennington, Kowalski, see if you can spot the torpedo boat or can tell me where he is in relation to the helo. They've got us bracketed."

He put the helicopter in a descending, skidding turn. A hand gripped his shoulder. It was Van der Jagt, standing between the pilots.

Van der Jagt pointed. "There's the boat, twelve o'clock low!"

"Got him. Bennington, get ready and hose the boat down as we pass."

Josh saw the gray-white water at the stern as the boat's screws churned up the gulf before he saw the shadowy gray shape. On the stern, the gunners were struggling to bring their dual 23mm turret to bear on the approaching helicopter that was swooping toward them at 110 knots.

Josh saw the tracers from the mini-gun stab out into the night. Bennington's first burst was right on target. Sparks from bullets ricocheting off the turret's steel flew in all directions. A second, longer burst stitched along the centerline of the ship. As they passed by, Bennington hosed down the bridge and the closest torpedo mount.

Josh banked hard to the right and leveled out to give Bennington a chance to rain bullets up and down the torpedo boat's deck as the helicopter crossed the traditional T.

Bennington's voice was clear over the intercom. "She's starting to burn. I see a fire aft and flames around the starboard torpedo tube."

Josh maneuvered the helicopter so that he could see the boat now dead in the water. "Bennington, I'm going to roll around to come up the starboard side, three to four hundred yards away and at two-hundred-fifty feet. See if you can really stoke the fires."

Two clicks were followed by a stream of tracers and a hum. Josh was head down, focused on the instruments, when the cockpit lit up with a burst of yellow-white light, followed by a second one. The cyclic was almost yanked from his hands as the HH-3A shook and vibrated as if it were about to come apart and rolled uncontrollably to the left. Josh quickly got it back level.

"Sir, the boat blew up! I think one of the torpedoes got cooked and set off the other one. There's nothing left but debris floating in the water."

Both pilots scanned the gauges. Nothing seemed amiss. No warning lights, all gauges were indicating normal. Both paid special attention to their highly tuned asses. All either could feel were the normal vibrations and noises as the helicopter beat its way through the night sky.

Josh could feel his heart rate start to slow down. "That was scary," he said that to no one in particular.

He got a "No shit,", an "Amen to that," a "No kidding," and two mike clicks in response.

* * * * *

Four and a half hours later, Josh stood in front of Montemayor's desk in the ready room. The RA-5s were not flying again until later in the morning. The only people in the room were the detachment's petty officer of the watch and the two officers.

Montemayor handed Josh the closed-book NATOPS exam and said, "Go find a quiet corner over there and finish this if you want to become a HAC. You've got an hour; then I'll be back to pick it up and grade it."

Wednesday, December 9th, 1970,
0830 Local Time, U.S.S. Ranger

Ten officers and 40 enlisted men stood in formation in front of Lieutenant Commander Montemayor on the hangar deck of the *Ranger.* The second of six *Forrestal*-class carriers built in the 1950s and 1960s, the San Diego-based *Ranger* was the first one designed from the keel up to have an angled deck, and the eighth U.S. Navy ship to have the name.

The officer-in-charge called for this formation at the beginning and end of flight operations as a muster. If he had to say something to the entire detachment, he could do it when they were all in front of him at the same time. After counting noses, Montemayor looked over the group.

"I want to put to bed some rumors. First, we're not going to Honolulu for the holidays. We'll be out here on the *Ranger* for another two, maybe three weeks. The good news is that we're going to spend part of the Christmas holiday in Cubi. Now for the bad news. We probably won't get a replacement for Mr. Richardson until we come out for our next line period, so it means we will be short a pilot. Richardson is doing O.K. in the hospital at Cubi and will be flown back to the states in the next day or so."

Cheers broke out, for Richardson had been a popular officer. Montemayor continued.

"Now I want to make an important announcement. Despite his best efforts to demonstrate that he is totally unqualified, last night Lieutenant Junior Grade Haman managed to convince me that he is worthy of being a search and rescue aircraft commander. The designation takes effect immediately, but we won't take off the training wheels right away. Whenever possible, he'll be flying with another HAC until we get to back to Cubi."

Montemayor waited until the congratulations died down. "Just remember, some of you may have to fly with him, so don't let him get a swelled head! Dismissed."

Josh was surrounded by officers and crewmen who shook his hand and even pounded him on the back. After exchanging some good-natured insults, he broke free and followed Montemayor to the ready room. He had a question to ask.

"Sir, I thought you had to get the commanding officer's approval to designate me as a HAC?"

"I don't. As the detachment officer-in-charge, I can make that determination and just tell the CO what I am doing. He reserves the right to veto my recommendation, but he's not overturned one yet, and I don't think he will this time. Anyway, I sent the message last night, and the answer came back today, saying *approved*. Just so you know, you made it faster than any other pilot in this squadron. Just keep doing what you are doing and you'll be fine. I've got air crewmen lining up to fly with you, and that, my friend, is a very, very good indicator that you deserve to be a HAC."

Monday, December 14th, 1970,
1300 Local Time, the Pentagon

The annual budget battles were over, and yet the Chairman of the Joint Chiefs knew that infighting would continue. He often wondered why the services couldn't put aside their bickering and cooperate.

As was customary, he waited until the other members were seated in the conference room before he entered. Even though they also wore four stars on the collar, the generals rose to their feet when he appeared. Standing when a senior officer entered was a 190-year-old tradition that the U.S. Navy had adopted from the Royal Navy. With a nod and "Seats, gentlemen," the chairman gave the traditional response to that gesture of respect.

Greetings and good wishes for the holiday season were exchanged, and a number of lesser topics were discussed before the Chairman tapped the desk with his pen.

"The president has agreed to allow a limited number of over flights of southern China. The operative word is *limited*: they will only be authorized one flight at a time. The Secretary of Defense wants us to brief him in detail on the planned route, timing, etc., of each overflight, at which point his team of *experts*"—sarcasm was heavy in his voice

—"will offer their input. Air Force, since you operate the U-2s and SR-71s, this is your action item. Any idea how you want to do this?"

"Actually I do, sir. A team from the Ninth Strategic Reconnaissance Wing at Beale Air Force Base has come up with a plan. To minimize the chance of a shoot down, they'll want to use the SR-71s staged out of Kadena Air Base in Okinawa. As soon as this meeting is over, I'll have them send it so we can run the plan by the Secretary of Defense."

"Good. My only advice to the team is that they need to realize the geniuses in the office of the Secretary of Defense will want to make changes, most of which will be dumb, just to prove they're on top; so be prepared to overcome objections. And bear in mind, if a plane, or worse, a pilot gets bagged, there will be hell to pay!"

Chapter 10 – RAID SUPPORT

Josh was sitting in the corner of the ready room that HC-7 Det 110 shared with the squadron that flew the RA-5C Vigilante. The sleek, twin engine jet had started out as a supersonic bomber but had been converted to a photo reconnaissance airplane. As a bomber it wasn't great, but its payload, speed and range made it ideal for recce missions. The "Viggie" had a reputation of being hard to land on a carrier, and ready room junkies often gathered around the monitor to watch the landings. Pilots had told Josh it was a delight to fly and a handful in the "groove", the final approach to the carrier.

The squadron RVAH-12 (reconnaissance, heavy attack), also known as the Speartips, consisted of eight crews for five two-seat airplanes. If all its officers were present, this still left extra space in the ready room designed to seat 30. When Detachment 110 was on board the *Ranger,* HC-7 operated out of the rear corner.

"Mail call!"

The two words galvanized everyone in the room. Announced over the ship's intercom, it got the attention of every member of the ship's crew, stirring hopes for news from home and care packages. Moments later, the detachment's yeoman came into the ready room carrying a dirty, faded yellow bag with 'U.S. Mail' stamped in black. He pulled out a stack of letters, grinned at the eager faces around him, and started calling out names.

About halfway through, he handed four to Josh. Two were from his parents; the other two, numbered 7 and 8, were on flimsy mail gram stationery. Danielle's tight, perfect penmanship was unmistakable.

With nothing to do and his next mission not scheduled to launch until midnight, Josh headed for his stateroom to devour the contents.

In number seven, Danielle informed him that she was going to Laos and Cambodia for several weeks, and she feared that letters to or from an American FPO would be opened. Josh checked the post markings and saw that both letters had gone from Singapore to the San Francisco fleet post office and on to Yankee Station. Number 7 had been sent just before Danielle left for Laos; number 8, sent two weeks later, was short and to the point.

> *Josh,*
>
> *I just got back from Vientiane and Phnom Penh—it was both work and a chance to visit with my family. My parents and brothers and sisters are doing fine, but all are afraid of what the Pathet Lao and their North Vietnamese allies will do if they conquer Laos. You know my views on this terrible war, and Pathet Lao rule of my homeland will not be good for any of us.*
>
> *I am running out of space on this mail gram so I will get to a happier note. I will be working out of Singapore for the foreseeable future and will fly up to Manila to visit you the next time you are in port there. You can call me at either the embassy or my apartment, and I will get on the first flight I can to Manila, where we can spend a few precious days together. Call me when you get the chance. I really want to see you again. You have my number, use it!*
>
> *Danielle*

Wednesday, December 16th, 1970,
0745 Local Time, on the U.S.S. Ranger

The flight deck still smelled from burned jet fuel and burnt rubber, even though the last aircraft had trapped aboard 20 minutes ago. The *Ranger* had slowed to a leisurely ten knots to save fuel as it moved through the placid gulf. Flight operations had ended and the flight deck crew were moving airplanes so some could be brought up from the hangar deck and others brought below.

Re-spotting the deck was one part Argentine tango, with well-defined, precise moves, and one part organized chaos in which the only person who knew the final layout was the flight deck officer. He sat in a small compartment at the forward end of the structure known as 'the island'. He presided over a two-tiered Plexiglas table that had the layouts of the flight deck on top and the hangar deck below. On it were placed silhouettes of each type of airplane with its side number, precisely correlating to the actual planes' locations on the deck. On top of the silhouettes were color-coded nuts that indicated the plane's status. Green nuts were for those ready to launch, and these dominated the board. Other colors were also in evidence. Red signified down, i.e., in need of major repairs; blue: maintenance to be performed between launches; purple: needs fuel; yellow: needs to be repositioned; white: needs ordnance; these were on the twenty-odd planes that would remain on the deck to be readied for the next launch.

In the midst of all this movement, Josh, as well as a few other hardy souls, jogged fore and aft, trying to get some needed exercise. As they ran, the joggers dodged tractors towing airplanes and tried not to slip on oily spots or trip on the tie down chains that stretched from airplanes to the pad-eyes on the deck.

Pad-eyes were dimples in the deck about ten inches round and three inches deep with steel X's welded across the opening. To secure a plane in place, crewmen would hook one end of tie down chains to the rebar X of a pad-eye and the other end to a tie down point on the airplane or helicopter, and then ratchet the chains tight.

Josh stopped when Petty Officer Van der Jagt appeared in front of him. "Mr. Haman, the boss wants you to meet him in the ready room ASAP."

"Do I have time for a shower?"

"No, sir. I don't think so."

"Then lead on."

No one gave Josh, who was wearing sneakers, shorts and a sweaty t-shirt, a second glance as he followed Van der Jagt down the passageway of green linoleum tiles that ran the length of the ship. Joggers were a common sight. Equally common were the skinned kneecaps they earned when they tripped over a tie down chain or some other piece of gear on the flight deck and the abrasive non-skid surface ripped off several layers of skin.

"What's up, boss?" Josh asked when he pulled up in front of Montemayor. 'Boss' was the unofficial title often given to detachment officers-in-charge or aircraft commanders in multi-seat aircraft.

"We've got a good deal."

Josh gave Lieutenant Commander Montemayor a quizzical look.

"Thee and me are going to fly to Da Nang. We've been summoned for some kind of meeting. Since, I gather, you have not yet, in your long and extensive career as a Naval Aviator, ever planned or flown such a mission, you are going to be the HAC."

"Sir, I have been in and out of Da Nang a couple of times." Josh stopped before he said it had been with Mr. Higgins.

"Ahhh, I suspected that. However, how many times have you flown there with a load of ten passengers, cargo and mail, and started from more than one hundred and fifty miles out to sea?"

"None, sir."

"I thought so. This is something we do all the time in the H-3. The HS guys often operate one hundred miles or more from the carrier, so over water ops are, or should be, no big deal. It is why the helo has two engines and a boat hull. So call the air transport officer and get a manifest and an estimate of the cargo's weight. Once you have that, figure out where you are going to put everyone and do a weight and balance. This is not just an exercise, because if they load the helo the wrong way, we'll have center of gravity problems. Also, it's a good habit to have the air crewmen handle all the boxes and bags as they are loaded. Remind them to sense check the weight of each. It is not uncommon for the post office guys to not put the weight on each bag. They just give us a total weight, and it's not always accurate, so you may have to adjust your calculations."

"Yes, sir. When do we launch?"

"The air boss will announce helo flight quarters at 0900, and he expects us to be on our way shortly thereafter, or my ass will get reamed when we get back. So we do not want to disappoint him, do we?"

"No, sir. I'll meet you at the airplane at 0815, which will give us time to supervise the loading, preflight and go over the weight and balance."

* * * * *

While they were waiting for the go ahead to start engines, Josh tossed a small bag into Montemayor's lap.

"What's this?"

"That's the chart bag for the dumb co-pilot. The chart has all the headings marked, as well as a fuel plan in there for the dumb co-pilot to monitor. The HAC will be busy flying the helicopter."

Montemayor was holding up his fist with an extended middle finger and laughing when they heard the Air Boss announce that the helicopter was cleared to start its engines.

"You know, Haman, you're getting to be a real wise ass. If you're not careful, you'll get all the midnight launches."

"I can't wait, sir. But let's not piss off the Air Boss."

Two hours later, Josh taxied the H-3 to a spot on the visiting aircraft ramp at Da Nang. Directly in front of them was a jeep, and at the wheel was a driver wearing an olive drab t-shirt, fatigue pants that had been cut into Bermuda shorts, a web belt with a .45 in the holder and several pouches of ammunition around his waist. An M-14 rifle was visible in the back seat.

Josh saw a gold bar on the driver's fatigue cap. His sandy blond hair and broad, muscular shoulders reminded Josh of the surfers he'd seen on the beaches in San Diego when he was going through the RAG.

The ensign watched from his seat as the passengers headed into the terminal and the bags of mail were tossed onto the back of a pick-up truck. Then he put one hand on the frame and the other on the dash and propelled himself out of the jeep. He walked up to the two pilots as they were coming down the ladder, came to attention and saluted. "Lieutenant Commander Montemayor, I'm Ensign Marty

Cabot. Thanks for coming."

Montemayor returned the salute. "Ensign Cabot, this is Lieutenant Joshua Haman."

Cabot nodded, not needing to salute again. "Thanks for coming on such short notice. I'll take the two of you to the meeting and then, if you like, to the club for a meal. It's up to you if you want to spend the night. There will be another jeep to pick up your crew in about five minutes."

Josh got into the back seat of the jeep and put the M-14 across his lap.

Marty turned around. "Be careful, flyboy, it is loaded."

"I saw that. I checked to see if there's a round in the chamber, and the safety is on."

"You noticed?"

"I did. I treat every firearm I am handed as if it is loaded until I know otherwise. This one is ready to fire. I also found the bandolier of six extra thirty round magazines."

"Well, mister helo driver, please don't shoot me in the back as I'm driving."

"I don't plan to," Josh grinned.

The drive took about 15 minutes before Cabot down-shifted and stopped in front of a razor-wire topped, double chain link fence with three feet between the two rows of metal. A man with an M-14 slung over his shoulder came out of a sand-bagged guard post, and Josh saw a manned M-60 machine gun pointed at them. After fiddling with the latch, the man opened the gate and Marty drove to a building that looked more like a blockhouse than anything else. On a nearby boat ramp, Josh noticed several Swift boats on cradles and several others in the water.

Josh handed Marty the M-14; Marty also slung the bandoleer over his shoulder before saying, "Follow me."

Another guard checked their names and identification cards against a list before he allowed Marty to lead them to a conference room. "The rest of the attendees will be here in a few minutes. Can I get you anything? Coffee, soda?"

"Water would be nice. Where are anyway, and why are we here?" Josh figured the worst Ensign Cabot could do was tell him to shut up.

"Welcome to the Navy Special Warfare Command, Vietnam's Da Nang's compound. You're in a secure conference room. Outside is an overhaul facility for all the Swift boats we use in this area of South Vietnam. They're moving in a month or so to a much bigger facility in Cam Ranh Bay. I'm a SEAL platoon leader who just got told I was going to support our Vietnamese allies on a series of special missions. More I can't tell you yet. We think we may need your help, and today we want to figure that out. If you can help us, we'll read you in and get started. If not, at least you've gotten a chance to stand on dry land for a few hours!"

Cabot's soft accent confirmed that he was from Southern California, not Georgia or the deep south. Josh took a long swallow from the bottle of cool water Cabot handed him.

"So, Haman, you handled that M-14 like you knew what you were doing. Or were you just imitating what you see in the movies?"

"When I picked it up, I looked for the safety and saw it was on. Then I slid the bolt part way back to see if it was loaded. It was. I don't know if that indicates I know what I was doing. I just thought it was being safe. Like I said, until I know differently, I treat every gun as if it is loaded."

"Ever fire one before?"

"No, but I've fired the M-1 Garand a lot."

"You hit what you aim at?"

"Yes. I'm more accurate than most."

"How do you measure that?"

"Honest answer is that I shot expert with both the pistol and the rifle while I was an ROTC Midshipmen. But that's target shooting, which is a lot different from what you do out here."

"Amen to that." Marty was about to say something when the door opened to the conference room, revealing two individuals wearing the same "uniform" that Marty Cabot had on.

"Attention on deck," Cabot said crisply.

"At ease, gentlemen," said one. "I am Captain Stan Rainer and I'm the senior SEAL in Vietnam. Thanks for coming. Take a seat; we'll be here a while."

Captain Rainer casually waved his hand in the direction of the other man. "This is Master Chief Hausner, my leading chief petty officer. What we're about to discuss is his idea, because he has friends in the Navy's helo community. For the record, this briefing is Top Secret, specially compartmented information. I know that both of you are cleared, but what you hear today cannot be discussed outside this building. We'll do the official paperwork later if this goes further than this meeting. Understood?"

"Yes, sir." The two aviators responded almost in unison.

"Good. Here's our problem. We're ably supported in the Mekong River delta by HAL-3, the Navy helicopter light attack squadron that operates off old World War II landing ship tanks and other places. But their UH-1s don't have the fuel to go where we want to go or carry enough people. If the shit hits the fan, the Hueys don't have the fuel to loiter around or a hoist to pull people out of the jungle. Refueling adds time, and all kinds of insertion and extraction risk. Master Chief Hausner thinks, based on what he has been told, the H-3s you fly might be the answer."

"How so?" Montemayor didn't move his bulky frame.

"We want to go two hundred to two hundred and fifty nautical miles, one way."

The lieutenant commander rubbed his head. "How many people would we be carrying?"

"Six, sometimes eight. I can envision missions where there could be as many as twelve."

"It would be crowded in the back, but possible. What do we do once we get there?"

"Drop your passengers off and return to a base. Then, a few days later, fly back into the same area and pick them up."

"Do we have to hover to drop them off?"

"We have to work that out. The SEAL team and the helo crew will have control over selection of the landing zones."

Josh grabbed a piece of paper lying on the table, pulled a pencil out of his sleeve pocket and started writing numbers on a piece of paper.

Montemayor turned to his co-pilot. "What are you doing?"

"I'm running a quick scenario with two different fuel burn rates."

"Without checking the NATOPS manual?"

"Oh, I'd confirm it by studying the manual, but if we stayed low and around ninety knots, we could do it. Four hundred miles should be easy. Four-fifty round-trip would be a stretch. Sir, if you figure an average fuel profile of one thousand pounds an hour, and three hundred pounds to hover, that leaves us landing with about five hundred pounds. The fuel low-level lights might be on when we landed, but that wouldn't be the first time that happened."

"You sure?" Montemayor was eyeing Josh skeptically.

"Yes, sir." Josh wanted to sound as confident as he could. He turned to the senior SEAL. "Can you give me an idea of where you want to go?"

"Specifically, no. Generally, yes. Marty?" The captain called. The young officer stood up and pulled on a string attached to a roll suspended on the wall, revealing a map of Laos, Cambodia, and North and South Vietnam. The captain went to the map and drew a circle on three places on the map with his forefinger. "Northwest of the DMZ in Laos, here in North Vietnam, and here in Cambodia. "

"Why can't the Army provide bases for the Hueys to use?"

"They can, but Hueys are really noisy."

"The H-3 is not exactly quiet," Josh replied. *There is something else they don't like about the Huey, but what was it? It can't just be noise and short range.*

"It is the H-3's range and passenger-carrying ability that got you invited here."

"Do you want to go in daylight or at night?"

"We'd prefer night," Marty answered before the captain could speak.

"Can we pick our own routes in and out and where we want to drop you off?"

"Routes, yes. We'll work with you on LZs as long as they are within an acceptable distance from our objective."

"Do we have to fight our way in or out?"

"We hope neither. The goal is to sneak in and out. More than likely, however, the bad guys will know that you put my team in and will want to try to find us, so the extraction may be hot."

"Will close air support for extractions be available?"

"Yes, we can make that a requirement. Since the Commander, Military Assistance and Advisory Command, came up with this idea, he'll support it and make sure we get the close air support we need," Captain Rainer responded quickly.

Montemayor turned to his newly minted aircraft commander. "Josh, what do you think?"

"I'd like to make a trial run, boss. Not a real mission, but let's put twelve SEALs and their gear in the H-3, fly two hundred miles to a helipad some place south of here, and land to simulate a drop off. Then we fly back and see how much fuel we burn." Josh turned to face the captain. "Will we have the ability to develop our tactics and techniques, or are they going to be forced on us?"

"Marty's team will get the target area and a rough timeline from me based on tasking from our boss. It'll be up to him and whoever flies the helicopter to figure out how to get in and out within the desired timeframe. Once on the ground, Marty is on his own. I'll provide the command and control, and task the close air support."

"Josh, when do you want to have a go at the dummy run?" Montemayor asked.

"Sir, today is as good as any, if the SEALs can come up with 12 guys and their equipment who want to ride in a helicopter for four hours. I'm assuming Ensign Cabot or the Master Chief will want to go along for the ride."

"Why 12 all of a sudden?" Montemayor wasn't following Josh's thinking.

"Because I want to simulate the max load to see how much more fuel we'll burn. Then I'll check it against the charts in the NATOPS manual.

"You're on." Captain Rainer turned to address his two SEALs. "Marty, tell your team to get ready, and Chief, find two extra guys who want to go on a boondoggle. Lieutenant Haman, how soon can you be ready to go?"

"Give me 30 minutes to plan a route and come up with a fuel plan."

"Great. Let's have a quick bite while Marty and I round up 10 more guys with nothing better to do than to take a sight-seeing ride." The captain looked at his watch. "It's 1107. How about we get lunch and launch at 1300?"

* * * * *

That evening, clouds obscured what moon there was. Cruising at 1,000 feet heading roughly northeast toward the *Ranger*, Josh thought it was dark, really dark out over the Gulf of Tonkin. He was searching for any source of light outside the helicopter when he remembered Higgins's description of how to get someone who hasn't flown over the sea at night to understand how dark it really is. "Go into a closet, close the door around you, and pull a towel tightly around your eyes. Then you'll get an idea of a cloudy night at sea. "

Josh had never tried it, but he thought the description was apt. He made a mental note that someday, when no one was around, he would test the comparison.

He was also musing about a thought that had come to him when he was looking at the wall map in the conference room, planning the test run. His eyes had gone to the location of the Michelin rubber plantation, and he'd made a quick estimate of how far it was from Da Nang. The helo could make it easily, but they'd need to stop for fuel either on the way there or the way back.

"That was impressive." The words over the intercom came from Montemayor and interrupted Josh's train of thought.

"What was impressive?" Josh had figured Montemayor's silence meant he was just tired. By the time they landed on the *Ranger* near midnight, they'd have flown almost nine hours since taking off this morning. Josh himself was tired but exhilarated.

"How quickly you figured things out. It wasn't just the flight planning, but the immediate grasp of what they were trying to do, and how you worked with Captain Rainer. Still, are you sure you want to take this on?"

"Yes, sir."

"You'd need a crew and a couple of extra guys for maintenance. They'll all have to volunteer."

"Sirs, you'll only need the maintenance guys." The voice of Bennington came on over the intercom. "Van der Jagt, Kowalski and I are volunteering right now. We want to go with Mr. Haman."

"Petty Officer Bennington, duly noted. This won't happen overnight, though. Captain Rainer will have to send his request up through the chain of command, and they'll have to find a helicopter. I'll let our skipper know that you have volunteered and I'll strongly endorse it. At that point, it will be out of my hands. The squadron commanding officer may want a more experienced HAC and co-pilot. And I just can't afford to let all four of you go until we get replacements. We're short-handed enough as it is."

Thursday, December 17ᵗʰ, 1970, 1056 Local Time, on the U.S.S. Ranger

Josh meandered toward the ready room after sleeping a good eight hours, despite the banging of the catapults and the clanking of chocks being dropped on the steel deck above his stateroom. The junior officer bunk room he presently occupied was situated under the number three catapult. The *Ranger*'s catapults took the jets from zero to one hundred and forty or fifty knots in less than two hundred feet. The noise of the shuttle rumbling and whooshing as it pulled the airplane down the deck made it an undesirable stateroom, which is why transients such as the Det 110 aviators bunked there.

The cat caused accelerations in the order of six or seven g's. One F-4 pilot told him "it cages your eyeballs."

The *Ranger's* air wing was shut down while the ship refueled and took on supplies from a tanker and a supply ship. The process was called underway replenishment. During an "unrep", the carrier and the other ship steamed about two hundred feet apart at matching speeds. A leader line was shot from the supply ship to the carrier and tied down. It was then used as a guide to allow the ship to winch across the fuel hose. Usually two or three hoses carried the Navy Distillate #2 black oil. It was heavier, darker and thicker than kerosene and had its own pungent, oily smell.

While the ship was refueling, which it did every three or four days, H-46 helicopters transferred food, weapons and other supplies. The helos picked up sling loads from the supply ship and placed them on a cleared space on the angle or the aft elevator. From there, the loads were broken down and carried below.

At these times, the only movement on the flight deck was the repositioning of planes for the first launch that night and the swapping of those that had to go into the bay for maintenance. And the only noise Josh could hear in his stateroom was the occasional clang and bang as a chock was dropped on the flight deck a few feet above his bunk.

Along the way he stopped by the Integrated Operations and Intelligence Center (IOIC) to see what was being planned for the night's strikes, but found they were still working on them. It would be another hour or two before the IOIC assigned the targets and the aviators started planning their missions.

Out of habit, the first thing he looked for in the ready room was the clipboard containing messages that Lieutenant Commander Montemayor wanted the officers to read and initial once they digested the contents. Specific assignments were placed in a man's "in" box, usually with a note from the boss. If you did your work, you never saw the papers again. If you didn't, you got the sheets back with more notes.

"Anything new?" Josh asked the young yeoman who spent the day updating the detachment's personnel records and official correspondence. All the detachment's files were stored in a large steel cruise box that the detachment carried wherever it went. *HC-7 Det 110 Admin and Personnel* was painted in large red capital letters on the light gray lid.

"Yes, sir. Bennington made chief. Make sure you note in his log book how unworthy he is, so that during the initiation he can be questioned at length. Chief Slaughter said that he was going to insist that you be Bennington's defense counsel at his initiation. Oh, yes, make sure you congratulate Chief Slaughter, because he made Senior Chief."

"Really." Josh didn't exactly know what a chief's initiation entailed, but he'd heard some stories. Apparently it was an honor for an officer to be requested as a defense counsel.

"Sir, one more thing. Mr. Montemayor told me to ask you to stay in the ready room until he gets here. Apparently, he has something to discuss with you and it is important. I'll call his stateroom to let him know you are here."

Josh had no sooner settled in his seat when he heard a chain rattling and looked up to see Petty Officer Bennington walking into the ready room. Draped around his neck was a heavy chain and the pale green book that the Navy used for logs.

"Congratulations, Petty Officer Bennington. I hear you made chief."

"I did, sir. Thank you." Bennington came to attention. "Sir, I am required to give this summons to you."

"Summons?" Josh had no idea what the air crewman was talking about.

"Yes, sir. Please read this and acknowledge it by signing it and giving the summons back to me, sir."

"Acknowledge what?"

"Sir, please just read the summons." Bennington looked around the room, clearly embarrassed and uncomfortable. A crowd of enlisted men and officers had gathering behind him, many of them with grins on their faces. *So that's how it is, eh?*

Josh shifted in his chair, cleared his throat as he adjusted his voice and spoke in a louder, command voice. "Petty Officer Bennington, I am not sure you are worthy of being a chief. You are not giving me a clear explanation of what this summons is about. An experienced chief petty officer would provide an officer with all the information he needs to know." Josh was enjoying Bennington's obvious discomfort. "Tell me, Petty Officer First Class Bennington, what is this summons for? Am I being charged with a crime?"

"No, sir. I have requested that you be my defense counsel at my initiation. I was told that I had to officially invite you, hence this summons."

"Bennington, all you had to do is ask me or put in a formal chit. A summons suggests that I committed a crime or need to appear as a witness."

"I am just following orders, sir."

"Ahhh. A good chief should follow orders. But I know a few who don't. Which one are you going to be?"

Bennington jaw dropped and he flushed bright red. Josh decided to let the petty officer first class stew for a few seconds. Making chief in the U.S. Navy was a really big deal. Every officer knew that they were the backbone of the Navy and, as a practical matter, ran it. Officers gave orders, but the chiefs got things done no matter how difficult. "Tell me why should I accept?"

"Sir, it is an honor."

"Only if you are worthy of being a chief."

"I am, sir. I will be an outstanding chief. Mr. Haman, please open, read it and sign it, saying only death will keep you from attending and acting as my defense counsel."

Josh ripped open the envelope and found a very official looking piece of Navy correspondence. He made a show of using his finger to underscore each word as he read, and could barely keep from laughing. *Only a Navy chief could write something like this.* After nodding his head a few times, to make it appear as if he was mulling over the contents, Josh pulled a pen out of his flight suit's sleeve pocket and made a flourishing show of signing the acknowledgement form.

As he handed back the signed form, Josh reached for the log book around Bennington's neck that, among other things, listed his "high crimes and misdemeanors."

"I think I need to make a note in your log book about your failure to inform me of my additional duties, as well as your failure to fully inform and prepare me for my duties as your defense counsel. And I believe I have a few witnesses who will sign your log book and attest to your incompetence, for which *I* shall have to defend you!"

"Hear hear!!!" came from the group. Bennington slewed around and then turned back to Josh. The look on his face said as clearly as words, "I've been had."

"I'll make my entry and you need to allow all these witnesses to add their own."

Lieutenant Commander Montemayor boomed over the chatter. "Lieutenant Haman, when you get done writing in soon-to-be Chief Bennington's logbook, come over and sit down!"

Josh knew an order when he heard one. He moved to one of the six chairs grouped around the back corner of Ready Seven. Each chair had a metal fold-out desk that was usually down at the side.

"You're very popular. You must have made quite an impression yesterday."

"What do you mean, sir?" As a junior officer, being popular wasn't always a good thing.

By way of an answer, Montemayor handed Josh a manila folder. When he opened it, he found three messages. The first was from the Commander, Navy Special Warfare Forces, Vietnam; the second was from the Commander, U.S. Pacific Fleet, ordering the Commander, HC-7, to detach Lieutenant (select) Joshua Haman with a helicopter, crew and soon-to-be designated supporting maintenance personnel to form HC-7 Detachment One Seven One, as soon as practical but no later than January 4th, 1971. The new detachment was thereafter to report to the Commander, Navy Special Warfare Forces Vietnam in Da Nang for mission tasking.

"Oh, wow." It was all Josh could say.

Montemayor stuck out his hand. "Congratulations, this is your first command."

Josh's hand disappeared in Montemayor paw. "Thank you, sir."

"My pleasure. You'll do well. Just so you know, as soon as we arrive in Subic, you are no longer part of Det 110. Be prepared, because you're about to get all kinds of help and suggestions from people who are well meaning and trying to be helpful. But most won't have a clue about what you are being tasked to do, much less how to do it." Montemayor paused. "Read the last message."

"Yes, sir."

Montemayor watched Josh's face slowly light up as he read. "The wetting down will be in Subic Bay on a different day than the chief's initiation. Get out your checkbook, because I have already started a guest list! May I be the first to congratulate you?" Montemayor held out his hand. "This message is enough to frock you until your official date of rank. You'll still get paid as a lieutenant junior grade until you are officially promoted, but at least you can wear the insignia. We'll get the paperwork done so you can get a new ID card, and I'll formally frock you at quarters tonight. Go get some railroad tracks at the ship's store."

"Yes, sir..." Josh thought for a second. "Sir, I need a favor."

"And that is?"

"I want *and need* your advice. I don't know anything about forming a det."

"I'll provide it on one condition."

"And that is, sir?"

"My recommendations and suggestions will be in the form of choices. We can talk about the options, but at the end of the day, *you* have to decide. That's part of being a leader, whether it's a det officer-in-charge or an aircraft commander or a squadron CO."

"No problem. When can we start my training?"

Montemayor laughed. "How about after lunch?"

Same Day, 1754 Local Time, Washington, D.C.

Captain Stan Wilson stood in front of a bank of four pay phones near the corner of 10th Street and Pennsylvania Avenue, Northwest, in the heart of the capital district. He was trying to control his anger and debating what he would say to his boss, the Chief of Naval Operations.

He waited until the only person using one of the phones in the middle hung up. With the phone bank to himself, he stepped forward, put in his dime and dialed a number. Captain Wilson was the Chief of Naval Operations' aide, and he called the admiral's direct line. It was a number that only a select few knew.

"Sir, Stan here. I'm going to be late. I have to go back to my apartment in Alexandria and change clothes before I can join you at the reception."

"Why?"

"Sir, I was on my way to pick up my wife and I got stopped by a group of anti-war protesters. I got egged and spat on."

"Say again, *what* happened?"

Captain Wilson grimaced. "Sir, as I was walking into the building where my wife works, a group of anti-war protestors cornered me. Each time I started to move in any direction, they blocked my way and taunted me, using language that would make a sailor blush. Two of them spat in my face. Others smacked eggs into my dress blues. When the protestors saw a couple of policemen coming, they dispersed."

"Are you O.K.?"

"Physically, I'm fine. But sir, I am mad as hell. While they have every right to oppose this war, this is not the way to express one's opinion. Their conduct was... was... disgusting, sir. It was no way to treat someone who has volunteered to put his life at risk for this country."

"Did you do anything that will make you look bad?"

"No, sir. I took their abuse and tried to ignore it. The only thing I did was ask them to get out of my way."

"I'm glad you didn't do anything that will affect your career. Are you going to file a police report?"

"Sir, will it do any good?"

"Probably not. Would you recognize them again?"

"Yes, sir. I'd remember the faces of some of them, particularly the two that spat in my face."

"Good, I'll set up an appointment with the Naval Investigative Service. You can give them a description and they'll make a sketch. They might already have pictures. I'm sorry this happened. What they did is both disgusting and out of line. Unfortunately, it is a sign of the times. Look, go home and change clothes. Take your wife out to dinner and I'll see you tomorrow. Throw your uniform and everything else you were wearing into the trash and the Navy will pay for replacements, along with the dinner. I think I can survive a Christmas cocktail party without you keeping my glass full and the riff-raff away!"

"Aye aye, sir."

"Stan, are you really O.K.?"

"Yes, sir. I'm fine. I'd rather be back flying missions over Hanoi and being shot at than go through what I just did. I'm hard pissed."

"Look at it this way. If you'd slugged one of them, I would be sending a lawyer down to the police station to get you bailed out. Or worse, I might be escorting your wife to the hospital because you got beat up by a mob. In this case, your self-control showed your courage. Take a shower and have a few drinks. Taking them on isn't worth the risk or the possible damage to your career. As difficult as it may be to understand, you did the right thing."

"Sir, a shower may cleanse my body, but it won't make my anger or the disgust I have for these people go away. *That* will stay with me for the rest of my life."

Friday, December 18th, 1158 Local Time, Beijing

The GRU officer stamped his feet as he tried to warm them up. The soles of his Russian-made uniform shoes were supposedly designed for this type of weather. So, why was he cold? Could they have been made with sub-standard materials? Raiskov would not have been surprised if some factory manager was making a few extra rubles by either skimping on insulation or using a cheaper substitute.

At home during the winter they wore their warm field boots with their uniforms. However, here at the embassy, the senior officer had said *no boots*: "Field uniforms are a sign that we were at war, and that is not the impression we wish to give"—particularly after last year's series of so-called border clashes. Anyone who had been there knew that they'd been real pitched battles, with artillery duels in which hundreds were killed on both sides.

Everyone inside the restaurant was wearing a coat. *Damn*, Raiskov thought, *this is like Moscow.*

The maître d' bowed ever so slightly from the waist before speaking. "Colonel, General Chia asked me to tell you that he will be a few minutes late. I have a table in the back for you."

Soon Raiskov was seated and sipping green tea. The empty chair in front of him allowed the GRU officer to survey the patrons and conclude by their clothing they were not the average Chinese workers. Without being obvious, he concentrated on conversation at the next table. From what he could gather, the two men worked in the Ministry of Defense.

He was almost done with tea when the maître d brought a second pot of tea along with a small bowl of soup. A few minutes later, Chia walked through the doorway. The maître d' pointed to the table in the back and Chia headed his way.

"I am so sorry to keep you waiting, Comrade Colonel." Chia held out his hand as Raiskov stood to greet his host. "But it could not be helped. I hope my cousin treated you well."

Ahhhh, there is a family connection. "He did. I am just finishing a bowl of sweet and sour soup."

"Good, let us order because I am very hungry."

"It is cold here, like Moscow." Raiskov had arrived in Beijing last spring and had not experienced winter in the People's Republic capital city.

"Yes, Beijing winters are worse than elsewhere, because the damp wind comes right from your Siberia. We don't get as much snow, just a damp, penetrating cold. But then again, you're a Russian, so you should like this weather."

"I'm from a part of the country where it gets cold, but not like this. I was miserable when I was going to the university in Moscow."

Chia was halfway through his bowl of noodle soup when he stopped. "My comrades found the messages you gave us to be quite interesting."

That means they validated the information through their own sources. "We're glad you found them valuable. I have brought you another set." Raiskov reached into his blouse pocket and pulled out another envelop and slid it, unopened, across the table.

Chia left it there. "And what are in these?"

"The American president has approved flights over southern China. When they will start is not known yet, but we know they are coming." Raiskov thought he saw a flicker in the Chinese general's poker face.

"Are they still looking for missiles on trains?"

"Yes."

"We both know there are none."

Raiskov thought silence was the best answer.

"The missiles you have sold us are deployed around Beijing and other sensitive areas."

Like along the Ussuri River, so they can shoot down my countrymen. You still have the T-62 you pulled out of the Ussuri River. It is our latest tank and we want it back. I've informed my superiors that right now it is in one of your tank factories, in pieces so machinists can examine every part and make a clone. The Chinese are very good at that. "We thought you might want to redeploy them to the south and possibly shoot down one of their airplanes."

"That is not for me to decide. I just study intelligence on our potential enemies and occasionally make recommendations."

"It was just a thought."

"Intelligence officers don't have random thoughts. Everything we say is based on careful analysis. Is that not so, Comrade Colonel?"

You are thinking that this is a formal suggestion from my

government to yours. And your training tells you to ask why and develop scenarios, which you will discuss with your superiors. I would like to be a fly on the wall to listen to those conversations. "It was just that, a thought. It is an opportunity for the People's Liberation Army to demonstrate its capabilities and its desire to defend its airspace. It is not a formal suggestion from my government." *If he believes my last statement, then he is not qualified to be in his position.*

Chia picked up the envelope and stuffed it into his uniform breast pocket without opening it. "My government thanks your government."

Same Day, 1856 Local Time, Moscow

The restaurant was almost empty. It wasn't the foot of snow on the ground or the bitter cold. It was just too early for those who could afford—and were allowed—to eat at restaurants that catered to senior GRU officers.

"This place will cost us a month's pay." Pavel Miranov looked around after they were seated. "Are you sure we can be here?"

"It is a free country, isn't it?" Maxim Goncharov laughed as he spoke. "Plus, if we eat slowly, the scenery will become very nice."

"Maxim, do you only think about women when you are not working?"

"Oh no, I also think about women when I am at work. Which one am I going to call for a date? Which one can get into bed? Which one might be a good mother of my children? So, what else is there? We work so we can afford to play. I like to play with women." He sipped his beer. "Well, I like to do more than play."

"Yes, but after today, we are lucky that we are not on a train to the Gulag."

"It is all the more reason to eat here. It may be our last good meal. It may also be my last piece of ass with a beautiful woman!"

"Be serious, Maxim! We told the generals *of the Second Directorate* that we could not build a working KY-7 without American parts. American circuit boards don't play nice with those made in the Soviet Union. Then you had to go and add that our programmers are not skilled in writing American style computer code. That is *not* what they wanted to hear!"

"Maybe it is not one that they wanted to hear, but it is the truth."

"But we *failed!* That is never a good thing to do in the GRU."

"Pavel, I don't think they were surprised. They know how far behind we are in computer design. All you have to do is look at our equipment and what was in the American machine to know that. Our computers are not as fast, they can not do as much, and our software does not have the same functions. And the KY-7 is, by American standards, an old design. When I was in Vietnam, our comrades there showed me samples of electronic equipment they took from downed airplanes. It convinced me that it will take a decade or more for us to catch up, if we ever can."

"So you don't think we are going to the gulag?"

"Well, if it is tonight, I will either be so drunk I won't be able to comprehend what they are doing, or they are going to have to rip me out of the arms of a beautiful woman."

Saturday, December 19th, 1970
0814 Local Time, on the U.S.S. Ranger

Josh laid out a fresh set of khakis, taking a little extra care to make sure the two silver bars that indicated he was a lieutenant in the U.S. Navy were properly positioned on the collars. Since today was a stand-down day for the *Ranger,* no flight operations were scheduled for another 20 hours. The only activity of the day was an underway replenishment scheduled to take about four hours.

His two roommates, both detachment pilots, had long since left for the ready room. Josh had been the last to get up, since he'd flown the last sortie of the night. He was standing, freshly showered, enjoying the relative quiet. Now that flight operations were over, the "roof" was a lot quieter.

A black rotary phone sat on a small platform welded to the ship's frame. Its jangling tone sounded like a phone from the 1920s, which, he mused, was probably when the original model was designed.

"Lieutenant Haman."

"You're a popular guy, Mr. Haman. You are so popular that you are causing work for other folks in the detachment on what is supposed to be our day off." Josh recognized the voice of Lieutenant Commander Montemayor. "Get your flight gear on and meet me on the flight deck as soon as you can. We're going to Da Nang to see your new SEAL friends. I've been a good co-pilot and done all the planning. Chief-to-be Bennington and petty officers Van der Jagt and Kowalski are threatening to shoot me if they are not on the helicopter." He hung up without waiting for a reply.

Josh was dressed and in the ready room three minutes after he hung up the phone. "Boss, what happened?"

"I got this." Montemayor stuffed a folded message into Josh's helmet bag. "You can read it when we get airborne. Oh, by the way, the captain is not turning the ship, so whatever wind is blowing is what we get to work with. If I were a betting man, I'd say a five to ten knot tail wind."

"Got it." Josh walked toward the front end of the angled deck. The calm, blue-green water gave no hint of the wind's direction, so he licked a finger and held it up to gauge the wind. Montemayor was right. It was coming from the stern, and the helo was on the angle pointed forward.

The *Ranger* was only about 150 miles east of Da Nang when the H-3 took off. Once they were cruising at 1,000 feet and 100 knots, Josh turned over the flying to his officer-in-charge and fished around in his helmet bag to find the message.

He read tit twice. "What's pre-detachment planning and qualification?"

"I thought you would never ask. I haven't a clue, so I thought I would tag along and find out, since I'm the one who will have to explain it to our commanding officer."

This time when they landed there was a small air-conditioned van waiting at the transient ramp. The driver, an enlisted man wearing shorts made from fatigues, and a dark green t-shirt, white socks and boots, came up to Josh as soon as he came out of the helicopter. "Mr.

Haman, Mr. Cabot asked me to take you right to our building."

In the conference room, there was a list of topics on the wall. Most had to do with logistics, but two—helipad and fire-arms qualifications–caught his eye. *Yes, the big black helicopter needs a place to roost.*

Marty had a yellow pad on the table in front of him. Josh could see there were notes spaced every few lines. *So they must be questions and he's leaving room for notes. That's a good technique, I need to remember that.* Marty looked up and without preamble asked, "Josh, if we cleared some space around the boat ramp, could we use it as our own helipad?"

"As long as there's electrical power to start the helicopter and run the maintenance equipment, it should work. We also need a source of jet fuel. And it would be nice to have a building where we can stow our gear and work in the shade and out of the rain. Why?"

"Well, there will be times when we don't want you to communicate with the tower to tell them we are taking off. We just go. If we have to, we'll have someone from our operations center tell them by phone after we've departed the area. So what do you need for a helipad?"

"A place that is hard surfaced, at least a hundred to a hundred and fifty feet wide, with a clear shot at the water. If we have some concrete to act as a mini-runway, say two to three hundred feet long, that will be even better. Oh, it also has to be free of obstacles like telephone poles and electric power lines."

"Good, we think the east end of the boat ramp will be just fine. The building there has 25-foot high doors that should be big enough. The ramp is open, yet sheltered from view by sand dunes. The telephone poles end just before they get to our building."

"Sounds workable. Can we go out and have a look?"

"Sure, we can do that in a few minutes on the way to the qualification event."

"O.K., Marty, I'm game. What the hell is a qualification event?"

"Well, anyone who will be flying as a crew member will have to be familiar with all the weapons we carry, as well as the enemy's.

They must be willing and trained by us to use them in combat. If we ever have to land and walk out, we want you to be familiar with our tactics and the weapons we carry. In short, you and your crew are going to get a crash course in how to be a SEAL, and we are going to find out very quickly if any of you know how to shoot."

"Makes sense." Josh thought this was a good idea.

"Good, because if any of your crew are not willing to do this, they're out. If they can't shoot and aren't willing to learn how to hike through the jungle the way we do, we don't want them. Keep that in mind as you pick your air crew."

"I will." Marty didn't know they were already picked.

"Now, rumor has it that you are pretty good with a pistol and a rifle as well as a mini-gun. Is that true?"

Josh laughed. "Where's Van der Jagt? I'll kill him!"

"True or not true?" Marty was enjoying the discomfort of the young aviator.

"It is true I qualified as an expert marksman with a perfect score for the pistol and a very good one with the rifle. I've won a few bets with my shooting. But that was at targets, not in combat."

"Good, we'll have a little contest after we visit the boat ramp and we'll see how good you really are. And I see the rest of your team have arrived, so we can begin our inspection. Shall we?"

Marty led the tour of the boat ramp and the adjacent building. It took 15 minutes before Chief-to-be Bennington pronounced them good enough. As they walked out of the hot, humid building onto the sweltering brightness of the ramp, Bennington turned to Van der Jagt. "When we get back here, your first responsibility is to get the two window air conditioners in those offices spitting out ice cold air. We're also going to need to get some big fans to get some air circulating. Your annual evaluation depends on it!"

* * * * *

Josh wasn't surprised when the van pulled into a dug out area of a sand dune that was set up as a firing range. It took an hour for Master Chief Hausner to run Josh and the three enlisted crew members through a series of pistol and rifle drills and announce they had passed the initial test.

When they finished, Marty walked up to Josh. "Now the fun begins. This is called Marty's Soda Can Challenge. Here's the deal. I set up six soda cans on a two-by-four held up by two target stands." He pointed at a narrow frame made from wood beams. You get one magazine plus one in the chamber for a total of eight rounds. You have to hit the soda cans directly, not hit the wood and knock them off. You have sixty seconds to hit as many as you can. The winner is the one who hits the most cans with the fewest rounds. We start at five yards, then move back to seven, then ten, and finally fifteen yards. If you haven't lost by then, we then go back to twenty yards. Loser buys dinner or, in this case, an IOU for dinner, because you guys have to head back to the boat today. Understand the game?"

"Yup. Whose .45 do I use? All I brought with me is my little snub-nosed .38 survival pistol."

"No problem, Josh. You can pick any one of the .45s you just fired."

"I'll shoot the same one you do, snake-eater. If you can do it with your .45, so can I."

"You're very confident, mister helo driver."

"So are you. You think you'll win because it is your game."

Master Chief Hausner placed a stack of loaded magazines and a box of loose rounds on the table next to the .45, which had its slide pulled back. "Sir, Mr. Cabot doesn't lose very often. In fact, I can't remember the last time Mr. Cabot lost. We, on the other hand, have lost a lot of beers because we keep trying to beat him, but can't."

"Well, then, I guess I will have to change the record. Marty, you go first. Show me how it is done."

The SEAL fired six rounds; each one hit a can. He racked the slide to eject the round and popped out the clip before he handed Josh the empty weapon. "Heat's on, helo driver. Six rounds, six cans."

"Piece of cake." Josh stepped to the line and took several breaths and then squeezed off six rounds, rapid fire. There were no cans standing on the two-by-four.

At seven yards, the result was the same. At ten yards, Marty took seven rounds.

"You gave me an opening. Time for you to start writing your IOU." Josh fired five rounds, each knocked a can down. The sixth hit the can, but it didn't go down, even though it was leaking fluid.

"It's not down. You have to knock it off the bar."

"O.K." Again, Josh took a deep breath and exhaled as he squeezed the trigger. The can flew off the two-by-four. "Now what?"

"We move out to fifteen yards."

"I don't want to put pressure on either one of you young gentlemen," Master Chief Hausner put more loaded magazines on the table, "but no one, not even Mr. Cabot here, has gotten all six cans with eight rounds at fifteen yards. Mr. Haman, you are the first non-SEAL to get this far. Congratulations."

"Thank you, Master Chief. There is always a first time." Josh was smiling, but inside his stomach was churning. His competitive juices had been flowing since he emptied the first magazine. "Master Chief, do you have a spare bottle of water? It is really hot out here."

"Sure." A 16-ounce bottle flew in Josh's direction. He caught it one-handed and guzzled it down. "Marty, I'm ready to make you look bad."

"Are you always this confident and arrogant?"

"Confident I can win, yes. Is that arrogance? I don't know. Go for it, snake eater, give it your best shot. I don't want to put any pressure on you, but you're about to lose."

Marty smiled but didn't say a word. Already, he liked this guy a lot.

When he stepped to the line, Marty was all concentration as he toed the line and got into a balanced firing position before triggering all eight rounds. Five cans went down. He handed the hot pistol to Josh. "I've never gotten all six with eight rounds. But then again, no one else has either."

"Well then, watch how it is done." Josh slipped a round in the chamber and released the slide before he slid the magazine into the butt of the pistol. He was careful to balance himself, weight forward on the balls of his feet. Josh took two deep breaths and exhaled. On the third, by the time the air left his lungs, he was zoned in, with the sight sights lined up on the top third of the first can. When the first round went off, it was a surprise, but after each round, he aimed the muzzle at the next can and squeezed the trigger. Six rounds and six cans in 20 seconds.

He grinned, flipped the .45 to grasp it by the hot barrel, and held the grip out to Cabot. "Marty, I saved two rounds for you in case you need them. Oh, by the way, I like German beers and fine California wines. Either will go nicely with my filet mignon, medium rare, and a baked potato with all the fixings!"

Saturday, December 26th, 1970,
2146 Local Time, Manila

From their balcony on the eighth floor of the Hyatt hotel and casino, Josh and Danielle had a clear view of the city's waterfront. Reflected light from the buildings along the waterfront shimmered in the gentle rolling waters of Manila Bay. To the left, one could see an occasional plane approaching Sangley Point, Naval Air Station, located on a spit of land at the end of the Cavite peninsula. To the right, anchored ships swayed with the swells and the tide.

Josh was wearing a pair of jogging shorts and Danielle, snuggled up to him on the beach chair, was wearing just her bikini bottom. Only the bottle of wine and two half-filled glasses were left from their room service dinner, and these were on a small table within arm's reach.

Josh held up a glass. "For the umpteenth time, thank you for coming."

"I've never been to Manila before and I've had a wonderful time. It's been my pleasure."

Josh gently stroked her inner thigh. "Did anyone tell you that besides being beautiful, you are also smart and fun to be around?" He spoke in English now. For the past five days Danielle would start each conversation in the language they had to speak, alternating between French and Russian, and occasionally English.

"That sounds very American, but I will take it as a compliment."

"I don't want this to end."

"Neither do I, but you have a war to go back to, and I have a job and a family in the middle of that same war to worry about. After I get back to Singapore, I will go to Vientiane for a few weeks to see my family and to attend meetings at the embassy. I am going to be promoted. Now I am the third assistant commercial attaché or something like that. The ambassador hasn't told me my title yet, but I am going to be more than just an interpreter."

"That is wonderful! But I will worry about you when you are in Laos."

"No need. I know what I am doing, and I will try to stay away from the Pathet Lao. Fortunately, I will be covered by diplomatic immunity."

"Yeah, but bullets can't read passports and don't understand the niceties of diplomatic protocols. Neither do the Pathet Lao. They shoot any American pilots they capture."

"I take your point." She leaned over and kissed him. As she did, her breasts pressed the top of his chest. "I'll be careful."

"You do know what kissing leads to, don't you?"

Josh felt her hand slide down to his crotch. "Women can be just as eager as men."

"Show me."

Forty minutes later, both were soaked in sweat and panting as they lay on their backs on the king-sized bed. "You're amazing," Danielle gasped as she came down.

"No, you are. I can't believe how turned on I am. Just your scent makes me want to make love to you."

"I am glad."

Josh padded out to the balcony and retrieved the bottle of red wine and both glasses. He emptied the bottle, making sure the glasses were filled with equal amounts of wine, then handed one to her. "To a great long weekend and many more to come."

"Many more." Danielle sipped the wine and put her hand on his cheek. "So what's next? When will I see you again?"

"I get my Magic Carpet flight in a couple of months. That's a whole eight days. The Navy will fly me to Hong Kong, Honolulu, Sydney or Singapore for a full week. Who knows, maybe we can steal another weekend in between, either here or in Singapore. Next time, I'll pay for the ticket."

"What about Saigon? The French embassy is in Hanoi and we have a consulate in Saigon."

"Maybe, but it may be too dangerous. Plus, I doubt I will ever get down to Saigon. If I do go, it will probably be on very short notice and just for a few hours."

"It can't be any worse than Laos." Danielle looked him in the eyes. "Then what?"

"We get a lot of time together to figure out if we should be together as a couple. I am sure your father will approve. This war will not go on forever."

"My father likes you." She rolled off the bed and reached into her purse. "He wanted me to show you this the next time we met. I've been waiting for the right moment. This is it." She dug through her purse and handed him a worn card laminated in plastic, along with a small metal disk on a leather thong stained with sweat and dirt.

"What is it?"

"His identity card and disk from the Legion."

Josh looked at the disk and the card. The picture, albeit of a much younger man, was still recognizable. Under the words 'la religion' was the word 'Juif.'

"Your father is Jewish?"

"Yes. There aren't many Jews in Laos, but he celebrates Jewish holidays and practices the religion in his own way."

"So what religion are you?"

"I have none. When I was at the Sorbonne, I tried to answer that question and went to churches and synagogues. Growing up, I studied animism and Buddhism as well as Catholicism in the missionary school, but nothing satisfied me. You could say I am still looking."

"Why didn't you tell me sooner? You knew I was Jewish."

"Yes, I saw the Star of David you wear with your identity tags, but I didn't know what to say. My father and I talked about it and he said, 'Tell him,' but I didn't. I just wanted to be with you and not discuss religion. We can talk about it more the next time we get together."

"Give these back to your father and tell him I understand. My father fought in World War II alongside Jews who refused to put their religion on their dog tags. He did, and said if he were ever shot down, he planned to fight it out, because he was not going to a concentration camp. I admire your father's courage for not hiding his religion."

"My father grew up near Verdun, which was demolished during World War I. Papa was in French Morocco when the war started, and he made his way to England to join the Free French Forces. Then in 1942 he rejoined La Legion."

"I'm impressed."

"So again, what's next?" Danielle looked into Josh's eyes, searching for an answer.

"We keep writing letters and I will call you when I can. We meet in Singapore or Sydney or Hong Kong for a week and then we plan from there."

"You promise me you will come for a whole week?"

"Yes."

Monday, December 28th, 1970,
0742 Local Time, Subic Bay

Josh had settled himself in detachment 171's pre-deployment office at one of the two grey desks that had seen better days. This space had been set aside for the det; it was where parts, tools and all sorts of other things could be kept separate from the rest of HC-7. Already, there were three empty cruise boxes aligned against the wall, with check lists taped to the inside of the lids. One had *Det 171 Maintenance* stenciled on the front and sides, the others said *Det 171 Admin and Personnel* and *Det 171 Operations.*

The largest pile on his desk were the logbooks of the three helicopters, from which he would choose one. The next largest pile was made up of personnel and training records. Some men had volunteered for the detachment, others would be assigned. Almost as big was the pile of unread and unanswered messages. He'd been issued a clipboard, but the stack was much bigger than the metal clip could hold.

The latch rattled as the door opened.

"Good morning, sir. Did you have a good time in Manila?" The round face of Senior Chief Slaughter appeared between the door and its frame.

"I did. Thank you for asking. What did you do for Christmas?"

"Not much. Had dinner at the Chief's club with the guys, then went into Olangapo for a few drinks and was back by midnight." The chief entered the office. "I stopped by to ask if you'd picked a bird yet. Also, the chief's initiation is tomorrow night. If you want, I can brief you on what you are expected to do as Bennington's defense counsel."

"On the initiation, I'll track you down later today. I understand I'll need a stack of dollar bills."

"Yes, you will, and you don't want to run out. Bring a hundred dollars or more for fines. It all goes into the chief's fund for guys going on emergency leave. And make sure you bring your sense of humor, because nothing you say or do will be right. You'll also hear from some of the other chiefs on what it was like to train you, so you'll be abused almost as much as Bennington."

"So I am much as much a target as the new chief?"

"Yes, sir. We'll tell stories about you every time the judge and jury deem it necessary. And, that, I can promise you, will be often."

Josh made a wry smile. "Grrrreaaaat."

"Sir, I'm confident you'll do fine. You wouldn't have been asked if we thought you might be offended. Mr. Montemayor will be there as well, and one or two other officers from the air station. At least you don't have to pay for any booze or food."

Josh winced. A hundred bucks was a lot of money. "O.K. I'll be ready for whatever happens." He reached over and hefted one of the log books. "As for your question, I think we'll take Big Mother 22."

"Why?"

"Color me superstitious, but it got me home that day Mr. Richardson was hit. The helo gives me good vibes."

"I'll make sure it's ready. The repairs are done and we're running a D check now, and we should finish that before New Year's weekend. Then it'll need a series of maintenance test flights."

"Great. We're supposed to be on the *Oriskany* when she pulls out January 3rd. Will it be ready?"

"Yes, sir, I don't anticipate any problems." The chief nodded in the direction of the personnel files on the desk as he picked up the log books for the three helicopters. "Have you picked your people yet?"

"Not yet. First I have to get through the pile of messages that arrived overnight. It's amazing; judging by all the paperwork, you'd think we were preparing to start World War III, not an eighteen person, one helicopter det."

"Want some help in picking the people?"

"Yes, but let me make some choices and then I'll get with you and Bennington to see if I they're good ones. I already know who the air crewmen will be. If I choose anyone else, I'm liable to get shot."

"You'll have a great det chief in Bennington. He's well respected amongst the other enlisted guys and the air crewmen. You'll need another senior petty officer first class to be in charge when you guys are flying. And, by the way, Bennington thinks you walk on water."

"I hope I don't disappoint him."

"You won't, sir." With that comment Senior Chief Slaughter left, closing the door softly, leaving Josh with only two piles—the messages and the personnel folders. It was progress!

It was three hours later when a soft knock on the door interrupted Josh's typing on a message form. "Come in," he called.

"Lieutenant Haman?"

"That's me."

"I'm Bill Braxton. I'm interested in joining your new detachment as your co-pilot."

Josh came around the desk so they could shake hands, then

pointed to another chair in the office. "Come in, sit down." Josh wasn't expecting Braxton until after lunch, but this was a welcome break from the drudgery of answering messages. He'd already talked informally with the other two candidates HC-7's commanding officer had suggested. They were both acceptable, but neither excited him. "Why do you want to volunteer?"

"It sounds interesting."

"Bill, what do you know about what we are going to do?"

"Nothing other than it will involve landing SEALs in strange places."

"Do you have any experience doing this?"

"No."

That makes two of us. "Do you realize that you won't be able to talk about what we will be doing outside the det?"

"No, but I guess that is understandable. But that makes another reason I want to join. It'll be different."

"Yeah, and it may get you killed."

"Josh, we're all gonna die sometime."

"I'd prefer it to be later rather than sooner."

"Me too."

"Bill, are you married or engaged?"

"Good lord, no! There's plenty of time for that when I get back to the States."

"How much time do you have in the H-3?"

"Only what I got in the RAG and a couple of fam flights out here. So, to be honest, not much. Maybe eighty hours in the H-3, and I just got my wings in August."

"Is there anything in your background that may prevent the Navy giving you a Top Secret clearance via a special background investigation?"

"Nothing that I know of, other than my great, great grandfather was a general in the Confederate Army." Braxton's South Carolina drawl, which was evident when he normally spoke, became more so.

"It didn't keep me from getting into the Academy."

"So you're a ring knocker?" Josh noticed the guy wasn't wearing a class ring. He didn't wear his own Norwich ring when he knew he was going to go flying, and this afternoon would be the first maintenance test turn of Big Mother 22.

"Yeeahhhsss," he drawled. "Class of '69. Why?"

"It seems that everywhere I turn in this man's canoe club, I run into one."

"Well, they pump about twelve hundred graduates a year, so there are a lot of us around."

"Bill, how'd you get into HC-7?"

"I was voluntold to fly helicopters. It was either that or become an officer on a Swift boat, so I decided to be a helo pilot. This was despite the fact I had the grades to go jets and wanted to fly F-4s. Instead, I was 'encouraged' to volunteer for this squadron."

Shit, I've heard this story before. "Any regrets?"

"No. If I had to go to war, at least I wanted to have a choice in the matter. This is the first time in the Navy I've been able to make my own decision instead of being... *encouraged* to pick something."

"Interesting. Just so you know, I sort of stumbled into this assignment." Josh leaned back in the chair.

"That's not what I hear."

"What do you hear?" *God, the rumor mill is already active, and lord only knows what they are saying.*

"A couple of the other pilots said that you wowed some SEAL captain and he moved heaven and earth to get you assigned as the detachment officer-in-charge, despite the fact that you are the most junior H-3 HAC in the squadron."

"Well, that's not too far from the truth. What else have you heard?"

"That you're pretty cool under fire."

"I'm scared shitless, like the rest of the guys in the helo."

"Josh, that just means you're sane and very normal."

"How would you know?"

"My father was a dive bomber pilot in the Pacific during World War II. He flew SBDs, and then the beast which was officially known as the Curtis Helldiver. We've talked a *lot* of flying in combat. He says, if you are not scared when you climb into the airplane, you don't understand what is happening around you and you'll get people killed unnecessarily. The trick is to overcome your fears and do what you have to do."

"My dad told me the same thing. He was in the Army Air Force during World War II and Korea, and he just got home from Vietnam."
I like this guy. He seems to have a good head on his shoulders.

"So, Josh, where did you go to school?"

"Norwich University, up in Vermont."

"Oh, I've heard of it. Isn't Norwich one of the private military colleges like the Citadel?" Braxton didn't wait for an answer. "I wanted to go to Annapolis since I was a kid, and my dad, who is a retired captain, helped me out. It didn't hurt that our Congressman went to our church. I knew if I had the grades, I'd get an appointment. Still, I had a list of Plan B schools with Navy ROTC in case the Academy didn't take me. The Citadel and Norwich were two of them."

"Why did you want to go to Annapolis so badly?"

"I grew up reading everything C.S. Forrester ever wrote. I think I've read every book in the Horatio Hornblower series a dozen times. And then there are the books by Patrick O'Brian and Alexander Kent. I've read them all at least three times. I love reading military history. It gives one great perspective."

Josh laughed. "I've read the same stuff and am determined to learn from them so as not to repeat the mistakes of the past."

"Me too."

"Bill, are you familiar with firearms?"

"I qualified expert with the pistol. Plus, I grew up hunting, deer, duck and geese. Why?"

"The SEALs want us to be able to shoot as well as they do."

"Great. Sounds like fun. I like to shoot!"

"So again, why this det?" Josh was trying to get to the heart of this potential co-pilot.

"You want a serious, straight answer?"

"I do. Our lives depend on it." Josh was trying not to be melodramatic, but he was serious. He wanted to hear the truth and then decide. Most of the answers he'd heard from the other pilots were, well… bullshit.

Braxton leaned forward and put his hands on the top of the desk. "From what I understand, we're going to be on our own and in control our own destiny for the most part. To my knowledge, which I admit is very limited, no one in the Navy has done this before, so we'll be pioneers. I like that. We have to figure it out as we go."

"I like challenges, too." Josh paused. *I've got to say this.* "And if we succeed, it will be good for your career."

"That too. But here's the way I see it. Assuming we succeed, which really isn't just an assumption, because I am allergic to failure, then we'll be the only ones who know how, and we'll have to teach those that come behind us. It will separate us from the pack on our fitness reports."

"You realize that there really is a high likelihood that we may get killed."

"I do. But at least we'll have a choice on how and why. My gut tells me that we'll make our own decisions and be able to tell those higher up in the chain of command to piss up a rope if we need to."

Josh laughed. "O.K., you're on. I'll take care of the necessary paperwork. Welcome aboard." They shook hands. Then Josh shoved the pile of enlisted personnel records across the desk. "You can start by picking the ten to twelve enlisted men who will make sure we always have a helo ready to go. The ones that are already in the det are Chief Bennington and Petty Officers Van der Jagt and Kowalski. Kowalski is an ordnance man and Van der Jagt is a metal bender. We need to be able to maintain an H-3 on our own with little or no outside support. So pick accordingly."

"But I don't know any of these people!" Braxton protested.

"That's exactly why you get to make some recommendations. You won't have any biases. After you've picked them, we'll go over them with Senior Chief Slaughter, who runs the maintenance shop here at Cubi, and Chief Bennington, the senior air crewman. That means we'll need another E-6 who can make chief to run things when Bennington isn't around. They'll have an opinion on each man and I want their input before we make the selections."

Tuesday, December 29th,
1900 Local Time, Subic Bay Naval Base

According to the "summons," the uniform of the day for the Chief's initiation was summer white. Senior Chief Slaughter had counseled Josh over a cup of coffee that he should not wear his newest or best uniform, because there was a good chance it might get dirty, even ruined. He'd warned, however, that being out of uniform, or wearing one that was already ratty, would be costly. "So," Josh had hazarded, "officers who are defense counsels pay." The Senior Chief smiled. "You got it; and remember, don't check your sense of humor at the door."

Josh rummaged through the uniforms hanging in his closet and pulled out the oldest uniform that was starting to yellow. Nevertheless, it was neat, pressed, and free of stains or mended tears. When he started to assemble it, he realized he needed a set of lieutenant shoulder boards. A quick trip to the air stations uniform shop solved that problem.

The Filipino clerk at the Navy Exchange Uniform Shop had a knowing look in his eye as he watched Josh go through the drawers with all the ribbons and metal devices. When all the selections were made and paid for, the clerk asked if Josh wanted him to assemble the ribbons. Josh nodded and watched as the Filipino expertly assembled his ribbons. He'd been in theater long enough to earn the Vietnam campaign ribbons, so now he had two full rows.

With his uniform assembled and on, he headed out the door of the BOQ. As he got into a taxi, he made sure that he had his wad of dollars, all 120 of them, in his front pocket.

Josh walked up to the door of the Chief's Club, took off his bridge cover, and tucked it under his left arm before entering. The unofficial official rule was, anyone walking into a bar in a Navy club with his hat on buys everyone in the bar a round. It was, as some of his friends had found out, an expensive mistake, one he was not going to make. If Josh goofed at the Chief's Club, he'd never hear the end of it, even after he retired. He'd be known as the "dumb lieutenant who walked into the Chief's Club bar with his cover on."

Inside, it looked like any other officer's club, but this was the Chief's Club and he was unsure of protocol. But before he could take another step, he was met by a Master Chief Petty Officer wearing full dress white: choker, white gloves, and medals. The Chief, who was a bit thicker around the waist than he should have been but didn't have the beer belly that distinguished some chief petty officers Josh had met, bent over and stared at Josh's name tag, then stood up with an artistically contrived look of confusion on his face. "And who be you, sir?"

"I am Lieutenant Haman, and I'm here for the chief's initiation as Petty Officer Bennington's defense counsel," Josh replied evenly, to make sure he sounded polite and respectful.

The Master Chief waved at a Senior Chief standing slightly behind and to the left, who handed him a clipboard. In his other arm he was holding a large fishbowl containing dollar bills. The Master Chief flipped the pages back and forth, running his forefinger up and down the pages as if he were looking for something. Then he touched his tongue to his finger to moisten it and again flipped through pages before he found what he was looking for.

"Ahhhhhhh, Lieutenant Junior Grade Joshua Jonathan Haman is here. Yet I see, sir, by your uniform, you are masquerading as a lieutenant. Can you resolve this non-trivial discrepancy and prove that you are real lieutenant, sir?"

"Master Chief, I am a lieutenant junior grade but since I am in a billet that should normally be filled by a full lieutenant, my commanding officer used his privilege and authorized me to wear the rank of full lieutenant. The term describing this action is called frocking. If you are interested, I can show you my ID card to verify that I am authorized to wear the rank of lieutenant."

The Master Chief turned to the Senior Chief. "Do you think this officer is a fake lieutenant?"

"Maybe, Master Chief."

"Hmmmmm. Did I hear the fake lieutenant tell me he was frocked? Or did he say fucked? Is he fucking or frocking? I'm confused."

The Senior Chief replied, "I think you should ask the fake lieutenant to explain the difference between frocked and fucked, frocking and fucking."

"Excellent suggestion, Senior Chief." The Master Chief turned his attention to the young aviator standing in front of him. "The fine for confusing the Master Chief is five dollars. Now, Lieutenant, tell me, what is the difference between frocking and fucking and being frocked and fucked?"

Josh took a deep breath and figuratively jumped off the deep end. "Frocking is the term used when a commanding officer decides to allow an officer has been selected for the next rank to wear and enjoy the privileges of the rank to which he has been selected. The officer does not, however, get paid at the new rank until he gets a date of rank. Once he is wearing the new rank, the officer is considered to have been frocked. Is that clear?" Josh fished out his wallet and handed the Master Chief his green ID card, also known as his Geneva Convention card. It listed him as a lieutenant.

"It appears," the Chief said sententiously, "that our records may be inaccurate, which, as a Master Chief, I find hard to believe. Chief's are never wrong, are they, Lieutenant?"

Trick question and a tough one. "In my brief career, I have not yet found one to be wrong."

The Senior Chief leaned forward and said, "Master Chief, the fake lieutenant is a diplomat."

The Master Chief waved him off. "Now, Lieutenant, help me to understand the difference between fucking and fucked?"

"Master Chief, fucking can be used as a verb, participle or

adjective. If one uses fucking as a verb, that suggest that one is having sex, or, in the political sense, giving someone else the shaft. As a participle, fucking refers to the act of sexual intercourse. If, on the other hand, I were to say, 'Look at that fucking helicopter,' it would be an adjective and could be considered negative or positive, depending on the context. One would have to know more about the content of the conversation to understand the use.

Josh looked at the Master Chief and then the Senior Chief, both of whom were smiling. He continued with the second part of the answer to, hopefully, avoid another fine. "Fucked is often used in the figurative sense as in, 'I've been fucked,' which is another way to say, I've been screwed. The use of the word fucked adds a degree of emphasis, because being fucked is worse than being screwed." Josh stopped and looked at the Master Chief, who was doing his level best to keep from laughing.

"Mr. Haman, that was fucking outstanding. I believe that I used the word as an adjective. Now, your fucking fine for attempting to further confuse the Master Chief is another fucking five dollars. You can determine whether or not I am using the word as an adjective, participle, or verb later. Most of us chiefs are fucking lucky to have passed English in grammar school."

The Senior Chief held out the bowl. He turned to Josh and spoke with a smile, "I'm impressed, Lieutenant. My associate has suggested that you are very diplomatic. Well, I'm a gunner's mate, and I like the diplomacy that comes out of the barrel of a sixteen inch naval rifle, which you aviators would call a very big gun. Don't you agree, Lieutenant?"

"I do, Master Chief."

"Fine for agreeing with me is one dollar." Josh pulled out his wad of bills, which the Master Chief made a show of noticing. "With all due respect, the court will rule as to whether or not you are a fake lieutenant or not. You may appeal, if you so wish." As if on cue, the other Chief appeared with the fishbowl. "Sir, the fine is one dollar for masquerading as a real lieutenant and another dollar for showing me what could be a forged ID card. You court fee for admittance to the bar so you can defend that worthless piece of shit Bennington is five dollars."

The second chief came to attention next to Josh and held out the bowl as if he was presenting arms.

"So, I own the Chief's Benevolent Fund nine more bucks?"

"Your math, sir, is quite correct. It is good to know that the junior officers they are producing today in some of finest universities are good at math."

Josh counted out another nine dollar bills and stuffed them into the bowl. This was, just as Senior Chief Slaughter had said, a kangaroo court. Anything he said or did would get him fined. *Just keep your sense of humor.*

"Sir, may I ask what was your route to a commission in this Master Chief's navy?"

"ROTC." Josh spoke briefly, wondering what the Chief would make of this answer.

"Excellent, sir! Since you got a free education and did not have to get dirt under your finger nails by working your way through college, your fine for not being a working man is five dollars."

Josh peeled off five more bills and deposited them in the fishbowl.

"And may I ask the fake lieutenant where he got his degree?"

Josh was enjoying the way the Chief twisted any answer, even though this interrogation was costing him a fortune relative to his pay. "Norwich University."

"And, sir, where is Norwich University located? It sounds limey, as in British."

"Vermont, Master Chief."

"And are you a Yankee?"

"Yes, I was born in Vermont."

"Yankees pay a lot of taxes. Your tax is two dollars."

Two more bills went into the bowl.

"Thank you, Mr. Haman. Please enter the courtroom. It is the first door on your left. You will find a wide variety of libations and an array of food that would make a prince feel proud. Two words of caution, sir. First, do not attempt to buy a drink. If you do, it will really cost you. Tonight, the Chiefs are buying. Second, the Chief wannabes are in a corral on the side of the room. Do not attempt to feed them. They have their food and have been instructed on how they are supposed to eat it."

"Thank you, Master Chief."

Josh found the cloak room and deposited his hat on a pile of others, glad that his last name was stamped in black indelible ink on the band. On the way to the courtroom, he smiled ruefully at how quickly the Master Chief fleeced him of twenty-five dollars. He hoped the remaining $95 would be enough to get him through the rest of the proceedings. Running out of cash, Chief Slaughter had warned him, was a big no-no.

Josh opened the door to the room, took a few steps in, and stopped. In front of him, a stage supported a very large desk, on which were piled a stack of green log books; Josh assumed Bennington's charge book was one of them. The chair behind the table looked more like a throne. In front of the desk were three rows of chairs, a folded piece of paper on each, one of which, according to Chief Slaughter, would have his name. For a second, he had a flashback to the disposition board. The chief's initiation was similar in many ways, but this was supposed to be good natured fun, if a bit warped.

As he turned around looking for the bar, he heard a gurgling sound. In a small pen were six men wearing nothing but adult diapers and flip flops. The diapers, Chief Slaughter had explained, were reminders that they were still babies when it came to knowing what to do as a Chief Petty Officer.

All six were on their hands and knees in front of two bowls. One was filled with green liquid; the other was filled with what looked like a mushy, soggy mix of Corn Flakes, Grape Nuts, Puffed Rice, Cheerios and other cereals. All six men wore headbands with dogs ears attached to them: some floppy like a poodle's or golden retriever's, others upright like a German Shepherd's.

The chief lording over the selectees gave an order and the man closest to Josh sat back on his haunches, held his hands in front of him as if he were begging, and howled loudly. Several of the chiefs standing nearby clapped in appreciation.

One by one, each new chief shifted to a begging position and barked or howled like a dog. Bennington was on the far right and gave Josh a pained look. Pieces of the cereal stuck to his face and green liquid was down his chin. He made an attempt to bark several times, sounding more like a dachshund than a German Shepherd, then went back to eating from his dog dish. *At least it's corn flakes*, thought Josh. It could have been much worse. With a shock he realized that every Chief present, and every one he had ever met, must have gone through a similar ordeal! He shook his head at the surreal image of Chief Slaughter in diapers.

This rite of passage meant that they would no longer wear bell bottom dungarees to work in the U.S. Navy. The next time they put on a uniform, they would wear the same khaki worn by officers, with the Chief's anchor insignia on their collar. For enlisted men this was a big deal. In one of Josh's ROTC classes, an officer had said, "Officers may lead the Navy, but the chiefs actually run it."

"Mr. Haman."

Josh turned around and saw Senior Chief Slaughter standing there with two bottles of San Miguel, holding one out toward him. Condensation was already made the dark brown bottles wet. "Sir, I believe you are fond of San Miguel."

"Thank you, Senior Chief, I am."

"Tonight they're all on me. All us chiefs who got promoted were assessed a portion of the cost. The new chiefs don't have to pay, they just get abused."

Josh took an appreciative swallow and said, "This sure beats lapping up green I-don't-know-what from a bowl."

Slaughter laughed.

Josh tried to look around without making it obvious or showing his discomfort at not quite knowing what he could say or do. There are some lines between officers and enlisted men that one doesn't cross. But the real difference between him and Chief Slaughter was experience. Each Chief had spent fifteen to twenty years in the Navy; he'd been commissioned barely two years!

"Sir, if you are looking for other officers, there won't be many. Besides Mr. Montemayor and you, I think there will be two, maybe three more."

"I guess I am in the inner sanctum."

"Sir, that is an excellent description. Sir, the buffet and bar are in an adjoining room. If you will follow me, we can get something to eat."

"Great idea."

An hour later, precisely at 2000 hours, a bell's tone signaled that the initiation was formally to begin. Josh, with a plate of food in one hand and a beer—his second—in the other, found his chair. He put the tented name tag on the floor and sat with his plate on his lap. Two other officers, one with wings, sat in the row along with him. Montemayor was sprawled over two chairs at the end. Josh wondered who he was here to defend. The big Indian almost never said anything; how could he defend a candidate?

After the six soon-to-be chiefs were led to a space to the left of the stage, the judge walked onto the podium and took his seat at the table. He was the same Master Chief who had greeted Josh at the door. Being the most senior enlisted man of the two bases, by date of rank, meant he was automatically the judge unless he declined the honor. After examining the books on the desk, he pounded the gavel. The room became absolutely quiet.

The Master Chief stared out at the room and then turned his attention to Officer Row. "You!" his finger pointed at Josh. "Who gave you permission to eat in my courtroom!"

Josh was trying to come up with a good answer. He wasn't fast enough.

"No one eats in my courtroom." The Master Chief held up a glass of what looked like whiskey. "We only drink alcoholic beverages in my court. Who are you?"

"Lieutenant Haman, Master Chief."

"Ahhhh, the lieutenant junior grade masquerading as a lieutenant. How many different items are on your plate?"

He looked down. "Four, Master Chief."

"Fine is four dollars. One for each item. What are you drinking?"

"Beer."

"Good. How many do you have?"

"One, Master Chief."

"You should have two. We're two-fisted drinkers in this club. Fine for having only one beer is one dollar. Bailiff, get this officer another beer." The Senior Chief with the bowl appeared out of nowhere to receive Josh's penalty. "Lieutenant, why are you here? This club is only for chiefs."

Josh put his plate down, fished out the five dollars, deposited them into the bowl and stood up. "I was invited, correction, I was *summoned* to appear as Petty Officer Bennington's defense counsel. The gods of the Navy have determined that he should be a chief and I am here to defend that decision."

The Master Chief smiled at this answer. He looked down at the log books spread in a row before him. "Ahhhhhh. Bennington. Aviation Electricians Mate First Class Bennington." He opened one book and started paging through it, made a show of reading what was written. "Hmmmmm, these are pretty serious charges. Lieutenant, are you sure you are up to it? From what I read, Bennington is hopeless. He will be found guilty."

"Guilty of what, Master Chief? The only thing that Bennington is guilty of is being a top notch sailor. That's why I believe I can get Petty Officer Bennington a fair hearing."

The Master Chief scowled. "That is a very good answer. Too good. Fine is one dollar for being a smart defense counsel."

The bowl reappeared and another buck went into it. The Master Chief waited until the payment was made and the Senior Chief returned to the end of the stage.

"Good. Then let's start with Bennington. Where is that sea dog wannabe?"

Bennington was led to the front of the room, barking as he walked, and carrying the two dog dishes: one full of beer dyed green, the other with Corn Flakes. Josh started to laugh but forced it down, afraid that laughing would get him fined. Tradition and rituals were going on here and he had to play along. Despite the financial pain, he was enjoying this!

The Master Chief glowered at Josh. "That's not a very strong bark. Counselor, the fine is five dollars for not training Bennington to have a strong bark. How do you think he will be able to do his job as a chief without a ferocious bark? Do you think it would be better a better bark if he were a chief?"

"Yes, Master Chief, I can teach him to bark."

"Please bark for me, Lieutenant."

Josh did as he was asked, loudly.

"Not bad. Still, it needs improvement. Fine is two dollars for only having a collie bark, not a German Shepherd's."

The Master Chief looked around the room while the fine was collected. "Who can speak to this fake lieutenant's qualification to be a defense counsel?"

Senior Chief Slaughter emerged from the crowd on the side. "Master Chief, I can."

"Speak."

"Lieutenant Haman has been known to go into a large reception full of important people. Instead of filling himself full of food and drink and making a fool out of himself, he finds one of the most beautiful women there and disappears with her."

"Go on. And you know this for a fact?"

"I do, Master Chief, I was there."

"And did the fake lieutenant close the sale?"

Senior Chief Slaughter looked over at Josh, who hung his head and shook it slowly from side to side, knowing what was coming. "I can't speak directly because I did not follow them, but having seen the two of them together, if I were a betting man, I would bet on yes, and many times. As further evidence, the two of them just spent five nights together in a hotel in Manila, and rumor has it that the only time they emerged was to eat, and most of their meals were delivered by room service."

"Are you sure of this information?"

Senior Chief Slaughter came to attention. "I am, Master Chief. I saw them with my own eyes and have even met the young lady. On the good looks scale of one to ten, she's a nine plus. Besides being beautiful, she has brains. She graduated from the Sorbonne in Paris and speaks seven languages."

"And she likes this fake lieutenant?"

"Yes, Master Chief. I think there is a wedding in the future."

The Master Chief leaned over the table and looked Josh. "Well done." He turned to Chief Slaughter. "Any other qualifications?"

"Yes, Master Chief. Mister Haman is a very good shot with a pistol."

"Which one? The one between his legs or one that uses gun powder and fires bullets?"

"I cannot vouch for the former, but one would assume he has demonstrated his skill with the gun between his legs in satisfying the aforementioned lady because she can't seem to keep her hands off him. But with the latter he bested a cocky snake-eater ensign who now owes him a steak dinner with all the trimmings and all the booze he can drink. In a feat of marksmanship, he demonstrated prowess with a .45. In fact, wannabe chief Bennington witnessed the event, as did four others from HC-7 Detachment 110, and I am told there were several other snake-eaters present, one of whom was a Master Chief."

"In-ter-es-ting." The Master Chief pointed the hammer end of the gavel at Josh. "Tell me, fake lieutenant, why do you think Petty Officer Bennington should be allowed to be a chief petty officer in the United States Navy?"

"Master Chief, he's very good with the mini-gun..." Josh wished he hadn't said that as soon as the words left his mouth.

The Master Chief leaned forward with a furrowed brow. "Sir, are you telling me that this future sea dog has a little dick? You are fined ten dollars for suggesting that a future chief petty officer has a small penis."

As he peeled off ten dollars, Josh tried to think of what to say. "Earlier this month, Bennington single handedly sunk a North Vietnamese torpedo boat. He chewed it up so bad that the warheads on the torpedoes exploded."

"That's another ten dollars for telling stories that are unbelievable. You can't sink a ship with a mini-gun. You need a naval rifle to do that and their bores are measured in inches. Lieutenant, you need to convince the court that this man deserves to be a chief."

Montemayor stood up. "I was in the helicopter, Master Chief."

"Lieutenant Commander, that's ten dollars for butting into a conversation. So you are saying that this sea story is true."

"It is, Master Chief."

The Master Chief turned back to Josh. "The lieutenant commander's fine still stands. Tell me what else?"

"In October of last year he gave an excellent brief to a Singaporean admiral on how our rescue air crewmen are trained and how they do their job. Then, in November, I was the co-pilot on a rescue mission and we got shot up pretty bad. The aircraft commander was wounded very badly and Petty Officer Bennington saved his life."

"So, fake lieutenant, you let a petty officer first class brief an admiral?

"I did, Master Chief."

"Are you telling me that this man is qualified to be a chief?"

"I am. I have so much faith in him that he is going to be my detachment chief."

"You, a fake lieutenant, are going to be a detachment officer-in-charge?"

"Not going, am already. Master Chief."

"Good God, the Navy is letting babies lead. Fifteen dollar fine for telling the truth and convincing me that Petty Officer Bennington will make a fine chief."

The Master Chief waited until Josh paid his fine. "Unchain Petty

Officer First Class Bennington."

A chief came forward with a key, unlocked the chains, and put them on the floor. The judge addressed Bennington directly. "Aviation Electrician's Mate First Class, are you going to uphold the finest traditions of not only the Navy but also those of us who are known as chief petty officers?"

"I am, Master Chief."

"Outstanding. Anoint the new chief."

A chief petty officer came up behind Bennington and poured a pitcher of beer over his head, while all around him chiefs shouted with laughter and applauded. The Master Chief pointed his gavel at Bennington. "You are out of uniform, Bennington. Get into a proper chief's uniform and report back to me in thirty minutes. There's a bag by the door with your name on it and a proper set of whites. You get to use the club's shower, soap and towels. Get your petty officer ass out of here and report back to me as a chief petty officer in the United States Navy."

"Yes, sir!" Bennington took off for the door like a scalded rabbit.

"You, fake lieutenant, I'm not done with you yet. You're fined ten dollars for allowing an enlisted man in this room who was out of uniform."

Josh reached into his pocket and pulled out the sadly diminished wad of dollar bills. The Master Chief leaned forward. "I made a pretty good dent into it, didn't I?"

"You did, Master Chief. I plan to donate the rest to the Chief's Benevolent Fund."

The Master Chief gave Josh a thumbs-up. "Out-fucking-standing. You are going to write Chief Bennington up for an award for sinking that torpedo boat, aren't you?"

"Already done, Master Chief."

"Thank you, Lieutenant. Good luck and God speed. Who's next?"

Thursday, December 31st,
0925 Local Time, Cubi Point Naval Air Station

When they came back from lunch, Braxton organized a work

space at the table with a second typewriter and was soon pecking away. He shook his head and sighed. "With two typewriters, the detachment will either be twice as productive or generate twice the amount of paperwork, I'm not sure which."

That pronouncement made, he returned to a message addressed to Commander, Naval Special Warfare Forces, Vietnam, naming the two officers and 12 enlisted men that would make up HC-7 Detachment 171.

Braxton was signing endorsements to the orders when he stopped suddenly, and slowly held up an open folder. "Josh…"

His detachment officer-in-charge made a tick mark on the message he was reading and looked up at his new co-pilot.

"Petty Officer Van der Jagt has an interesting letter in his jacket. It says that if he has any discipline problems while in the Navy, they are to be reported to some court in New York City. Care to tell me about that? Is this guy going to be a problem?"

"No, Van der Jagt is a model sailor. Just look at his evals. For your information, right now, he has more time sitting in the co-pilot seat flying with me than you do!"

"Care to tell me about those adventures?"

"Later. We have lots to do. Here's the *Reader's Digest* version." Josh was almost through the story when a familiar face peered around the door. It was Lieutenant Commander Montemayor.

"Josh, Big Mother 22 will be ready for a thirty minute test hover in an hour. The guys had to replace the tail rotor gearbox. Plan on starting pre-flight around 1030. I'll go with you as the co-pilot, so by the time all the check flights are done, I can sign you off as a maintenance test pilot."

"Got it."

"And I just got a call from your new boss. Marty Cabot is on his way to Subic. He should get here about the time we finish with the flight. He has much to discuss with you and has to go back first thing tomorrow. Apparently it is urgent, so I guess you're going to have to hit the ground running."

* * * * *

While they were waiting for the HH-3A to be pulled out of the hangar, Montemayor pulled Josh aside. "Last night Senior Chief Slaughter told me that he did something he thought he never would do. He turned over to the Naval Investigative Service the log he kept on Det 104, in which he noted the times that Higgins downed the H-2 to dodge missions when in fact it was fully mission capable. Along with the log, he kept copies of the yellow sheets signed by Higgins that downed the helicopter. At some point, probably in Hawaii, the results of that investigation will marry up with those of the board. Who knows what will happen, but it will not be good for Higgins. I'm telling you this so you know."

"Yes, sir. I never saw the messages, but I know Higgins did it several times while I was on the det."

"Apparently, it happened more times than any of us knew, and Senior Chief Slaughter took it as a personal affront to his ability to maintain a helicopter." Montemayor looked around and saw Van der Jagt coming towards them. "One more thing. You did well last night."

"Thank you, sir."

"I want you to remember a couple of things. First, it is an honor and a sign of genuine respect that you were invited. They like you, more importantly they trust you. As a result, as long as you do nothing to break that bond, these men and the men who work for them will go through the gates of hell for you. Higgins never had it. He had positional respect that comes with his rank and position, but he never earned their trust. Their trust in your ability to lead means they will never quit on you, even if it means they are dying or about to die. Even then, they'll be sorry because they'll think they are letting you down by getting killed or seriously wounded."

Josh bowed his head, then looked up at the lieutenant commander and nodded.

"Second, the chief's initiation is a rite of passage, but if you think back through the evening, despite all the good natured abuse you were asked to endure, neither the Master Chief nor any of the other chiefs ever crossed the line that separates officers from enlisted men. Your authority as an officer was never challenged. And, despite the amount of liquor that flowed and that some of them were drunk on their feet, all of the chief's maintained their military bearing. Follow me?"

"Yes, sir."

"One more thing. You were allowed in their inner sanctum and what they really wanted to show you was how big a deal it is to make chief in this man's Navy. When they put on that khaki uniform, every sailor knows that at one time, they wore bell bottom dungarees and Cracker Jack Whites and Blues on liberty. They are the link between you and those airman and petty officers who literally have your life in their hands. If they don't do their job well, you can die when your helicopter rolls itself in a ball without ever taking a bullet."

* * * * *

Marty's wash khakis were already wrinkled when he got off the plane. Between the heat and humidity of Vietnam and riding in the back of a C-130 for two hours, whatever stiffness the starch gave them was gone. As he walked down the ramp, his aviator sunglasses fogged as the lenses, still cool from the air-conditioned transport plane, met the humidity of Subic Bay.

The SEAL wanted a quick bite rather than a formal lunch, so Josh introduced him to the snack bar, a.k.a. the greasy spoon in the terminal building. They quickly wolfed down bacon cheeseburgers, French fries and cokes. Nothing was said about Det 171 and its mission tasking. Instead, Marty kept the conversation social.

On the way back, Josh wanted to show off his new toy, so they walked through the hangar before heading to their "office." He stopped abruptly when he saw a half-sunk ship painted in dull, brick red under the aircraft commander's side window. He looked around and spotted Van der Jagt pumping grease into a tail rotor bearing.

With his left hand on his hip, he pointed his right forefinger at the symbol. "Van der Jagt, what is this?

"Sir, we were credited with sinking a torpedo boat. So we thought we would let everyone know. I can paint it over if you want, sir."

"When did you paint it on?"

"Right after we took possession of the helo, sir.

"Whose idea was it?"

Van der Jagt looked down at his feet and then looked at his detachment commander, trying hard not to look guilty. "Several of us came up with the idea."

"I like it, and more importantly, we earned it. Leave it there, and let Chief Bennington and anyone who asks know that I approved it."

Once they were settled in the office, Marty turned to Josh and asked, "When can you get to Da Nang with the helo?"

"January 4th for sure. We leave on the *Oriskany* January second and should be in the gulf 48 hours later. It's only about five hundred miles as the crow flies. I can cram what I can into the H-3 and launch about two hundred miles out from Da Nang, but it will take two trips. Or I can send the maintenance guys and their gear over as soon as the bird is up. Why?"

"We got our first op."

"What is it?"

"Hang on, I'll get to it. Do you have everything you need?"

"So, far yes. It's amazing, our requisitions must have a pretty high priority. We ask and someone provides. We're going to get our personal weapons tomorrow, then go to the range to zero them in."

"Good. What are you getting?"

".45s and Korean War vintage M-1 carbines. They're M2s with a selector that allows us to pick semi or full automatic fire. We like them because they are light, compact, reliable, and accurate out to about two hundred yards. Plus, we can carry a lot of ammo for them."

"Good. Get at least a dozen magazines for each weapon and make sure they are the 30 rounders. Bring what ammo you can get, but don't worry if you can't find enough. The South Vietnamese use them as well, so there's lots of ammo for them around."

"Got it." Braxton made a note in a little green book he kept in his vest pocket. Josh had assigned him to handle administration and logistics, which Josh defined as people, paperwork and parts. Josh kept operations and maintenance. Messages? Josh had to sign off on them all, but now he only had to write the ones for his areas.

"Where are we going?"

Marty pulled a map out of his briefcase. Josh handed him some worn-out, four inch diameter nuts, the kind that kept rotor blades attached to the rotor head. Marty plunked them down on the corners as paperweights.

"You need to figure out how to get from Da Nang to here," he stabbed the map where Laos, Cambodia and South Vietnam met, about one hundred and fifty miles southwest of Da Nang, "up in the mountains."

"On the Laotian side of the border, or in Cambodia?"

"It doesn't matter, because there's no fence marking the borders. The insertion landing zone we'd like to use is in Laos. Our preferred extraction one is, if not in Cambodia, damn close."

"That's along the Ho Chi Minh Trail."

"Indeed. The roads and trails go around this mountainous area."

"Why here?"

"We're setting a trap."

"For whom?"

"Several Army Long Range Reconnaissance teams are running into trouble. Sometimes they go in and we never hear from them again. Others get on the ground and are running from the time they get off the helicopter. We think the NVA has a unit or two in the area that specializes in hunting them down."

Josh and Baxter looked grim, but Marty looked grimmer as he continued. "We also suspect that there is a leak someplace in their chain of command. So here's the deal. We're going in to hunt for their pursuers and give them a bloody nose. And because of our suspicions, secrecy on our part is paramount. Other than the people directly involved, we're not telling anybody anything."

"Marty, why doesn't the Army do this? It's their people."

"It's a long story, but here is the gist of it. For a while the high mucky-mucks in Saigon didn't think there was a problem, because these missions are high risk, so if you lose a few teams, oh well. But it's happening all the time now. They're trying to sort out if they have a leak, but while they do, the Special Operations Group approached us for help, and I think we can provide it."

Josh sat back in his chair. *The Army's been doing insertions for years, but apparently they're not covert enough. Still...* "We got the *Navy*'s O.K. to help the *Army*?"

"Yeah. Believe it or not, it wasn't hard. This isn't a football match. Special ops guys are getting killed and we're leaving guys behind, and that's not acceptable. The trick will be to find the bad guys and call in airstrikes. Alternatively, we draw the NVA into a short, sharp engagement at a time and place of our choosing. After we ambush them, we withdraw, maneuver, and then set up another ambush again before we disappear into the jungle. Your job will be to pull us out before we run out of ammo and get overrun."

"Why do you think the NVA won't hear us coming a mile away."

"Because the NVA knows the sound of a Huey, but I'm guessing they'll think an H-3 is just transiting to or from a base in Thailand. Better yet, you figure out a way to get us in without their knowing where you dropped us off."

"We may surprise them the first couple of times, but not over the long haul. We need to figure out how to get in and out quietly, so to speak." Josh drummed his fingers. "How many people will we be carrying?"

"I'd like to carry 12 on this mission. Six to eight would be the norm."

"Space may be a problem. Fuel won't be."

"I understand. That's why I am here."

"What about the LZs? Do you have any pictures and locations?" Josh wanted to know in advance as much about the landing zones as possible.

Marty pulled out sealed light brown envelope stamped *Top Secret* on both sides out of his briefcase and put it on the table. Josh handed him an orange switchblade that had a hook-shaped parachute shroud cutter on one end and a four inch blade on the other. The knife made short work of the envelope, and Marty dumped out a half in thick pile of 8" X 10" black and white photographs.

"Here's what we got. Tomorrow, or the next day, a courier will bring another batch, which will have more detail. I've marked the ones I like and numbered them in order of my preference. They all have the grid square marked, as well as the latitude and longitude. We need to agree on the landing zones, then we'll adjust the plan."

Josh picked up a photo and examined the black and white image. "Do we have to land?"

"That would be our preference. We can fast rope out if you want."

"Day or night?"

"We would prefer night, right after dark or, if we have to, a couple hours before dawn."

"How soon do you need a plan?"

"Josh, we've got to have one when you arrive in country. You work on the route, pick the LZs, and let me know which ones they are. Meanwhile, I'll do the ground portion. This mission has got a lot of eyes on it. I'll give you a template of a message so you can just fill it in the numbers. Do not deviate or change it. The LZs are listed by number but with no geographic data. To someone other than your crew and my team, the message will be just meaningless numbers."

"Got it. As soon as we get to Da Nang, I want to have your guys practice getting on and off the helicopter for speed. Minimizing the time on the ground or in a hover is the key. I want to flare, touch down, and get going again within a minute. Thirty seconds would be better."

As soon as he said it, Josh wondered, *How the hell am I going to do that?* He looked at Braxton, who had his poker face on. *He doesn't know any more about this than I do!*

"Marty, my preference would be to land to pick you up. A hoist will take too long, and I don't think you want to dangle on the end of the rope for a couple of hours while we fly home. So extraction LZs have to be at least seventy-five feet wide—I'd prefer a hundred—and about twice as long. If it's smaller, it takes longer to get in or out and a lot more power. We need room to accelerate and climb over the trees. Insertion LZs should be the same size, unless you want to fast rope in."

"Understood." Marty slid a piece of paper across the table with several ten-digit numbers. "If you need anything, call any one of these Autovon numbers. We have a secure phone at our end. Do you have one?"

"I wouldn't know one if I saw one."

"If we talk on an open line, we'll have to dance around the topic. You know what I mean."

"I think so." *Another skill I am going to have to learn. These guys are paranoid about security, which is a good thing!*

"Good. Josh, I've got a couple of other stops. How about meeting for dinner?"

"Sure. What time?"

"1900. Cubi O Club. Meet you at the main bar. I'm buying to pay off my debt."

Monday, January 4th, 1971,
0730 Local Time, Norfolk Naval Air Station

The raw wind coming off the Atlantic was blocked by the dark blue woolen greatcoat, officially known as a bridge coat, that Higgins had kept from his days at Annapolis. Despite the 20-degree temperature and the wind chill in low single digits, he was toasty warm as he walked up the steps to the Naval Air Station's operations office.

He'd arrived late Saturday night after taking two days to drive from Madison, Wisconsin. After leaving the Philippines, Higgins had used up every day of leave he had on the books to delay reporting as long as possible.

At home, he'd decide what he was going to do.

First, once he got situated, he'd fire off a letter to the admiral heading the Bureau of Naval Personnel and ask for an early out. Higgins knew the Navy was granting them, so why not him? After reading the fitness report written by the commanding officer of HC-7, and Captain Danforth's letter to the promotion board, Higgins was sure that he wouldn't make lieutenant commander. Between the pilot disposition board and the fitness report, it was clear that the Navy didn't want him and the feeling was mutual—he didn't want to stay in. Letting him out before his six year commitment was up would be good for both parties.

Second, he was going to register to take the Law School Acceptance Test as the first step in getting into law school. He'd already bought two books to help him prepare. He'd scored 1350 on his SATs, so he was confident that he would do well, and from reading the law school catalogues in the Madison Public Library, he was sure that his grades from Annapolis would be good enough. Once he had the scores, there were several law schools in the Norfolk area that offered night courses, so he could start even before he left the Navy. After he got out, he could go full time and live off his GI Bill.

Third, he needed a social life. Higgins didn't have a girlfriend, and he wanted one. In high school, he'd gone steady with a girl named Marcia, but he'd left for the Academy, and she'd gone to Vanderbilt, and the time between letters had gotten longer and longer and finally stopped. Social events in Annapolis had been fun, but none of the women he'd met had interested him. He'd dated a school teacher in Subic Bay, but he'd quickly figured out that she was more into one night stands than a steady relationship. Maybe, since he won't be going to sea, he could find someone in Norfolk at a church young adults group.

After being a "civilian" for almost six weeks, just seeing the Marine guard at the gate was a rude reminder that he was re-entering the Navy. The next came when he checked into the BOQ. The Filipino behind the desk was an instant reminder of HC-7. Higgins didn't want to live in the BOQ; he wanted a place of his own, well away from the Navy. And he didn't want to lose the untaxed pay known as Quarters Allowance. If he lived in the BOQ, the government kept the money. If he lived off base, the allowance would cover at least half of the cost of an apartment.

On Sunday morning, Higgins picked up a copy of the local paper and drove around Norfolk, looking at apartment buildings and getting a feel for the area. The only other time he'd been to the big east coast naval base had been as a midshipman on a bus tour after his first year at the Naval Academy.

His orders were to report to the Commanding Officer, Naval Air Station Norfolk, Chambers Field, for duties in base operations and as a station pilot. The operations offices occupied the top two floors of the building that housed the transient terminal. Higgins looked at the directory board, found flight operations, and walked up the three flights of stairs.

The only man in the office was wearing service dress khaki and gold oak leaves on his collar—a lieutenant commander. A name plate indicated this was Albert "Bud" Norris. Higgins rapped on the door jam three times before he approached the desk with the air of confidence befitting a graduate of the Naval Academy. "Mr. Norris, I am Lieutenant Steven Higgins, reporting for duty as a station pilot."

The dark haired officer stood up and stuck out his hand. "Hi, Steve. It is good to meet you. I'm the assistant operations officer." Norris didn't look the part of a Naval Aviator. When he stood up, Higgins could see he was short and stocky—some would say pudgy —but when they shook hands, he had a firm grip. "What squadron are you coming from?"

"HC-7."

Norris glanced at Higgin's ribbons and noticed a Distinguished Flying Cross and several Air Medals, plus the usual rows of campaign medals. "What did you fly?"

"H-2s. Both the single engine A and B as well as the twin engine C model."

"That's great. That's just what the doctor ordered! I know we're short a helicopter pilot, and one was scheduled to come after the first of the year. So that must be you. I just got back from leave, and Commander Maastrich is out until the eleventh. I'm his stand-in until he returns, and I'm buried with paperwork."

"Yes, sir." Higgins didn't know what else to say.

"Go over to the base's Administrative Office; they'll take your orders and pay records. Then, they'll give you a check list of places to go, people to see. You need to do that first. Medical is important, because they need to take your medical record off your hands and give you an 'up chit' so you to start flying. When you are done, come see me and bring your training jacket. It should take you most of the day, so why don't you come back tomorrow. I'll leave a note for Commander Maastrich to let him know you've arrived. He checks in with his administrative assistant every day."

"Thank you, sir. Any idea of what I will be flying?"

"Well, we've got an old H-2A that is being sent to back to the factory to be converted to a D model, and I hope we don't get it back. We just got the first of two K model Hueys. I presume you flew the T-28 in the training command, like everybody else who didn't go jets."

"Yes, sir, I did. I haven't flown a T-28 since I hit the boat in the training command, but I've flown the A, B and C models of H-2, and my NATOPS checks for all three are still current."

"Good. Hopefully, we won't have to fly the H-2 anymore, but I'll keep that in mind. We need pilots to fly in the T-28 with those who are getting their four hours a month. We'll get you checked out in both the front and back seat, and you'll fly as a safety pilot. And the ops oh is pretty liberal about letting you take them on cross-country hops. Two- or three-day trips over weekends are not a problem. A lot of guys around here use the T-28 to fly to Dallas, Chicago, or Atlanta to visit family, or for interviews with Delta, Braniff, United or American Airlines."

"Sounds good." Higgins tried to sound excited. He had never thought about flying for an airline. He'd heard the pay was good after the first year.

"After a while, we'll get you checked out as a co-pilot in the C-117. We've got three, and we need more pilots to fly them. The C-117 is a bigger, souped up version of the C-47 and they're a lot of fun to fly. Ever flown a tail dragger?"

"No, sir, I haven't."

"Well, you'll learn. We have daily log runs up and down the coast. We also have the northbound trips that stop at Quantico outside

DC, Lakehurst in New Jersey, Quonset in Rhode Island, and to New Brunswick in Maine, then come back the next day. The southern one goes south to New River, North Carolina, Myrtle Beach in South Carolina, Jacksonville, and then Key West, where they spend the night. That's a great run! Ever been to Key west? All the pilots want that assignment. Pensacola and Meridian are also places we go. We run a regular airline."

"Sounds interesting." *They're going to fly my ass off. I was hoping to spend less time in the cockpit, not more. I have to get out of this canoe club as soon as I can.*

"It is a great flying job. Our guys average forty to fifty hours a month. You can get more if you want!"

Higgins didn't say anything.

"Oh, you'll probably be assigned as the GCA and tower officer. That's the billet that's open. Who knows, Commander Maastricht may decide to swap everybody around. See you when you get back." Norris looked down at the stack of messages in front of him, signaling that the discussion was over.

Same Day, 1330 Local Time, the Pentagon

In front of each chair was a document bearing the logo of the Office of the Secretary of Defense and a factual summary of the war in Vietnam laid out in stark terms—casualties by service, aircraft and helicopters lost, rounds of all types expended, fuel consumed, and an estimate of the enemy killed. It went on for three pages. On the last page were metrics—to use one the Secretary's favorite words—that gave us a scorecard—another favorite word of the former auto executive. It ended with a summary of the dollar cost to the taxpayers of the United States.

Everything the secretary of defense did was reduced to dollars and cents. He had no idea of what it was like to be shot at. To him, it was all about numbers. People didn't matter.

Winning was measured, not by how many enemy were killed or the cost to kill them, or how many bullets it took to eliminate one enemy soldier, but by taking their territory, cutting off their supplies, and hitting them so hard that the enemy finally quit. *We are doing none of that. It is all about body counts, ordnance expended and sorties flown.*

When the members were seated around the table, the Chairman spoke. "I was told by the Secretary of Defense to give you this document. You can peruse it at your pleasure. I am not going to waste our time discussing its contents.

Chapter 11 – ENHANCING A REP

Friday, January 8th, 1971,
2345 Local Time, South Vietnam

As Josh strapped into the aircraft commander's seat, conflicting emotions flooded his system. One was exhilaration, but the other was churning his gut. It was called fear. This was his crew's first SEAL insertion and extraction mission, and he couldn't erase the nagging feeling that, despite all the preparation, they really didn't know what they were doing. They all agreed that the plan was sound but all admitted that it was breaking new ground. *No one in the Navy has tried what we're about to do with an H-3! I don't want to fail myself or more importantly, fail the men in my det. I don't want to, correction, I WON'T become another Higgins.*

From a mission planning perspective, it was a perfect night— enough clouds to cover the moon but none low enough to fill the valleys. There was enough light so that the rivers and filled rice paddies glowed faintly in the darkened terrain 3,000 feet below. They climbed that high to stay out of the range of small arms fire.

The flight plan called for them to drop down to 40 feet above the trees and fly at 60 knots. One nautical mile a minute made route planning and navigating easier. If Josh felt comfortable, they would increase the speed slowly. On each knee board, they had a card with a table that showed the nautical miles covered in a minute for 70, 80 and 90 knots.

They used the trees to mask the noise of their passing. In informal and very unscientific tests, they'd found out that full growth trees dissipated the noise made by the engines, main rotor and tail rotor blades. So, the closer to the trees, the better. Night time, when the human eye struggled to see shapes because there wasn't the contrast provided by color, also made the helicopter harder to detect visually. At least, these were the theories that they were about to test.

As they started to descend, Josh remembered Marty's words as they'd boarded the helicopter, "We've got a good plan with lots of back-up. Remember, you're just the taxi driver. Just drop us off, and come when you're called!"

Behind him, bathed in dull red light in the dimly lit cabin, the only shapes he could make out were Kowalski, who was sitting behind Braxton, and Marty, who had his back against the armor plate riveted to the "broom closet" where the actuators that controlled the pitch of the helicopter's five main rotor blades were housed.

Conversation was limited, only headings, time to turn, and fuel state versus the flight plan, until they got to the fifth waypoint, the last of a series of dog legs designed to disguise where they were actually headed. Braxton was scanning the top of the forest to make sure they didn't hit a tree sticking way above the canopy, while Josh was flying the helicopter on instruments. Airspeed. Heading. Needle and ball to keep the helicopter in balanced flight. Look out. Then glance back to the cockpit and do it all over again. It was repetitious and required concentration. It was also a reminder that very precise flying was hard work.

Braxton had a picture of the LZ on top of the console and every so often he'd compare it to what he could see outside while his finger marked their position on the strip chart, on which headings and distances between each waypoint were noted in black marker. "Josh, the LZ should be on our nose in about ten minutes. Guys in the back, get ready."

Josh tried not to be distracted by the scuffling and moving around in the cabin. The noise was sensed more than it was heard.

Braxton was scanning the ground on the left side of the helicopter. "Shit, we just passed it. Turn left and come back around."

Josh took the helicopter, now lighter by 2,400 pounds of fuel than at take off, up to 150 feet above the trees before he rolled and banked. The landing zone was barely discernable: it was just a lighter shade of green-black.

Josh flared the helicopter and into a hover. According to the radar altimeter, the belly of the helicopter was 40 feet off the ground.

"Rope going out and SEALs are going down." Bennington's voice was muffled by the mask he wore.

It felt like ten minutes, but in reality it was less than 30 seconds when Bennington's voice came over the intercom. "SEALs are all out. I got a thumbs-up. Tail is clear. Let's get out of here."

"Leaving." Josh made the helicopter climb strait up for fifty feet before accelerating and then descending down to 40 feet above the trees and a steady sixty knots.

Braxton gave him the coordinates for their return flight and warned, "We're going to skirt the Ho Chi Minh trail air defenses. My gut says stay close to the ground until we get into South Vietnam, and then we can climb back to three thousand feet."

"I agree, Bill. Let's hope we don't stumble on anyone who can put a bunch of AK-47 rounds in our belly. I'm going to kick it up to eighty knots."

"There's one other danger…"

"Which is?"

"I hope bar at the Officer's Club is still open!"

Sunday, January 10th, 1971,
0549 Local Time, North Vietnam

Visibility in the jungle was a love/hate thing for Marty. He loved that you could be ten feet away from your enemy and they couldn't see you. He hated that they might see you when you could not see them, which was, on most occasions, fatal.

He'd been in country long enough to respect the jungle. If you knew what you were doing, it could be an endless source of food and water and material for shelter. It could hide you. On the other hand, it could be your implacable enemy and imprison you until you died, lost, hungry and very much afraid.

Marty curled his body around the trunk of a tree and braced his elbows on a root as he used his binoculars to study their ambush's kill zone. Eight members of his team were deployed along the longest side of the clearing, which was shaped like a trapezoid. At the smaller end of the odd shaped field of grass, Marty and three others were looking straight down the depression.

Earlier in the day, they'd engaged a North Vietnamese company for a few seconds and then faded away, back into the jungle, hoping the enemy commander would follow.

If the pursuing commander of the NVA soldiers was cautious and reconnoitered this ridge top, he would probably back off and called in artillery, if they had some available, or look for a way to lay siege. An aggressive commander would think that he had his enemy trapped and follow.

There was only one way up the 40-meter wide ravine, thick with elephant grass that offered little concealment and no cover. The NVA might think it was an extraction site for one of the small teams the Americans sent in. The rock outcropping at the top of the ravine was the logical place for a defender to make his last stand before being extracted.

Depending on his vantage point, someone looking up the ravine might or might not notice the large grouping of rocks just inside the tree line on the east side of the clearing; from there, defenders would have a clear shot at anyone in the ravine ten meters below. On the west side, the line of trees gave a false promise of an escape route; behind the trees was a 35 meter-high cliff.

In three locations that appeared to be logical entry points, the SEALs had placed booby traps: claymore mines with tripwires and grenades to act as early warning indicators.

Marty wanted to avoid close combat. Once the NVA got to within 20 to 30 meters of their position, it was time to leave.

As he lay there, two thoughts kept running through his mind. *Did Hausner and I overlook anything? When and where is Murphy and his law going to show up?*

The bang of an exploding Claymore followed by screams shattered the pre-dawn stillness. The tinny clang of the spoon of a fragmentation grenade was followed a second later by another bang and more screams.

Fight's on, but where are *the bastards?* Fire discipline was paramount, and the SEALs knew better than to start firing until they had good targets. In the slowly growing light, a ground level fog hid anyone creeping through the elephant grass. Marty make sure the fire selector switch of his Heckler & Koch MP-5 was in the three round burst position as he rose to a kneeling position, keeping his body behind the two-foot diameter tree.

He eased the German-made assault rifle forward and snugged the stock into his shoulder. Still no targets.

A ripple of distinct thunks from mortars surprised him. Marty made himself as small as possible and waited for the explosions when he heard a second volley fired. The first set of mortar shells exploded in the treetops, showering him with leaves and pieces of branches.

Only three shells penetrated the dense foliage and exploded on the ground. How many of his guys were hit by the shrapnel? He pressed the switch on his throat mike. "Casualties?" His men knew that he only wanted to know if anyone was down. If you weren't hit, you didn't need to say anything. Marty heard nothing. *So far, so good.*

Marty counted 16 explosions around his twelve-man team's little nests, then there was a pause before another ripple of four more thunks as mortar shells left the tube, followed by another four. He saw the first two red flashes, but the rest were obscured as a dense white smoke filled the ravine.

So that's their plan. Rush at us through the smoke and hope enough get through to overwhelm us. The NVA commander has at least a company-sized force, that explains the mortars. But how many shells does he have? Mortars, even 40mm ones, and their shells are heavy as sin to lug around in the jungle. Shells will be at a premium.

The rising smoke and knee-high fog curling around the elephant grass turned charging NVA soldier into silhouettes, just like the targets the SEALs used during training. At fifty yards, Marty's first burst of three smacked into a man's chest. Another shape, another burst. It was mechanical: see a shape, shoot a burst; see a shape, shoot a burst. Ten targets, ten bursts. Reload. Shoot only when you have a target. *Maintain fire discipline. Conserve ammunition.*

The grass hid the number of men dead or dying and he didn't hear the next volley of smoke rounds explode, he only noted that the cloud was now denser and closer. More shapes, more bursts, more dying men. Then the North Vietnamese stopped coming.

He pressed the throat mike up against his larynx. "Update. Casualties and ammo."

After listening to reports from five two-man fire teams, he keyed the mike again. "After the next rush, we exit stage left as planned." Double mike clicks acknowledged his order; he tapped his fire teammate. "Radio."

Thumbs up said it was on.

"Any Ballot Box or Nail, this is Gringo 6, over." Marty waited for an answer. There was none, so he keyed the mike again and repeated his transmission. Still no answer. He tried a third time with the same result.

A burst from a PK machine gun chewed up the earth ten feet in front of him. The next one went way over his head. Another one methodically started stitching their position at the head of the ravine with 7.62 millimeter rounds. More bursts. Someone was directing the pattern of fire, targeting specific locations.

Rescue may or may not be on the way, but it was time to retreat. "Teams one and two, pull back and crawl up the ridgeline to the rest of the team."

Another burst tattooed the tree he was using for cover. Marty felt his pack jerk, followed by a warm wetness. Marty reached back, hoping not to feel warm blood.

Same Day, 0827 Local Time, Pleiku, South Vietnam

Josh watched a strange twin engine turboprop with a bubble canopy park in front of base operations. The olive-drab airplane had *U.S. Army* painted on the aft fuselage in matte black. A fuel truck pulled up and the driver started pumping fuel into the plane before the propellers came to a stop. While one man stayed with the plane, another headed to base operations, where Josh was looking at the latest weather maps.

The Army pilot filled out a form and then looked Josh over, spying the gold wings on his name tag. "We don't get many Navy guys around here. What are you flying?"

"The HH-3A out there on the ramp."

"Oh. The black helo?"

"That's it."

"What kind of missions do you fly?"

"Combat search and rescue and special operations." A pause. "Why?"

"Just curious. They may need you. I just finished a mission over the trail and there's a helluva firefight going on. Some kind of recon team's in trouble. Call sign of the team is Gringo 6—" If the aviator wanted to continue the conversation, it would have to be with the duty sergeant, because Josh's was running to the H-3.

An hour later, Big Mother 22 was 2,000 feet above the rising terrain and approaching the area that contained the extraction LZs. The different shades of deep green gave the jungle its own camouflage look. Chief Bennington was standing between the two pilot seats when Bill keyed the intercom. "So what's the plan?"

"We're going to get Marty and his guys out."

"How?"

"Don't know yet." Privately, Josh feared they would either be too late or not be able to get in at all. His own words to Marty came back to haunt him: *If you get in trouble, I'll move heaven and earth to get you and your team out.*

"So the plan is to figure it out when we get there, so it will be a surprise to the bad guys?"

"Yup. Bill, give Nail Five 572 a call. He's the forward air controller who is supposed to be in this area. We should be in range by now."

Five minutes passed before Nail Five 517 answered, telling them that he'd relieved 572. He was surprised that Big Mother 22 was a helicopter, not a jet loaded with bombs to drop. Josh told him that they were there to pick up Gringo 6.

"Welcome to the party, Big Mother. You guys figure out what you want to do and I'll bring the close air support. Last contact with Gringo 6 was an hour ago; you can see the smoke from the last bomb strikes at your two o'clock. Gringo 6 said they were evading toward primary pick-up point Stowe."

Bill tried to reach Gringo 6. No answer.

Josh keyed the mike. "I don't know how long it will take Marty to get to Stowe, but we'll be orbiting for a couple of hours. So let's minimize our fuel burn by slowing the rotors and making gentle turns. We need at least twelve hundred pounds of gas to get back to Pleiku. Right now, we have thirty-five hundred pounds in our tanks. We need to make it last as long as we can."

"Josh, I'm estimating from the location of the smoke that they're between one-and-a-half and two kilometers from Stowe. If they're evading, it could take the rest of the day."

"Yeah."

"So...?"

"As I see it, we have three choices:

"Option one: We orbit until we know from Marty how long it will take him to get to Stowe and then figure out the best way to make the pick-up.

"Option two: Orbit until we have six hundred pounds of fuel and then go get gas at Kon Tum or Dak To. Both are a lot closer than Pleiku and we would arrive there with about two hundred pounds."

"Option three is something we haven't thought of yet."

"Josh, you really don't know what we're going to do, do you?"

"Nope. Not until we hear from Marty. Then we'll figure it out. Meanwhile, we burn as little gas as possible. Figure out the headings and the time needed to get to Kon Tum and Dak To."

"Will do."

"Bill, do you want the good news?"

"Is there any?

"Always is. You just have to find it. But here it is. The Air Force uses JP-4 instead of JP-5. It burns hotter, is slightly lighter and gives us more power. Not much, but enough. That means we can go farther on the same amount of fuel. So, when you are done with your navigation duties dig into the NATOPS manual and see what you can figure out. If I remember correctly, it gives us an additional five percent. It's a question on the closed book NATOPS exam. Meanwhile, I'll fly and try to keep from hitting anything."

Josh was staring out at the building clouds to the west, knowing that as the day progressed they would get bigger and make things really shitty if they turned into heavy thunderstorms. The rain and cloud cover would affect the close air support operations and make it more difficult to navigate and find Stowe.

No one said anything. Despite being deep in country, flying a race track pattern with three minute legs was boring. And yet, each man knew there was a high probability that the landing zone was going to be hot, very hot.

Then the radio crackled. Josh listened and could tell Marty's voice was heavy with tension and fatigue.

"Big Mother, Gringo 6 is midway, west side. Bad guys closing. Hurry. We've got wounded."

Josh spotted the clearing and rolled the helicopter into a steep descent that sent them plunging six thousand feet per minute. Tracers that looked like a series of red golf balls leapt out from the jungle as the North Vietnamese gunners hosed the sky, trying to hit the plummeting helicopter. The streams of bullets stayed behind the turning and descending helicopter as the North Vietnamese gunners struggled to acquire their target. Return fire from the helicopter's six-barreled mini-gun, short streams of green tracers, looked like Morse code as they chewed up the trees around the source of the red tracers.

"Josh, you've got full power. Gear down and locked. The landing checklist is complete."

The H-3 groaned and shuddered as Josh forced it to level off and stop. Two rocket propelled grenades trailing a plume of smoke and fire streaked past the nose of the slowing helicopter as it touched the ground.

"S'okay!" Kowalski called over the noise. "I got this!" He

hammered away with the M-60.

"Big Mother, we're coming out of the trees. Cover us."

"I see them." Bennington's voice was calm as he spoke between bursts from the mini-gun. "Mr. Cabot has got one guy over his shoulders. Two others are carrying a stretcher."

The pinging sound of AK-47 rounds going through the thin aluminum skin sounded like rain on a tin roof. The thwacks when they hit something other than thin aluminum were the ones that caught Josh's attention.

"Twenty seconds." Bill fired 30 rounds from his M-1 carbine in two long bursts as he spoke. He yanked out the empty magazine and replaced it with a fresh one and sprayed the jungle.

"Wounded are on board." A long burst from the mini-gun. "We got all twelve. Let's get the fuck out of here."

Josh didn't need any encouragement. As soon as the helicopter was off the ground, he dumped the nose and added power to accelerate. Scant seconds after they lifted, the ground where they'd landed erupted. Then there was a thump followed by the sound of tearing metal, but the helo kept accelerating.

"What the hell was that?" Dirt from the explosion was splattered against the windscreen and Josh moved his head to see between the clumps of mud.

"Sir, the right main mount is all screwed up. The wheels are turned about forty-five degrees to the right, and it's dripping hydraulic fluid," Van der Jagt reported.

"Josh." Bill pointed to a dial on the panel. The utility hydraulic system was showing zero pressure. "You don't have any brakes. And the hoist won't work."

"Any other damage?"

"No, sir." Van der Jagt walked forward into the cabin and stood between the pilots, gripping the handholds on the back of the pilot seats. "I can't see anything else that thousand mile an hour tape won't fix. The chief and the SEAL medic are working on the wounded."

"Good. Bill, you fly. Keep it at two thousand feet and ninety knots. I think we have enough gas to get to Pleiku. Van der Jagt, give Mr. Cabot a headset."

Van der Jagt headed back.

"Josh, I'm on. Thanks for coming to get us. It was starting to get pretty ugly."

"What happened?"

"We drew them into an ambush site, but they hit us with a mix of smoke and explosive mortar rounds before they rushed us. We bugged out by rappelling down a hundred foot cliff and headed for the extraction zone. That's when we ran into another company-size force that was coming to reinforce the one we chewed up. After we punched them in the face and moved away, we were down to pistol ammo and one belt for each machine gun. Then it was a race between them finding us and you getting us out."

"How bad are the two guys who were hurt?"

"They should both make it, if we can get them to a hospital soon. The guy on the stretcher has a stomach wound."

"If we need to, we can stop at either Dak To or Kon Tum to get them to a hospital sooner. But once we're down, we probably can't take off again without major repairs. The advantage of Pleiku is that they have more maintenance facilities and probably a better equipped hospital."

"Give us ten minutes and we'll let you know."

"Josh," Bill demanded, "how the hell are we going to touch down with our landing gear shot to hell?"

"Carefully? I have no idea! How are we on fuel?"

"We should have enough to make Pleiku—barely. That's if my calculations for the JP-4 fuel work out."

Van der Jagt stepped forward to address the pilots.

"Mr. Haman, sir. The chief says we can wait until we get to Pleiku. And I have an idea."

Twenty minutes later, with less than 200 pounds of fuel left, Josh slowly flared the helicopter to a 40-foot hover. On one side of the landing zone were two ambulances, a fire truck, and a fireman in a hooded silver suit manning the foam cannon. On the other side was a pile of pallets and two mattresses.

Josh could feel the oleo strut on the left side begin to absorb the helicopter's weight when he stopped the descent, maintaining a hover to keep the damaged right side level with the left. "O.K, Chief," he called to the back, "get everyone out. And hurry!"

Once the crew transferred the two wounded out of the helo, three airmen on the ground quickly slid two piles of pallets, each topped by a mattress, under the helicopter. As Van der Jagt gave Josh the cut sign, the right engine began to unwind from fuel starvation, followed quickly by the left one. Just before the rotors stopped, they heard a loud crack caused by the wood one of the pallets breaking under the weight of the helicopter as it settled. The helicopter lurched to the right but stopped, at a twenty degree angle of bank. The only noise was the cackling of the engines as they cooled down. They'd made it.

Monday, January 11th, 1971,
1152 Local Time, Beijing

The small gap between the handle and the door, sized for Asians, wouldn't let Raiskov's fingers in his thick gloves get a good grip on the door handle. A strong wind blowing straight south from Siberia added to his misery. Acrid smoke from the coal fired furnaces that heated most of the buildings in Beijing blew up and down the streets. On days like this, it was so thick that you could taste it, so strong it made your eyes water, and so dense that it coated your coat with ash.

He had to take a glove off to turn the handle, and then the door stuck in its frame. Frustrated and wanting to get out of the cold, away from the coal smoke, Raiskov grabbed the edge of the door with both hands and forced it open. *This godforsaken country doesn't know how to build for winter or cook food that will stick to your bones!*

Nevertheless, the Russian was all smiles when he shook hands with Brigadier General Chia.

They were a study in contrasts. Raiskov was broad-framed, with thick, dark hair that showed his Black Sea heritage. He certainly wasn't the blond, blue eyed Soviet officer whose parents had lots of Viking genes. Chia was slim, wiry, and shorter by a noticeable number of centimeters. He was emotionless in conversation and never raised his voice. He met Raiskov because he was told to do so. The GRU had approached Chinese intelligence with an offer to provide information on U.S. Navy operations in and around the Chinese coast, in keeping with the principle that "the enemy of my enemy can be an ally." Since Chia handled special projects, the relationship with Raiskov was his.

Chia waved to a table set apart from the others, one that gave them extra privacy. "Have some green tea," he said politely. "It will help take away the chill."

What Raiskov really wanted was a cup of hot coffee laced with something stronger. A bowl of borscht would also be nice right now, much better than the thin egg drop soup favored by the general. "Thank you, General, I'll take some." He knew not to ask for sugar. Cuban sugar was scarce and expensive.

"You should like this weather. It is just like your home."

"One never likes a Russian winter. You just learn to endure it. And I am from the Crimea where it is warm; well, at least it is warmer than Moscow."

The Chinese nodded at this. "I grew up near Shanghai, where it rarely gets cold. Ahhhhhh, here they are. I ordered some steamed dumplings because I know you like them." Chia sat straight up with his hands in his lap and waited as the round wicker basket was placed in the center of the table. Once the waiter left, he opened the lid and pushed it toward the GRU officer as if to say, you first.

Interesting. Is he softening me up? What does he want?

"My country," Chia said next, "is grateful for the messages you are giving us. It is a sign of the strong fraternal relationship between socialist countries."

"We are just trying to help our comrades in the fight against capitalism." *He wants something.*

"I have a favor to ask."

Ahhhhh, Raiskov thought, *here it comes.*

"You know that, sometimes, fraternal countries have... differences."

Yes, my country and yours have almost gone to war more than once since the Great Patriotic War. We still shoot at each other. The last full scale battle with artillery and tanks was March of 1969. The People's Liberation Army attacked the KGB Border Guard outpost on Zhenbao Island in the Ussuri River that is the border between Eastern Siberia and the People's Republic of China. "Differences' is a polite way to say 'rival claims' to territory.

"And yet, we have smoothed out those differences."

General Chia, are you sure about that? I am not. We do not trust you, And I would be astonished if you trusted us. Moscow's second worst nightmare is millions of soldiers from the People's Liberation Army storming across the Amur and Ussuri Rivers and seizing control of the airplane and submarine factories near the mouth of the Amur. That's why we started sending tank patrols into your country. That's when we lost one of our brand new and very secret T-62 tanks.

Raiskov nodded politely and continued to look at Chia to show that he was paying attention. *I can outwait you.*

"We see from the American press reports that our Vietnamese comrades are having great success with your Divina missiles. These are the ones you have so graciously provided us..."

You and I both know that they are export models and don't have the same capabilities as the ones we use.

"...so we would like to learn from our neighbors to the south and ask you to facilitate an informal tour during which we could watch how they use their missiles..."

"General, are you asking me to see if the Vietnamese will allow you to watch how they use the Divinas to shoot down American fighter-bombers?"

"Yes. Exactly that. We will only send a small observation team to watch. No more than a half dozen officers. And we will send more of the equipment that they need, such as trucks and cheap oil, in addition to all the ammunition and weapons we ship them."

I doubt they'll allow you into their command centers no matter what you give them. "General, I would have to check. But I am sure we could provide you with our analysis of their tactics, as well as

American counter measures. As you know, we have advisors there." Raiskov gave a dumpling his attention, then asked the questions his superiors wanted answered. "Would you willing to return our T-62 tank as a gesture of good will?"

"Those reports would be a good way for us to prepare for the visit, but reports are not as valuable as seeing our brothers *actually* use the missiles."

So this is what they really want. He didn't answer my question about the tank. Let's see if I can make some progress. "General, I can't set up those meetings. It is beyond my power, beyond even those within our embassy here in Beijing. I could, however, use the return of the tank as leverage."

"But you know who can convince the Vietnamese of the value of letting us visit."

You've got to be kidding. The Vietnamese hate the Chinese! You've invaded them and the only reason you are helping them now is because they are killing Americans. So what game, General Chia are you playing? "I will see what I can do."

"Please check. It will mean a great deal to the relationship between our great socialist nations."

Shit, my country is doing all the giving. These guys always have their hand out. And he still had to deliver and discuss the thick envelop of decrypted messages in his great coat.

Thursday, January 14th, 1971,
1046 Local Time, Da Nang

The good news was that it wasn't the rainy season in Vietnam. The better news was that the Army had stand jacks that could hold the weight of the H-3. The even better news was that it wasn't summer, so instead of it being close to 100 degrees Fahrenheit, it was a more comfortable but still very humid 75. Using the Mark 1 eyeball and a couple of long levels on the cabin floor, they got the H-3 mounted on jacks and level.

After looking at the damage, the decision was made to replace the bolts as well as the strut that went from the top of the fuselage to the sponson that held the landing gear. This was in addition to rebuilding the structure inside the sponson itself. This was done more as a precaution than as a necessity.

Back in Subic Bay, it took almost a day and a half to take off the landing gear strut from an H-3 that was undergoing major maintenance at Cubi and fly it to Pleiku along with the necessary pieces of aluminum. Once in Vietnam, by the end of the second day, Senior Chief Slaughter, who came with the parts and a couple of extra men, pronounced the HH-3A ready for a ferry flight to Da Nang where they would finish the repairs.

When they touched down on the former boat ramp, the enlisted man who handled their personnel paperwork drove up in a battered jeep. "Welcome back, sir. Captain Rainer asked me to come get you."

"O.K." Josh turned to his co-pilot. "Bill, I'll be back. You take care of the post-flight." As soon as Josh climbed into the passenger's seat, the young sailor popped the clutch and left a short strip of black rubber on the concrete.

The air conditioning in the ops building was a welcome relief. Josh passed the armory, assaulted by the smell of gun oil and solvents. The odors permeated much of the building, but as one person put it, it kept the weapons handy and it was a better smell than the jungle.

As he tapped on the door frame of Captain Rainer's office to announce his arrival, Josh saw a second officer sitting in a chair. Rainer called him in. "Lieutenant Haman, this is Captain Latham from the Pacific Fleet's judge advocate's office. He wants to have a word with you. Do you want me to listen in?"

Josh was puzzled, but not alarmed. "Sir, I don't have anything to hide, so sure, please feel free to stay. Captain Latham, what can I do for you?"

Captain Latham, who had a great tan from playing 18 holes four days a week on one of the many courses in Oahu, was a quarter inch over the minimum height for the academy. As he had aged, his mid-section had expanded and now instead of being stocky, he was pudgy. The cloth around the buttons was stretched and strained. Josh was sure he couldn't pass a PT test if his life depended on it.

He did not stand up but addressed Josh perfunctorily from his chair as if he were a king addressing a commoner. "Lieutenant Haman, I don't believe in beating around the bush. I reviewed the board's findings, as well as Commander Ryerson's endorsement. I am here to officially let you know that based on your actions, I am going to recommend a general court martial. The charges will be conduct unbecoming of an officer, refusal to follow orders, attempted mutiny, and a couple of others. I can give you a list of the charges by the Uniform Code of Military Justice Article that will be filed against you. You led a mutiny on the *Sterett,* and that, Lieutenant, the Navy cannot allow."

"Sir, ..." Josh was so stunned that he was groping for words, "... with all due respect, I was cleared by the board."

"Let me finish, Lieutenant. I came all this way to tell you in person, and to recommend that Captain Rainer find a replacement for you so you can spend the next few months preparing for your trial. You should be officially charged in a week or two after I get back to Hawaii. Then you will be transferred to Hawaii and confined to the Pearl Harbor Naval Base, where the trial will be held. You will be able to select a lawyer from the Judge Advocate General's office, or you can hire one of your own."

"Sir, what about Lieutenant Higgins? Is he going to be tried for..."

The pudgy captain stood up and poked his finger against Josh's chest. "What happens to Lieutenant Higgins is of no concern to you. Your focus should be on your court martial."

"Captain, sir." Josh stepped back to create some distance and clasped his hands together behind his back as he tried to control his anger. There was no way he was going to let this asshole goad him into doing something really stupid, like hitting him. Anger is one thing, assault is another. "That's unmitigated bullshit and you know it. What I did was based on a legal order from Captain Danforth. If we hadn't taken off, Lieutenant Olgethorpe would be rotting in the Hanoi Hilton, right along with the other pilots Higgins..." Josh revised what he was about to say, "...was reluctant to go and get. We took off because there was a pilot down. Higgins didn't want to go and that is clear in the board's testimony. I am sure that they will be happy to be witnesses during the trial."

"We shall see. The rules of evidence, or the judge, may not allow the board's report."

"Captain, sir, I will be able to call witnesses and they will testify."

"Lieutenant, I am telling you that when you took off you disobeyed a direct order from your superior officer and aircraft commander, and you struck him. And that, Lieutenant is what will get you sent to Leavenworth or drummed out of the Navy."

Latham sat back down in his chair, pleased to have made his point. He was already starting to sweat from the exertion and the humidity, despite the air conditioning.

The legal officer had spent the first four of the five days he'd been in country at the Naval Support Activity in Da Nang. It was just enough to qualify him for the combat zone tax exclusion that made the first five hundred dollars of his base pay tax free. He used his position as the Pacific Command's senior legal officer to justify the monthly trip. It also was the basis for his qualification for the Vietnam campaign ribbons.

"Sir, is the Navy going to try Higgins for cowardice in the face of the enemy?"

"That is a pretty strong accusation against a fellow officer who has a fine record. I suggest you engage your brain before your mouth says something else that you'll regret, Lieutenant. I've heard that you were cocky and insubordinate. Your attitude proves it, and you're crossing a line that you'll regret." Latham turned to Captain Rainer. "I don't know how you tolerate such behavior from a junior officer.

Josh waited until Latham was facing him again. "Am I? I think not. Captain. I saw Higgins exhibit a yellow streak a mile wide, *and* falsify government records. That will come out in the trial. By the way, Captain Latham, what year did you graduate from the academy?

Latham flushed visibly and pulled a handkerchief out of his back pocket to wipe his sweating face. "What are you insinuating,

Lieutenant Haman?"

"Captain, sir. I'm not insinuating anything. I am curious; how far are you ring knockers going to go to protect one of your own who is a coward and unfit to be in the Navy?"

"Are you accusing Lieutenant Higgins of being a coward?"

"No, sir, I don't have to accuse him at all. The facts speak for themselves. He refused to do his duty in the face of enemy fire and, as a result, at least one Naval Aviator is missing in action and presumed to be a prisoner of war. There were two other witnesses in the helicopter as well as several others from the Air Wing 19 on the *Oriskany,* to say nothing of those who listened to the radio transmissions. So, no, Captain Latham, I don't have to prove anything. It is a documented fact."

"Lieutenant, you're an insubordinate bastard who needs to be taken down. I can't wait to get your arrogant ass on the witness stand. I plan, no, I *will* get a conviction that will send you away to pound big rocks into little rocks at Leavenworth for a long, long time!"

Rainer stood up and stood between the two officers. "Captain Latham, I think your mission has been accomplished. This discussion is over. My driver will be happy to take you back to base operations or the BOQ, wherever you so desire. We're done here. Lieutenant, you stay in my office until I return."

Captain Rainer escorted Latham to the jeep. When he came back to his office Josh was still seething.

"That was interesting, Lieutenant. Montemayor gave me a copy of the board's report. That's one of the reasons you are here. You're not going to Hawaii to be court martialed. Get your helicopter fixed so you can do what you came here to do. Meanwhile, I have a phone call to make and a P-Four to write."

Friday, January 15th, 1971,
0847 Local Time, Norfolk

There were three NATOPS manuals in a neat row at the front of the desk, aligned so that their tops were parallel to the edge of the desk. Three open book exams were precisely matched to the sides and top of each manual.

To the left were three labeled wire frame baskets—In, Out, and Hold. Next to them a stapler and a tape dispenser were positioned so their fronts were in an exact row aligned with the bottoms of the baskets. The only other accessories on the desk were two phones: a black one for general use and a red one with two buttons. One button connected Higgins directly to the tower, whose air traffic controllers reported to him, and the other was his link to control center. Both phones had their fronts neatly aligned.

After he read each of the day's "In" messages, Higgins stood the stack on its end and tapped it on the desk to make sure the papers were in a neat, precise pile. As he moved each paper from one basket to the other, he repeated the process to make sure nothing was out of line.

The black phone jangled. Higgins, without taking his eye off the message he was reading, picked up the handset of the 1950s rotary phone. "Higgins." He listened for a few seconds. "Yes, Mrs. Hinsley, tell Commander Maastricht I'll be right there."

Higgins entered the ops officer's office with a practiced air of confidence and ease. "Commander Maastricht, Lieutenant Higgins reporting as ordered."

The commander was leaning back in his chair, tapping an envelope against the table.

"Lieutenant, I just got this letter, which took weeks to wind its way through channels. There are more endorsements than you can shake a stick at. You are to undergo a psychiatric exam to determine whether or not you should continue flying in the Navy. The letter directs you to report to the chief medical officer at the Naval Air Station. I am not going to probe into what precipitated this, but until you are cleared to fly, I am keeping you off the flight schedule so I don't have to officially ground you. Meanwhile, I want you to go ahead with the NATOPS exams for the T-28, C-117 and the UH-1 so we can continue your transition to those aircraft. I am not going to cancel your orders for Pensacola next month to attend the Huey ground school. If you are cleared by the shrinks, you start flying again. Any questions? If not, that is all."

"No, sir." White-faced and tight-lipped, Higgins spun on his heel and headed back to his office. *I don't remember the board recommending a psyche evaluation for me. Who did? I just want to finish my commitment and get the hell out of the Navy. Maybe if I act a little crazy, they will give me an early out.*

Chapter 12 – SAM THIEVERY

Saturday, January 16th, 1971,
1038 Local Time, Da Nang

The HH-3A was resting in the former boat repair facility. A neatly lettered and hand painted sign on the front door bore the legend: HC-7 Detachment 171 Maintenance Facility. Inside, two offices were kept cool by four window air conditioners. Two large, six foot diameter fans blew air from the back of the hangar out the front to create circulation, so instead of hot, humid, still air, those working on the helicopter were treated to a breeze of hot, humid air.

Off to one side, the damaged main mount was lying on a pallet and the torn aluminum structure that held the landing gear was clearly visible. Soon, it would go via crate back to an overhaul facility where it would be repaired, salvaged for parts, or discarded. The white paint of the newly installed landing gear on the right side clashed with the dirty, dented, worn one on the left.

After giving the newly painted sponson a cursory inspection, Josh walked back to headquarters, past the two rows of barbed wire, three watch towers and sandbagged fighting positions manned 24 hours a day by SEALs. Inside, Braxton handed him an analysis of the North Vietnamese air defense system with the locations of all known surface-to-air missile sites.

"Whenever we ask for info on anti-aircraft artillery, we get stuff on missiles." Bill tossed another message on the table. "Shit! We need the locations of the guns that can kill us, the 23 through 57 millimeters. I know they can't give the location of every twelve point seven millimeter gun in the country, but the bigger stuff, come on!"

"Now you know why I started keeping my own chart," Josh said. "The carriers have heavy guns plotted from reconnaissance photos. I asked them for photos that showed the smaller stuff and they were more than happy to give them to me. Then it only took a few minutes to plot locations."

"Then maybe we should take a trip out to the carriers on Yankee Station and see what they have."

"Good idea. Send a message and ask for the info." Josh picked up another message. "What's this?"

"Oh, it is more on the SA-2 missile and how it works, but there are caveats throughout the message saying they are not sure of this or that. The way I read it, they're guessing."

"So why don't we steal a missile and a control van and find out?"

"How would you do that, Lieutenant?" Captain Rainer's familiar voice came from behind his back.

Josh turned around to face Rainer. "Sir, I was just wondering out loud. If our intelligence folks are not sure what makes an SA-2 tick, why don't we go steal one? It shouldn't be that hard."

"So, Lieutenant, answer my question, how would you do it?" Captain Rainer sat down.

Friday, January 22nd, 1971,
1146 Local Time, Beijing

The restaurant that catered to foreigners was along Embassy Row. Since it was his turn to pay, Raiskov wanted a change in venue, and he wanted a nice meal on the Kremlin's ruble. To get Chia to eat someplace new required negotiations with the reluctant Chinese general that further convinced Raiskov the tables where they usually sat were bugged. This time, however, Raiskov got to pick the place to eat, and the table. In some ways, he thought getting that concession from Chia was a victory.

Chia's arrival turned heads. Generals of the People's Liberation Army didn't come here very often. Raiskov could see more than one patron making a mental recording of the general's face and rank for further investigation. As the Chinese general approached, Raiskov stood up and held out his hand, which Chia took in a firm grip. Raiskov held the Chinese officer's hand a few seconds longer to see if it was moist, which would tell him that his guest was nervous. It was just cold.

"Thank you for coming. Have you been here before, General?"

"No, I haven't." The subtle movement of the brigadier general's head and eyes suggested that he too was gathering data.

"Well, it is supposed to be the best Western-style restaurant in Beijing, but my comrades tell me that if it was in Hong Kong it would probably go out of business."

Chia didn't smile; there were lots of places in his country where people considered themselves lucky to get any food at all. The waiter appeared and poured cups of tea.

Chia looked up at the waiter. "I will have the filet mignon, medium, and a baked potato with sour cream, chives, and bacon if you have it."

Raiskov's eyebrows rose in spite of himself.

Chia was halfway through his steak when he shifted the conversation from a discussion of U.S./Japanese relation. "So, do you have a package for me?"

"I do. There are two envelopes."

"Two. Very interesting. Why two?"

"There so many decoded messages we think you should know about. One set authorizes actual flights over southeastern China. The other envelope contains information about American fleet movements around Taiwan."

"What are the American imperialists doing there?"

Ahhh, he is more interested in the island of Taiwan than Americans flying over his own country. "It is an exercise with their air force and navy. One of their carriers, the *Constellation,* is participating, along with some of their fighters and bombers based in Guam, Korea and Okinawa."

"Do they say where the exercises are going to take place?"

"Yes. Most of the time the carrier will be north and east of the island. Then, sometime late in the war games, the carrier and its escorts will be coming into the Taiwan Strait. They will continue south on to the Philippines after the end of the exercise."

"Any military exercise in the straits is a provocation."

Raiskov didn't answer. He was intrigued by the general's interpretation. *Flying aircraft over another country without permission* **IS** *provocative. Having a fucking, publicly announced military exercise in international waters is not.*

"Are they still interested in finding the non-existent missiles on rail cars in my country?"

"If you are asking if I think they will attack trains inside the People's Republic, the answer is no. The American President will not risk widening the war. But if they think missiles are transported on those rail lines, they will try to destroy them as soon as they are on the Vietnamese side of the border."

"That would not be good for our Vietnamese friends."

"No, it would not."

"Have you heard from them regarding that matter we spoke of?"

"Yes. They are…" Raiskov struggled for a word, "…*reluctant* to host a delegation. You can imagine why?"

"No I cannot. Tell me." There was a hardness in Chia's voice that Raiskov had not heard before.

"I don't know what they said; I am only the messenger, but I was told that they would think about it." *Why would they share air defense secrets with a country that has attacked it repeatedly?*

"Press them. And the Soviet Union needs to tell them it will get expensive if they refuse."

"I think my government would be more, shall we say, aggressive in encouraging our fraternal allies, if we got our tank back."

"Get us the visit and maybe we can talk about your tank. You have hundreds, maybe thousands of them by now. Why are you so worried about one tank that we had to pull out of the river?" Chia put down his knife and fork, which Raiskov observed he used with practiced efficiency. "I have to go. I do not want anyone seeing me receive anything from you. You can understand why," he added with the barest trace of irony. "So I will have someone get the envelopes from you at your office. Good day."

Monday, January 25th, 1971,
0934 Local Time, the Pentagon

The Chairman of the Joint Chiefs waved the Chief of Naval Operations over toward the black leather couch in his office. The Chief had requested this meeting, pressing for the earliest time the Chairman had available.

"So, what's so urgent?"

"Boss, I think I have a partial answer to the missile question."

"And that is?"

"We steal one. A couple of bright young officers came up with a foolproof, well, no plan is that, but a very good plan to capture an SA-2 and a control van intact. Neither the guys at CINCPAC nor COMMAACV could punch holes in the plan, so their recommendation is we go forward with it." The CNO waved a folder that contained the briefing package. "I had a couple of my own guys go over the briefing and, other than nitpicking, they liked it and wanted to go on the mission. That's the best qualifier I know."

"Then tell COMMAACV to do it."

"Yes, sir, I just wanted to let you know. You won't see anything in the message traffic. The guys who came up with are paranoid about secrecy."

"They should be. Thanks for the heads-up. I am not going to take this to the president, because we're conducting raids up and down the coast, so this is nothing new. Just let me know when it goes down so I can tell him the results."

Thursday, January 28th, 1971,
2235 Local Time, Gulf of Tonkin

The phosphorescence of the wake was like a bright shaft of an arrow to the arrowhead that was the dull black shape of the U.S.S. *Dubuque* moving through the calm waters of the Gulf of Tonkin. The helicopter deck aft of the superstructure had two landing spots, each large enough for an H-53. Below the helo pad was a well deck that could be flooded to launch amphibious assault vehicles transporting

Marines.

The H-53 looked like the Air Force version of the H-3, but it was much, much bigger. It had a maximum take off weight of 45,000 pounds—more than twice that of the H-3. Its rotor blade diameter was just over 72 feet, 17 feet greater than an H-3's. More importantly, for this mission, it could haul a load of 13,000 pounds.

From their orbit a quarter mile to starboard and 200 feet above the water, Josh could see two H-53s squatting on the flight deck, their anti-collision lights flashing as they took on fuel. A half-mile behind the *Dubuque,* a third H-53 was circling, waiting its turn to land and top off its fuel tanks. Big Mother 22 had already refueled from the *Sterett* steaming nearby.

As soon as he saw the third H-53 lift off, Josh rolled Big Mother 22 to a course that would pass astern of the ship and allow the bigger helicopters to join in an echelon. Big Mother would lead and navigate; the three Marine helicopters, Pegasus 30, 31, and 35, would be doing the heavy lifting.

They were slightly ahead of schedule. Nevertheless, he pulled the mike switch back into the transmit mode. "Thunder, Big Mother 22 is inbound."

Thunder was the U.S.S. *Newport News,* a heavy cruiser built after World War II that still mounted nine 8-inch guns in three turrets—two forward and one aft. It had a secondary armament of twelve five-inch guns in twin turrets, three on each side. Even though they were nearly ten miles away from the cruiser, Josh could see the flash of its big guns, then feel the helicopter shake from the concussion a few seconds later.

"How accurate do you think those eight-inchers are?" Braxton asked.

"Hits within fifty feet of point of aim are no problem. The A-6s from the *Oriskany* can call the shots and help the ships adjust their shooting. The plan is to take out the 37- and 57-millimeter positions we plotted, which are in open revetments along our route. They should knock most if not all of them out. Now, while everybody's distracted, we've got a missile system to steal."

The ripple of flashes in the distance grew brighter as the *Newport News* hammered away at the North Vietnamese triple-A positions, walking the six hundred pound shells along Big Mother's ingress and egress route, firing from nearly three miles offshore. The smaller flashes of the five-inch guns were engulfed by the flames from the eight-inchers, which lit up the sky.

Josh keyed the intercom. "Marty, you awake?"

"Yeah, talk to me."

"We're going feet dry in about five minutes. That means we'll be at the site in ten."

"Got it. We're ready to go."

The four helos swept across the coast. The air smelled of burnt explosive mixed with seared wood. Off to their right, fires burned where just a few minutes ago there had been a 57- millimeter gun battery. At intervals there'd be a flash as a round of ammunition cooked off.

Josh rotated the mike switch to transmit. "Pegasus 31, less than three minutes."

That was the signal for Pegasus 30 and Pegasus 35 to drop back and orbit off the beach until they were called. Two clicks from the trailing Marine helicopter provided an acknowledgement.

The pale sand of the SA-2 missile launcher site popped into view, even though there was very little moonlight. Josh flared, rolled left, and hovered 40 feet, 50 feet from two control vans. Holding Big Mother steady, he could feel the shifts in weight and balance as eight men leapt out.

"SEALs are all out, go, Go, GO!" was his cue to climb to 500 feet and orbit. He could just make out Pegasus 31 landing in the cleared area between one of the missile launchers and a trailer bearing an SA-2.

Josh glanced to the side and saw a man come out of the van, stop, and put up his hands. Before he could even wonder about this, Bennington's voice came over the com. "We've got bad guys coming out of a building down the road."

"I'll swing round and give you a clear line of fire," Josh replied. Soon Bennington had the mini-gun humming as it spat out 7.62 millimeter rounds at the rate of 4,000 bullets a minute, the chief using short bursts to keep the barrel from overheating.

"Big Mother," Marty called in, "Gringo 6 reporting vans secured, but we have a problem."

"Gringo 6, what's that?"

"Six Russians have surrendered. I'm going to take them prisoner because I can't just shoot them."

"Ask them if they want to go to America!"

"Are you serious?"

"Yup."

"None of them speak English, and none of us speak Russian. We're trying Vietnamese."

"We'll pick them up, and I'll talk to them."

"Josh," Bill interrupted, "we have to call in the other two birds before the gooks figure out what we're doing."

"Take care of that, Bill."

No sooner had Pegasus 30 and 35 acknowledged when the radio hissed again.

"Big Mother 22, Pegasus 31. We're getting the missile and trailer inside the helo. The guys will winch it in so there is no need to sling it. Be ready to go in less than five."

"Big Mother 22 copies."

Josh was surprised by the lack of enemy fire or movement, until he scanned the horizon. All six battery positions that had ringed the site were obliterated. Where had been AAA guns were now only smoking holes and debris. *Looks like Thunder's gunners were on the mark. I'll be sure to tell them.*

"Oh shit! This is Pegasus 35, 30 just crashed!"

"Say again?"

"Big Mother 22, this is Pegasus 35. I think Pegasus 30 hit something with his tail pylon when he flared. The bird whipped round and down, and it's not going anywhere now. Too dark to see the damage, but I can see the crew moving toward Gringo 6. Looks like they're carrying one."

"Pegasus flight, Big Mother 22 will get 30's crew when we pick up the SEALS. Can you handle the load?"

"Guess we'll find out, won't we?" Josh could see one of the SEALs standing on top of one of the two vans that controlled the SA-2s. He was holding up the looped ends of the sling on the pole. The H-53 dropped down and he guided the sling onto a hook on the belly of the helicopter and the helo rose, lifting the van.

"Pegasus 35 is up. I hope this thing weighs what they said it would."

Josh knew that the estimate of the van was 14,000 pounds, which just so happened to be 1,000 more than the max sling payload of the A model H-53. However, when consulted, the pilots in Marine Heavy Helicopter Squadron 463 had said that they should be able to pull it off, because by the time they got on site the helos would be down to half fuel. That math was about to be tested. *Yeah, and what if it's the sling that gives out?*

Slowly, the van came off the ground, and the H-53 headed for the Gulf.

"Josh, what do you want to do with the Russians? There's six of them, plus the Marines, plus the SEALs."

"Take them with us."

"Where?"

"In the cabin, where else? It'll be cozy, but we'll manage."

As Josh landed, he did the math. He was committed to take 23 passengers—eight SEALs, nine Marines and six Russians. On a good day, with some planning, they were authorized for twelve. He figured they could sit on each other if they had too. And that was pretty much what they had to do. Marty squeezed himself forward so that he was sitting between the two pilot's seats.

"Josh, don't go near the H-53." Marty was grinning. "We put two bricks of C-4 in the cabin and two in the fuel tanks on ten minute fuses; they should blow any minute."

"Got it." With that, he executed a rolling take off on the hard sand. The overloaded H-3 groaned and complained, the rotor rpm drooped to 98 percent, but it lifted off. Once the helo was airborne, Josh banked away and headed out to sea. Behind him, a series of explosions ignited a fireball, consuming the downed helicopter.

Five minutes later, Bill keyed the mike to report in. "Hammer 702, Big Mother 22 is feet wet. Everyone is accounted for and we have six extra passengers."

"Say again, Big Mother 22."

"Big Mother 22 has 28 souls on board. Leave at that. We have a Marine that needs medical attention on arrival." The last thing Braxton wanted to do was explain the Russian supercargo over the radio. activated the pilot's intercom. Speaking of the Russians...

"O.K., genius, we land, get rid of the Marines, gas up and go home. What about the Russians? Where are we going to put them, or do with them? They can't live forever on this helicopter."

"While we're getting gas on the *Dubuque,* I'll go talk to our Russians. Hey, Marty, have you figured out their ranks?"

"I think we have a captain, a couple of lieutenants, and maybe the rest are warrant officers or sergeants, but I could be wrong."

Josh thought for a few moment, then keyed the mike. "Van der Jagt, Kowalski and Chief Bennington, listen up!"

"Yes, sir." The chief spoke for the two enlisted men.

"Here's the plan. Once we get aboard the *Dubuque,* you need to hop out and cumshaw six sets of fatigues or dungarees or overalls while we take on fuel. Make an educated guess to the size but make sure you get something the Russians can wear. Once you get the new clothes, the Soviets can change in the cabin and we can provide a bag for them to store their uniforms. We need to do this because if they any of them have to get off the helo, they have to look like Americans, at least from a distance. Chief, you need to find me a phone on the flight deck that connects me to the bridge and then go get box lunches for everyone. My math says we need 19—five of us, eight SEALs and six

Russians. Kowalski, you supervise the refueling. Bill, you stay in the seat because the rotors will be turning and I get to talk to the Russkies. Marty, your SEALs should get off to stretch their legs, but leave one with me to guard the Russians. Chief, before you get out of the helo, put the spare headset on the senior Russian so I can talk to him and he can talk to me without shouting. Everyone got it?"

A series of two clicks provided the answer.

"Great. Now we have a plan. Bill, be a good co-pilot and give me control back and do the landing check list. Looks like they've got the van on the deck and the first H-53 has gotten gas and is orbiting. We're landing on the aft spot."

Five minutes later, Josh climbed out of the pilot's seat and joined Marty, who was sitting on the ammo tray with his MP-5 on his lap. The six Russians were sitting on the floor with their hands tied together and their arms around their knees. Marty pointed the barrel at one of the faces. "He's the captain, I think."

Josh gestured for the man to stand up and handed him the Mickey Mouse ears with the boom mike. Once they were on his head, Josh handed him the mike switch. "*Tovarich*, what is your name and rank?"

The Soviet officer's head moved and his eyes widened when he heard his native tongue. "I am Captain Abram Mishkin of the Soviet Anti-Aircraft Artillery Forces."

"Captain, I am Lieutenant Joshua Haman, United States Navy. Are you the most senior officer?"

"*Da*."

"Do any of you speak English?"

"*Nyet*, no English."

"Who are the other men?"

"Lieutenants Victor Zhiglov and Valentin Bazin; Warrant Officers Bogdan Lubachev and Vadim Onegin; and Sergeant Boris Protosov. All from the anti-aircraft artillery forces. We fire missiles at your planes."

"Do you understand you are now prisoners of the United States of America?"

"*Da*."

"The United States and the Soviet Union are not at war. Do you want me to arrange for you to be transported back to the Soviet Union?"

The Soviet officer looked around at his fellow Russians and then made sure that none of them could see his face. "Me, *nyet*! The others, I don't know, but I think yes."

"When we get to a base in South Vietnam, each of you will be asked this question in private. I can't make any promises, but those who want to go to the United States may be allowed to go. The others will be sent back to the Soviet Union. Do you understand?"

"*Da.*"

"Good. Please tell them the question now so they have time to think about it."

Josh waited while Captain Mishkin shouted the question to each of the men. They're eyes opened wide and some of them stared at Josh.

"Captain Mishkin, one more thing. Tell your men that if any of you try to escape or interfere with our flying this helicopter, you will be killed. I will not tolerate any act of violence by any of your men. Do you understand?"

"*Da.*"

"Good, tell your men."

Mishkin turned and shouted at his men. All of them nodded their heads.

Captain, do any of you have to go to the bathroom? You won't have access to a bathroom for another three hours."

After another shouted exchange, the Soviet captain said, "Yes, Lieutenant, we need to use toilet."

"O.K., in a few minutes, we will bring different clothes and then escort you, three at a time, to the toilet."

"Thank you."

"When we are airborne again, we will feed you."

"You have kitchen on helicopter?"

"No, it will be prepared meals from the ship's kitchen."

The Soviet officer gave Josh a puzzled look. Before Josh could say anything more, a pile of dungaree uniforms was tossed onto the cabin floor.

"Mr. Haman, the chief said the box lunches will be here by the time we are ready to go, and he's already spoken to the captain of the ship. Bennington knew him as a young lieutenant commander when he was flying H-34s. We're also going to get a bucket of vanilla ice cream and a cooler full of cokes."

Josh thought, *Captain Miskin, welcome to the West and the American way of war!*

Three hours later, after they landed at Da Nang, Josh was dog tired when he walked around the helicopter. He'd been up for the better part of 24 tension-filled hours and could feel his body start to fade as the adrenalin began to wear off.

"Marty, please take the Russians back to the compound. Chief, let's get the helicopter tied down and put to bed. We get some shut-eye and then come back later in the day to give the helo a once over."

"Sir, what we going to do with the Russkies?" Van der Jagt was leaning on the handle of the mini-gun in the cargo door.

"They come with us. The SEALs will put them up in one of their empty enlisted bunk rooms, lock the door and guard them. Our Soviet friends won't be able to go anyplace, and Marty can talk to his fellow SEALs so they know to keep their mouths shut. That goes for our guys as well. Tell the Chief to pass the word that the penalty for talking is that either Lieutenant Cabot or I will cut their balls off with a dull serrated knife."

"Got it."

"Van der Jagt, could you get Captain Mishkin, please? I need to tell him what is happening so he can tell his men."

"Sir, you are being awful nice to these bastards. Six hours ago, they would have shot us down."

"Don't worry, there is method to my madness."

* * * * *

Eight hours later, with six hours of sleep under his belt, Josh was sitting on a bench just inside the barbed wire of the officer's compound. The Russians were locked in rooms for the night, and armed guards were posted outside their rooms.

"Lieutenant, I may talk?"

The question, spoken as it was in Russian, told him who the person was even before Josh looked up.

"What's on your mind, Captain?"

The Soviet officer was wearing a set of Navy-issue bell bottom dungarees and the light blue top. He pointed at the gold Star of David that Josh's father had worn during World War II, hanging on the chain that held his dog tags.

"I saw six-pointed star last night. You Jew?"

"I am. Why?"

"I, too. Very difficult to practice religion in Soviet Union. KGB not like Jews. Do you speak Yiddish?"

"No, but I speak German, why?"

"My parents taught me Yiddish. Interesting language. You write in Hebrew script. Only speak at home or with other trusted Jews. You go to schul?" Mishkin used the Yiddish word for synagogue, even though he was still speaking Russian.

"Yes, when I am not here in Vietnam."

"Schul in Leningrad monitored by KGB. We pray at home. Quietly." The Soviet officer bent over and looked Josh straight in the eyes. "I want to go to Israel. Every year at Rosh Hashanah and Passover, we pray that next year, in Israel. My parents would understand and be happy if I went there and not come back to Soviet Union. Can you arrange?"

"What about the others?"

"They want to go back to Soviet Union. They don't know better. I do. Parents lived in Latvia before war. Fought as partisans after Nazis came. Then Russians came and forced us to move to Leningrad. Family business no more. Father now work in shipyard. Mother works in city office. They like owning business better. More freedom."

"How could you get a message to them telling them where you were without the KGB finding out?"

"We have ways. Father and mother have friends and relatives in Finland. I not want to go back. Can you arrange emigration to Israel?"

"I don't know. Will you tell us about the SA-2? That will help."

"*Da*. Everything I know. Tell Israelis too."

"Good. Captain Mishkin, I will see what I can do, but you see my rank. I can't promise anything."

Monday, February 1st, 1971, 0822 Local Time, the Pentagon

The bullpen, Jeffrey Gainesville noted, was very egalitarian. Commanders sat next to lieutenant commanders who intermingled with captains. Small, chest high partitions divided the clusters of desks and did little to reduce the noise of a half a dozen IBM Selectric typewriters clattering away. He was using a light metallic blue IBM Selectric to put the finishing touches on a report.

Captain Grainger peered over the cube wall next to him. "Are you finished with it yet?"

"Just about, sir. I need another five minutes."

"Two things: number one, I don't know if you've heard yet, but we borrowed an SA-2, along with an electronics and control van. Our guys picked them up right under the North Vietnamese's noses. It was a Navy/Marine Corps op and no one got killed. Apparently, they got a defector out of it as well. And number two, we got us a super-secret project. We're going to get moved out of here to our own space in the basement. So finish up that report post haste and then we'll go downstairs and get officially read in."

"Is there going to be any message traffic about the SA-2?"

"Nope. Apparently the raid was the brain child of some young lieutenant helo driver. The CNO said that there will be a lot of red faces who wear light blue uniforms. *They* told the chairman it couldn't be done."

"Sir, do you know the name of the helicopter pilot?"

"They mentioned his name, but I don't remember. But it was an odd-sounding name. I think it began with an H?"

"Was it Josh Haman?"

"Yeah, that's it. Do you know him?"

"I do. He was on the *Sterett.*"

"Was he the guy who took off by himself and picked up a pilot right off the beach?"

"Yes, sir. That's him. There's a lot more to the story, but that's what happened."

"You need to tell me the rest over a beer."

"Yes, sir. May I have my five minutes?"

"Sure, I need to get a cup of coffee."

An hour later Jeffrey Gainesville was sitting in a room with three other officers and two civilians. Since he was the most junior officer in the room, for this project he would be the SLJO, or 'shitty little jobs officer'. What made it worse, he was the only surface warfare officer. Grainger was an aviator, as was one of the commanders. The third wore the large gold emblem designating him a SEAL. Being low man on the totem pole wasn't that unusual; what surprised Gainesville was the presence of the two men not wearing any sort of military uniform, but maybe they were CIA.

He was even more surprised when the Chief of Naval Operations entered the room and explained the new mission.

"The Air Force thinks the North Vietnamese get most of their missiles by trains coming through the People's Republic of China. None of our aerial reconnaissance photographs have found any evidence to support this theory, but the Air Force argues that we just haven't taken pictures of the right trains."

The CNO was trying to sound impartial, but Jeffrey was pretty sure he detected some underlying bitterness.

"So the president has authorized a mission to take a peek at one rail yard by putting eyes on the ground. If that is successful, then we're going to look at another yard. The yards are outside of Mengzi and Nanning in southeastern China. Your job is to determine if a SEAL team sneak and peek is feasible or not. If it is, you need to tell us what assets we would need to carry out the mission, as well as how you would carry it out. Later today, several boxes of photos, charts and other material will arrive. This project is code-named Southern Charm. It cannot be discussed outside this room without my express permission. If we deem it feasible, then we will get the folks who will actually go on the mission to develop the detailed plan and execute it. Questions?"

Captain Grainger raised his hand. "Yes, sir. Can we task any asset, or is this just a Navy op?"

"If you think it is feasible and if you think another service asset is essential, then I think the Chairman will make it available. I would, however, prefer if we stay inside the Navy."

Jeffrey wondered whether CNO was being parochial, or was thinking: *If the Air Force thinks the ops is so damn-all important, they should step up and do the job themselves. If they're not up to it, let the Navy do it without interference.*

Same Day, 1453, Local Time, Hawaii

The Pacific Fleet Commander's office was housed in a three-story building constructed in the early 1930s, in the days before air conditioning or tinted glass, as part of the expansion of the Pearl Harbor naval base. The roof's overhang and the wide porches provided shade, and the large windows overlooked vistas of the harbor crowded with ships. Captain Lester Latham was sitting in a chair at the end of the porch that doubled as a waiting area in front of the N1's office.

A Hawaiian native, whom the lawyer assessed with a practiced eye to be in her thirties, came out onto the porch. "Captain Latham, Admiral Hastings will see you now."

Latham knew that normally the N1 on the Pacific Fleet staff was a two-star admiral, but Hastings was a rising star and had gotten the billet right after he took a carrier battle group through a successful Mediterranean cruise. The word on the staff was that the A-4 pilot was a shoe-in for a second star.

"Captain Latham reporting, sir. Good afternoon." He had no idea why the admiral wanted to see him. Hastings had said nothing to him during the morning staff meeting.

Latham did, however, want to get back inside so he could enjoy the air conditioning. He knew he'd sweat too much sitting on the porch and his armpits would show it. As the chubby captain walked inside, he looked at his watch and hoped this wouldn't take too long; he had a tee time set for four so he could get nine holes in before it got too dark to find his ball on the fairway. Latham was proud that his handicap, thanks to playing almost every other day, was down to single digits. He often thought that by the time he retired, he'd be close to a being a scratch golfer.

Admiral Hastings looked up from the papers on his desk and greeted the captain, but did not invite him to sit down.

"Captain, I just finished reading your endorsement and strong recommendation for a court martial of Lieutenant Haman. I see it was accompanied by all the paperwork that would authorize a general court martial. Would you humor me with an explanation?"

"Yes, Admiral, sir. It is pretty simple. The lieutenant disobeyed a direct order from his detachment officer-in-charge, who was also his aircraft commander. Lieutenant Haman pushed Lieutenant Higgins away, which is the same as striking a superior officer, and took off after he was ordered not to go. The men of the detachment then kept Lieutenant Higgins in a small room near the hangar against his will. That constitutes mutiny. What happened on the mission, from a legal standpoint, is irrelevant."

"So you want to court martial him?"

"Yes, sir. Without a doubt. It will send a message to others who may hesitate to obey the orders of their superior officers."

"Do you really believe that is necessary?"

"Yes, Admiral, I do."

"Did you read the pilot disposition board's report?"

"I did, sir. They glossed over the legal aspects. They hung their hat on the fact that Haman thought the mission was authorized when he took off. But if you look at the *Sterett's* log, it wasn't. The note authorizing the mission isn't made until several minutes and entries later."

"Did members of the board have a legal officer advising them?"

"Yes, sir, they did."

"And his recommendation, comments were..."

"Sir, Lieutenant Nash, that was the name of the legal officer, is very junior. At the time, he'd been out of law school for less than two years."

"That does not answer my question, Captain. I was asking what did Lieutenant Nash write in the report? He was in the room for all the interviews as well as with the board during their deliberations."

Latham swallowed hard. "Sir, Lieutenant Nash's written opinion was that when Lieutenant Haman took off, he believed that the mission was authorized."

"By whom?"

"The captain of the ship."

Admiral Hastings sat back in his chair and then picked up several sheets of paper with a yellow note clipped on the top. "Do you know what this is?"

"No, sir."

"Captain, allow me to enlighten you. The handwritten note on the top was given to my boss, the Commander, Pacific Fleet by CINCPAC himself. It directs us to award a Distinguished Flying Cross or a Silver Star to Lieutenant Haman. I've been told to make the call on which medal. It also directs me to have the commanding officer of HC-7 write a meritorious fitness report on Haman and evaluations for the enlisted members of his crew that will be sent via the chain of command to CINCPAC for endorsement. He will send them to the Bureau of Naval Personnel with personal endorsements for inclusion in their personnel files. The rest is the paperwork needed to award medals, because each member of the crew is to be given a Bronze Star with a Combat V for the rescue. The medals are to be awarded as soon as possible. Now, do you still think we should go ahead with the court martial?"

"Yes, sir, I do. Sure, it was a great rescue in a difficult situation. But the medals don't change the facts of insubordination and mutiny."

"Captain Latham, I was afraid you would say that. Mutiny is a very strong word. So is cowardice. Have you ever stopped to think about the consequences if the court martial happened? As soon as the word got out, it would turn into a circus. A smart defense lawyer will take his case to two courts—the one we convene and the court of public opinion. I can just see the headline in the *New York Times:* "Navy court martials aviator hero". We'd spend weeks trying to get the egg off our face."

"Sir, I disagree. The public knows officers shouldn't strike their superiors, and they know what mutiny is. The facts will show that Haman was in the wrong."

Hastings shook his head. "Captain, this is the third or fourth time since I have been sitting in this chair that you've taken a legal position that, to be honest, wasn't smart, wasn't good for the Navy, and wasn't enforceable or legally defensible. By the way, I heard about your confrontation with Lieutenant Haman at Da Nang."

"I was there to tell him that he needed to prepare for his court martial and that in my legal opinion as CINCPAC's senior lawyer and legal officer, he will, in all likelihood, be found guilty."

"Captain, you had no authorization to tell him he was about to be hauled in front of a general court martial. That request wasn't even on my desk when you had that conversation. It was still on *yours!* You *assumed* it would be approved without even discussing the subject with me. I shouldn't have to remind you that orders to convene court martials have be approved and endorsed by me, and then by my boss, before we begin the proceedings or notify anyone that their lives are going to be turned upside down and inside out by a court martial. Your recommendation had not been approved at the time, and it has subsequently been denied. Just so you know, my denial is being endorsed by the Commander, Pacific Fleet and the Commander, Pacific."

Hastings stared hard at Latham, who was sweating profusely.

The admiral reached for a folder on the edge of his desk. "Captain, you were out of line when you went to see him and you went over the cliff when you threatened him with a court martial. You should have known better after 26 years in the Navy and 24 as a legal officer."

Admiral Hastings opened the brown file folder and looked at the papers. The top one was the endorsement from CINCPAC that had been delivered in a sealed envelope by a courier just after lunch.

"Captain Latham, you've had a good career, but I think it is time for you to retire. Turn over your case load to the rest of the legal team. That's an order. There's a letter in here signed by my boss making it official. I'll work with the bureau to get a replacement out here as soon as possible. That's my problem. I expect to see your resignation letter on my desk in 24 hours. You're being given 60 days of terminal leave, starting next Monday, and your retirement orders are in here along with the leave papers." Hastings paused as he put the papers back in the folder and handed it to the man who was now the staff's former legal officer. He noted that Latham was not able to conceal the shock on his face.

"Captain Latham, you are a good lawyer, but sometimes you lose your way. The Navy thinks it is time you move on."

"Sir, does this mean I am relieved as the Pacific Fleet's senior legal officer?"

"Yes it does. I suggest you use the terminal leave time to find a job with a law firm. It'll pay you a lot more than this man's Navy."

Hastings wished the knot in his gut and the churning in his stomach would go away. Ending a man's career is never easy. *But,* he reflected, *that was exactly what Latham had been planning to do to someone else.*

Tuesday, February 2nd, 1971,
1246 Local Time, Da Nang

Lying on the table was the draft of a message summarizing January's flight operations. Next to it, Josh had December's message as a reference, and he was using a piece of scrap paper to do the math. While he trusted Chief Bennington to add correctly, this way he could truthfully say, if asked, that he had indeed checked.

Josh was about halfway through the columns when the phone rang. He only started to pay attention after he overheard Van der Jagt say, "Yes, sir, he's right here and I'll get him."

Josh walked over to the phone and took the offered handset from Van der Jagt. "Lieutenant Haman."

"Josh, Captain Rainer here. I just got off the phone with my counterpart at the Army Special Operations Group. They've got an Aussie recon team that's on the run, and the Army Hueys can't get into where they are because of the weather. They wanted to know if you'd take a shot at extracting them."

"Where are they?"

"Right in the area where Cambodia, Laos and North and South Vietnam come together. It wasn't a secure phone, so he wouldn't give the coordinates."

Josh took a deep breath. Before he answered, Captain Rainer spoke again. "Josh, you don't have to go. They can't task us. It's an unofficial request."

"Sir, where can I get more info on this unofficial request?"

"Marty is pulling together what he knows about the area right now. If you're not going to go, I'll have him stop. If you decide to go, he'll brief you, and once you get to Pleiku someone from the Special Operations Group detachment from Kontum will give you the details. All I know is, we don't have much time to get them out."

"Captain, we'll go and do our best." Josh nodded to Van der Jagt, who grinned back

"Josh, thank-you. I'll let them know you're coming."

*   *   *   *   *

What had started out as light rain shortly after take off had turned into a deluge. The wipers on the H-3 were useless; they were flying on instruments at 90 knots and 3,000 feet.

"Josh," Bill alerted him, "the TACAN says Pleiku is thirty miles out. Do we have a plan yet?"

"So far all we know is that there's an Aussie SAS team on the run in the jungle. We're supposed to get a briefing from the Army folks, who supposedly know about where they are. Then we go pick them up."

"Sounds like the beginning of a plan, assuming that these guys have a clue where the Aussies are."

"They have to tell us three things before we take off, besides the radio frequencies and the Aussies' call sign. We need a way to authenticate that the guys on the ground are in fact the people we've come to get. Two, a relatively precise location, or at least where they were inserted. From Marty's briefing, that's right on the edge of the trail, which means lots of anti-aircraft guns whose gunners will think we are a big, fat, slow and inviting target. And three, how are they normally extracted? It's easier to rescue people in the way they practiced, rather than by trying to teach them how under fire."

"Amen to that."

"Big Mother 22, Pleiku Approach. You are cleared for the approach. Weather at Pleiku is five hundred foot overcast with moderate rain. Winds are three-two-zero at ten. Contact Pleiku Tower on three-one-zero-point-two after you pass the outer marker inbound."

Josh read back the instructions from the approach controller.

When they shut down on the ramp, Josh looked out at the streaming rain. *Moderate, hell!!!*

Kowalski dropped the passenger door and ran around to the starboard side to supervise the refueling. He was wearing a poncho, which meant he was going to get less wet than those who dashed for the nondescript van parked beyond the tips of the rotor blades. The good news was they were getting a bath in 85 degree air.

*   *   *   *   *

"This is a lot easier in daylight than it was at night," Bill commented. Josh was flying just a few feet above the trees at 90 knots, about100 feet below a ridge line.

It took nearly an hour to get to the area where they had been told the Dingo 5 Australian Special Air Service team was operating. Support was also on the way, call signs Dagger 77 and Nail 512.

"Josh, we're here. Or at least I think we're here."

"Call Dagger 77 and Nail 512 and see if they are in the area. We've got about five minutes until they are supposed to be listening. Everyone, I am going to fly around; let's look for clearings we can use."

Neither Nail 512 or Dagger 77 responded to their initial call. Then, just before they were going to try to reach the Aussies, a voice came on the air.

"Big Mother 22, Dagger 72 is orbiting about ten miles south of your briefed area at four point five."

"Hey, how'd he know our area? And, why is he using the call sign Dagger 72?" Bill asked.

"Good question, but we don't ask him. If it's a trap, based on intercepted messages or interrogation info, we'll know soon enough. Or it could be his new sensor monitoring orbit. For now, we stick with the plan and try to contact the ground pounders.

"Dingo 5, this is Big Mother 22 on fox mike. Do you copy, over?"

Over the radio came the sound of a new voice. "Big Mother 22, Dingo Five. G'day, mate." The accent was unmistakable.

"Dingo 5, Big Mother 22. Are you up for a helicopter ride?"

"Any time you want to take us."

"Dingo 5, tell me the best beach in Sydney, over?"

"Bondi, without a doubt, mate."

"Dingo 5, Big Mother 22, tell me why?"

"The sheilas, mate. Nothing better than sheilas in bikinis and cold beer."

"Dingo 5, who do you like to beat most in rugby?"

"Either the Pommeys or the Kiwis, take your pick. Now can you bloody well come get us? We can talk about rugby, beer and sheilas later!" The electronics of the radio transmission didn't do much to hide the speaker's irritation.

"Dingo 5, give us a slow short count, over."

The Australian complied with a slow count down from five to one and then back to five, with a one-second pause between each number.

"Got him" Bill informed Josh. "Twenty degrees off our nose to the right. Basically our two o'clock."

"Dingo 5, this is Big Mother 22, mark me on top. No smoke."

The two clicks told the crew of Big Mother 22 that Dingo 5

understood. Josh headed the helicopter toward a mountain top about five miles away to use as a reference point.

"Big Mother, we hear you. Now, now, NOW!!! You passed us on your left side about 50 meters."

"Dingo 5, stand-by." Josh climbed and turned. "Guys, did you get a good idea of where they were?"

"This is Bennington, sir. Not really. It's all trees. But there's a clearing where we could get them out by hoist, about 200 meters from where I think they are. If you swing around to the left, I can direct you over it."

Josh slowed the helicopter as they came close to the clearing and activated the radio again. "Dingo 5, can you hear Big Mother 22?"

"Affirmative, mate."

"Head toward me. Let me know if you have any trouble."

"Right oh. On the move."

Josh decided to try something. "Dagger 72, Big Mother 22. I need you to join me at my party to act as FAC. Use TACAN channel ninety-nine. Over." Josh pulled the top of the rocker switch back to speak on the intercom. "If he's real, he'll come back and acknowledge with a distance. If not, I suspect we won't hear from him again."

There was no response from their mystery caller. Instead: "Big Mother 22, this is Nail 512. I just arrived on the scene. Have four Sandys with me. We'll join you in about three mikes, and the Sandys will orbit out to the east, over."

Josh maintained a slow orbit in sighting distance of the clearing, 1,000 feet above the valley. "Everyone, there's eight of them, so that means three hoists, twice with one man on each prong of the jungle penetrator. The hoist is rated for six hundred pounds, so this will max it out. At about sixty seconds per hoist, that's a full three minutes. My guess is we're going to take some hits. I don't want to get shot down. Do what you can to suppress the enemy fire, and everyone, put on your armor. I don't want anyone going home in body bag. This could get really ugly."

Josh heard both the mini-gun and the M-60 as Van der Jagt and

Kowalski fired test bursts.

"We're ready in the back. I've got the hoist wire coiled and ready to throw out for the first pick-up," Bennington reported.

"Big Mother 22, Dingo 5. We're at the clearing, but we've had to dodge a bunch of gooks. Ready for pick-up. Understand torso harness is best."

"Affirmative. Be there in a minute. Use your D rings to clip on to the hoist."

Josh dove down to the tree tops until he was 100 yards from the clearing and then flared. As soon as the helicopter started down, Bennington called out, "Hoist is on the ground! First three hooking up."

A stream of tracers shot across the nose of the helicopter from left to right, answered with a clatter by the M-60. Bill grabbed the M-79 and twisted in his seat to fire grenades.

"First three are on board. Hoist going back down."

Ping, ping, pa-ping. Despite the noise suppression of the head sets, Josh could clearly hear the sound of bullets going through the skin of the helicopter. He pushed himself back into the seat between the armored wings on either side. The thick breast plate leaning against his chest was supposed to stop AK-47 rounds, as long as they weren't fired at point blank range.

Smack! Smack! Two hard punches struck his chest. The impact caused Josh's arms to twitch on the controls and the helicopter slewed drunkenly in its hover. He glanced down, looking for blood, and saw two small holes in the Plexiglas just above his feet.

"Steady hover, steady." Bennington's voice was as calm as if he didn't have a care in the world hanging half out of a helicopter 100 feet off the jungle floor, with a mini-gun spitting out rounds just over his head and the North Vietnamese doing their best to shoot down the helicopter and kill him.

"You O.K.?" Bill leaned forward, looking for blood.

"I'm fine, I think. Breast plate did its job."

"That's good to know." Bill went back to aiming the M-79. He'd already fired more than half of their twenty-four grenades.

"Second three are on board. Boss, we're taking heavy fire from the left rear quarter and Van can't get the mini-gun around that far."

"Nail 512, this is Big Mother 22," bellowed Josh over the radio. "Can you see the tracers? We're taking heavy fire and lots of hits from our six o'clock."

"Big Mother 22, Sandy 58 and 52 are rolling in with guns. Bad guys are much too close to you for anything heavier."

Ping, ping, SMACK. "Shit, I'm hit."

"Who's hit?"

"Kowalski, sir."

Josh turned his head in time to see one of the Australian soldiers pull Kowalski back and man the M-60. The young petty officer's flight suit was dark with blood. The Aussie started firing short bursts from the M-60 as if he'd been trained to do it.

"Last two on the way up. Let's get out of here," came Bennington's voice at last.

In the background, Josh could hear the mini-gun hum in two-to-three second bursts.

Josh sent the HH-3A climbing and accelerating before he keyed the mike. "Nail 512, Big Mother 22. When we get to four thousand, can you look me over? We took a lot of hits."

"Big Mother 22, Nail 512 is on the way."

Once they were clear of the area, Josh turned over flying to his co-pilot. Before loosening his shoulder harness, he spun the chest plate around and saw that not two, but three rounds had struck it. Turning around, he could see Kowalski lying on the floor with his left arm in the air. Bennington was kneeling by his side.

"Chief, how's Kowalski?"

"His left forearm is pretty mangled. I had to put a tourniquet on it just above the elbow to stop the bleeding. He took another round right on the edge of his armor that went into his pectoral area. I've got a pressure bandage on it and one on the arm."

"Josh, the fuel gauges are doing something weird...." Bill tapped the gauge for the aft tank.

"What do you mean, weird?

"Well, one minute it shows one thousand pounds, the next it's full, and then the it's down to a couple hundred. I saw the low fuel light come on as well. What do you think?"

"Maybe we took a lot of rounds in the aft tank, or a round hit the sensor, or a wire and it is shorting out. Chief, Van der Jagt, can you smell jet fuel in the cabin?"

"There's a faint smell, sir, a little stronger than usual. Give me a second and we can pull off one of the access covers."

"Bill, we're 20 miles from Pleiku. You keep flying and I'll give them a call and tell them we have wounded aboard."

"Do you want to go back and land in Kon Tum?"

"No, because once we shut this puppy down, it will probably be down for the count. If we can fly it, we go back to Da Nang. If not, we become guests of the Air Force and Army again."

The smell of kerosene filled the cabin. "Sir, we have some fuel sloshing around in the bay from the aft tank. Forward tank seems to be O.K. We must have been tattooed pretty badly in the belly. I could hear the hits."

"Got it. Thanks, Chief."

Friday, February 5th, 1971,
1046 Local Time, the Pentagon

Three levels below the main floor of the Pentagon, the room looked like any other military operational planning center. Maps were pinned to the walls and photos taped to charts and bare places on the wall.

Jeffrey Gainesville had been listening to the debate amongst the officers on how to get a reconnaissance team into the People's Republic of China. He heard the same ideas over and over again. Worse, positions were hardening as egos got involved. He decided to speak up; he could scarcely make things any worse.

"Captain Grainger, may I ask a simple, maybe even stupid question?"

"Go ahead, Jeff, fire away."

"Sir, with all due respect to the SEALs and aviators in the room, you're not going to fly the mission or be on the ground. Why don't we ask someone who does this for a living for their opinion?"

"May I assume that you have someone in mind?" Captain Grainger's sarcasm was almost as thick as the smoke-filled air.

"I do. He's in Vietnam right now writing the book on how these operations should be conducted. If anyone can figure out to carry this off, this guy can. And he even has the necessary clearance."

"Mr. Gainesville, we don't need any more theoreticians. We need a doer!" interrupted a Naval Intelligence officer known as Commander Tom.

"Sir, have you heard of the raid that acquired an SA-2 intact along with the electronics and a missile control van?"

"I have. The exploitation and analysis is going on right now at China Lake. They've also got a defector from the Soviet Anti-Aircraft Artillery who is explaining how the equipment is used."

"Well, sir, the officer who came up with the plan AND executed that mission is who I would like to get. And since he's busy, I suggest that some of us pay him a visit."

"Mr. Gainesville," Captain Grainger leaned forward to address him directly, "why don't you pack a box or two, then give him a call to let him know we're coming. And just where are we going, so the CNO knows when someone asks?"

"Da Nang."

Same Day, 1538 Local Time Honolulu

Latham gazed down at the summer white uniform shirt. He was standing in the spare bedroom of the three-bedroom apartment in downtown Honolulu that the Latham's had called home for the past two years. It was with sadness that he realized that now that his retirement ceremony was over, it was probably the last time he would take it off. He decided to leave it there with the shoulder boards, name tag and ribbons still attached.

Next to him was the last box of documents he had copied. If anyone had checked his briefcase when he left his office each day since being relieved, they would have had grounds to charge him. *But what could the Navy do? Retire me? Reduce me in rank?*

Beside the box was a hand written list of addresses of officers and men he thought were wrongly convicted of a crime, or run out of the service without what he thought was due process. They had been given the choice between a general discharge without benefits or a court martial, and they would be his first list of prospective clients. He figured that he had two months to find a law firm to take him on, and he could bank his pension. If worse came to worse, he could hang out his own shingle.

In the politically charged anti-war atmosphere in the U.S., all he needed was one case to embarrass the Navy. That would make his reputation. With his knowledge of how the Judge Advocate General office worked, he felt it would be easy. With that motivation, he started typing.

Chapter 13 – NEED TO KNOW

Monday, February 8th, 1971,
1852 Local Time, Beijing

It had been dark for almost an hour and a half when Colonel Vasily Raiskov walked into the bar at one of the nicer hotels in the embassy district. He thought it was humorous that access to the hotel by Chinese nationals was restricted. In fact, if one was a citizen of the People's Republic, one needed a special pass to enter.

By suggesting a meeting at the hotel, Raiskov would be able to determine if Chia had the influence, even power that he thought he did. It was also part of his attempt to wean Chia away from the protected environment of the restaurant where their early meetings were held.

The official brief on the brigadier general was that despite his young age, he had far more power and influence than a man of his rank should have. The GRU wanted to find out how much. Recruiting him to be a spy was out of the question, what they wanted was a man they could use to send and receive messages that were best kept out of diplomatic channels.

Some in the embassy thought he was married to the sister of a member of Mao's inner circle. If he was, the GRU could not find any proof no matter how hard it tried. The fact that, after a bit of hesitation, Chia agreed to have a drink with him meant that he was sure he could get permission.

The bar was just off the entrance and Raiskov took a stool where he could see door. They wouldn't talk at the bar, but it gave him a chance to get a drink under his belt before Chia arrived.

As soon as the Chinese general opened the doors, several hotel security people, who he assumed were plainclothes policeman, swarmed to block his path inside. As soon as the first one got close enough to see, Chia held up his identity card in one hand and the special pass in the other. Within seconds, the security people melted away and Chia saw the waving Raiskov.

With his glass of whiskey, Raiskov motioned to a table in the back. "Welcome. It is good to see you. What would you like to drink on the GRU's ruble?"

"A fifteen year-old, single malt scotch whiskey. I am told the bar has some."

Raiskov swallowed hard. One, drinks like that were expensive, which meant he would have some explaining to do. Two, where did Chia learn about single malt scotches and three, how did he know the bar had them?

Chia held up his glass, "Socialist comrades in arms." Their glasses touched.

Raiskov decided to ask a question that had been on his mind for months. *The man had a taste for things American. The steak dinner was one. His use of a knife and fork was another. And now, Chia knows the differences between scotches. If he did, then it confirms the fact that he is an up and comer in Chinese intelligence.* "Were you ever stationed at your embassy in Washington?"

Chia looked directly back at the Russian. "So Colonel Raiskov, what was so urgent?"

I think I saw a reaction in his eyes even though the muscles in his face didn't move. So the answer is yes. What's the harm in telling me unless he was undercover? I will have The Centre check out my hunch. It was not in my brief. "I have some interesting news for you. My country has agreed to ship you some of the latest generation Divinas. These are new models that have an infrared homing capability so that if the missiles' own radar is jammed, it still will find its target."

"Interesting. And when will we get them?"

"I am told that they, along with some additional launchers, will be shipped next month."

"We have heard that before and it took almost a year before the missiles arrived. Even then, they were missing parts."

Raiskov tried not to react. That was not an uncommon tactic by the Soviet Union to meet its commitment, yet use the delay to extract some extra concessions or use it to send in "technicians" who were really intelligence officers. In some cases, the, shipments were held up because the country could not produce the weapons that would pass inspection after final assembly. "This time, I am assured, this shipment will be different. The missiles will be delivered on time."

"Why?"

"Because my country wants you to deploy them in the south so you can shoot down American reconnaissance planes."

"So, I want to make sure that I understand the conditions. We are being given advanced versions of the Divina missile with the requirement we deploy them in the south and use them to shoot down an American airplane?"

"Yes, but the last part is up to your government. My government will give you the flight paths so you can be ready."

"If and when we decide to create an incident with the American Imperialists, it will be up to Mao Tse Tung to make that decision, not anyone in Moscow."

"I understand. I am just unofficially conveying my government's wishes which will be passed through official channels. We also want our tank back. We think this is a fair trade—a new version of the Divina missiles for a damaged tank."

Chia took another sip of his scotch. The glass was two fingers full when it was delivered, now it was only half that much. "So what do you hear from our socialist comrades in arms to the south."

That again. He won't give up. The Vietnamese have told us that they will not allow Chinese officers to visit any of their command centers under any circumstances, nor watch how they use the Divina missiles.

"General, may I be blunt?"

"Please do. Frankness between friends is always a good thing."

"They are more than reluctant. They have refused."

"That won't go down well with my superiors."

"I'm sorry, but that is the truth."

"You could cut off their supply of missiles."

"That is not an option. We cannot allow a socialist country to be bombed by the imperialist Americans and not help it defend itself."

"Then neither is shipping them to Vietnam through my country, nor is there any chance of getting your tank back."

"General Chia, I will pass that on to my leadership."

Chia swallowed the last of his scotch. "Deliver the messages the same way as last time. I must go, Colonel Raiskov. Thank you for the drink."

Wednesday, February 10th, 1971, 1746 Local Time, Da Nang

The four engine JetStar gleamed in its silver and blue paint that mimicked the paint scheme on Air Force One as it taxied to a spot right in front of base operations. The bright sun and the glare from the polished aluminum made it painful to look at without sunglasses. As the airplane was chocked and the engines wound down, Josh drove a van out to a spot just in front of the airplane's nose.

Jeff Gainesville's bent over body was making its way down the air stair behind a captain. Both were laden, and it was obvious that the briefcases they were carrying were heavy. The captain spoke before Josh had time to extend a welcome.

"You must be Josh Haman! I am Captain Stan Grainger."

"Yes, sir, I am. How do you do, sir!"

"Jeff has been bending my ear about how you are god's gift to helicopter pilots for the past fifteen hours."

"He lies a lot!"

The captain laughed. "We have three boxes that we need to get secured, as well as these briefcases."

"No problem, sir. We'll take them to our compound and get them logged in. We have a vault to store special intelligence properly."

"Good! What's next?"

"Sir, right after we store the classified material, we'll get you checked in at the BOQ and have dinner. We can start first thing in the morning."

"Why not tonight?"

"Sir, Lieutenant Cabot isn't here and we need his input."

"Where is he?"

"In Saigon with Captain Rainer. They were summoned by COMMAACV for a meeting. I'm expecting them back on the evening flight from Tan San Nhut."

"It is good to see you." Jeff Gainesville dropped the two boxes into the luggage area of the van and hugged his former roommate after shaking hands. "How are you doing?"

"Great. The detachment is my first command. We've had some excitement, but in a perverse sort of way, what we're doing is fun. And no one bothers us. They just tell us what the mission is and we figure out how and then go do it."

It took about an hour to complete the tedious process of verifying each box's inventory as they logged each item of classified material and then put the documents and photos back in the boxes to be stored in their vault. Then from the compound it was a fifteen minute drive to the officer's club and another ten before they got to a table in the corner. Beer, on the other hand, did not take long to arrive. After they clinked bottles, Jeff took a swig and pointed the top of his beer bottle at his friend. "I want to hear about the raid."

"I do too." Captain Grainger held up his beer bottle. "I heard through the grapevine that the Air Force had been telling everyone that it couldn't be done. I would have paid big money to be a fly on the wall when CNO briefed the rest of the joint chiefs."

it didn't take long to tell about the mission. Josh finished his account with, "The only bad news was that one of the '53s crashed, but we got the crew out."

"What's this I heard about a defector?" Captain Grainger asked, as he emptied his beer bottle and put it on the table. "The intelligence officer said we captured an officer who was familiar with the SA-2 system."

"We captured his whole launch crew: three other officers, a warrant officer and a sergeant. His name is Avram Mishkin and he approached me about defecting. The rest we put on a C-130 at Da Nang and flew them to Vientiane, where we turned them turned over to the Soviet embassy."

"How'd the van and the missile get back to the states so fast?" Jeff asked as their steaks arrived.

"We put them on the *Dubuque* because it had a flight deck big enough for two CH-53s. It took them to Subic, where I guess they were probably put on a C-141 and flown back to the states."

"How much enemy fire did you take?"

"Almost none. The *Newport News* chewed up most of the sites. I think we caught them by surprise. I'll show you the post-strike photos. It is pretty impressive. After we left, both the A-6s and the ship worked over the missile site just to make sure they won't be using it for a long time."

"Out-fucking-standing..." Captain Grainger signaled for another beer, and for a while conversation lagged as they all turned their attention to their dinner. After they had done justice to the steaks and baked potatoes, Josh addressed the captain.

"Sir, may I ask a question?"

"Shoot."

"I understand from Jeff's letters that you report to the CNO. Is that true?"

"It is. I am just one of many captains and commanders assigned to him to run special projects. Why?"

"Sir, in the days after we captured Captain Mishkin, I got to know him pretty well. He's a Latvian Jew and he defected, not so much to help us, but as the first step in his journey to get to Israel. Telling us all about the SA-2 was a means to that end. I made that clear both verbally and in writing to the officers who came to debrief him. He's a Soviet Jew, and if you don't know it, they are persecuted by the KGB just like they were by the Cossacks and the Cheka in the days of the Czars. The

NKVD seized his family's import/export business, evicted them from their home in Riga and forced them to move to Leningrad."

"So what do you want me to do?"

"I've tried to find out where he is. I gave him my parents' address and my FPO and told him to write to me and let me know if he needs help. Yesterday, I got a letter from him, and I think, from his description, he's at some base in the deserts of California and no closer to Israel. I made a commitment to him but I don't have the rank to help."

"He's probably at China Lake. Here's what I will do. I'll call the CNO and ask him to find out where he is and see when we can turn him over to the Israelis."

"Thank you, sir."

"With the agreement to do that good deed," Grainger stood up, "I think I will trundle off to bed and leave you two to chat about old times."

Friday, February 12th, 1971,
1030 Local Time, Norfolk

The Navy's sprawling base in Norfolk actually had two base commanders—an aviator for Chambers Field, the Naval Air Station, and a surface warfare officer who ran the base, with the senior of the two men acting as the complex's commander.

The commanding officer of the Naval Air Station's office had the corner office on the top floor of the base's administration building that gave him a panoramic view of the base's runway complex, squadron hangars, and the rework and overhaul facility.

When Higgins walked in, the captain's administrative assistant was not at her desk, having taken a vacation day to make it a four-day weekend and take advantage of the Federal holiday on Monday, February 15th. So he stood in the doorway and rapped on the molding. "Captain Brinley, you wanted to see me, sir?"

"Lieutenant, please come in and close the door." The captain pulled two folders to the front of his desk and stood up.

The documents had arrived Thursday form the legal office. Once he'd reviewed the contents, Brinley had told the legal officer that he would deliver the message personally. As a member of the Class of 1948, the contents made him sick to his stomach. It would have been bad enough if the man standing in front of him was a reserve officer, but to read this about a fellow academy graduate? It was beyond disgusting. Higgins was an affront everything he believed and to the men who gave their all in the service of their country. He knew what he was going to say was going to be unpleasant; he decided to get right on with it rather than beat around the bush and try to soft-pedal the message.

"Lieutenant Higgins, it is my sad duty to inform you that I have been directed by the Chief of Naval Personnel to inform you that you are to be separated from the Navy involuntarily, effective Monday, 15 February, 1971. You will be given a general discharge for administrative reasons and therefore will not be eligible for G.I Bill benefits."

"Sir, I don't understand." Higgins struggled to hold on to his composure.

"Lieutenant Higgins, this is difficult enough for me, so let me put this in words of one syllable that aviators can understand. What I am telling you is that you are being kicked out of the Navy. And the Navy wants you gone as soon as possible."

"But what about the psychiatric evaluation?"

"That has been cancelled."

"Why?"

"I think you know why." The captain looked down and picked up the second, much thicker folder. "You do have another option if you choose to accept it."

"What is that, sir?"

"A general court martial. Here is the paperwork ordering me to convene the board, along with all the charges listed. It also has a summary and a short description of the evidence against you that the Navy will present at your court martial. If you are convicted of any of the charges, you will spend a lot of time at Leavenworth."

"Sir, if I may ask, what are the charges?"

"I won't give you all the mumbo jumbo from the Uniform Code of Military Justice, but they range from knowingly falsifying government records to conduct unbecoming an officer, assault on a fellow officer, and the worst one, cowardice in the face of the enemy. I've read the specific charges and descriptions of the evidence. If I were a member of the jury, I would send you away for a very long time."

"Sir, I didn't do anything wrong."

"That's not what the Navy thinks. It is apparent to me that the Naval Investigative Service has spent a lot of time piecing together the evidence. It is pretty detailed and very damning. The trail of strong endorsements for the court martial if you don't accept the general discharge goes right up through the chain of command. It starts with the Commander in Chief, Pacific Fleet; the Commander in Chief, Pacific; the Chief of Naval Operations; and on to the Chief of Naval Personnel. What this tells me is that they are prepared to make an example out of you."

"Sir, so those are my only choices?"

"They are. Once we finish our conversation, I will escort you down to our base legal officer who will fill out the paperwork based on the option you choose. If you accept the discharge, you have to be out of the BOQ by Monday morning. If you accept the court martial option, then you will be restricted to the base and will have to muster in person four times a day at 0730, 1230, 1730 and 2130 at the base shore patrol office. Failure to do so will force us to put you in the brig until the court martial."

"Captain Brinley, how long do I have to decide?"

"The Navy needs to know your answer now. I don't like having this conversation any more than you do, Lieutenant Higgins. After you give me your answer, you get to sit with the legal officer and sign the forms for your discharge. Or, if you elect the court martial option, he will formally charge you and you can spend the next month or two preparing for your trial. The choice is yours."

The captain was wearing ribbons that indicated that he'd flown in combat in both the Korean and Vietnam wars. The top medal was the Silver Star with a small star on the ribbon that indicated he had won it twice. He considered the man standing numbly in front of him. "I'll tell you what. Have a seat in my outer office while I have a quick chat with someone. When I come back you need to tell me what you want to do. In the meantime, you might find this interesting reading." The captain handed Higgins the court martial authorization and endorsements along with the specific charges.

It was 20 minutes before the captain came back trailing a young lieutenant wearing the insignia of rank on one collar and the Navy's Judge Advocate General's office on the other. Higgins followed the captain into his office while the legal officer stayed outside.

"Sir, may I speak frankly?"

"Please do. But I must tell you, it won't change anything."

"I tried to prevent a mutiny, sir. My co-pilot disobeyed a *direct order* from me and took off on an unauthorized mission. I tried to prevent him from doing so and the rest of the detachment joined him and threw me to the deck and then confined me against my will."

"Lieutenant, I am not going to debate what happened with you. If you are convinced you are innocent, then take the court martial option. My advice to you is to accept the discharge and get on with your life. The way I look at it, you are getting a second chance even though you fucked up big time; this is one of the consequences of your actions. The other is that several of our fellow aviators are either in the Hanoi Hilton or dead because you didn't have the balls to attempt a rescue. Whether they come home or not, you will have to live with the consequences of your actions for the rest of your life–and so will they."

Captain Brinley, who'd led an A-4 squadron on two combat cruises, took a deep breath. He had to get an answer and get this man out of his office because he wanted to throw up. He didn't want to spend any more time on this very unpleasant task. "Lieutenant Higgins, which option are you going to accept?"

Saturday, February 13th, 1971,
1730 Local Time, Da Nang

By the time Jeff Gainesville and Stan Grainger were escorted into the planning room, the maps and charts from other operations were either removed or covered with black drapes. While they had the necessary clearance levels, they were not cleared for information on SEAL operations in Vietnam.

Two 4' X 8' sheets of plywood were placed in the corner of the room on makeshift easels to mount photos and maps. The briefcases and the three boxes were in a neat row on the table.

After the introductions, and after the cups of coffee were filled, Captain Grainger unsnapped the briefcase he'd placed on the table before he sat down.

"Before we begin, are these all the people who would be involved in planning a covert mission?"

Marty looked at his boss. "Sir, I think we need to get Chief Hausner in here."

"I agree. So, Captain Grainger what's the project?"

"It is Top Secret, specially compartmented intelligence under the code named Southern Charm." The captain from the Pentagon slid a pink self-copying form across the table to each individual. When he saw Josh's quizzical look, he took the time to explain that by signing this form, he was agreeing not to divulge, at the risk of criminal prosecution, any information covered under the code name Southern Charm. The terms of the form said that the restrictions would hold for the rest of his life unless declassified by the Department of Defense. "Welcome to the world of special operations. Sooo, fill this out and sign it. Then I will tell you more about Southern Charm and why Mr. Gainesville and I flew half way around the world to meet with you."

As each form was completed, Grainger looked at it, signed it, and passed the completed form to Jeff Gainesville, who slid them into a manila envelope. "Before you ask, no, you can't have copies. One copy will, however, go into your clearance file maintained by the DIA."

"O.K., so what's the mission?" Josh was already tired of the "I know something that you don't know" game.

"The president has authorized a mission to take a close look at two rail yards, putting people on the ground to see if they have trains carrying missiles into North Vietnam. There is, apparently, a vigorous debate on how many missiles are coming in, and from where. The Air Force insists that there is a second source via the two rail lines that come in from the People's Republic of China. The Navy disagrees with the Air Force. The Army says they don't have a dog in this hunt. The Air Force says it doesn't have the assets to execute the mission. The Navy got the short straw and has to carry out the reconnaissance."

Grainger took a swig from his coffee mug. "The rail yards that they want looked at are outside two cities, Nanning and Mengzi. Both are well inside the People's Republic of China."

"*Where?*" Josh blurted the word out in his surprise.

"You heard me, Lieutenant, the PRC, as in People's Republic of China."

"Isn't that what we have U-2s, SR-71s and satellites for?"

"Yes, but the photos they have been taking are inconclusive, that is to say, the Air Force can't *prove* their theory and we—the Navy—can't *dis*prove it. All the photos prove is that there are trains in the yards and sometimes, if they are flat cars, we can see what they are carrying. What the Air Force wants is for someone to look inside the rail cars."

Josh leaned forward, "So let me get this straight, sir. We have very specific rules of engagement that prevent us from flying or bombing targets within twelve miles of the Chinese border. If one violates them, we are subject to disciplinary action that could result in a court martial. Yet you want us to figure out a way to penetrate Chinese air defenses, not once, but four times on each mission—in and out for the insertion and in and out for the extraction. And if Marty and his guys get into trouble, then I have to do it when the Chinese Army is alerted that we're coming."

"We understand the challenge, Lieutenant. The restrictions for entering Chinese airspace will be waived for these missions."

"That's comforting! So if we make it there and back, we won't wind up in Leavenworth for the rest of our lives. If we don't, then we're either dead or the unwanted guests of the PRC."

Captain Rainer made a face and forged ahead. "Figuring out a way to fly in and out of the PRC covertly is why we're here. Your friend, Jeff Gainesville, said if anyone could come up with a plan on out how to get in and out, you were the man. So here we are. We will share everything we know and see if you can come up with something viable."

"Thank you for your confidence, Captain Grainger," Josh said evenly, unsure if he was being sincere or sarcastic. "*Viable* is the operative word. I think I can speak for Marty on this; neither one of us are into suicide or one-way missions."

"We're not intending to send you on one."

"Good, sir, because if I thought you were, I'd refuse to go. Having said that, I love a challenge. So the exercise is to figure out a way in and out. Then what?"

"We present the plan to the joint chiefs. They will review it and, if they like it, they take it to the president who gives the mission either a thumbs up or down. If it is up, you go."

"O.K., Captain, but I am going to lay out some ground rules, and they are non-negotiable. If you cannot agree in writing or if they are violated, then find someone else."

"Those are pretty strong words coming from a lieutenant."

Josh started to ignore the comment but decided to make a point by stating the obvious. "It is our asses on the line, not yours, not anyone's in the Pentagon, so we have the right to lay out some ground rules. So here they are. One, no messages of *any* kind from anyone to anybody about what we are about to do. Two, telephones are used only to schedule meetings, not to discuss the mission. Three, all briefings on the mission are face-to-face by the principals, who are in this case the two of you, Captain Grainger, Marty, Chief Hausner, Bill Braxton my co-pilot, and me. Four, Marty's team and my crew get to approve any changes that any, repeat *any*, senior officer wants to make, and that includes the President of the United

States. If we can't agree, then find someone else. Five, my crew and Marty's team get to volunteer after they know where they are going. If they want out, they can opt out with no harm to their careers."

Grainger's eyes narrowed with surprise and annoyance at Josh's demands. "You are pretty junior to be making demands that are not open to discussion of officers a lot senior to you."

"Sir, with all due respect, they are not demands, they are absolute requirements and there will be zero tolerance for errors and no exceptions. And, for the record, to restate the obvious and what I said before, if this mission goes, it is Marty's team and my crew's asses that are on the line. The rest of you get to go home at night and sleep with your sweethearts while we may be dead in some god forsaken rice paddy in China, or rotting in one of their prisons with little or no hope of coming home, not to mention being the ones who set off an international incident, and we all know how badly that could go. So, yes, Captain Grainger, they can be construed as demands or requirements. It just depends on one's perspective."

Captain Grainger looked at the other four-striper in the room. Rainer was smiling, and he decided to come to Grainger's rescue.

"Captain Grainger, Lieutenant Haman is absolute right. Secrecy is paramount. You also need to make some guarantees, such as if they are captured, the State Department does whatever is necessary to get them back. Or, if the shit hits the fan, the President of the United States directs the Joint Chiefs to move heaven and earth to help them. No guarantees, no go. I support that. I don't want any hand wringing about how we can't help these brave men. That's bullshit."

"I'll see what I can do."

"Captain, that's not good enough." Josh was on a roll and not finished. "You agree in writing on behalf of CNO to them right now or no planning, and you can go find someone else. If you want to wait until you can talk to him or he needs us to put this in writing, we can wait."

"I'll say this much, Lieutenant Haman, I admire your courage in telling me politely that it is your way or the highway. Type the letter and I'll sign it and get the appropriate approvals."

"Before you sign it, I want to tell you one more thing."

"This should be interesting. What else could there be?"

"Sir... there will be people who know about this mission even though they won't be going on it. If it goes bad and they find out that anyone violated the requirements, they will hunt those responsible for the security breach down. When they find them, these individuals will cut off their balls with a dull serrated knife before they kill them very, very slowly. Captain, that is not a threat, it is promise made by some of the people in this compound. You *don't* want to mess with them or screw their friends. They're very protective that way."

Monday, February 15ᵗʰ, 1971,
1640 Local Time, Da Nang

Over the weekend, the planners used a Tactical Pilotage Chart J-11, cut up and taped to a plywood board, to plot routes. The latitude and longitude of potential landing zones were indicated with pins, and string ran from each pin to a corresponding photograph of the area. The left side of the room was dedicated to the route to Mengzi; the right side showed the way they planned to get to the rail yard outside of Nanning.

Captain Grainger called the CNO to request the negatives so they could make enlargements of the rail yards, potential anti-aircraft positions and landing zones. A few hours after the call, the watch officer at the National Reconnaissance Office called back with the name of a petty officer who would act as both a courier and a photo interpreter, and his ETA at Da Nang.

On the table in front of him, Josh had the NATOPS manual held open to the charts used to calculate fuel burn with a loaded .45 magazine. He was using an E-6B circular slide rule to build a fuel table that was based on helicopter weight, airspeed and altitude when he heard the conference room door open behind him.

"Mr. Haman, I have a P-For for you." The enlisted man was standing the door holding up an envelope.

Curious, Josh took the envelope and sat down to open it. he

extracted a sheet of paper and began to read.

FROM: CHIEF OF NAVAL OPERATIONS

PERSONAL FOR: OFFICER IN CHARGE, HELICOPTER COMBAT SUPPORT SQUADRON DET 171

SUBJ: CAPTAIN AVRAM MISHKIN, SOVIET ROCKET ARTILLERY FORCES

(SECRET/NOFORN) BE ADVISED THAT CAPTAIN MISHKIN CURRENTLY IS PROVIDING VALUABLE INFORMATION IN HIS DEBRIEFING AT THE NAVAL STRIKE WARFARE CENTER, FALLON, NEVADA. HE IS NOW A MEMBER OF THE ISRAELI MISSION AT THE CENTER AND HAS AN ISRAELI PASSPORT SO THAT AT THE END THE DEBRIEFING, HE CAN TRAVEL TO ISRAEL AS AN ISRAELI CITIZEN. WE EXPECT HIS DEPARTURE ON OR ABOUT FEBRUARY 22. GREAT WORK GETTING US AN SA-2 MISSILE AND CONTROL VAN. WELL DONE.

Josh's loud, "out-fucking-standing" caused heads in the room to turn.

"Captain Grainger, thank you. Captain Mishkin is at Fallon and will be going to Israel shortly."

"Is that what is in the P-For?"

"Yes, sir, it is from CNO. Again, thank you."

Tuesday, February 16th,
1426 Local Time, New York City

The hotel in Manhattan on the edge of Greenwich Village was easy to find. Finding a parking place was not, because the hotel didn't have its own parking garage and most of its clientele came and went by cab. Higgins drove around the block several times before he found one, a few blocks away.

After he'd stuffed all his uniforms into a couple of large plastic bags, he'd been surprised how little was left. His civilian clothes fit with room to spare into his parachute and B-4 bags, which he decided to keep as his sole souvenirs of his four years at the academy and nearly four years as a Naval Aviator. It was when he looked at the partially full bags that he realized how rarely he'd worn anything other than a uniform or a flight suit.

Leaving the Naval Air Station, his first stop had been a thrift shop near the Naval Base that bought used uniforms. Higgins had headed north feeling as though a heavy burden had been lifted off his shoulders. He waved his arms and shouted. *He was out!*

Higgins sat on his bed in a room on the tenth floor and opened the *New York Times*. On page two of the first section, he read, and then sat up and re-read, a story that was on the top center of the page. One name stood out. Not finding the listing in the white pages, he tossed the four-inch thick book onto the bed, called Information, got the number and dialed.

The cab ride took less than ten minutes and dropped him off in front of a dingy-looking apartment building in the West Village. He pushed the bell next to the name and the buzzer opened the door. He then had to walk up eight flights of stairs.

A bearded man who needed a haircut opened the door and stared silently at him.

"Hi, I'm Steve Higgins. I called about half an hour ago."

"Hi, I'm Barry Winthrop, please come in. Over there at the table are Harry O'Brien and David Bernstein. Welcome to Vietnam Veterans Against the War."

Thursday, February 18th, 1971,
1356 Local Time, Da Nang

The four planners—Josh, Bill, Marty and Master Chief Hausner —spent the morning checking and rechecking the two sets of mission plans. Just after lunch, Josh put down the circular computer which he had been using to check their fuel burn calculations for the umpteenth time, and asked, "You guys ready?"

"Ready as we'll ever be," Marty said. "Let's bring the heavies in and see what they think."

Three chairs—for Captain Grainger, Captain Rainer and

Lieutenant Commander Gainesville—were lined up in front of one of the plywood sheets. On it was a chart of North Vietnam and Southern China covered by a sheet of Plexiglas. Two neat piles of photographs with notations on both the front and back were on the table. Once the men were seated, Josh stood before them.

"Sirs, before we begin, I'll cover some of the security precautions we want to take from this point forward. First, all the LZs have been given a name which is a brand of snow ski. Not something we expect anyone outside this room to know or think of. The lowest three digit number is the primary landing zone, and as one goes up in length, they become the secondary and tertiary LZs. In other words, Kneissl 195 would be a primary LZ and Kneissl 200 would be the next preferred one. From this time on, we will only use those terms when we talk about the LZs. We're the only ones who know the conversion from ski length to its actual location."

Marty, who was standing at the end of the board, could see the smiles on the audience faces.

"Second, conditions on the ground will be in terms of Marty's favorite sport, surfing. So, if he says surf's up that means things are good. We have others, and we will write out the explanations so that those involved in radio communications will know what we are talking about, but we think by the time the Chinks figure out the code, we'll be long gone. Plus, we see it as reusable because even if they figure out that a ski brand is a landing zone, they still don't know where it is."

Josh looked down at his list on the knee board he was holding in his hand. "Third, we're going to use a series of light signals on the pick-up. While the radio is usually a better option, for security the fewer transmissions the better. In reality, I think we'll probably use both and just minimize time on the air, because finding an LZ in the dark by dead reckoning is going to be difficult. And last, everyone will carry their green Geneva Convention cards and wear dog tags and nothing else."

The captain from the Pentagon jumped in. "What challenges do you foresee?"

"Captain Grainger, sir, these missions are not short on problems.

We'll get to them. But first, I want to share one important tidbit we learned about Soviet surveillance and tracking radars. The radars they use for the twenty-three, thirty-seven, fifty-seven and eighty-five millimeter guns supposedly can't track a target that is flying at eighty knots or below. There is a gray area between eighty and ninety. By the time you pass ninety, they can lock on to the helicopter."

"Josh, is that a fact or just someone's theory?" asked Jeff Gainesville. He had in mind several occasions when theory had translated inaccurately to fact—with deadly consequences.

"Sir, it is in the intel I've been reading. Most aviators gloss over it because a guy flying a jet has got other, serious problems if he is that slow. But the A-1 drivers know it because they can zoom up, slow to ninety or even eighty and still keep flying. It is not recommended, but they can do it. For us, I think we can turn it into a tactical advantage by keeping our penetration speed below eighty knots where we know they have radar coverage."

The captains exchanged a glance. "Good to know. Go on."

Josh stepped back to the map. "We'll brief both the Nanning and the Mengzi missions in two parts. I will go over the route in and out, as well as how we're going to stage the pick-up. Then Marty will cover the ground portion of how he will conduct the reconnaissance. Our preference is to do the sneak and peak at the yard outside Nanning first, and then Mengzi. Nanning is a shorter flight, and we think there are fewer triple-A positions, which reduces the time in and out. The bad news is that we have to take off and land from a ship which has to remain in the area until we go back to pick up Marty and his guys. The area is full of fishing boats and is close to Chinese territorial waters. If the Chinese fishing boats report seeing us, it may raise a few eyebrows in Beijing."

Josh looked at the chart for a few seconds. "Mengzi has warts of its own. To get there, we have to fly in and around mountains that are four to eight thousand feet tall. I can tell you that the H-3 won't be happy at those altitudes; it was designed to operate at sea level. The only good news about flying that high is that we burn a lot less fuel. The subject of fuel leads me to my second point about Mengzi. It is a long way from Udorn. To make the trip, we'll need the external tanks that are supposedly available for the H-3. They will give us about six hours flying time with a twenty minute reserve. That's enough to get there, but we'll be on fumes when we return to Udorn. So, to fly this mission with any kind of fuel safety margin, we have to get gas at one of Air America's landing strips, the Lima Sites in northern Laos. Or we can fly Air Force H-3s that can refuel in the air from a C-130. That adds some transition training on our part and would delay when we can go. Or, better yet, since they want to have a look at the sites, they can fly the mission themselves!"

There were smiles from the audience at Josh's reference to the Air Force's desire to have a look at the trains.

"Haman," Captain Grainger rejoined, "CNO wants this as a Navy-only mission. The Air Force said that they don't have the capabilities or assets to carry it out."

"Sir, that's bullshit. I think they don't want to fly it for the same reasons I am reluctant to go. With all due respect, from a flying perspective it will be difficult; the risk of something bad happening is very high. If Mr. Murphy shows up, you'll be sending letters out that start with 'Dear Mr. and Mrs. So-and-So, I have the sad duty to inform you...' And then, because of the classification, you won't be able to tell the families anything about why their loved ones are dead. Or we can become long-term guests of the People's Republic of China. I am not sure which is worse—spending a few years in one of their prisons after being tortured and beaten, or being killed outright."

Josh stopped for a few seconds. The thought was sobering, and he wanted the others to know the risks. "Anyway, if we get the go ahead, we need two sets of the drop tanks in case we have to dump them on the way in or out. Without at least two sets, the mission is a no go, simple as that. As it is, we're going to have to pick the route to save gas, and even then we're on the edge; we may have to stooge around to get to the LZ, or worse, fly around bad weather. Keep in mind that each mission means four trips through Indian country, two in and two out. Each time we go in, we increase the chances the Chinese will react and try to bag us, *and* capture Marty and his guys.

Each mission is on the margin of being doable. Both of us, given a choice, would prefer not to go. As I said before, they're very, very high risk. But if we go, here's how we plan to do it."

Heads nodded as Josh started to describe the route to Nanning.

Friday, February 26th, 1971,
0845 Local Time, the Pentagon

The Chief of Staff of the Air Force was ushered right into the office of the Chairman of the Joint Chiefs of Staff, who had left on his dark blue blouse with the gold braid around the sleeves and his medals under his wings. The Chairman pointed to the chair opposite his desk, rather than the couch that would indicate a more informal conversation.

"General, thanks for coming down on such short notice. I wanted to tell you that the guys at CINCPAC have gone over the plan to put a team on the ground in Nanning and at Mengzi and have given their thumbs up. I want to ask you, are you still sure you want to put a team on the ground just to look at railroad cars that we are pretty sure do not contain missiles?"

"It is the only way we can prove or..." The general paused before he used a word he didn't want to say. "...disprove our theory. So, yes."

"You realize, you are putting eleven men, five in a helo and eight in a reconnaissance team, at risk inside the PRC based on your service's skepticism of some pretty sound analysis based on really good photos."

The Air Force general stiffened a bit, but didn't say anything.

"I ask because I am going to the President and the National Security Council Monday morning to get their approval. If they say yes, then we will authorize the mission that same day."

"Admiral," the Air Force general was being formal, not using first names, just as his boss wasn't; this wasn't a friendly conversation. "When I am going to get a brief on the mission?"

"You're not. You don't have a need to know any of the details. You provided the mission tasking; the guys who are going to carry it out did the planning. The fewer people who know the details, the better. The team wants it that way and I'm okay with that."

"Is there an Air Force intelligence officer on the team that will be on the ground?"

"No. Our guys will know a missile when the see one."

"Then how can we be assured that they will be looking at the right rail yards?"

"Because the Air Force picked them. The sites have been photographed at the insistence of the Air Force, by Air Force U-2s and SR-71s, and Air Force Intelligence officers have said they are the ones the mostly likely to have missiles on the trains."

"Was anyone from the Air Force involved in the planning of the mission?"

"No." The admiral leaned forward and laid his hands palms down on the green blotter that covered the polished cherry wood desk. "General, you don't get to have it both ways. You can't claim that your boys can't do the job, demand that the Navy do it for you, and then insist to be in on the planning. And if you are looking for an excuse to crawfish out of this, I am not going to let you. This mission and the second source of missiles idea has been driven by the Air Force, not by the Navy, not by the Marine Corps, and not by the Army. Because I am not convinced this mission is necessary, I have prepared a letter that you will sign, acknowledging that you have read and received it. It will go in the files. If the mission goes wrong, it will go public; and you're going to have to take the heat and explain why the Air Force has been demanding it."

"I thought we all agreed to it."

"No, General, we are all going along with it because the Air Force is adamant that it wants to confirm its theory. We've used satellites, drones, U-2s and SR-71s, and so far *nothing* we've seen even remotely corroborates the theory. Other than lowering Air Force estimates of how many missiles have been fired, this is the only thing left. So, we're going to go in once to take a look at Nanning and then, if necessary, Mengzi. Granted, it is only a point in time, but we've collected enough intelligence to know when the yard is full, and that's when they will be there." The chairman paused again. "So I ask you one more time, do you want the mission to go?"

The General, who had been a World War II bomber pilot, took a deep breath. "Yes, sir, I believe it is worth the risk." He pulled the letter toward and took thirty seconds to read the two paragraph letter before he picked up the offered black U.S. government issued ball point pen and scribbled his name on both copies.

Chapter 14 – MISSIONS TO CHINA

Tuesday, March 2nd, 1971,

1935 Local Time, Da Nang

The two boxes that contained the planning material were now sealed and stored alongside the three original ones from D. C. in the vault. Everything had been boiled down to a folded up strip chart—one for Nanning and one for Mengzi—clipped to the kneeboard card: the fuel plans, the photos of the insertion and extraction LZs and their two alternatives.

Jeff Gainesville and Stan Grainger left on the a special air mission plane. The only thing left in the room was the Plexiglas-covered map, wiped clean of all grease pencil markings, and the two stands with 4' X 8' sheets of plywood that were now blank.

The last words the admiral leading the evaluation team had said to them was that they were to stand down until they heard whether or not the mission was a go, which meant there was nothing else for them to do.

Josh was coming back from another session on the gun range one morning when Captain Rainer handed him a form.

"You've been in country almost six whole, fun-filled months. You're eligible for your one-week magic carpet flight. Pick your destination and fill out this form. I'll submit it, and once we know whether or not your mission is approved we'll get it scheduled."

Josh headed for the planning room, nodded to Marty, who had the same blue form, quickly filled his out, then started writing a note to Danielle.

"Where are you going?" Marty.

"Singapore. You?"

"Hawaii. My wife Ma'i will meet me there. She'll probably get there before I do and stay longer because her folks live on the Big

Island."

"On a different subject, we should hear from Washington in a day or so. Marty, what do you think our chances of going are?"

"Maybe a little better than 70 percent. Based on what Captain Grainger said, some Air Force heavy wants this to happen and is applying pressure at very high levels." Marty sighed and rubbed his head.

"As for the sneak and peak itself, the odds of success are a lot lower. There are no real good places to hide, which is why I cut the time on the ground to four days. First night we insert and move to a hide, then it is a night's walk back and forth. A day for a contingency and then you come and get us. I have two worries. One, there is no bat phone I can use to call for help. That means, once we leave the helo, we are *really* on our own for four days. And two, getting there and back is going to be dicey."

"Yeah. There's not much triple-A there, but who knows how pissed the Chinese are going to be. It is not the insertion that is bothering me, it is the second trip in to pick you up. If the Chinese are halfway competent, they'll be waiting."

"Vacation is over, guys." Captain Rainer walked into the planning room. "I just got off the phone with the guys at CINCPAC. You're on your way. They've given you 72 hours to execute the insertion phase to Nanning. If you can't, we need to let the powers-that-be know it has been delayed and why. At that point, a determination will be made on when the next window will be. Courier arrives tomorrow with the sealed orders for the *Oklahoma City* and the *Sterett.*"

"Yes, sir, I'll go find Bill. We'll go up to the weather office and see what we can learn. My guess is that we go to the *Oklahoma City* tomorrow, take a nap, get gas and then head north that night."

Marty stood up. "I'll get the guys to start packing."

* * * * *

While they were sleeping, or trying to sleep, the *Oklahoma City* slid east to a position in the vicinity of 107 degrees, 40 minutes west longitude and 23 degrees, 30 minutes north latitude. It was not the first time the ship had been in those waters, so the North Vietnamese and the Chinese, if they were tracking the movements of the guided-missile cruiser, wouldn't find it unusual, even though it was only ten miles from the edge of the air defense buffer zone between the PRC and North Vietnam.

What was different this time was there were two helicopters on board. One H-3 had its blades folded and was pulled forward and tied down next to the Talos missile launcher. Another was parked on the helo deck. If the North Vietnamese could have read the dull black numbers on the matte gray paint, they would have seen its side number to be 22. And, if they looked closely at the nose on the left side, under the aircraft commander's window, they would have seen the silhouette of a sinking ship with its bow sticking out of the water. Under it was the date, 12-8-70.

After a routine take off, if one can call 'routine' lifting off in a helicopter that is several thousand pounds over its designed maximum take off weight from a blacked-out cruiser steaming 15 nautical miles from the country with the largest army in the world, Big Mother 22 headed north, 100 feet off the water. Bill Braxton took a moment to admire the brilliance of a half moon and a sky filled with bright stars before he went back to the task at hand—navigating.

"Josh, from here it is due north, zero-zero-zero until we go feet dry just west of the megapolis of Bai Long. If we hit our mark, we should pass about two miles to the west of the village and then it is only about 90 miles to the LZ. Based on the weather guesser's brief, we should see some high clouds around the time we cross the beach. How much they obscure the moon and for how long is unknown."

"Got it." Josh held the blacked-out helicopter to a steady 90 knots. He knew that ten miles after they crossed the beach, they had to make a dog-leg through a strip of mountains where low clouds could obscure the valleys. *So far so good. No fishing boats out at this time of night.*

They flew on in silence. The reflective blackness of the gulf transitioned to the uninhabited blackness of the land. The only communication between the two pilots were those needed to navigate. The pilot not flying kept track of the fuel burn and monitored the engine instruments. To give each other a break, they swapped flying every twenty minutes or so.

Bill peered into the darkness after looking at the map. "I just saw one vehicle on the road. It is heading away from us, so we should be safe crossing behind it, unless the Chinese drive around in the dark with no lights on."

Focused on flying, Josh merely acknowledged the comment with two clicks.

About 25 miles into the People's Republic, the passage through the notch in the ridgeline of the Shihwan Dasran mountains gave way to an open plain. Descending from the 3000-foot elevation, Josh kept the helo 100 feet above the ground and at 90 knots, confident that at this altitude the helicopter wouldn't be detected by radar because it was part of the "ground clutter."

"Well, let's see if the Chinese are broadcasting near the Nanning airport." Bill spun the crank on the ARN-6 receiver which could, if they knew the frequencies, let them listen to local Chinese AM radio stations. "We want to pass about three miles to the west of the airport and the beacon. Then we pop over the ridge and then a mile to the northeast to the LZ. We have less than 15 minutes to go."

Josh made a slight dogleg to the southeast to parallel a major road until he saw a break in the traffic and then crossed it, still holding a steady 90 knots.

"The beacon's not on, or if it is, we have the wrong frequency." Bill had been going back and forth trying different frequencies before he gave up and flipped the switch to the off position.

"O.K. We shouldn't need it."

"Josh, if we miss our turn point, we'll see the rail road and then we can turn back to the LZ."

"Got it." Josh keyed the intercom. "Marty, we're about ten minutes out. Good luck, my friend, and I will, God willing and the creeks don't rise, come back and get you and your guys."

"Thanks. Good luck on the way back. See you in four days."

"Josh, the LZ is on the nose in five miles."

But it wasn't. They had to circle around and find the wide draw in the ridgeline that was going to be the SEALs' hiding place. Down below, just before the contour lines on the Tactical Pilotage Chart showed the terrain flattened out, there was a large L-shaped wood that they'd found on one of the U-2 photos. Behind it, Josh pulled the H-3 into a hover and the SEALs went down the thick, three-inch-diameter manila rope.

"Sir, this is Chief Bennington. We got a thumbs up. All eight guys are on the ground safely. Let's go."

The route south, back to the safety of the gulf, was roughly 15 miles to the east around the eastern end of the Shihwan Dasran ridge and then south to the coast, crossing into the Gulf of Tonkin 11 miles to the east of where the helicopter had entered the People's Republic of China. They had been cruising for about 30 minutes when Bill spoke up.

"This is spooky. It is almost as if we were flying cross-country in the rural parts of the U.S. There are lights on in the villages and a few trucks on the roads, but no fire control radars, no air traffic control radars. The radar warning receiver hasn't made a peep. Where and when will Mr. Murphy try to apply his law and screw things up?"

"Maybe he doesn't have a visa to enter the People's Republic of China. How long to feet wet?"

"Eight minutes."

Three hours and just over 20 minutes after they took off, the HH-3A touched down on the familiar deck of the *Sterett,* which was the other ship holding the racetrack pattern. It was close to the spot in the gulf where they had launched.

Wednesday, March 3rd, 1971,
1041 Local Time, Beijing

The office Chia used was down the hall from the commanding officer of the General Staff Department of the People's Liberation Army. There was no name or title on the door. He had been selected for special projects while he was a member of the Second Department—

the Army's intelligence agency. After spending four years going to Stanford University, Chia had returned to the People's Republic and become one of the general staff's experts on the United States.

It helped his standing that his father was a survivor of the Long March of 1934-1935, in which Mao's forces escaped annihilation from the Nationalists. The 9,000 kilometer trek took them through the mountains of southern and western China to a sanctuary up near the Amur River in Shaanxi province. His father was one of the seven thousand survivors of the one hundred thousand people that started the walk. He'd emerged as one of Mao's trusted brigade commanders, which is why his son was allowed to go to the United States for four years. His own ability to get things done discretely and well was what got him promoted ahead of his peers.

Everyone around him knew that he was the equivalent of a major general in an army that supposedly had no ranks. With regard to his meetings with Raiskov, neither the general staff nor he wanted the Russian to know his real rank or position.

The phone rang; he picked the receiver up after the third ring and said one word. "Chia."

"Comrade Chia, I have someone on the phone from Guangzhou military region headquarters. He says it is urgent and that he was told to call you immediately."

"Put him through." Chia knew his aide and administrative assistant was a very good judge of what he should take care of and what needed the general's attention.

"Comrade Chia, sir. Last night, we had numerous reports of a helicopter flying in and around Nanning. I checked with all our local air force and army units and they did not have any helicopters airborne. All our helicopters are accounted for and there were no authorized flights, so we think it was an intruder."

"Did any of the observers who reported this mysterious helicopter actually see it?"

"No, sir, they did not. We only had reports from citizens who heard the rotor noise in the middle of the night when we are not normally flying."

"Thank you. Please call me if anyone in your region actually sees an unusual helicopter. However, until you are authorized to do so, do not shoot at it. That's an order. Do you understand?"

"Yes, sir."

Chia hung up. *So the Russian was right. The Americans are interested in our trains. I wish the Central Military Commission had not rejected my idea of creating dummy missiles and putting them on the trains. The Americans would have bombed them as soon as they entered Vietnam. That would have taught our comrades to the south a lesson, and maybe gotten us the visit we wanted.*

Saturday, March 6th, 1971,
2213 Local Time, on the U.S.S. Sterett

The *Belknap*-class destroyer was pitching and rolling in the swells as it plowed through the Gulf of Tonkin, which was being beaten up by a squall. By the time they climbed into the helicopter, Josh and the rest of the crew were soaking wet. It had been a tough three days, not knowing if their friends in Gringo 6 were alive and waiting for pick-up, dead, or being tortured in a prison. No messages could get through, so they manned up, hoping that an hour and 42 minutes after they lifted off the *Sterett* they would be landing in a meadow someplace south of Nanning and helping their friends on board.

Just as the rotors engaged, Josh felt the ship heel over and then steady up on a course that put the gusty winds 30 degrees off the port side. Despite its size, the ship corkscrewed as it plowed through the quartering sea. The movement was very noticeable on the helo deck, 40 feet above the water.

Before he'd boarded the helicopter, Josh had talked to the watch officer, who'd estimated the winds over the flight deck would be 20 knots, gusting to 30. The wind speed was just at the outer edge of the rotor engagement window. Until they picked up speed, the gusts could cause the blades to flap up and down and hit the helicopter's tail pylon or the deck.

The good news was that they would need less power to lift off the helo deck. But a sudden gust could cause the helicopter to drift, and there was only six feet of clearance between the tips of the rotor blade and the hangar. Hitting the hangar with the rotor blades could result in them all dying in a fireball on the flight deck.

To take off safely, Josh raised the collective quickly. As soon as the helicopter became light on the main mounts, he eased the cyclic to the left to keep the blades away from the hangar.

Once the H-3 was safely airborne, the *Sterett* headed west; the *Oklahoma City* would pass it about five miles to the south as they exchanged positions. The cruiser had a better equipped hospital, as well as another helicopter which could be used as a search and rescue bird once Big Mother 22 was close to the Tonkin Gulf. Its crew was forbidden to cross the beach into the People's Republic; however, Josh was confident that, if needed, they would come a few miles inland. The question in the back of his mind was: what's a 'few'?

The rain got heavier as Big Mother 22 headed north, airborne at cherubs two and 90 knots. Just after they went feet dry, the water beating on the windshield slowed, then stopped ten minutes later. As they came out from under the cloud deck, Josh could see stars in the clear sky overhead. The route north this time took them through the same pass, but instead of going directly north, they made a westerly dogleg for 12 miles and then headed straight for the landing zone, hugging the terrain at 100 feet and covering the flat ground at a mile and a half a minute.

Twenty minutes later, Bill, who had been examining the blow up of the landing zone with his flashlight, announced, "Everyone, keep your eyes peeled for a light. I've got the FM radio tuned to the briefed frequency, and the UHF is on the standard Search and Rescue channel. Josh, if we see the next road, we've gone three miles to far."

"Big Mother 22, Gringo 6. You just passed us. We're at your four 'o'clock, about a mile."

Bill clicked the mike twice while Josh rolled the helicopter into a 60-degree bank and then steadied. The soft glow of a white light was then replaced by two green flashes and a steady red.

"That's them."

Josh flared the helo and let it descend so that the wheels on the main mounts were just touching the ground, then added enough power so it would not settle because he was afraid they would sink into the soft, rain-soaked earth.

Thirty seconds later, Bennington slammed the back door shut. "Everyone's on board. Go, *go*, **GO!!!**"

Once they were headed south, Josh turned the flying over to his co-pilot and turned in his seat to look back into the darkened cabin. Marty's face glistened with slimy wet mud that Josh guessed he was using to make sure his white face didn't show in the dark. "How'd it go?"

"Walk in the park. There's no real security in the yard. We got into dozens of box cars and they're all stuffed with ammo. It's no wonder that the NVA has plenty to shoot. We found everything from pistol to 85-millimeter artillery rounds, along with hand and rocket propelled grenades."

"Any SA-2s?"

"No. We looked at four trains that either came in the yard or were there when we arrived. No SA-2s no SA-2-related equipment. I wish we were allowed to leave behind a little C-4. The yard would burn and explode for days!"

"Anybody see you?"

"Not that we could figure out. We got sniffed by a couple of scrawny stray dogs and stumbled across some wild pigs, but that's about it. The trains arrive in the early evening and shut down. I think they switch crews because just after sunrise they chug on out. The scariest moment was yesterday morning when one of those fabric-covered bi-planes flew over the ridge and then circled the area where we were hiding. After that, we put our Claymores out and expected trucks to disgorge hundreds of Chinese soldiers. We were prepared to fight it out, but no one came."

"Get any pictures with the infrared cameras?"

"Yeah, we used up all twelve rolls of the film we brought with us. The Air Force is going to be disappointed."

Sunday, March 7ᵗʰ, 1971,
1953 Local Time, Madison, WI

The large late spring snowflakes quickly covered the grass and then the sidewalk. By the time the Higgins family finished dinner, the snow was three inches deep.

"What was in the package from the Navy?" Robert Higgins settled into his favorite chair in the den after he shared the remaining wine with his son.

"My discharge papers."

"You still haven't explained to me why you got out of the Navy so fast. I thought your commitment was a full four years after you finished flight training and they weren't giving academy grads early outs."

"It is, but I got out early."

"Did you get accepted to law school?"

"I did. With my grades at the academy, my test scores and because I am a veteran, the school fast tracked my admission. Officially, I start in the fall, but I am going to take courses this summer to get ahead of the game. Money will be tight, but as long as I can live here I'll be able to live off my savings."

"What about the G.I. Bill? That should at least cover the tuition and give you some spending money."

Steve Higgins looked down. He'd been dreading this conversation with his father, who'd been a combat engineer until an artillery shell filled his body with shrapnel, six days after he landed at Anzio in January, 1944. Even to this day, almost 30 years later, he didn't take off his shirt in public because he didn't want to answer questions about the jagged scars all over his side and back. "I don't get G.I. Bill benefits."

"Why not?"

Steve gave him a short, stylized, and slanted précis of what had happened. At the end of it, his father was holding his head in his hands and he was no longer looking at his son.

Finally the older man looked up. His eyes looked both tired and sad. "Steven, I don't think you are telling me the whole story, not that

I want to hear it now. Son, I know that the military doesn't just kick out an officer, particularly a graduate from one of the service academies, with a general discharge for administrative purposes and deny veterans benefits without a very good reason."

The former Army captain had been awarded a Silver Star and a Bronze Star for his actions clearing minefields and obstacles under fire on the first day of the landing, plus a Purple Heart for his wounds. He said, "There has to be something deeper. From what I know, they offer a discharge of this type with no benefits in lieu of a court martial or some other type of legal action. My guess is that you were given that choice and took the discharge. Am I wrong?"

Steven Higgins, former Naval officer and Aviator, didn't answer.

Robert grimaced as if he were wounded again. "You didn't make rescues because you were afraid. That makes the person living in my house masquerading as my son a…"—Robert Higgins paused for a few seconds because the word was hard to say—"… coward."

The older man rubbed both his temples and didn't hear a denial. "I don't like what we are doing in Vietnam. It is the wrong war with the wrong mission, but anyone who puts up his right hand and takes the oath to serve makes a commitment to his country to do his duty. What happened to you? Where is the young man full of pride in his uniform, his service and his country?"

Steve looked up. "Dad, that person is dead. He died off the coast of Vietnam."

Robert Higgins stood up slowly, using the armrest for support that he would not normally need, and headed for the door. "That discharge and what caused it will haunt you the rest of your life. And I have to live the rest of my life knowing the son I raised and love is a disgrace to his country, his service and to his family."

Monday, March 15th, 1971,
1330 Local Time, the Pentagon

The Chairman of the Joint Chiefs of Staff was sitting at the head of the table as the others arrived. In front of him were five manila envelopes. As each officer arrived, he acknowledged their presence.

When all four service chiefs were seated, he looked up, smiling.

"Gentlemen, before we get to our agenda, I have some good news. Thirteen of our finest servicemen accomplished a unique feat of intelligence-gathering. A week ago, a Navy helicopter flew 120 miles into the People's Republic of China and deposited eight SEALs on the ground, who spent the better part of four days watching a rail yard outside of Nanning. At the appointed time, the helicopter picked them up and flew them back out. No one got a scratch and there was not a round fired in either direction."

He looked around the table and saw three broad grins. The Air Force Chief of Staff barely forced a tight-lipped smile. The chairman began to slide the manila envelopes around the table. On purpose, the Air Force Chief of Staff got his last.

"In the envelope is a sample of the infrared pictures the SEALs took. While there, they inspected five trains that were either in the yard when they arrived or came in during their mission. As you can see, there was lots of ammo, medical supplies, and artillery pieces, but no, repeat *no* SA-2s or any related missile-handling equipment in the yard or on the trains."

"This doesn't mean they are not using this route, it only means that they weren't there when the SEALs were there." The Air Force general had spent most of World War II in the U.S. until he was sent to Europe—*after* the Allied Air Forces had wrested control of the air from the Germans.

He continued, "While this was a very good operation, the Air Force was not involved in either the planning or the execution of the mission, nor the interpretation of the photos. Bottom line, I think what they brought back is, well, inconclusive."

The chairman's eyes got icy cold and he clasped his hands in front of him as he reminded himself that these meetings were supposed to be collegial. "General, a copy of the written report by the SEALs is in the envelope. I suggest you read it."

"I will, and I will also ask for Air Force Intelligence to give me their input. My gut feeling is that we're going to have to go back again every so often so that we can verify that the Chinese are not allowing the missiles to go through their country."

"General, you don't give up, do you? Every shred of evidence we have suggests that the only way the missiles are getting into Vietnam is via ship. None, repeat none, have ever been seen at the rail yard outside Ha Giang in Vietnam, nor in Nanning in the PRC. Mengzi is the only other possibility."

"And it is my understanding, Admiral, that we are planning a mission there as well."

"Yes, we have a mission plan and all it needs is presidential approval for them to launch. It is a much more difficult mission because the yard is at extreme range of the H-3."

The general smiled at this opportunity to make a point about the unique Air Force capability. "Navy H-3s have that limit. Air Force H-3s, which can be refueled in the air from Air Force C-130s, do not."

"General, if I remember correctly, in this very room, you said that the Air Force doesn't have the spare assets to take on a mission of this type. So the tasking for both the air and ground portions went to the Navy. They've done an outstanding job."

"We still really don't know one way or the other."

The Admiral slammed his palm down on the table. "What do you want us to do, station men inside a neutral but hostile country to inspect their trains?"

The Air Force general realized he had just crossed a line.

"General," the Chairman took out a single sheet with the presidential seal in the upper center. "The president authorized one mission to each location. No more. We're half done. This letter I am about to give to you in front of four witnesses comes from the president of the United States. In a nut shell, he orders you to use every, and that means *every* means and aircraft in the U.S. Air Force inventory to get those guys out if something, God forbid, goes wrong on the mission to Mengzi. That means no excuses. It means every asset, airplane and member of the U.S. Air Force will be committed to getting them out or die trying. If it means you fly the plane, then you do it. Is that clear?"

"Yes, Admiral," the general replied stiffly, "it is crystal clear. The Air Force will do its part."

The chairman slid the piece of paper to the Air Force General. "I hope so. The original letter is in the classified archives of the president. The fact that you have received this letter will be in the minutes of this meeting."

The Air Force general looked at the single sheet, but did not touch it.

"So, General, do you still want that mission to Mengzi?"

"Yes, sir, I think we don't have a choice. We have to go."

"Are you sure? My bet is that we don't find anything."

"Sir, my recommendation is that we go. We have to determine if they are using the railroad. Air Force intelligence is convinced that they are. We just have to find those missiles."

"What does he mean, 'We'? murmured the Chief of Staff of the U.S. Army to his Navy counterpart, who grimaced.

Friday, March 19th, 1971,
0746 Local Time, Da Nang

Captain Rainer was still trying to get his blood pressure down after reading a message from someone inside the Navy's Supply and Logistics command. It requested a detailed explanation of why his unit had far exceeded its allowance for ammunition for training purposes. The author of the message noted that until a satisfactory answer was received, the unit would not be authorized to order ammunition or explosives. He started to pen a sarcastic answer when the phone rang. he picked it up. "Rainer."

"Karl, Stan Grainger here. Good morning."

"I guess it is good evening in D. C. How are things there? Are you on the golf course yet?"

Grainger chuckled; both of them knew that Pentagon tours for Navy captains meant long hours during the week and lost weekends researching the answers to what were often dumb questions. "Never a dull moment. This will take just a minute, but I thought I needed to give your guys a heads up."

"What's going on? Do I need to switch to a secure phone?"

"No, I don't think so. CNO just passed the word that your guys need to stand down for about a month while some folks think about the second trip."

"O.K., we can do that. We've got other work they can do."

"No they can't. CNO was very specific. He wants these guys on the shelf until the go/no-go decision is made. They're not to participate in anything that involves risk of capture."

"Stan, I can send them on their R&R trips which will keep them all out of harm's way. The paperwork is already in the system."

"Good idea, Karl. What do you need?"

"Let's get them priority for flights and funding to go now."

"I'll get Gainesville on it right away. Black shoes are good at paperwork drills!"

Chapter 15 – NOT SO MAGIC CARPET

Friday, April 3rd, 1971,
2033 Local Time, Singapore

The candles on the small table were half gone. Their flickering light in the light spring breeze wouldn't be noticeable to any passer by eleven stories below, but to the two diners, they lit a romantic dinner on the small balcony.

Josh put his chopsticks down, the bowl picked clean of Hunan chicken, vegetables and rice. "Danielle, it has been a wonderful week. I can't tell you how much I enjoyed it." He was about to get into the discussion that both had been avoiding for most of the week. But, Josh knew it had to happen.

"So, what's next? I'm half way through my first of two years out here. I have lots of leave, and I want to keep seeing you and no one else."

"I feel the same way," Danielle replied slowly, "but I don't want to make any commitments until I know my parents and younger sister are safe. My brothers have good jobs in Bangkok, but the rest of my family is still in Laos. That's why the embassy is allowing me to go to Vientiane next week. I have long stay visas for my parents and sister for Singapore. I *have* to convince them to get out. I keep telling my mother if she leaves, she can always go back but my pleas fall on deaf ears. I want to give it one more try."

"In your heart of hearts, do you think they'll leave?"

"No. My father wants out, but he won't leave my mother."

"When are you leaving for Vientiane?"

"Monday."

"When will you be back in Singapore?"

"In a week, I hope. At most two weeks. The embassy doesn't want people there unless they have official business. They are doing me a favor because they all know my father."

"Will you do me a favor?"

"What is it?"

"The moment you arrive back in Singapore, write me a letter and call that number I gave you to leave a message for me. I won't be there, but I will get it. This way, I will know you are safe. Please promise me you will do this."

"I promise I will do that."

"Thank you." Josh leaned over the table and kissed her.

Wednesday, April 7th, 1971,
0717 Local Time, Laos

The noise and concussion from exploding mortar shells rattled the house and sent everyone scurrying. Danielle grabbed her sister's hand and they dashed down the stairs and out to the Citroen parked under a small shed. Jacques Debenard, carrying a Danish-made Madsen submachine gun and a bandoleer of ammunition, ran through the house looking for his wife and peering cautiously out of windows. As smoke made it harder and harder to discern shapes, he glimpsed indistinct forms heading towards one of the shed, and followed them.

Shrapnel from exploding mortar rounds sang over Danielle and Gabrielle's heads and smacked into the wooden beams with dull thuds. Mortars ripped jagged holes in the metal that protected the car from the rain and sun. They lay flat on the ground, waiting for the barrage to stop. Looking over her shoulder, Danielle watched as two shells crashed through the roof and set the house on fire.

"Where's mother?" Danielle asked her father appeared and crouched by the car.

"I thought she was with you!"

Danielle turned toward the house and saw her mother stagger from the burning frame of what was left of the building, her body engulfed in flames. She took a few steps and then collapsed to the ground in hail of bullets. Danielle ran toward her mother, oblivious to her father's scream to stop and to the bullets flying in both directions, some from the Loyalist forces occupying the plantation, others from the Pathet

Lao, and some, she suspected, from her father trying to give her cover.

Danielle got within a step of the prostrate form that was her mother when she felt an agonizing, burning pain in her left thigh and realized that she was falling. She fell next to her mother's smoldering body. Danielle remembered her father holding her, saying *Everything will be all right.* The last thing she saw were Pathet Lao soldiers standing in front of her father and 15-year-old sister, pointing their AK-47s at them.

Friday, April 9th, 1971,
0836 Local Time, Da Nang

Josh was at the SEAL facility, sitting at one of the two desks in the room that his helo det used for an office. The other gray steel desk was pushed against the far wall so that the Selectric typewriter's cord could reach the wall plug without an extension cord. It was used by the Detachment 171 yeoman who handed all the personnel and administrative paperwork, as well as sorting, typing and filing the messages that came in droves every day.

The room was large enough to accommodate all 14 members of the det. Its other benefit was that it had a phone that went through the Da Nang switchboard, which gave it a link to the outside world. With it, they could make official calls. Some were to Cubi to get the latest squadron gossip or ask for stuff to be put on the daily flights between Cubi and Da Nang; most of the calls went to Da Nang's huge supply depot, which carried most of what they needed and could order what they didn't have.

From memory, Josh dialed the number of Det 1 in Cubi. On his list was an urgent request for a box of molybdenum disulfide grease cans. Da Nang was out, and without this special type of grease they were, after the next ten hours of flying, grounded.

"HC-7 maintenance office. Petty Officer Davis speaking. This is not a secure line."

"Davis, this is Lieutenant Haman. Is Senior Chief Slaughter around?"

"Yes, sir, he is out in the hangar someplace. But before I send someone to find him, sir, I got a phone call this morning from the French embassy in Vientiane…"

Josh's heart raced. "What did she say?"

"Sir, it wasn't a she, it was a he and he said he was the French Ambassador to Laos. When I told him you weren't here, he asked me to give you this message. His exact words, sir, were 'Danielle Debenard and her father Jacques were taken prisoner by the Pathet Lao two days ago. The embassy is doing everything they can to get them back but as of the moment, their fate and whereabouts are unknown.'" The young petty officer paused. "Does that have anything to do with the missions Det 171 is flying, sir?"

Josh couldn't see for the tears running down his cheeks. He forced himself to say "No, Davis, it doesn't. Please tell Senior Chief Slaughter to put a case of moly D on the next plane to Da Nang. We're out. Something has come up. I gotta run." He put the phone down and it was all he could do to keep from throwing up. *Goddamn this war. I told her it was too dangerous. Now I may never see her again because they'll see her as French, not Laotian.*

Monday, April 12th, 1991,
0906 Local Time, Washington, D.C.

His new office was small, but it was in the trendy Georgetown area of Washington DC and belonged to a well-known firm of litigators. Through the window that took up nearly three fourths of the back wall, the new occupant could see the Potomac River between a gap in the buildings. The room had a freshly cleaned smell that was accentuated by a faint whiff of furniture polish.

A contemporary wooden desk finished in a dark rosewood stain nestled against the wall opposite the entrance. Behind the desk was a matching credenza that had two rows of file drawers that ran the full length of the wall and whose top was just below the window sill. It was perfect place to put the few pictures he'd brought with him. Catty-corner to the desk was a small table and two side chairs finished in cordovan leather. This office, bigger than any he'd had before, was one of many set aside for partners at Loeb, Feinberg and McKinley.

A passerby looking in the window would have noticed that the occupant was overweight and had close cropped hair. His brand new suit was large enough so that it would button around his belly without straining. When he took off his coat, it revealed that his pants were held up by a pair of red and black suspenders that complimented his tie and contrasted with his starched white shirt. His cloisonné cufflinks had a bright blue background with four gold stars arranged in a diamond.

He studied the files in manila file folders that were packed into the two boxes and began to load them, one by one, into the hanging folders already in the top drawer of the credenza. A third box contained a clock and several framed pictures from his past life that went on the top of the credenza.

Loeb, Feinberg and McKinley was a small law firm of litigators who liked helping those they referred to as "the little people" wronged by big corporations or government agencies. The senior partner, Chad Loeb, liked to tell prospective clients that they were a law firm that liked causes. They picked only those cases that interested them, preferably one in which the defendant had deep pockets. To take on a new client on a contingency, two of the three partners had to vote yes.

The firm was very successful and had an unusual philosophy about bringing in new talent. Rather than continually add partners as their reputation and revenue grew, they added only a select few who were, after they proved themselves, paid very well. But they were partners in name only; all the decisions were made by Loeb, Feinberg and McKinley. Anyone who wanted ownership was free to go to another firm.

At the last official partner's meeting in March, the three had been all smiles when they reviewed the balance sheet. Bonuses for the first half of the year were going to be very nice. The founders took sixty percent of the bonus pool, the other attorneys who divvied up 35 percent of the bonus pool would be grinning ear-to-ear at the high seven-figure numbers. The remaining five percent went to the administrative staff.

The healthy profit margin allowed the firm to take on selected pro-bono cases in keeping with their ACLU background. Some of these cases led to larger law suits that paid well in contingency fees. Their most recent pro-bono cases had been defending draft dodgers and two anti-war activists who tried to burn down a Federal office building. That work got the firm excellent publicity—the lawyers they beat would call it notoriety—that served to further the reputation and influence of Loeb, Feinberg and McKinley.

The partners were ambivalent about the war, but if it generated high-paying work for the firm, great. If not, there were plenty of other sources of clients. The partners—Chad Loeb, Saul Feinberg and Andrew McKinley– felt that draft dodgers had interesting stories, but they wanted something more.

After the financials had been reviewed, Chad Loeb, the senior partner, had tossed a letter on the table. "I think we've found our next challenge and a new line of work." The result was a new brass plaque with the name engraved and filled with black ink beside the door of office where the new occupant was unpacking. It announced him as *Lester Latham, Associate Partner*. The word 'Associate' would be removed after he proved himself by bringing in new clients and generating revenue.

Already on his desk was a draft of a letter to fellow ring knocker Steven Higgins that outlined why he thought he had a case against the Navy. Latham knew that Drysdale and Danforth were close friends and had been Academy roommates for three of the four years they were at Annapolis, and he was sure that under cross-examination, they would admit that they'd discussed the board's findings before it was released. This would invalidate the board and its recommendations. Therefore, Latham reasoned, any actions taken by the Navy against Higgins were based on a biased board and consequently invalid. Therefore, Higgins was entitled, according to his logic, to an apology, a revised discharge that would give him VA benefits, and a substantial monetary settlement, some of which would wind up in the Loeb, Feinberg and McKinley bonus pool.

Tuesday, April 13ᵗʰ, 1971,
1146 Local Time, Da Nang

Despite three aspirin, Josh's head felt as if the pounding behind his eyes meant that his head was going to explode as he emerged from the small bunkhouse where the officers slept. His dark aviator glasses hid his blood-shot eyes and minimized the pain the bright sun was inflicting. The night before he had drunk half a bottle of scotch and another one of bourbon before he'd passed out, still dressed, on his bed.

He wanted to be alone and didn't want to talk to anyone, so he volunteered to make the trip to base operations to meet the flight from Cubi and get the case of molybdenum disulfide grease cans. The day before, only a couple of cans had arrived, with a note that they would send a full box the next day.

He hoped by the time he got back his headache would have subsided. If not, he planned to take a jog to work up a sweat and purge his system. It would also allow him to be alone.

The headache didn't subside, but it didn't stop his mind from coming up with the outline of a plan during the run. After a shower, he walked over to the main building. His head still hurt, but the pounding was definitely lessening.

"Bill, what do you think of taking an all-expense paid trip to Laos?"

Braxton regarded his flight commander with some concern. "Josh, let me remind you that other than routine maintenance flights, we're grounded?"

"I know that, but we're not going to take the H-3. There's a daily flight from Da Nang to Vientiane. We can go there, meet with the Air America guys, and get them to fly us up to Prabang Luong to check it out. All we need is a set of official orders. Technically, I can write them. If you want, we can ask Rainer to endorse them."

"So you want to go into a town where it is tough to tell the good guys from the bad guys without a score card? Do you really want to go that bad?"

Josh swallowed hard and in a soft voice said, "Yes. I'll go by myself if you don't want to come."

"No, you'll need some adult supervision. Before we go, let's get Rainer's approval and then I'll cut the TAD orders. This way, we'll have our asses covered. How long will we need?"

"Make them for five days, but we'll really only be gone for three. I've got a number to call to coordinate things with the Air America guys in Vientiane.

"Where did you get that?"

"Base ops. I talked to the pilot of the C-123 that makes the daily trip and he said there is always room for two more guys. He said the Air America pilots are always looking for a reason to do something other than carrying food and supplies. I'll ask them to fly us around to look at the Lima sites. With orders and a day's notice, we can get reserved seats, and since we're pilots, we can ride on the jump seats in the cockpit."

"Why do I think there is more to this trip than just going to take a look at a Lima site in northern Laos?"

Thursday, April 15th, 1971,
1948 Local Time, Vientianne

Josh wasn't surprised that no one from the Laotian government came out to met the C-123. In addition to their dog tags and green ID cards, both Josh and Bill had their passports stuffed in the back pockets of their jeans. In an odd sort of way, Josh wanted his passport stamped because it would be the only proof that he'd been to Laos.

After a twenty minute ride from the airport, during which the Air America driver used a combination of horn, steering, throttle and braking to keep from hitting traffic that ranged from water buffalo-pulled carts, bicycles, mopeds, and scooters to cars and large trucks, they stopped under the hotel's portico. The brochure said it had been built as a small luxury hotel in 1932. Fading, peeling paint suggested that the hotel had seen better days. It did, however, have a pool; and, from what he was told by the American driver, a four star—by Laos standards—restaurant that served classic French food with a Laotian twist.

They had nothing to do until the morning; they had been instructed to be ready to leave the hotel at 1100 for a flight to Prabang Luaong, just under 100 miles due north, then 100 miles to the east to Lima site 36, and then another 100 or so back. The driver made no mention of what type of airplane they were taking, he just told them to be in the lobby at 1100 ready to go.

Fragrant smells of basil and sesame from the hotel's La Belle Epoque restaurant filled the lobby and wafted through the open windows of their fourth floor rooms. After dinner, Josh suggested they take a walk through the hot, muggy air and find the road that ran along the Mekong River that separated Thailand from Laos. From one of the riverside food vendors, they got brown bottles of cool, but not icy cold, Thai Singha Beer.

After he took a sip, Bill faced his aircraft commander and tapped him gently on his chest with the top of the bottle. In his South Carolinian drawl he demanded, "Josh, what's eating at you? You haven't been the same for the past few days. Impatient, grouchy, curt, rude would all be words to describe your behavior. It can't be because this is the day your tax return is due, because we don't have to file taxes while we are out here. So what gives?"

Josh had been wondering how long it would take for Bill to say something. He had tried to shove Danielle's capture into a locked compartment in the back of his mind, but every so often like a cuckoo clock, it snuck out and had to be pounded back into place. Apparently, he hadn't done a very good job of concealing the struggle.

"Danielle, her father, and I am guessing her sister and mother, were captured by the Pathet Lao last Wednesday."

Bill swallowed hard, gently put the bottle on a nearby table and slammed the heels of his hands into Josh's chest. Josh, at just over six foot and 160, was a good 40 pounds less and a couple inches shorter than his co-pilot. The impact caused him to stagger back.

Bill came forward with fire in his eyes. "So, the trip to Prabang Luaong and Lima 36 is just a cover for a reconnaissance. You want to mount your white horse and go rescue her. Is that it?"

Josh made no move to defend himself. "No, not exactly. I want to see if I can find out where the Pathet Lao are holding her and her family. Then I'll figure out what I'll do next."

Bill loomed over his boss, who had also become his friend. "You do know that the Pathet Lao execute any American pilots they capture. Not hold, not turn over to the North Vietnamese after they torture them. No, they execute, as in kill!"

"I know."

Braxton poked a finger at Josh's chest. "Then why are you—no, why are *we* here? You're not suicidal."

Josh kept his hands at his side, not wanting to further aggravate his co-pilot. "I was not trying to deceive you. You didn't ask. But you're right, I should have told you. Look, I want to do something. Sitting around at Da Nang, not knowing whether she is alive or dead, is eating me up."

Bill retrieved his beer and took a swig. "So what's the next step? You're here, I'm here. We've got two, maybe three more days."

"I have an appointment tomorrow at nine a.m. with the French ambassador to see what I can learn. He was more or less expecting a call from me. After that, I don't know."

"You should have told me. I don't like being deceived."

"If I told you, would you have come?"

"Probably, but I would have liked to know why." Bill tapped Josh's chest with the top of his beer again. "Let me decide, not you. Look, when we fly these missions, we have talked about the risks and understand them. That way, I get to know how, what and why, and I get to make suggestions. In other words, I know what the fuck is going on and I, not you, decide whether or not I am going. This is different. You didn't tell me the real purpose of this trip. The trip to the Lima sites is a side show. And, to be honest, I'm pissed, really pissed, because this is a major breach of trust. You're lucky I don't beat the shit out of you."

"I'm sorry. I thought I offered you a chance not to come."

"No, you didn't. All you asked was if I wanted to go. We are, whether you like it or not, part of a crew, who, by the way, will follow you to hell and back. All you have to do is tell them the mission, let them have their say, and launch. This was selfish and stupid. It is obvious that I have to be the adult in the room. But here's the odd part. I am glad I am here so I can, hopefully, prevent you from doing something *really* dumb. "

"Like what?"

"Like going off and trying to rescue Danielle all by yourself. You *will* need help. Marty and the boys are just a few hours away and would, if given the opportunity, leap at the chance."

"Understood. So do you want to come with me to the embassy in the morning?"

"Sure, why not? I won't understand a word, but you can translate, and we'll see how good your French really is."

Friday, April 16th, 1971, 0900 Local Time, Vientianne

It didn't take long to wind their way from the hotel to the French embassy, whose large, tri-color flag flying over the entrance made it easy to find. On the way, Josh was surprised by how few men in uniforms there were for a country involved in a civil war and by the number of Europeans on the streets. Listening to some of them speak when they stopped for traffic, he knew that they were not just Frenchmen or Americans. He also heard German, and was not surprised to hear Russian as well. As they walked up to the embassy, Josh guessed that the older parts of it dated back to the late 1800s, after the French carved the current country out of what used to be known as Siam.

The outside building on the appropriately named Rue de la Mission had seen better days. The paint on the foot-thick wall surrounding the building was fading noticeably—Josh figured that the French didn't want to spend money updating building that they may have to abandon soon. The steel gate that blocked the driveway also was in need of a coat of paint. It was guarded by two armed French soldiers.

Josh suspected there were more soldiers on the grounds who

remained out of sight but were ready to respond to an attack. On either side of small guard post next to the main gate, there were two lines. In front of a sign that said *"Visas,"* a long line that snaked around the corner. No one was in the line below the sign that said *"Visiteurs."*

A soldier checked his passport against a list of names on a clipboard, and after Josh told him that Braxton was with him, the soldier held up his hand.

"Monsieur Haman, attendez une moment, s'il vou plait. Quelqu'un du bureau de l'ambassadeur vient de vous escorter."

Josh wasn't surprised that the soldier didn't attempt to speak English when he told him to please wait, someone from the ambassador's office was coming to escort him. He translated for Bill, then thanked the guard in French. Standing just inside the gate gave Josh time to admire the garden, which was manicured to perfection. *Interesting set of priorities*, he mused, comparing the well-maintained garden to the state of the walls.

Their escort arrived a diplomatic five minutes later and led the two Americans through several corridors and up a flight of stairs to usher them into an office that was larger than many living rooms. It was furnished modestly; Josh guessed the furniture had been made from local woods by local craftsmen. Their guide suggested they have a seat at the small conference table and said the ambassador would be there in a few minutes. Somewhat to Josh's surprise, this proved to be the case, as two men entered the room.

"Bonjour, Lieutenant Haman." The ambassador was a short, dark-haired man, impeccably dressed. "Allow me to introduce Colonel Henri Pantenaude, our senior military attaché." He spoke in French, and Josh responded in the same language.

After exchanging introductions and shaking hands with the ambassador and the French colonel, both Americans sat back down.

"You are here on official business, yes?" The ambassador had switched to his guests' language; like most Frenchmen, he clung to the idea that French was the language of diplomacy and love, and English was the language of business. "Allow me to say how sorry I am to hear about Danielle. She told me about you. I gather you spent time together in Singapore."

"Yes, sir, we just spent a week together."

"Ahhhhh, *amour*. It does cloud things a bit." The ambassador paused and sighed wistfully as he spread his arms, then clasped his hands in his lap in a gesture of futility. "We will miss Danielle. She was a very capable interpreter whom we had just promoted. And I have known her father for many years. He was awarded the *Legion d'Honneur* twice, along with many other decorations. Alas, we do not know what happened to them, only that a staff member at the plantation called the embassy to inform us that they were captured during a battle between the Royalist forces and the Pathet Lao. Why the Pathet Lao were there, we do not know. Then plantation was well south of where the main fighting is. On the other hand, the North Vietnamese have a sanctuary in Laos. Perhaps they thought he was a security risk."

"Sir, do you know if they were killed?"

"He was sure they were taken alive. That was a week or so ago. Anything could have happened since then. The Pathet Lao do not like westerners and often they kill them for no reason."

Josh nodded his head. "*D'accord, monsieur ambassadeur.* I know that. Do you know in which re-education camp the Debenards are being held?"

"Lieutenant, you are not here planning a rescue mission of the Debenards?"

"*Non, monsieur ambassadeur,* we are not," Josh forced himself to say calmly.

"*Bon.* No attempt should be made for the simple reason we do not know where they are or if they are still alive." The ambassador nodded to the colonel to indicate it was his turn to speak.

"Lieutenant Haman, if I may. We know that the Pathet Lao take captured foreigners to several small camps just west of the Vietnamese/Laotian border. Right now, they have several hundred Europeans, mostly French, Belgian, Swedes and Germans who were working in Laos and who got swept up in the war. They do not allow the International Red Cross or diplomats to visit those camps, or we would know their exact location. All we have is a general idea that we get from the locals who are afraid of the Pathet Lao. Finding out who is at which camp is impossible without going to each camp and meeting each prisoner."

"What do they do with the foreigners?"

"If they don't kill them outright, not much. At first, if they think they know something valuable, they will interrogate them. Then, they try to extort money from their employers or families. But beyond that, nothing. From what we have heard, they live in poor conditions. They grow their own crops for food that is enough to keep them alive. Very little medical care or medicine is available to them."

"Why don't they just release them?"

"Good question. I wish I knew. Well, they are Communists, and that explains a lot."

Josh heard condescension in the colonel's voice, but these same Communists had kicked the French out of Indochina and were killing lots of Americans. "Colonel, are they holding any Americans?"

"None that we know of. The Pathet Lao kill most of the Americans they capture. The Pathet Lao think that even the Americans working for the Agency for International Development are really spies working for the CIA. For that reason, and the good work that they do, they kill them."

"How do you know about these camps?"

"Because every year or so, the Pathet Lao release a few people, generally after it is clear that their employers are not going to pay a ransom, or if they get a lot of money. These former prisoners suddenly show up in Vientiane, knocking on the door of their embassy, or if they don't have one, ours."

"How many camps are there?"

"We think at least three." The French colonel leaned forward. "The people whom they release give us the names of others that are held at their camp, but they are not sure of the location because they are blindfolded until they get to Vientiane."

"Do any of them try to escape?"

"Yes, a few have, but unlike your Dieter Dengler, they don't make it. Some are re-captured and shot to discourage others from attempting, others disappear into the jungle and are never heard of again. No one has ever come to us after escaping."

"Colonel Patenaude, how well do you know Jacques Debenard?"

"Very well. I served under him before he retired when I was a very junior *sous-lieutenant*. Since my posting here, I have come to consider him a good friend."

"Do you think he will try to escape?"

"He will consider his options very carefully. The Pathet Lao know who he is and how well regarded Colonel Debenard is by Laotians. They may see him as a threat, because if he ran for public office, he would win. The easiest thing for the Pathet Lao to do would be to just shoot him, but I don't think they will. He is held in much esteem and they could demand a high ransom for him. Or they might decide they need him. After this war ends, Michelin will listen to him. If Debenard says he can get the rubber plantations running again, they will give him the money to do that. Knowing Jacques as I do, I am certain he will not leave his family, so if he thinks that they will not survive in the jungle, then he will stay with them in the camp."

The French ambassador put his hand on his military attaché's arm and addressed Josh. "Lieutenant, if I may. I have phone numbers where I can reach you. If you want to give me an address or more phone numbers, we will keep them on file and will call you as soon as we find out anything. In the meantime, I suggest you go back to your squadron. There is nothing you can do here in Laos, other than get captured, or worse, killed. Either outcome would lead to... unpleasant consequences."

Josh nodded, taking the ambassador's point and realizing the meeting was over. There was nothing more they would or could tell him.

Same Day, 1707 Local Time

Josh was grinning as he climbed out of the back seat of the piston engine Helio Courier. The Air America pilot, a former Naval Aviator, had let Josh fly up to Prabang Luong and then had coached him through his first landing in an airplane with a tail wheel. The airplane swerved a bit as it slowed, but Josh had managed to keep it pointed down the runway.

The trip eastward to Lima 36 took nearly an hour. Before Josh made his second landing, the pilot let him circle the valley and pointed out the helipads up the side of the mountain, as well as the runway in the valley. After a quick stop to go to the bathroom and get something to drink, Josh climbed in the back seat so Bill could fly the 40 minute leg back to Vientiane.

As they were thanking the Air America pilot, a man whose gray hair was evident despite a high and tight haircut walked up to the two Naval Aviators. "Good afternoon, gentlemen, I'm Ralph Randall. Please follow me."

Josh knew an order when he heard one. The two officers followed the man into a small room in the back of one of the hangars used by Air America. Inside, Randall half sat on the only desk in the room and rested his palms against the edge.

"For the record, I run things around here. When I found out you were coming, I made a couple of phone calls. What I was told was simply *Do what they ask and give them what they want*. Not many people gets that kind of blanket clearance, and only when it is really important. Then my good friend Colonel Patenaude called me while you were airborne. So, do you two care to tell me what this is all about?"

Josh looked at his co-pilot before he provided a *Reader's Digest* version of the meeting at the French embassy.

"Lieutenant," Randall said, looking directly at Josh, "Jacques Debenard and I are very good friends. We go back a long way, to when he was in the Legion leading a regiment here in Indochina and fighting the Communists. Just like you, I am pissed at what happened. Trust me, everyone here at Air America, the CIA and the Air Force wants to find him and, if we can, free him. And every swinging dick around here who every met Jacques' daughter has been trying to get in her pants, without success, I might add.

Patenaude told me you seemed to be the exception to that rule. That being said, I am going to spell this out for you: finding and freeing him and his family is not, let me repeat that word, NOT your job or mission. We have enough to do around here without having to chase after a pussy-whipped Naval Aviator looking for his long-lost girlfriend. Do I make myself clear, Lieutenant?"

"Yes, sir."

"Good. I am glad we understand each other." Randall levered himself up onto the desk. "With regard to the matter that actually IS your business, I have arranged for you to meet with a Colonel Lee from the Nationalist Chinese Air Force after this chat. That's not his real name, but he is the commander of their 34th squadron, called the Black Bats. Their mission is to penetrate the People's Republic's air space on electronic and photo reconnaissance missions. If anyone knows anything about where I think you are going, he does. He may be able to give you some tips."

Josh didn't say anything; he didn't want to confirm Randall's hypothesis. His visits to Prabang Luaong and Lima 36 were enough to confirm an educated guess.

"Once you finish your chat with Colonel Lee, you will climb on-board a waiting Turbo Porter which will take you back to Da Nang. Right now, my driver is packing your bags and paying your bill when he checks you out of your hotel. Consider your stay on the house. Your bags will already be on the plane when you get there. Should you try to go *anywhere*, do *anything* other than what I described, after I order a search party, my next call will be to Captain Rainer, as well as to senior officers in the CIA. By the time we find you, assuming you are still alive, your Naval careers will be over. And by the time you land in the U.S. your administrative discharges will be handed to you and you will not be eligible to join the Reserves or get any VA benefits. Again, am I clear, or do I need to repeat myself?"

"No, sir." The words were spoken in unison.

"Excellent. Now, assuming you get on the Turbo Porter, this conversation and the one you are about to have did not happen."

"Yes, sir."

"Good. Just for the record, I was once a junior officer and tried to do stupid things. An O-5 or two had to slap me around a couple of times to knock some sense into my head. I survived and went on to bigger and better things. So will you. By the way, I have heard good things about you two or we would never have had this meeting."

Chapter 16 – DIVINE INTERVENTION

Thursday, April 22nd,
2019 Local Time, Over Laos

Glancing back into the cabin from the dimly lit cockpit, it looked like a black hole. With the helicopter blacked out, all visibility ended a few feet from where Josh was sitting; he could not see or hear any of the eleven men back there.

Outside, there was no moon and no clouds. Stars, because there was no ambient light, shone brightly. As Josh scanned the horizon, he marveled at the sheer beauty of the twinkling pricks of light that were an unfathomable distance away.

"Hi ho, hi ho, it is off to work we go," Bill warbled.

"Why are you so cheerful?" Josh was relaxed as he kept the H-3 at 1,000 feet and 90 knots. It was on autopilot, but he still kept his hands on or near the controls.

"I'm enjoying what I hope will *not* be my last day of flying and freedom."

"What do you mean by that?"

"We're tempting fate. We got in and out two times without a round fired. I would like to think, but know better, that no one saw us. Both this trip and the one to bring the guys back have warts all over them. Simple things like distance. If the transfer from the aux tanks fails, we do not make it back. We have only six hours and twenty minutes from light off to flame out. And I just hope the jet fuel we just picked up at the CIA Lima site in Luang Prabang doesn't clog our fuel filters. "

"Bill, the CIA guys assured me the fuel they fly in has the same rate of burn to match our calculations. And refueling at Luang Prabang, which is one hundred and ten miles closer to Mengzi, gives us a healthy reserve."

"I know, but I'm the designated worry wart of the detachment. Keep in mind, *I* did the fuel plan."

"Yeah, you were the one who was all excited and happy that the fuel charts said that at the higher altitudes we'll burn ten to twelve percent less fuel. For the four hours we'll be above the mountains, that's four to five hundred pounds of fuel, which translates to another half-hour of flying."

"Yeah, but what if the charts are wrong?"

"You can always complain to Sikorsky and the guys who did the testing when we get back!"

"You mean *if* we get back." Bill looked down at the chart. "We just passed over the Mekong River again. Maintain a heading of zero-one-five until we get to the mountains. We're now in uncharted territory, almost literally." He raided his voice and spoke as if he were a radio deejay. "Aaaand welcome to the PRC. This is the last country on our four-nation trip that started five hours ago in Thailand and takes us on a night sight-seeing trip by air over Laos, North Vietnam, and now the People's Republic of China."

Josh looked over his shoulder again. He knew, without seeing them, that the eight SEALs were sitting on the floor with their backs against the cabin wall, four on each side of the mini-gun ammo tray. Marty was the closest with his back to the "broom closet" where the hydraulic actuators for the main rotor blades were located. It was his usual position. He was wearing a set of Mickey Mouse ears with a boom mike he could use to communicate with the helicopter's crew. And, Josh knew, even though his eyes were closed, Marty was not sleeping. Josh suspected the SEAL was reviewing every aspect of the mission.

Glints off the reflective tape on their helmets told Josh that Bennington and Van der Jagt were well back in the cabin, sitting on one of the canvas bench seats. Just behind him, Petty Officer Third Class Billy Kelly, the replacement for Kowalski, was sitting on the step between the pilot and co-pilot seats. After Kowalski had been wounded, Chief Bennington went back to Cubi Point for a day to select a replacement. What had surprised Josh was that there was no shortage of volunteers. Chief Bennington had picked the nineteen year-old kid from Tennessee because of his attitude, and because they needed another ordnance man to replace Kowalski.

Marty stood up and Kelly moved over so Marty could stand between the two seats, or torture thrones as Josh often referred to them. The backrest joined the seat pan at a ninety degree angle, and after about three hours sitting in them, one's back hurt. After four hours, no matter how you shifted your body in the seat, there was no way you could get comfortable. The seats and the shock absorbers mounted on the frame were designed to lessen the chance that a pilot would break his back in a hard landing, not for comfort.

Bill Braxton shone his red lens filtered flashlight on the map and keyed the intercom. "Marty, we have about fifteen minutes to go."

"Thanks. We'll start getting ready."

"Josh, just so you know, we're good on the fuel burn. Roughly halfway through the flight, and we're almost two hundred and fifty pounds to the good. So, I guess the NATOPS manual is accurate."

Josh clicked the mike twice. "Marty, do you want go out via rope or a low hover and a jump out?"

"Rope, if you think it is faster."

"I do. We don't know how much shit the rotors would kick up. The satellite photos show a mix of dirt, grass and rocks."

"Rope it is from forty feet. Chief, did you copy?"

Two clicks of the mike acknowledged the choice.

"Marty, we'll be at the LZ in less than ten minutes. It's show time."

"I just hope we don't end up doing show and tell for the local PRC garrison commander."

Josh glanced back at his friend. "Marty, remember, we're coming back to get you. So be on time! Good luck. See you in four days."

As they traversed the valley, Josh looked down. "Shit! There's a village there with lights on." Seconds later, he turned left along the ridge southeast of Mengzi.

Bill pointed out the window. "LZ at eleven o'clock. Engines are spooled up to the max."

"Got it." In the thinner air, the helicopter responded more slowly than he'd anticipated. Josh had to flare hard to keep from overflying. The HH-3A came to a stop, forty feet above the rocky ground. A quick glance at the torque gauge told him that he still had some, but not much power to spare.

Bennington had his head and shoulders out the cargo door so he could see the area under the helicopter. "SEALs going out... All out. I got a thumbs up from Mr. Cabot. Let's go."

Josh used the remaining power to accelerate and climb. Grinning, Josh turned to his co-pilot and gave him a thumbs up, then called over the mike, "Okay crew, it's three more hours to Miller time. By then, Mr. Braxton and I will have a severe case of fanny fatigue."

Friday, April 23rd, 1971, 1526 Local Time, Mengzi

Chia gazed upward, craning his neck. The observation platform 70 meters above the ground had been built so engineers could look out over the marshlands north of the city. From that elevation, one could see which gates had to be opened to control the water levels in the two man-made lakes and turn the land into fertile rice paddies. But it would be a month or so before the rice seedlings were planted.

He was here with several officers of the People's Liberation Army to reconnoiter.

Before he began the climb up the steel ladder, Chia was given a torso harness to wear and a pair of light gloves. They were not for warmth, but to keep his hands clean. The ladders, he was was warned, were often coated with ashes from the smokestack from the coal fired furnaces in the smelting plants that extracted tin from the crushed rocks.

The ladder was inside a "tube" made from iron and spaced so it would be difficult to fall backwards. One of the officers reminded him was better to look up, not down until he got to the platform. Chia nodded, took a deep breath and started up. As he climbed, he could smell burnt coal and taste the acid in the ash flakes that got into his mouth.

It took less effort than he thought to get to the platform, and he moved to stand by the wrought-iron railings spaced at half-meter intervals above the wooden planks. From here, both he and the local PLA commander could see the loop of train track that branched off south of the city and ran around the swamps back to the main line. The loop was often used as a place to park trains and not block the main north-south track.

With the East German-made Zeiss 10 x 50 binoculars he had bought when he was assigned to the embassy in Berlin, Chia slowly scanned the surrounding area, looking for a logical place for the Americans to hide. He realized it would take days, maybe weeks, for local troops to search the hills surrounding the area, and he doubted the Americans, if they really were here, would hang around and wait to be captured.

He had come to Mengzi because it had been named in the messages delivered by Raiskov, and because there were credible reports of helicopter noise in the middle of the night. Together, it was enough for him to come south to take a look for himself.

Chia waited to speak until he and the garrison commander, another major general, returned to the general's office and were alone.

"General Chin, I do not want you to order any of your men into the field, even though both of us suspect that a team of imperialist American special forces landed in the hills southeast of Mengzi last night."

"But General Chia, we have two divisions within one hundred kilometers and a regiment of helicopters. Surely we could find and capture them! It is our sacred, sworn duty."

"Comrade General, one of the reasons I came down here was to deliver your orders from the general staff in person. You and your units are to stay in their barracks and do nothing out of the ordinary. If you see them, observe them and report. Nothing more. Do not attempt to capture them. Do not attempt to engage them. In short, leave them alone. Is that clear?"

"Yes, General, but I do not understand. My men will not like staying in their quarters and ordered to do nothing, knowing that Americans are here."

"You are not to tell them that Americans are here. If you are asked, say it is a training exercise by a special commando team from another military region. In fact, you are not to discuss our conversation or the true purpose of my visit with anyone. If anyone asks, I am here to review exercise plans." Chia took an envelope from his coat pocket and pulled out two sheets of papers. "Here are your written orders. Sign here. This will protect you. You can keep one copy and the other I will take back with me to Beijing."

General Chin read the document, nodded his head and signed both copies. "Sir, how long are you going to stay in Mengzi?"

"Until I am sure the Americans have left. My guess is that I will leave in two or three days."

"What are they looking for?"

"Divina anti-aircraft missiles."

General Chin laughed. "I have heard that we have some, but I have never seen them! I can assure you, none have ever passed through here."

"I know that, you know that, and now the Americans will know that. Trust me, the Americans knowing that fact will be a good thing for the People's Republic, because they will be less inclined to bomb our railroads as part of their war against our socialist comrades in Vietnam."

Monday, April 26ᵗʰ, 1971,
0046 Local Time, Mengzi

To Marty, it felt as if it were going to snow. At night the temperature dropped from a pleasant 60 degrees Fahrenheit to the 30s. They'd brought lightweight insulated jackets and ponchos, as well as four shelter halves, and a good thing they had. Huddled on the mountaintop, they were already cold when the rain started. Until they got enough branches to cover the shelter halves, the pelting rain sounded like someone beating a cheap snare drum. Even with the shelter, by morning nothing they had was dry and they were cold, wet, and uncomfortable.

Something wasn't right. From their hide, they could see the People's Liberation Army compounds that were south of the city and clustered around the airport. They had been in the area for three days, and nothing had changed. No trucks came out, and only a few helicopters flew around the valley and then back to the airport on what looked like training hops. No-one appeared to be hunting intruders. To Marty, it looked too, well, normal! *Way too normal.*

His instinct said to change location and head toward the secondary landing zone. The low clouds and ugly weather gave him the chance. But the rain and fog would make it very difficult for the crew of Big Mother 22 to see light signals, so he was sure that Josh would come on the FM radio as soon as he was in range, any minute now. Sure enough, the radio came to life.

"Gringo Six, Big Mother 22. Are you up?"

"Big Mother, this is 6. Pick-up at LZ Strato 203, copy?"

"Copy Strato 203."

Bill pulled a sheaf of photos out of the navigation bag and sorted through them to find ones of the new LZ. "Strato 203 is a huge open area with trees on the valley side. My guess is they are someplace along the tree line."

"Six, authenticate conditions." They had agreed during planning to minimize the use of call signs. The less time they spent on air, the less likely it was that hostiles would zero in on them

"Surf's up. Need wetsuits."

Bill clicked the mike twice. The comment about wetsuits meant they were cold.

Josh activated the intercom to give the crew the heads up. "Everyone, I'm not going to put the weight of the helicopter on the wheels. I don't want to get stuck in the mud. So you may have to haul them in. I think it will be easier if they come in the passenger door on the port side."

Two green and one red light flashed briefly at the edge of the tree line ahead. Bill rotated the mike switch to transmit and spoke tersely. "See you. Passenger door."

Josh lowered the helicopter until the wheels just touched the ground and held it steady, making micro-adjustments as the weight shifted, while eight mud covered, soaking wet, chilled and shaking SEALs slogged through the ankle deep mud to the passenger door and clambered up. He turned the cabin heat up to full to help warm his passengers. As soon as he got the all clear from Van der Jagt, they lifted off, quickly reaching their optimum altitude and the careful speed of 90 knots that, he hoped, would keep them from tripping radar sensors. He passed the control over to Bill,

Soon the helicopter was heading south, and Marty, his teeth no longer threatening to chatter, came on the intercom. "Josh, something's odd. There are People's Liberation Army units all over the place, but they never went on patrol. We counted twenty fighters and the same number of helicopters on the airfield, and not one came looking for us."

"What about the trains?"

"We looked at six. Security was almost non-existent. Anyway, we found nothing of interest. One had no military equipment we could find. The others had truck parts, engines and transmissions in crates, and ammo. Only one was full of 85-millimeter artillery shells."

"O.K. Hopefully, this will be the last one of these missions. Settle down, It's about three hours back to Luong Prabang."

Forty minutes later, they were descending a ridge in Laos into noticeably warmer air. Even at their altitude, the smell of the jungle and the pungent aroma created by rotting vegetation rose up to greet them. The outside air temperature gauge was now showing it was seventy degrees Fahrenheit, forty more than when they touched down in the mountains around Mengzi.

"Tracers, four o'clock low. Tracking us." Bennington's call was cool and calm, for all that the news was alarming.

Bill had just relinquished the controls as part of the pilots' routine to change roles every twenty minutes. Josh rolled the helicopter into a sixty degree bank to the left, held it for a few seconds to let the gunner adjust his aim, then rolled the helicopter in a skidding right turn to make it harder to track.

"Three streams that I can see. So far, they're aim is bad. Keep jinking." Josh knew by the change in the muffled tone of Bennington's voice that he now had the mask on that minimized wind noise. Bennington had the back door open and was probably lying on the floor looking out and aft. The others knew to brace themselves; the helicopter was going to maneuver violently.

A stream of green golf balls went by the nose of the H-3. Josh used erratic control inputs to jink back and forth and change altitude and airspeed to give the enemy gunners a four-dimensional problem. He couldn't dive; 100 feet over the tree tops left no room for that. *Fuck, we stumbled on an enemy position. Mr. Murphy has arrived!*

"Sir, looks like four gunners. My guess is 12.7 millimeter and maybe 7.62."

Ping, ping, ping, thwack, thwack, ping. Josh saw pieces of helmet and visor fly across the cockpit and his co-pilot loll to one side. "Bill's hit! Anyone else?"

"No, sir. Some half inch holes in the cabin and a couple of hits in the armor along the floor. No casualties back here."

"Are we leaking anything?"

"I can't tell yet. Van der Jagt is doing a security check. I am coming forward to get Mr. Braxton." Bennington crawled forward.

"Sir, he's still alive." Chief Bennington had his hand on Braxton's neck. He handed Josh the kneeboard with the strip chart and fuel plan clipped to it.

Out of the corner of his eye, Josh watched Airman Kelly and the Chief lift his unconscious co-pilot out of the seat. "Sir, we're going to close the back door and turn up the red lights to full bright while we look at Mr. Braxton."

Josh clicked the mike twice and studied each of the gauges to make sure nothing vital had been hit. No lights on the caution panel. So far, so good. He eased the helicopter up toward 1,000 feet above the ground. He definitely needed angels now.

"Sir, this is Bennington. The medic and I think Mr. Braxton will be O.K. Looks like a 12.7-millimeter round grazed his forehead. It is bleeding pretty badly, so I am going to use some monofilament fishing line to stitch it up. When we get back, a real doctor will have to re-do it. He won't be able to wear his helmet for the rest of the flight, but it is shot to hell anyway. So, if you don't mind, can you keep it straight and level for about five, maybe ten, minutes? I'll tell you when we're done."

"Go for it."

Van der Jagt climbed into to the co-pilot's seat. "What can I do?"

"Help me navigate and watch the gauges like a hawk."

Josh let the ground fall away and held altitude, mostly as a defense against small arms, but also to give himself some altitude in case something failed and he had to execute a full autorotation to touchdown. The last time he'd done a full auto had been with the TH-57 Jet Rangers over a year ago, during training command.

"Sir, Mr. Braxton is awake and sitting up. Besides the bullet wound, he probably has a concussion, but he wants to get back in the cockpit."

"The medic makes that call. Chief, what do you think?"

"Sir, I think we ought to keep him back here sitting down for a few more minutes unless you absolutely need him up there."

"I can do without him for the rest of the flight, if need be. Van der Jagt is up here keeping me company. He always seems to wind up in the copilot's seat just after the shit hits the fan."

Van der Jagt held up a middle finger.

The transmission high temperature and low oil pressure caution light came on, glowing balefully. The temperature gauge was moving up the dial and the pressure gauge was headed toward zero. The transmission's oil system was failing. The NATOPS manual protocol was to land as soon as practical.

Josh was debating whether to descend and look for a clearing or stay 1,000 feet above hostile terrain when the main transmission chip light came on. *Shit! That means something is coming apart in the gearbox.* Without the oil circulating it was only a matter of seconds before the transmission failed. *Okay, time to get the helicopter on the ground as soon as possible. But where?*

"Fuck! Everybody brace yourselves, we're going down!" Josh slammed the collective to the floor and eased the cyclic back to slow the HH-3 to the best autorotation speed of seventy knots. He knew that without oil, the H-3s transmission would run for between 30 and 60 seconds before coming apart. When its ring gears failed or the transmission seized, the main shaft would shear and the rotor head would come off the helicopter. The moment that happened, everyone in the helicopter would be dead: the sudden snap from the reduction in torque would break each man's neck.

"Mayday, mayday, mayday. This is Big Mother 22 going down along its planned route one point five hours north of planned gas stop. Repeat, mayday, mayday, any station, this is Big Mother 22, going down, one point five hours north along its route to its planned intermediate gas stop—"

The dark ground rushed up to meet them. Josh was aiming for the only clearing he could see within autorotation range, a quarter of a mile away. In the pale light of the growing dawn Josh could recognize it as a dry rice paddy. He eased back to trade airspeed for altitude so they would skim over the trees. As he lowered the nose, the helicopter shuddered. He heard the sickening sound of aluminum being ripped and torn apart. In a last ditch effort to stave off disaster, he yanked up on the collective, but he could feel the fuselage rolling and falling. He heard the rippling sound of metal being bent in ways it wasn't designed for. And then nothing.

* * * * *

Something was odd when Josh opened his eyes. It took a few seconds before he recognized the crackling of the engines as they cooled down. He was facing down and to the right, held in place by the seat's straps; a look outside told him that the helicopter was upright but canted about twenty degrees. He unstrapped and tried to get up, but the incline made it difficult, so he released the window and clambered out. He looked back, surprised to see the fuselage almost intact.

The passenger door opened normally, and he could see a mass of tangled arms and legs attached to groaning bodies. "Come on, everyone, let's get out." Josh grabbed the arm of the body closest to the door and found himself looking at Braxton's bloody face.

"Haman, did you fuck up the landing or what?"

Josh helped Bill to the ground. By then, Van der Jagt was already helping the groggy SEALs get out of the mangled fuselage.

Soon they were standing beside the wreck. Marty was the first to count noses.

"Where's Kelly?"

Josh went back into the cabin, ripped open the canvas curtain that separated the cabin from the tail cone for light, but found no one.

"He's not in here. I'll go look for him. Van der Jagt, please help Hausner strip everything out of the helo that we think we'll need. That's first aid kits, ammo, weapons, everything. Chief, check everyone over. Marty, we're in your world, we need a plan!"

The floor at the rear of the cabin by the cargo door was only a foot off the ground. After looking around, Josh saw a torn gunner's belt and started walking in the direction of the parts that trailed the fuselage. About fifty feet away from the helicopter, he found Kelly's body. His head was at an odd angle and there was no pulse. Josh picked him up and carefully slung him over his shoulder, walked back to the helo and he laid him on the ground. He looked at Marty and shook his head.

Marty took a deep breath, then addressed the men standing or sitting amongst the salvaged gear.

"I am assuming no one heard the mayday, so we're going to start walking south. Once we're overdue, which will be in about an hour and half, the mission plan says to start monitoring the SAR frequency at five minutes past the top of every hour for ten minutes. We've got the FM radio, two PRC-90 survival radios, plus spare batteries. Josh, you're the radioman and, if we need one, the FAC."

Marty turned to Chief Bennington. "Chief, you're the primary medic, and along with Van der Jagt you're also our heavy weapons fire team with the M-60. Where is Van der Jagt?"

"Sir, he's inside the helo, breaking up the belt from the mini-gun into roughly 200-round sections. Each of us gets two belts to carry, which will give us plenty of ammo."

"Okay, here's how we're going to move out." Marty looked at the circle of men around him. "One fire team of two SEALs will act as point. They will be followed by my fire teammate and me, then Chief Bennington and Van der Jagt with the M-60. Then two more SEALS. Josh, you follow with Braxton, and Master Chief Hausner will bring up the real with the two remaining SEALs. Any questions?"

"Marty, what about Airman Kelly?" Josh had placed his body just outside the circle of men.

"We'll carry him home; the stretcher bearers will be in the middle, just in front of Mr. Haman. We need to make a stretcher and we'll alternate as stretcher bearers. Put his weapon under him on the stretcher and divide up his ammo. We can put a couple of belts for the M-60 on the stretcher."

Van der Jagt disappeared and came out of the helo with one of the bench seats. "Sir, this will make it easy to carry Kelly. I've got some straps that we can use to tie his body to the stretcher."

Josh spoke up. "Marty, one last thing. We need to burn the helo. Any ideas?"

"Sir, give me a minute?" Van der Jagt disappeared under the belly of the H-3. A few seconds later, the pungent smell of jet fuel filled the area. Within seconds, he had a roaring fire under the H-3 that was already starting to burn the matte black paint.

"Marty, let's burn everything that shows where we've been. I'll keep the route map. We have a spare pilotage chart in the nav bag we can use for navigation."

"Good idea. The only stuff I'll keep is our notes and the film. If we think we're about to be captured, we can destroy them. We need move out as soon as possible. I want to cover as much ground as we can today."

Same Day, 1109 Local Time, Fort Myer, Virginia

The Chairman of the Joint Chiefs of Staff was getting ready to go out and play a round of golf on the base that had been built on land confiscated from General Robert E. Lee when the Civil War began. The ringing phone in Quarters Six, his official residence on the army post just south of the district, stopped him in his tracks as his aide ran to answer.

"Admiral, there is an urgent call for you from the Air Force Rescue Command Center in Udorn, Thailand. Apparently, they picked up a mayday from a Navy helicopter with the call sign of Big Mother 22."

"Get the Air Force Chief of Staff on the line in the next two minutes," the chairman ordered. "If you need to, run down to Quarters Seven and bang on his door to find someone who can tell you where the hell he is. Once you reach him, find Captain Stan Grainger and have them both meet me in the Pentagon command center ASAP."

As he got in the staff car, the Chairman had that churning in his gut that told him something bad happened or was about to happen. As he sat there for the short ride, he started thinking about what he was going to say to the Air Force Chief of Staff.

Same Day, 1643 Local Time, Laos

Josh had always thought this part of Laos was mostly jungle, but now, after walking for ten hours, he realized that it was plains and forests all mixed together. It smelled like any other damp forest. The one thing that was different was that it was much, much noisier.

It seemed that monkeys made the most noise as they jumped from branch to branch paralleling their course. He wasn't sure if they were mocking the string of Americans or were just curious. During survival school, the instructors focused on two types of animals—those that could provide food and those that could kill you. The latter category was filled mostly by snakes—cobras, kraits and vipers—and a few poisonous spiders. The instructors did also mention that the jungle was full of leopards who would view a single human as a nice meal.

By now, the oily black smoke from the funeral pyre that marked the location of Big Mother 22 was well behind them and hadn't been visible for several hours. Just before they left the rice paddy, Josh had taken a last look at the machine that had been so good to him and now looked so sad and broken as it was engulfed in flames. Burning it was like a cavalryman shooting his horse with a broken leg—

painful but necessary.

So far, they had not seen another human being; Marty thought that was a good thing, although at one stop he and several of the SEALs agreed that they were being followed, or at least watched. Their suspicion, based on honed instincts, lead them to change the way they advanced. Now Marty had a fire team several hundred yards out in front, scouting for potential ambush sites.

Every two hours, the group took a ten-minute break and Josh turned on the PRC-90, listened, made two broadcasts and listened again. Still no contact. They had been overdue now for at least six to eight hours. He was beginning to wonder if anyone at the Air Force Rescue Center at Udorn had read the contents of the sealed envelope that was to be opened if they did not return on time. He imagined Air Force bureaucracy trumping common sense, and the guy with the combination to the safe or the authorization to open the envelope either on the golf course, or in the bar, or out shopping because he needed his time off.

The string of men bunched up to switch bearers, then spread out in a circle as Marty scanned the terrain to the south, illuminated by the late afternoon sun. On the other side of the large clearing, he saw a clump of trees separated by a few hundred yards from the jungle. He looked at his watch and turned to the group. "Guys, that group of trees looks like a good position to bed down for the night. According to the map, there should be a stream on the other side where we can refill our canteens. There's enough daylight so we can set up our defensive perimeter before we try to get some sleep. We've covered almost fifteen miles, which is very good. After the radio check, we'll move out."

Same Day, 1824 Local Time, Beijing

Chia showed his pass and invitation and was ushered into the U.S. Embassy compound. He'd never been inside the building before, but before leaving his office the Chinese general had talked to several who had. They told him that the Americans flew food in from outside the country and that booze was plentiful. This time, it was his turn to be a guest at a U.S. embassy reception.

After getting his glass filled with four fingers of Glenlivet, he looked around the room and spotted the man he had come to see, recognizing him from the surveillance pictures. It took him only six steps to get in front of the man.

"Mr. Clifford, may I have a word with you in private?"

"Excuse me, I don't believe we have met. You are...?"

"Major General Dao Chia, Chief of Intelligence on the General Staff. My government knows that I am here and has approved what I would like to tell you. I believe you are the chief of station for the CIA. Am I not correct?" Chia's precise English with an American accent, plus his uniform, and his correct assumption made the American uncomfortable. He responded automatically.

"I am a commercial attaché and not with the CIA."

"Then would you please introduce me to the CIA station chief? What I want to tell him is time sensitive and very important or I wouldn't be this direct. I am sure he is here, because he wouldn't want to miss chatting with a half a dozen generals and other dignitaries of the People's Republic." Chia's tone of voice was even, forceful, and not at all apologetic. Four years at Stanford had taught him the nuances of addressing various ranks of the so-called American democracy.

"I can pass on the information to the appropriate person."

"Sorry, but what I have to give to the United States is much too important for a low-level embassy employee." Chia's cold stare told the American that he was serious.

"What happens if he, assuming he is here, doesn't want to talk to you?"

"Then you will miss out on some very valuable intelligence about our Russian comrades and their ability to read your encrypted messages. Or about an American helicopter that crashed in Northern Laos this morning."

"How long will this take?"

"Five minutes. Ten at the most. If you have many questions, then it will take longer. I would prefer if we went someplace private and I want to give the details directly to the CIA's chief of station." Chia knew that when Raiskov found out about this meeting, he would have a fit. By now, the senior GRU officer at the reception knew he was talking to the Americans.

"Please, stay here for a minute." Clifford left and talked briefly to another man, then lead the way into a small, empty room that looked like an office. "This is Mr. Smith."

Chia smiled, knowing it was not his real name. He also knew that Clifford *was* the CIA station chief and that this was a ruse. He would play along.

"I have three things for you. One, our Soviet comrades are reading your secret message traffic and are giving us copies. I am sure they are carefully choosing what they share with my country."

He put down his tumbler that had the emblem of the United States of America etched into the glass and pulled an envelope out of his tunic. "Here are several messages taken at random from what we were given by the Soviets." Chia waited while Clifford looked at the message; his eyebrows went up before he handed it to Mr. Smith.

"Second, apparently there are some intelligence analysts in the U.S. Air Force who believe the Soviet Union is shipping SA-2 missiles through my country to Vietnam. We know that from some of the message traffic that our socialist brothers in Moscow have given us. Please inform them that the Soviets are not transshipping missiles through my country and never have. If your Air Force continues to pursue their theory, it may lead to the United States taking actions it may regret."

Chia paused, waiting for a question. Neither American said a word, so he continued. "We believe that the Soviets are afraid to ship their missiles through my country because they think we will, shall we say, borrow one or two to see how they compare to the ones they sold us. Their technical support of the Divina, which you call the SA-2, ended in 1960. We used their design as the basis of our own missile, what we call the HQ-1, which we think is much better. HQ-1s are, as you know, deployed around Beijing and nowhere else. The reason I am bringing this up is that twice in this month, one of your helicopters penetrated our airspace, landed a reconnaissance team which inspected several trains and then was picked up a few days later. The second one left yesterday. From the messages we were given, we know the purpose of their mission. I just validated the results of their reconnaissance so you will no longer need to violate our airspace. Starting today, we will allow no more. I am here to warn your country that we will shoot down the next one that enters our airspace and imprison any crew members that we capture. They will be tried as spies, and if convicted, face the death penalty. In addition, if the over flights of my country continue, we will deploy missiles to the North Vietnamese border and will shoot at any airplane approaching it. This will add another threat that your fighter bombers have to face. And then, yes, there will be missiles on trains, not to go to Vietnam, but to support our own missile batteries. Do I make my country's intentions clear?"

"Yes, General," Mr. Clifford said softly, abandoning pretense. "They are very clear. We appreciate your candor."

"Thank you. We are doing this in the spirit of cooperation. We do not want to have the sort of unfortunate incident which would prevent your Secretary of State, Mr. Kissinger, from making his visit, or the one being planned by your President Nixon."

"General, we understand completely."

"Excellent. That brings me to my last point. Early this morning, we picked up a distress call from one of your helicopters whose call sign is Big Mother 22. We believe it crashed in Northern Laos. That is an area full of drug dealers and warlords who would view their presence as an unwelcome intrusion. They will try to hunt them down and kill them because do not like outsiders. They do not take prisoners. To use an American term, these men are real bad guys and your men are in grave danger. I am authorized to offer my country's help in finding the crew, and if we do, they will not be interrogated. We will repatriate them to the United States unharmed and as soon as possible. We will, of course, attend to any medical needs if they were injured in the crash."

"General Chia, that is a very generous offer. But I am not aware of a U.S. helicopter that crashed in Laos today. We just don't get that kind of information here at the embassy."

"I understand. We believe it was on the way home from the second of the two reconnaissance missions into my country that I just described. This one was near the town of Mengzi. The other was near Nanning. Please let me know if my country can help in the search."

"General, how well does the People's Liberation Army know the area where the helicopter went down?"

"We know it very well, Mr. Clifford. We are constantly hunting down the smugglers whose business is producing opium and then selling it to the highest bidder to turn into heroin. They do not respect international borders and sell their dope to anyone who will pay them. It is a constant battle keeping their poison out of our country. If you have no other questions, our business is finished and we can go back to your reception. I can't wait to taste the delicious food your embassy is serving." Chia paused and held up his glass. "And, drink more of your scotch."

Tuesday, April 27th, 1971,
0453 Local Time, Laos

Marty tapped Josh's foot with his toe and whispered. "Pass the word that we have some people approaching our hide and to get ready. No one is to open fire until they attack us. Right now, the guys with the starlight scopes have been watching them for about an hour and say they're now about 200 meters out."

Josh crawled to the large tree that was his designated fighting position. Before it got dark, Marty had assigned each man a position and set up the watch bill. Now, in the growing dawn, Josh could see shapes moving through the tall grass well enough to make out that they were carrying AK-47s and other weapons. At fifty meters, the intruders crouched down in the two-foot high grass and waited. He could see two groups of heads and guessed there were at least twenty in each.

With the fire selector switch in the semi-automatic position and the safety catch off, Josh dug his toes into the soft ground and made sure his left elbow was directly under the stock to give him a stable shooting position. He began scanning his sector.

"Grenade!!!"

Josh wasn't sure who yelled, but he saw the flash and felt the wave of concussion as shrapnel zinged over his head. A shadowy form in front of his sight stood up. He pulled the trigger twice and the man dropped. More human shapes rose up, fired, and advanced in his direction. He lost count how many double taps he fired and was surprised when the rifle clicked empty. Reload, slam the bolt forward, find a target, shoot. More targets popped up, fired, and disappeared in the elephant grass.

"Cease fire, cease fire." Marty's voice was clear. The morning stillness returned except for the groaning of some men in the field in front of them.

"Regroup and pack up." Marty's hissing voice was soft and sharp. "Be ready to move out in less than ten minutes when I return. You come with me." Marty pointed to his SEAL fire teammate. "Bennington, Van der Jagt, cover us with the M-60."

Marty moved out in a crouch with his teammate a few yards off to one side. He'd gotten about twenty meters from their position when a machine gun opened up. Marty was spun around by the impact and crumpled to the ground. Without thinking, Josh leaped up and ran toward his friend. He could hear the AK-47 rounds zipping by his head. Seeing one man with a red headband, he fired several times from the shoulder as he charged. The man dropped and Josh dove to the ground, where the other SEAL was already putting a pressure bandage on the wound in Marty's side.

The firefight started again as two grenades were thrown in their direction. The concussion slammed Josh's head into the ground. Sensing someone coming, he looked up and saw two men low crawling toward their position. A quick shot to the head stopped the first. As the other started to bring his AK-47 to bear, Josh pulled the trigger several times and the man's head dropped into a growing pool of blood. "I'll cover you. Drag Marty back," he called over his shoulder. The SEAL nodded, rolled Marty onto his back, and began dragging him while maintaining a low crouch.

When no one fired at them, Josh followed, moving low to the ground and taking advantage of the cover of the tall grasses. When he got back to their position, Josh crawled over to where Chief Bennington and the SEAL medic were redoing the pressure bandage on Marty's side. He could see the earth darkened and dampened by his friend's blood.

"Josh, you and Hausner have the con," Marty whispered.

"Marty, you're not dead yet, so shut the fuck up and let the docs work on you."

"I think they're going to rush us again."

For some strange reason, Josh looked at his watch. It was 0504. "Bill, try the radio."

Josh turned to Hausner, the senior SEAL after Marty. Josh knew any SEAL, regardless of rank, would know more about firefights than he did. "Master Chief, what do you think? Do we do the Fort Apache thing and dig in and fight it out, or try to move?"

Chief Hausner took a deep breath. "First we let Bennington do what he can for Mr. Cabot. If he thinks we can move him, great. We'll be slower, but at least we'll be a moving target, not sitting ducks. If we can't, then Fort Apache it is."

"I want to know who we are up against." Josh pointed at two of the SEALs. "Reconnoiter and see what you can find out. Don't stick your heads up and get shot!"

Two nods and the men moved out. Josh turned his attention to his wounded friend.

"Sir," Bennington said, "the good news is that it is a through-and-through wound. Bad news is, Mr. Cabot has lost a lot of blood. We can give him a man-to-man transfusion after I stop the bleeding. But no matter what we do, this wound will get infected in a hurry out here in the jungle."

Twenty minutes later, the two SEALs crawled back into the perimeter, dragging bandoleers and a mix of weapons. From the inside of his fatigues, one of them pulled a half dozen grenades and laid them on the ground. "Sir, you're not going to believe this." He handed Josh two sets of dog tags. "Two of the dead guys are Americans—one black, one white. I don't know about the rest, but they sure aren't NVA or Pathet Lao. They've got a mix of weapons, mostly AKs, but we brought back a real live Tommy gun and a Sten. I don't think they expected us to fight back as hard as we did. The survivors seem to have pulled back. My guess is that they have an observer back out there tracking us."

"Shit. I don't want to risk losing anyone trying to find the observer. Did you get all the abandoned guns and ammo?"

"Not sure. I think we got most of it. A bit later, we can crawl out and see what else we find."

Josh looked around. "Hausner, Bennington, they know where we are, so we have to assume they'll come back with more people. We're going to be here until it is safe to move Mr. Cabot. Let's spend the next few hours improving our position. We can distribute the guns and ammo. At least we have water, the field makes a good LZ in case the cavalry arrives, and we've got a defendable position. So let's deploy the Claymores. While we're at it, let's collect all the weapons and ammo from the dead guys."

"Yes, sir."

"Bill, try the radio. It's time."

Josh crawled on his hands and knees to where his friend was lying, his face pale and drawn. A narrow, plastic tube carrying dark liquid ran from Chief Bennington's arm to Marty's. Josh leaned over and spoke into his friend's ear.

"Marty, I'm not going to leave you or anyone else here to die in this God-forsaken place. Everyone except Airman Kelly is going to get home alive."

Marty opened his eyes. "Promises, promises. Do what you have to do, even if it means leaving Kelly and me."

"You're not listening."

"Contact." Bill's hoarse whisper turned everyone's head. He held out the radio and the earpiece to Josh. "It's Billiard Ball 71."

"Billiard Ball 71, this is Big Mother 22 Alpha, over." 'Alpha' told the listeners on the surveillance plane that they were talking to the aircraft commander.

"Big Mother, give me a long count."

Josh knew they were needed the long count to get a bearing on their location. Signal strength of his radio would give the crew some idea of the distance. He also knew to speak the numbers slowly. The risk was that any hostiles listening on the frequency could also get a fix on their position.

"Long count follows. Ten... Nine... Eight... Seven... Six... Five... Four... Three... Two... One... One... Two... Three... Four... Five... Six... Seven... Eight... Nine... Ten... Long count out."

"Alpha, we got a bearing. Stand by this frequency. Will call in five mikes for another long count. Copy?"

Josh clicked the mike twice and looked at his watch. He left the radio on and earpiece in while he waited.

"Big Mother 22 Alpha, long count." The call came exactly five minutes later.

"Billiard Ball 71, long count follows." Josh slowly counted down from ten and back up.

"Alpha, we have a rough fix. Authenticate. Year, make, model and color of your current car."

"1965 Porsche 356SC Coupe. Color is red."

"Roger. Will vector fly by for a visual as soon as we can. Working on pick-up. Say status."

"One KIA, one seriously wounded, and another wounded. We've been attacked once and expect another, over."

"Copy. Contact me at scheduled time unless status changes. We're working on air cover. Billiard Ball out."

Josh looked at Hausner. "They know roughly where we are, but they don't have a plan to get us or a pick-up time. Meanwhile, the bad guys know where we are. We need to dig in and be prepared for a tough fight. Lord only knows how long it will be before the Air Force comes to get us."

"Yes, sir. I'll take care of setting up the defense. Mr. Cabot chose well. Anybody that tries to take us out will pay a very high price."

"Good. Bill, you're now the radioman." Josh handed his copilot the radio and ear piece. "Check in on schedule. Remember, you're 22 Bravo, they will ask your authentication questions. If you don't think you can remember them, I'll take back the radio or give it to Chief Bennington."

Same Day, 1122 Local Time

Hausner was giving his update.

"Mr. Haman, the guys finished laying out the Claymores. We put two in the stream bed to alert us if they try to sneak in that way. We'll have a two-man fire team to watch it, but we're going to focus on the front side. There are 21 bodies out there, and trails of blood heading back across the field, but we don't know how many wounded. Our guess is it was originally about forty that came at us. Other than the dog tags and the wallets we picked up off the two Americans, there's nothing on the bodies to tell us who they are."

"O.K., Master Chief." Josh had slung the Thompson over his shoulder, giving him a third weapon after his M1 carbine and a .45. "Do you think they'll hit us again?"

"Not sure. What I am thinking is that they are watching us and hoping we move because if we do, we'll be strung out and much more vulnerable. Plus, they'll see the stretchers. So I say stay here and fight it out. Hopefully, the Air Force will get its shit together and get us out either this afternoon or tomorrow."

"When do you think they'll attack?"

"I'll bet either just before dark tonight or right around first light. Night attacks require a lot of coordination and can get confused in a hurry without good command and control. For that, you need radios. First light is easier for them, but they'll know it's also easier for us."

"What problems do we have that I don't know about?"

"Food is the biggest one. We'll split up the D rations we have left, but after they're gone, we'll have to scrounge for food and that will mean leaving the security of this place. The stream will provide water, but we have a limited number of halazone tablets, so if we're here much longer we'll have to start boiling the water."

"Got it. Bennington, how's Mr. Cabot?"

"So far, so good, sir. I'm glad we're not moving. I'll have the guys keep improving our defensive positions. We don't have much to dig with, but we'll make maximum use of what we have here."

Same Day, 1501 Local Time

The first vultures began circling about lunch time. Within an hour, the initial pair had been joined by over a dozen, but none had yet landed on the bodies to begin feeding.

Bill was watching the birds with Marty's binoculars. "I'll bet the bastards are discussing who will be the first to come down. Or maybe they're divvying up the bodies."

"Either that or they are thinking that if the humans keep killing each other, they'll be feasting for weeks." Josh pointed to his co-pilot's bloody forehead. "How's the head?"

"It hurts. Occasionally, I get a bit woozy, but I'll survive."

Josh tapped the radio lying nearby. Bill nodded and turned the radio on before he pushed the soft rubber earpiece into his ear.

On cue, the radio crackled. "Big Mother 22 Alpha, this is Billiard Ball 94. We relieved 71. Copy."

"Billiard Ball 94, this is Big Mother 22 Bravo. We're up."

"22 Bravo, where's 22 Alpha?"

"He's inspecting our perimeter, over."

"22 Bravo, authenticate. What plane did your dad fly first in World War II?"

"Sierra Bravo Delta, also known as the Dauntless. Where is our air cover?" Bill's head throbbed even more from the noise in his earpiece.

"Sandies should be overhead in five mikes for a visual. Say status." Sandy was the call sign for the Air Force A-1s that supported rescue operations.

"Same as before. Nothing's changed. We're expecting another attack by local hostiles, over."

A little later, Josh heard the beat of the engines of the A-1s before he saw them just above the treetops. He stood up and flashed his mirror. The pilot rocked his wings, then continued on for about a mile before climbing and turning to the south.

"Bravo, this is Sandy 46 with playmate Sandy 59, tally ho. Got the mirror flash. We're taking up an orbit at angels five. We have two hours of play time and then will be relieved. Plan is to have two Sandies overhead until pick-up, copy?"

"What time is the pick-up?"

"Will provide notice about ten mikes before the helos arrive."

Same Day, 1906 Local Time

Every thirty minutes two A-1s would make a pass over their position at altitudes between 500 and 1,500 hundred feet. It was frustrating to be kept waiting for pick-up, especially with two wounded men, but it was better than nothing. If nothing else, Josh figured, their presence had probably deterred the follow-up attack he'd expected.

"Big Mother 22 Bravo, Billiard Ball 11, over." An hour earlier, Billiard Ball 11 had relieved Billiard Ball 94.

"22 Bravo, go," Bill answered.

"Bad news, Bravo. One of the rescue helos is hard down. Air Force rules are we need at least two to make a pick-up in Indian country. We're working on getting another one in position. We will let you know when it arrives, copy?"

"22 Bravo copies." Discouraged, with a throbbing headache even worse than his hunger and fatigue, Bill turned to Josh.

"We're on our own tonight. They'll have some air support, but no pick-up until tomorrow."

"Not surprised." Josh walked over to where Marty was lying on the makeshift stretcher. "Chief, how is he doing?"

"Could be better. I've got him heavily sedated. The bleeding has stopped, but moving him will start it all over again."

"What's going on?" Marty's words were slurred by the drugs.

"We've got to spend the night here. Your job is staying alive. My job is to keep the bad guys away from you."

"You can leave me if you need to get out of here."

"Not on your life. I'm not leaving you in fucking Laos, so get used to that idea."

"Mr. Haman, we've got company." A SEAL on lookout in one of the trees called down, his voice soft but audible. He had been scanning the perimeter with one of the starlight scopes. "Three groups: one of about twenty is coming down the stream bed; two larger ones are coming at our front from two directions. Estimated numbers, a hundred and fifty or more, total. They may think that they can divide and conquer under cover of darkness." No one said what they all were thinking, that the A-1s would not be of any help, even if they returned.

"Thanks." Josh turned to Hausner. "Master Chief, pass the word not to fire until they rush us. We need to conserve ammunition. Hopefully the Claymores will discourage them."

"Mr. Haman, they've seen the airplanes, so their tactic will be to get close as quickly as possible and try to get in among us to prevent the use of air support. It could turn hand-to-hand. Sir, I suggest you stay back here as the command post, deal with the guys coming right at us, and I'll take care of the back door."

"Got it."

Josh turned to Bill, hoping his co-pilot couldn't hear his stomach growling. He wasn't sure if it was from hunger or fear or both. In the first firefight, he'd had the security of knowing that Marty was in charge and knew what he was doing. Now he was playing it by ear and relying on the Master Chief's judgment.

"Get on the horn and tell Billiard Ball we have company."

"Billiard Ball 11, this is Big Mother 22 Bravo. We have an attack forming of one hundred and fifty plus. There are two groups in the field to our north and one in the stream bed. Need air support as soon as possible, over."

"Big Mother 22 Bravo, this is Billiard Ball 11. Spooky 59 will be overhead in one zero mikes. He's been briefed on your position. Stay up this frequency, over."

"Tell Spooky 59 to hurry!"

The first of the Claymores in the creek bed flashed as it banged off. The other three followed in rapid sequence. The momentary silence was followed by a shrill bugle call. Josh just had time to remember that he'd read about bugles being used during the Korean War and to for Chinese human wave attacks before he heard shouts, and men appeared out of the grass, firing from their hips as they charged forward.

Josh pulled the trigger on the Tommy gun and heard a loud click. *Shit, I forgot to put a round in the chamber.* He yanked the bolt back, slammed it forward and squeezed off the first burst. The target went from charging to going backward as the four rounds tore through his body. *Whoa!!! That was cool.*

He shifted fire and dropped a man with each burst, but they were getting closer and closer. He had gone through the fourth and last magazine on the Thompson and started to unsling his M-1 Carbine when he saw a shape come swiftly at him with a bayonet. He jumped a step to the side and swung the rifle by the barrel, hitting the man in his chest. The blow caused his attacker to drop his AK-47. The carbine's stock broke in two, but the impact was enough to slow his attacker momentarily. The man had a wide eyed, crazed look as he rushed Josh, who yanked his .45 out of his survival vest and pumped two rounds into his attacker. The first round blew the man's arm off at the shoulder and the second sent him staggering backward before he fell.

The steady beat of short bursts from the M-60 stopped. Worried, Josh fell back to where Marty was hidden and saw Chief Bennington stagger and then spin around before falling down. On the way, he put two rounds from his .45 into a shape leaning against a tree reloading an AK-47.

Josh heard a yell and spun around to come face-to-face with a man charging him with a machete. Two rounds from the .45 put the man face down, sprawled at his feet in a growing pool of his blood. *Dumb bastard, don't bring a knife to a gunfight!*

The fading evening grey turned into a harsh white light as two parachute flares ignited 2,000 above his head. Out in the field, Josh could see the attackers freeze in their tracks. The M-60 started again, spitting out bursts that knocked several down. That's when a stream of red tracers from the three 7.62-millimeter mini-guns of a AC-47 churned up the field in front of Josh and then moved around to the stream bed, where it chewed up men. The steady stream of lead made a strange sucking sound as the bullets smacked into the mud.

Within minutes of the gunship's arrival, their attackers were running back across the field for cover among the trees. The weapons fire stopped. In the eerie silence that followed, the loudest noises were the groans and cries of the wounded and the drone of the two radial engines in the C-47 transport that had been converted into a gunship.

Braxton appeared by his side, "That was ugly. How bad off are we?"

"I don't know. How long can that gunship stay around?"

"He's got gas for another three hours. He didn't say anything about ammo, other than his relief was on alert."

"Where's Master Chief Hausner?"

"Right behind you, sir."

"How's the back door?"

"Closed. The Claymores took out a bunch, and then the AC-47 got most, if not all of the rest of them. We only fired a few rounds. How'd it go on this side?"

"We almost got overrun. There are dead bad guys all over our area. We need to check our ammo status and figure out how many of us are still alive and who's wounded. I saw Chief Bennington go down, but I don't know who else. The SEAL medic is working on him. We need to get all the guns and ammo from our attackers and get ready for the next attack."

Van der Jagt joined the three men. "The Chief took a round in the shoulder and another in the hip. The SEAL medic is working on him now."

Josh took a deep breath. The fragrance of the elephant grass was now tainted by burnt gunpowder and the rank smell of blood. After he studied the battleground, he walked over to the dense area in the clump of trees where Marty and Kelly's body were hidden and where, if it came to that, they would make their last stand. Marty tried to sit up, but Josh, kneeling next to the stretcher, gently pushed him back down.

"Josh, how'd we do?"

"O.K. We almost got over run, but between us and the gunship, we beat off the attack."

"Good." Marty closed his eyes.

"Mr. Haman."

Josh stood up and turned around. "What's up, Master Chief?"

"We've got two more wounded. As for ammo, we're down to two magazines for the M-16s per man, but we have enough AK-47s to go around, each with about four 30-round magazines. Not much ammo left for the .45s. I'd say enough for one more attack. After that, we're down to knives and fists."

"What do you recommend?"

"We sit here and wait. I've got a fire team out gathering more ammo from the bodies that are out there, but I told them not to go too far out. I'll have an AK for you and Mr. Braxton in a few minutes. It is going to be a long night!"

Wednesday, April 28th,
1971, 0605 Local Time

The noise and concussion from a treetop pass by a pair of A-1s woke everyone up, besides the two SEALs on watch. Josh grabbed the radio, turned it on and listened.

"Big Mother 22 Bravo, this is Billiard Ball 96, how copy? Over."

"Billiard Ball 96, this is Big Mother 22 Alpha, we hear you loud and clear. What's up?"

"Authenticate. Year, make and model of your first car."

"1965 Sunbeam Alpine."

"Big Mother 22 Alpha, helos are on the way. We have four Sandies orbiting, plus another gunship for close air support. Any change in status since firefight?"

"We now have one KIA, two seriously wounded and several

others injured. We're carrying out three bodies. Best pick-up area is to the northeast side. Ground is firm, just tall grass, over."

"Roger. Jolly Green 80 and 09 are on the way. They'll contact you when they are five minutes out. Did you say *three* bodies? Over."

"We found two American MIAs and we're bringing them home. Over."

Josh turned to his co-pilot and Marty's second in command. "Hausner, Bill, let everybody know the helos are on their way. We need to pack up what we want to take with us. I want to bring those two Americans home. They may be deserters, but they deserve to be buried in the U.S."

"Yes, sir, I agree." The Master Chief turned and waved his arm in the direction of the elephant grass. "My guys know where they are and will pick them up on the way out. I don't think the hostiles are going to have another go at us, not with the Sandies are around. I hope they will just let us go. There are at least fifty bodies out there, maybe more."

Chapter 17 – WHAT ARE FRIENDS FOR?

Thursday, April 29th, 1971,
1436 Local Time, Da Nang

They had scarcely reached the compound when Captain Rainer sent for the two pilots. After inviting them into his office, he closed the door and gave them time to settle themselves, watching them closely.

"Braxton, how long did it take them to stitch you up?"

"At Udorn or here?"

"Start with Udorn."

"About twenty minutes, sir. Hurt like hell because by the time they got to me, or I got to them, it was all swollen. They jabbed my forehead with a lot of needles and then cleaned it out before sewing it back up and giving me a hefty shot of penicillin, which made sitting down uncomfortable for a while. Anyway, I should be fine in a few days."

"Good." Rainer sat down. "I hear you guys had a conversation with Ralph Randall."

The two pilots nodded. Josh barely managed not to grimace.

"I'll bet he was in transmit mode."

Again, Josh and Bill just nodded. If Randall hadn't repeated their conversation to anybody, they weren't going to.

"He's an old Indochina hand. Cut his teeth with the Air Force's First Air Commando Group back in 1944, and he's been out here off and on since then. He left the Air Force right after Korea because he thought it was turning into a country club. Since then, when the CIA wants something done with an airplane anywhere in Africa or here in Southeast Asia, they call Randall."

"Actually, Captain, he was quite helpful."

"Besides chewing your ass off and flying you guys to Lima 36 and Prabang Luaong and getting you back here in one piece, what else did he do?"

"Set us up with a guy from a Taiwanese squadron who told us a lot about the People's Republic's anti-aircraft doctrine."

"Well, that tells me that you passed muster with Ralph."

"How so, sir?"

"He wouldn't have offered if he didn't think you guys were worth the trouble. I'm glad you didn't try to bullshit your way out of anything when he called you on the carpet. By the time you talked he probably knew the answers and was testing you. He can call anyone, I mean anyone, he wants. But I told him that if he stole you two, I'd come kick his ass. In Ralph's world, he'd rather be reining people in for pushing too hard than kicking them in the ass to do something. I see things the same way." Rainer paused. "So Josh, are you planning any rescues in Laos?"

Josh made a face. "No, sir."

"Why not?"

Is he *testing me?* Three reasons, sir. One, I don't know where Danielle and her father are. Two, if I did and they were in a camp with a lot of other people, assuming I could free them, how would I get them all to a safe place? You'd need a bunch of helicopters. Three, I don't have the people, planes, or equipment to make the rescue."

"You left out the one thing that is most important."

Josh was puzzled. "Sir, what's that?"

The next words were spoken in a voice of steel, and Rainer's eyes bored into Josh's. "You don't have the tasking or authorization. If you did, then you could develop the solution to all three of your problems."

"Yes, sir. I understand."

"Good. Let me give you a little history lesson. Patton knew his son-in-law was held in a specific P.O.W. camp in Germany. When he got close, he sent a column of tanks and trucks to rescue the P.O.Ws., who were mostly Americans. The raid got lost, shot up; it was, by all accounts, a disaster. It almost got Patton relieved, but by then

Eisenhower didn't want to make any changes because everyone knew the war was just about over. So you are not the first to think about going into Indian country to rescue a loved one, and I am sure you won't be the last."

"Yes, sir, I understand."

The phone rang on the back of Rainer's desk. "Now get out of here. Go write your after-action report. I've got work to do."

As they walked away, Josh knew the captain was right, but he also knew he's never be able to fly over Laos without thinking about Danielle, wondering what had happened to her...

Friday, April 30th, 1971,
1022 Local Time

Det 171 was a unit in name only; not only was it short an essential crew member, it was without a helicopter. As they were all downed, it gave them time to catch up with the detachment's paperwork.

Josh's fingers were flying over the keys on the typewriter when Captain Rainer stopped by. "How's it coming along?"

"I'm just about done, sir. I think this position paper on pairing a helicopter crew with a SEAL team for an entire tour will make pretty convincing reading. Not only have I outlined the reasons, I've also included the operational doctrine and a training syllabus based on what we learned. Hopefully, CINCPAC will approve our recommendations and have the guys at PACFLT implement them." Josh spoke the acronym PACFLT as 'pack fleet."

"Good. I am pretty sure they will. It was a good idea of yours and I think it should be sent up the chain of command. When do you think you'll be finished?"

"The first full draft should be done today and ready for your comments."

"Great, I can't wait to read it. I'll get the endorsement ready. Different subject, have you talked to the guys back at Cubi to find out when you're going to get another helicopter?"

"Yes, sir, the last time I spoke with them, they thought it would be by the middle of next week. As soon as they have one available, Braxton and I will fly back to Cubi with Van der Jagt and check it out. I'll call this afternoon and get the latest update."

"Let me know what they say. If needed, I'll get someone to light a fire under their ass, or I'll send you out to Yankee Station to commandeer one!"

Wednesday, May 12th, 1971, 1038 Local Time, Da Nang

It was only May, but it was already hot. Labor as it might at its coldest setting, the air conditioner in the gray van Josh was driving barely brought the temperature down to 95 degrees and 80 percent humidity. Given the van's worn-out shocks and the state of his passenger, rather than drive as fast as he liked, Josh drove slowly from the hospital to their compound. In the passenger seat, Marty was clearly uncomfortable, but it wasn't from Josh's driving. He'd just been released from the hospital and was weak and still in pain.

"So what did the docs tell you?"

"To take it easy for a month. The infection is gone. That was actually the most dangerous part. I have to go back every week so they can take a look at how I am healing, but I should be fine in two months because nothing vital was hit. The bullet grazed my liver, but it turns out livers are pretty resilient. In the meantime, I can't go on any missions. Captain Rainer said I am going to be the permanent duty officer until I head for Hawaii for two weeks. Hopefully, by then they'll start letting me exercise. I want to be able to go swimming and surfing while I'm there."

"That's good. You deserve the break."

"Thanks for picking me up."

"That's what friends are for. Without a helo, being a taxi driver is all I have to do!"

"Not picking me up at the hospital; getting me out of Laos, you dummy."

"Oh that!" Josh turned to look at his friend and smiled. *Good buddy, there was no way I was going to leave you in the People's Republic or lying in a field in Laos.*

"You know, you would make a great SEAL."

"No, I wouldn't. There's no way I would ride in a sub or one of those swimmer delivery vehicles. My claustrophobia would cause me to freak out."

"You'd learn to deal with it."

"I like flying better."

When Josh stopped in front of the entrance, Master Chief Hausner came outside to meet them. "Sirs, you need to hurry in. We have some senior officers here to see us."

"Where are Mr. Braxton and Chief Bennington?"

"Already inside. Van der Jagt took the chief for his daily doctor's visit earlier today."

"Sounds like a party."

The decision had been made at Udorn to fly Marty and Chief Bennington back to Da Nang where they had a better equipped hospital. Josh had waited outside the operating room, and then stayed with both of them in the recovery room until he knew they were okay. Bennington's wounds were less serious, and he was released for light duty seven days after surgery. Ever since they'd brought Marty to Da Nang, Josh had driven to the hospital, sometimes with a member of his team, other times just by himself to visit Marty three times a day.

Now Captain Rainer was the first to greet Marty as he came into the conference room filled with the members of Gringo Six and the crew of Big Mother 22. He then turned to Josh.

"I believe you know Captain Drysdale from the Pacific Fleet staff. And Captain Grainger and Lieutenant Commander Gainesville have decided to once again grace us with their company. I am beginning to think they like our hospitality! Captain Grainger, you have the floor."

"Gentlemen, I want to congratulate you on a job well done. There are really no other words to describe it. The most important news is that there will be no more missions into the People's Republic of

China. We got that word the day after you were picked up, and I think everyone in this room will agree that is a good thing."

"Amen." The word just escaped Josh's lips. Captain Grainger smiled at him before continuing. "I was unofficially told that the Chairman of the Joint Chiefs told the Air Force Chief, in polite terms I am sure, to shut the fuck up. However, I must again remind each of you that you cannot discuss these missions with anyone at any time. While I realize you cannot forget what happened, you can't talk about it, even amongst yourselves. I've got some administrative details I will take care of later, which will mean more forms that you will have to sign to that effect. Again, a job well done... Captain Drysdale."

"Thank you, Captain Grainger. I too want to add my congratulations. CINCPAC has directed Captain Rainer to write meritorious evaluations for the enlisted personnel and fitness reports for the officers. These will go into your service record, but there will be no narrative. The only notations in the Remarks section will be that it was for a highly classified mission, the award that you are about to be given, and the words 'must promote.'

Now, although a much more formal ceremony would be more appropriate, the powers that be would like to keep this as quiet as possible. Lieutenant Haman, it is my distinct pleasure to award you a Silver Star for your leadership and bravery during the battle at what Chief Hausner calls the Laotian Fort Apache. He said, and I quote, 'He never lost his cool, led when he had too, listened when it made sense, and most important, took care of his men. He would make an outstanding SEAL. I'd be proud to follow him anywhere.' In addition, both Lieutenant Junior Grade Braxton and you are being awarded the Distinguished Flying Cross for reasons that are obvious to all. Lieutenant Junior Grade Cabot, you've been awarded the Bronze Star with a combat V. All those who were wounded have been awarded Purple Hearts, and all the enlisted men have been awarded Navy Commendation Medals with combat Vs."

Drysdale handed out all the boxes and the certificates. "I believe that a few toasts are in order." He reached under the table and put two bottles of Macallan 25-year old single malt scotch on the table next to a row of glasses. "Gentlemen, before we leave this room, these should be empty."

Two months later, in July, 1971 Henry Kissinger, Nixon's National Security Advisor, made his secret trip to the People's Republic of China during a visit to Pakistan. It was then followed by President Richard Nixon's historic visit in February, 1972.

The Debenards disappeared into a Laotion re-education camp. Their fate, as well as that of many other foreigners held by the Pathet Lao and Khmer Rouge, remains unknown. Neither organization communicates with any international relief agency or embassies in response to requests for information on those that are being held against their will. What we do know is that the conditions in the camps were horrendous. In many ways, they were similar to the Nazi concentration camps, without the gas chambers. Instead of gas, the Pathet Lao and Khmer Rouge let disease, starvation and injuries from torture sessions thin the ranks of those they held.

Deck Diagram of the U.S.S. Sterett

DLG 31 STERETT

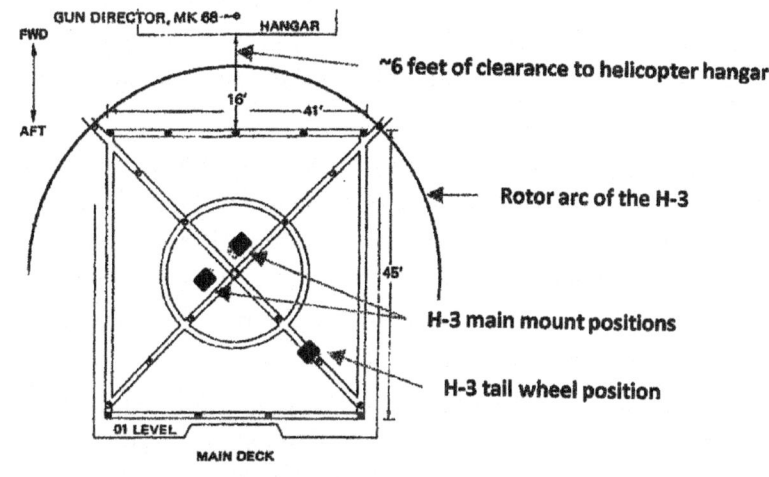

GUN DIRECTOR, MK 68
HANGAR
FWD
AFT
16'
41'
45'
01 LEVEL
MAIN DECK

~6 feet of clearance to helicopter hangar

Rotor arc of the H-3

H-3 main mount positions

H-3 tail wheel position

TOP OF 5" GUN APPROX.
8' HIGHER THAN HELO
PLATFORM LEVEL

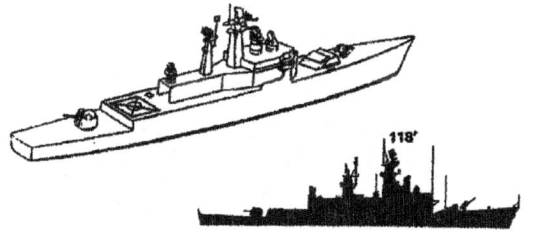

118'

FUEL - JP, HIFR   POWER - NONE   CERTIFICATION - VLA
NAVIGATION - HF/DF   CERT for NIGHT and
                                   DAY LANDING IAW
COMMUNICATION - UHF, VHF, HF, FM   VLA BUL 9-2
VOICE CALL - NUKJ   H-1, H-2
HELO DECK HEIGHT ABOVE W.L. - 20'   ORIGINAL   1-38

A Short History of U.S. Navy Combat Search and Rescue

To be polite, the U.S. Navy entered the Vietnam War in the early 1960s unprepared for the war it would ultimately be forced to fight. That is a bold statement, but the service just bought a fighter without a gun, designed to intercept Soviet cruise missile carrying bombers hundreds of miles from the carrier. It was called the F-4. Its pilots were told that "dogfighting" which is now known as "air combat maneuvering," was a thing of the past.

Embarrassing, well-publicized losses to North Vietnamese MiGs led to the creation of the Navy's Fighter Weapons School, a.k.a. Top Gun, and the kill ratio turned in our favor. Please note that the next three generations of fighters, the F-14, F/A-18 and soon to be deployed F-35 all have internal cannon, and air combat maneuvering is practiced every day in the fleet.

Down closer to the water, the Navy had ignored, if not forgotten, the painful lessons of the Korean War where early helicopters had proven their value by saving pilots that ditched near the carrier, as well as those who were downed on the Korean Peninsula.

The Navy *had* developed procedures and tactics, codified into doctrine, on supporting a vulnerable helicopter attempting to pick up a downed pilot over land. By the end of the Korean War these tactics were well known. Unfortunately, when the Navy arrived in the Tonkin Gulf off the coast of North Vietnam, they were long forgotten.

By the 1960s, overland search and rescue had become the responsibility of the Air Force. But the Air Force figured that it was going to be a long range bomber war and it too had to some extent forgotten what it learned about combat search and rescue in Korea. There's no glamour (and therefore little in the way of funding) in combat search and rescue because it happens only after you are shot down. To plan, fund, and carry out S&R missions, you have to first be willing to admit that rescues will be needed—an unthinkable admission!

Since the tactical aviation community ran Naval Aviation in those days, the majority of the money and focus went into the fixed wing squadrons of the carrier air wing. Combat search and rescue is a really big deal only if you're the one standing on the ground deep in Indian country look up into the sky searching for someone to come get you!

In the 1950s and 1960s, the Navy's helo community was a bastard stepchild of the Navy. Most of the money allocated to helicopters went into anti-submarine warfare which resulted in the H-3. Funds for development and evaluation of the equipment and tactics to support combat search and rescue were scarce. Helicopters are slow and noisy and, unlike jets, not very exciting. This made it harder to get Congressional backing for procurement unless the manufacturer or major systems manufacturers were located in the member's state. Funding for combat SAR evaporated because there was no perceived need—we weren't at war. Until Vietnam...

As late as 1969, I was issued a Mae West life jacket that was made in the1950s, when all our fixed wing brethren were using the new flotation system that was integrated into their survival vests! It wasn't until we were headed for Vietnam that we got the latest survival equipment. Even then, our vests had to be modified because they were designed to be used with g suits and torso harnesses connected to a parachute, neither of which we wore.

By the early 1960s, the carriers had plane guard helo detachments equipped with the turbine powered UH-2A/B. By then, all Navy helicopter anti-submarine or HS squadrons were flying the newly manufactured twin engine H-3 and for the most part, they flew off older carriers known as CVSs which concentrated on anti-submarine warfare.

While both helicopters were a major step up in performance and reliability from the piston engine helicopters they replaced, the UH-2A was, to be polite, an underpowered dog. Unless it was very cold, you couldn't hover at full mission weight and full fuel. So if you had to make a rescue right after you took off, you had to lighten the helicopter by dumping fuel so you could hover. Often, after you finished the pick-up, you didn't have the fuel to get home and had to stop land on a destroyer to get enough fuel to make it back to where you started.

Neither the H-2 nor the H-3 were designed for the missions we flew in South East Asia. They didn't have self-sealing fuel tanks, armor or defensive armament. In the H-3, if both the hydraulic systems were damaged, the helicopter was uncontrollable. If you were not dead when the hydraulic systems failed, you would be shortly.

The U.S. Navy needed a viable combat search and rescue capability so it mounted M-60s in the doors of SH-3As of the HS squadrons flying off carriers and ordered them to fly combat search and rescue. These squadrons did a very credible job using helicopters that weren't designed or really equipped for the mission. The lessons learned from their early rescue missions helped those of us who came along later.

Another interim solution was the upgraded HH-2B and then the HH-2C. The HH-2B was UH-2A with about 250 more horsepower, self-sealing tanks and seats, some armor around vital components and M-60s firing out the doors. The more powerful engine was a help, but it was still not enough. The HH-2B was still very underpowered.

The Navy told Kaman, the maker of the H-2, to convert forty A and B models to the twin-engine version that became the UH-2C and HH-2C. The second engine solved the power problem, external tanks on either side of the fuselage gave it about two-and-a-half hours of fuel and the HH version had armor, self-sealing tanks. Six of the Cs had a three-barreled mini-gun under the chin. The mini-gun was later removed because of the weight and space the ammo tray took up in an already small cabin. The HH-2C with the mini-gun is the helicopter flown by Josh Haman and Steve Higgins in the early part of this novel.

The Navy asked Sikorsky to provide a combat SAR version of the H-3, and twelve converted SH-3As re-designated HH-3As became the mainstay of the Navy's combat search and rescue operations in and around North and South Vietnam. In my first novel, BIG MOTHER 40, and in CHERUBS 2, this is the H-3 flown by the hero, Josh Haman.

I flew all of the H-2s described above except the HH-2B. Please note, if you go to my website—marcliebman.com—and click on the *From the HAC's Seat* box, you'll read about what it was really like to fly each one of these helicopters. I also cover some of the other issues we dealt with. I've got lots of flight time in almost all the models of the H-2 and H-3 flown by the Navy.

Organizationally, the Navy wasn't prepared for the war and the necessary combat search and rescue mission. In 1966, Helicopter Utility Squadron One or HU-1 was based in Atsugi, Japan. It provided helicopter detachments to ships in the Western Pacific. Its pilots and aircrew flew plane guard and logistics missions. They were neither trained nor equipped for the combat SAR role.

In 1967 the Navy realized it needed to revamp its helicopter squadrons on the West Coast. From its base in Atsugi, Japan, HU-1, which supported the entire Pacific Fleet, was split into five squadrons. HU-1 became Helicopter Combat Support Squadron One, or HC-1, and moved back to San Diego. Its mission was to deploy plane guard detachments to carriers based on the West Coast.

HC-3 and HC-5 were created to fly the new twin engine, twin rotor H-46s developed for the Marine Corps to move supplies back and forth between ships in a process called vertical replenishment. Helicopter Attack Squadron (Light) 3 or HAL-3 was created to provide helicopter gunships to Navy operations in the Mekong River delta. They flew ex-Army UH-1B Hueys outfitted with rockets and machine guns. The fifth squadron, HC-7, was created with the specific mission of providing a combat search and rescue capability to support the carriers operating on both Yankee and Dixie stations in the Gulf of Tonkin.

Headquarters of HC-7 remained in Atsugi, and a forward maintenance support detachment, known as DET 1, was set up at Naval Air Station Cubi Point in the Republic of the Philippines. This air station and the Subic Bay Naval Base functioned as staging areas for the Navy's operations in and around Vietnam. By ship, the Gulf of Tonkin was only two or three days away from Subic Bay. Once formed, HC-7 provided SAR support every day for over 2,800 days, which is seven years and nine months!

Det 110 from HC-7 provided a three-to-five helicopter detachment that operated from the carriers on Yankee and Dixie Stations. The detachment was on station continuously for 1,815 consecutive days. Crews and personnel were rotated from Cubi, but a core of qualified crews always remained on board a carrier with the helicopters. When the carrier headed back to Subic Bay or the States, then the det moved to another carrier on Yankee Station.

HC-7 was often tasked to provide a single plane detachment to helicopter-capable ships with helo decks large enough to handle the H-3. These were usually large destroyers that were later reclassified as cruisers.

By 1970, the U.S.S. *Oklahoma City (CG-5),* a World War II light cruiser converted to guided-missile shooter, took over as the North SAR ship. Its secondary mission was to provide radar surveillance and control of the strike formations coming from the carriers in the Gulf of Tonkin. It was usually about twenty-five miles southeast of the North Vietnamese port of Haiphong. The South SAR ship steamed closer to the coast between Quang Tri and Da Nang. These ships also provided naval gunfire support with their five-inch guns. The detachments on these North and South SAR ships usually had three-digit designators such as DET 103 or 104.

Early on, when HC-7 had a mix of HH-2Cs and HH-3As, the smaller HH-2Cs were sent to North and South SAR and DET 110 stayed on the carriers. However, as the war progressed, the HH-2Cs were phased out and the H-3s began to operate off the smaller decks, even though technically the ships weren't "certified" to handle them.

On some of the ships the H-3 like the *Sterett,* it was a very tight fit, with a rotor tip to a piece of the ship's steel structure of less than six feet. This made a night landing, or any landing when the ship was pitching and rolling, an exciting and mind-focusing experience.

When this novel takes place, HC-7 was still flying a mix of HH-2Cs and HH-3As. Even after several years of war, the Navy was still re-learning lessons about combat search and rescue and special operations.

Call signs for squadrons, air wings, carriers and other ships in the Tonkin Gulf at the time CHERUBS 2 takes place

During the time CHERUBS 2 takes place, the following ships, carriers and squadrons of their embarked air wings were deployed in the Gulf of Tonkin. The "modex" series are the letters seen on the tail of Navy aircraft along with the side number. At the time this book takes place, the typical carrier air wing on a larger deck, i.e. on a *Forrestal* or *Kitty Hawk* class carrier, had between seventy and seventy-five aircraft during a deployment made up of:

- Two 12 plane F-4 squadrons of fighters
- Two 12 plane A-7 squadrons of light attack aircraft
- One 12 plane A-6 squadron of medium attack aircraft
- A four or five plane photo reconnaissance squadron flying RA-5Cs;
- A four or five plane airborne early warning and control squadron flying E-2s;
- A detachment of two or three KA-3s to fly as tankers; and
- A three or four helicopter detachment for plane guard and logistics, flying either single engine H-2As or twin-engine H-2s

Naval aviation was in a period of transition, with the older *Midway* class carriers nearing the end of their careers, to be replaced by carriers from the *Forrestal* and *Kitty Hawk* classes. The *Ranger* is a *Forrestal* class carrier while the *America* is a member of the *Kitty Hawk* class. The first nuclear powered carrier, the *Enterprise,* was already making combat cruises.

Newer aircraft—F-4s, A-6s, A7s and E-2s—were replacing older aircraft in the inventory. On board the older *Midway*-class carriers, such as the *Oriskany*, the air wings were of similar composition but their squadrons usually flew F-8s instead of F-4s, A-4s instead of A-7s, and E-1s instead of E-2s. The actual mix of old and new depended on where the squadron and air wing was in its deployment cycle and how fast new airplanes could be provided. What follows are the actual squadrons, aircraft and call signs of the squadrons deployed to the Gulf of Tonkin when CHERUBS 2 takes place.

Ship or Squadron	Call Sign	Aircraft	Mission	Typical Number Assigned	Modex Series
U.S.S. Oriskany (CV-34)	Sea Lord				
Carrier Air Wing 19				62	NM
VF-191	Hell Cat	F-8J	Fighter	12	NM 100 series
VF-194	Red Flash	F-8J	Fighter	12	NM 200 series
VA-153	Power House	A-7A	Attack	12	NM 300 series
VA 155	Saddleback	A-7B	Attack	12	NM 400 series
VFP-63 Det 34	Corktip	RF-8G	Photo reconnaissance	4	NM 600—609 series
VAQ-130 Det 1	Gun Powder	EKA-3B	Electronic Warfare/Tanker	3	NM 610—615 series
VAW-111 Det 34	Hunter	E-1B	Airborne Early Warning and Control	4	NM 01X series
HC-1 Det 34	Guardian	UH-2C	Plane guard, logistics	3	NM 00X series

Ship or Squadron	Call Sign	Aircraft	Mission	Typical Number Assigned	Modex Series
U.S.S. *America* (CV-66)	Courage				
Carrier Air Wing 9				75	NG Series
VF-96	Silver Kings	F-4J	Fighter/attack	12	NG 100 series
VF-92	Fighting Falcons a.k.a. Falcons	F-4J	Fighter/attack	12	NG 200 series
VA-146	Blue Diamonds	A-7E	Attack	12	NG 300 series
VA-147	Argonauts	A-7E	Attack	12	NG 400 series
VA-165	Boomers	A-6A/B	Attack	12	NG 500 series
RVAH-12	Speartip	RA-5C	Photo reconnaissance	4	NG 600—609 series
VAW 124	Bullseye Hammers a.k.a. Hammers	E-2A	Airborne Early Warning and Control	4	NG 700 series
VAQ-132	Scorpions	KA-3B/ EKA-3B	Electronic Warfare/Tanker	3	NG 610—615 series
VQ-1 Det 1	World Watchers	EA-3B	Electronic Warfare	1	PR XX series
HC-2 Det 66	Angel	UH-2C	Plane guard/ logistics	3	NG 00X Series

Ship or Squadron	Call Sign	Aircraft	Mission	Typical Number Assigned	Modex Series
U.S.S. *Ranger* (CV-61)	Gray Eagle				
VF-21	Sundown	F-4J	Fighter/ attack	12	NE 100 series
VF-154	City Desk	F-4J	Fighter/ attack	12	NE 200 series
VA-25	Canasta	A-7E	Attack	12	NE-300 series
VA-113	Battle Cry	A-7E	Attack	12	NE-400 series
VA-145	Electron	A-6A/C	Attack	12	NE-500 series
RVAH-1	Sunbird	RA-5C	Photo Reconnaissance	4	NE-600—605 series
VAQ-134	Garudas	EA-3B/ KA-3A	Electronic Warfare/ Tanker	3	NE-605— 610
VAW-111 Det 7	Sea Bat	E-1B	Airborne Early warning	4	NE-700 series
HC-1 Det 1	Angel	SH-3A	Plane Guard and Logistics	3	Two digits, no airwing tail number

Ship or Squadron	Call Sign	Aircraft	Mission	Typical Number Assigned	Modex Series
U.S.S. *Oklahoma City (CG-5)*	Fireball	H-2 series, H-3 series	Anti-aircraft warfare, naval gunfire support, command and control	Up to 2 in a detachment	
U.S.S. *Sterett (DLG-31)*	Battle Torch	H-2 series	Anti-aircraft warfare, naval gunfire support, command and control	1 in a detachment	
U.S.S. *Newport News (CA-135)*	Thunder	H-2 series, H-3 series	Anti-aircraft warfare, naval gunfire support, command and control	Up to 2 in a detachment	
Helicopter Combat Support Squadron 7	Clementine	HH-2A	Combat search and rescue/ logistics	Deployed in single plane detachments	XX
	Clementine	HH-2C	Combat search and rescue/ logistics	Deployed in single plane detach-ments	XX

	Big Mother	HH-3A	Combat search and rescue/ logistics	Deployed in a three or four helicopter detachment called Det 110 on to one of the carriers on Yankee Station in the Gulf of Tonkin	XX

What follows is a short history of the ships other than carriers that are mentioned in the book. The information is current for when *CHERUBS 2* takes place. Some of these ships were significantly upgraded in the '80s and '90s or as in the case of the *Newport News,* scrapped.

U.S.S. *Sterett* (DLG-31) – The *Sterett* was a *Belknap* class of what was known as DLGs, or "destroyer leaders, guided missile." They were built when the Navy was forbidden to use the term "cruiser" as a ship designation. In 1975, the *Sterett* and its six sister ships were reclassified as guided missile cruisers (CG). Designated CG-31, the *Sterett's* primary mission was air defense as well as conducting anti-surface warfare against enemy ships. The class had a large bow-mounted sonar to give it some anti-submarine warfare capability. All of the ships carried Harpoon anti-ship missiles as well as anti-submarine torpedoes. The ship, which displaced almost 8,000 tons, had a twin-armed missile launcher forward of the bridge and a five-inch gun mounted aft on the main deck. The ships of the class were unique in that the helo deck and hangar were located on the "01 level", which meant the landing area was on first deck above the main, or "0 level." The *Sterett* was commissioned in 1966 and de-commissioned in 1994.

U.S.S. *Newport News* (CA-148) – Laid down in 1945 and finished in 1948, the *Des Moines*-class heavy cruiser had nine eight-inch guns as her main armament and a secondary battery of 12 five-inch guns. The *Newport News* was the last heavy cruiser built for the U.S. Navy. It was a 21,000-ton ship that could reach a maximum speed of 30+ knots. She made several cruises to the Gulf of Tonkin, where she fired her eight-inch and five-inch guns to support U.S. forces. Along with the U.S.S. *Providence (CLG-6) and the* U.S.S. *Oklahoma City (CLG-5),* the U.S.S. *Newport News* bombarded Haiphong Harbor in May, 1972, which is the last time U.S. Navy ships were employed in this type mission until Desert Storm. The *Newport News* was decommissioned in 1975.

U.S.S. *Oklahoma City (CLG-5)* – The *Oklahoma City (CL-91)* was one of 27 *Cleveland*-class light cruisers built for the U.S. Navy during and right after World War II. Its original main armament was 12 six-inch guns in four turrets, two forward and two aft, and had a secondary battery of a total of 12 five-inch guns in three dual gun turrets on each side. Originally, the ship was designed to provide shore bombardment and anti-aircraft defense for the carriers. The *Oklahoma City* originally displaced 11,800 tons when it was completed and commissioned in 1944. It was one of the six *Cleveland*-class cruisers selected for a major refit and conversion that removed three of the four six-inch turrets and replaced them with a missile launcher and its magazine where the aft turrets were located. Displacement dropped to around 10,000 tons. In 1960, the ship was re-commissioned as a guided missile cruiser CG-5 and designated as a member of the *Galveston* class. In 1972, the *Oklahoma City* became the first U.S. Navy ship to shoot down an enemy aircraft with a missile when it destroyed a North Vietnamese MiG-17. The cruiser served as the Seventh Fleet flagship until just before it was decommissioned in 1979.

U.S.S. *Dubuque (LPD-8)* – The initials stand for Landing Platform Dock. These ships were unique in that they had a large helicopter deck designed to allow two H-53s to land at the same time with room to spare. Forward of the two helicopter spots was a small hangar. Beneath the helo deck was a large well deck where amphibious tractors could be carried and then launched when it was flooded. The *Dubuque* was commissioned in 1967 and was the eighth of the twelve ships of the *Austin*-class of LPDs. It was decommissioned in 2011. It had a crew of about 420 officers and men and could carry approximately 900 Marines as well as all of their equipment.

GLOSSARY

1MC: The acronym stands for "First (or one) Main Communication" system. This provides a means of transmitting general information and orders to all internal ship spaces and topside areas and is loud enough that all embarked personnel are able to (normally) hear it. It is used to put out general information to the ship's crew on a regular basis each day

2P: Stands for 'second pilot' which on a helicopter is another way to say co-pilot.

AN-12: The AN-12 is a four engine, tactical military transport that was also flown in the Aeroflot, the Soviet national airline colors. It is very similar in size and shape to the U.S. C-130 and became operational in 1959. It could carry a 20,000-pound payload over 2,000 miles at 300-plus knots. Over 1,200 were built and many are still in service around the world.

Airdales: Navy slang for the aviation community, i.e. those who fly and support aircraft.

BEQ: Bachelor Enlisted Quarters a.k.a. "the barracks."

B-4 Bag: It was a folding bag issued to members of the U.S. Army to hold one full issue of clothing. Its unique design helped minimize wrinkling as well as enabling the bag to be its own self-contained "closet" when hung. From personal experience, it is easy to pack a B-4 bag with so much stuff that it is bulky and very heavy, almost too heavy to carry.

Bitt: A vertical post, usually one of a pair, set on the deck of a ship and used to secure ropes or cables.

Blackshoe: Navy slang for the surface warfare community, i.e. the ship drivers.

Buster: Term used by Naval Aviators to fly as fast as the plane or helicopter will go.

BOQ: Bachelor Officer Quarters a.k.a. "the Q."

Chokers: Navy slang term for "Service Dress White" which for officers and chiefs meant the white uniform blouse that fit tightly around the neck. In the days before stay press fabrics, the "choker whites" were highly starched and uncomfortable to wear until the starch broke down.

CIC: Combat Information Center. It is the nerve center of the ship where all the information from the ship's sensors is displayed and its weapons fired. In older ships like the *Sterett* during the Vietnam War, the information from all the sensors was plotted manually on a board and the CIC watch officer had to synthesize and build a picture of the "world" around the ship in his head. Today, technology has automated the process and provided displays that give the watch officer a clearer picture of what is happening.

CINCPAC: *(the acronym is pronounced as "sink-pack).* The acronym stands for Commander-in-Chief, Pacific and is the four-star admiral in who has operational control of units deployed in an area that ranges from the east coast of Africa to the mid-Pacific.

CINCPACFLT: *(the acronym is pronounced as "sink-pack-fleet").* The acronym stands for the Commander-in-Chief, Pacific Fleet who reports to the Commander, Pacific Command, a.k.a. by the acronym CINCPAC. All Navy units in the Pacific area of operations report to CINCPACFLT for administrative purposes when not assigned to other operational commands, such as Seventh Fleet.

COMMAACV: *(the acronym is pronounced "com-mac-vee).* The acronym stands for Commander, Military Assistance and Advisory

Command, Vietnam. All Air Force, Army, Marine Corps, Navy and allied units operating in Vietnam reported to this individual.

CTF-77: Commander, Task Force 77. Term is used to refer to the individual by his title rather than his name. During the Vietnam War, CTF 77 was the designation for the unit in command of the carriers and supporting ships in the Gulf of Tonkin.

Dieter Dengler: Lieutenant (junior grade) Dengler was a U.S. Navy A-1 Skyraider pilot and a member of VA-145 on board the U.S.S. *Ranger* when he was shot down over the Miu Gia Pass in Laos on February 1st, 1966. He was captured the next day by the Pathet Lao. After being beaten and tortured, he escaped on June 29th, 1966. Dengler spent 23 days in the jungle before he was able to signal an Air Force plane which helped get him picked him up. During the ordeal, he'd lost almost eighty pounds.

ECMO: (*pronounced Eck-Mo*) Stands for electronic countermeasures officer.

Ex-pats: Ex-patriates. Slang term used to describe businessmen and women who are given long-term assignments in a foreign country.

Feet Dry: Term used by Naval Aviators to describe flying from over the water to over land. It is the opposite of "feet wet."

Feet Wet: Term used by Naval Aviators to describe flying from over land to flying over land. It is the opposite of "feet dry."

Great Patriotic War: The Soviet Union's official name for World War II.

Ground Controlled Approach (GCA): An approach in which a ground controller guides the pilot of an aircraft using radar images that show the plane in relation to a glide path and left or right of the centerline of the runway. The GCA was used to guide planes down to runways when the ceilings were 200 feet over the ground and the visibility one-half mile. In most countries, the GCA has been replaced by more modern systems such as ILS, MLS and GPS in which the controller is not needed.

GRU: GRU or Glavnoye Razvedyvatel'noye Upravleniye is the foreign military intelligence main directorate of the Soviet Army General Staff of the Soviet Union. It was the Soviet Union's largest foreign intelligence agency and, like the KGB, is divided into a series of directorates. The Second Directorate is responsible for collecting intelligence from foreign countries and its primary target is the U.S. The Third Directorate concentrates on Asia. The GRU also has a Fleet Intelligence section that tracks naval activities around the world with the primary focus on the location of U.S. carriers and submarines. All information collected is processed under the Chief of Information who has 12 sub-directorates. One of them is the Ninth Directorate that is charged with exploiting technology captured or acquired by the GRU. The GRU, like the KGB, has its own "private" army which in this case are the Spetznaz troops whose rigorous training gives them similar capabilities of the U.S. Green Berets, Navy SEALs and Marine Recon units.

Fox Mike: Radio terminology for FM radios that operated on frequencies between the 60—90 MHz. In Vietnam, the U.S. and allied forces used FM radios for voice communications that operated just below the FM radio bands familiar to most Americans.

HAL-3: Helicopter Light Attack Squadron 3. This was a unique squadron formed during the Vietnam War to provide close air support of Navy SEAL and maritime interdiction operations in the Mekong Delta. They flew surplus UH-1B Hueys that were converted to gunships and carried 2.75 millimeter rockets and 7.62 millimeter machine guns. HAL-3 detachments operated off old World War II vintage LSTs (landing ship tanks) as well as air bases. It was formed in 1966 when HC-1 was broken up into five squadrons: HC-1, HC-3, HC-5, HC-7 and HAL-3.

IFF: Identification, Friend of Foe. Equipment allows radar operators to determine which aircraft are "friendly" and which ones are not.

JEST: Stands for Jungle Escape Survival Training. The course started with a day of classroom training and then migrated to a captive camp in which the students were taught techniques for surviving in the jungle. Then attendees spent several days being chased by Filipinos and Americans trying to evade capture enroute to a mythical evasion/rescue point. If you made it there without being captured, you got something to drink and eat before being tossed into a "simulated" PoW camp in which all the guards were dressed in either North Vietnamese or Soviet military uniforms. There one was treated as one would be if captured by the North Vietnamese or one of its allies. It took only one rifle butt smashed into your side to convince you that the next few days would be spent in a very realistic PoW camp where the guards employed many of the interrogation techniques used by the North Vietnamese.

Lima Sites: These were a series of bases throughout Laos served by both the U.S. Air Force and Air America. The sites, designated LS followed by a number, ranged from helipads scratched out of the jungle to bases with hard-packed dirt called laterite that were 4,500 feet long. The bases were used to supply those fighting both the North Vietnamese and the Pathet Lao as well as to support Air Force combat search and rescue and CIA special operations missions.

LSE: Landing Signal Enlisted. This person is a sailor who has been taught how to guide a helicopter onto a flight deck. Usually it is a member of the ship's helicopter detachment or squadron but on those ships where no helicopters are assigned, members of the ship's company are trained in the techniques and signals.

LZ: Landing Zone

Modex Numbers: A modex is a three-digit number used for United States Navy and United States Marine Corps aircraft. The first digit indicates the squadron within the carrier air wing and the next two are the aircraft number. During the Vietnam War, fighter squadrons are 1XX and 2XX and light attack squadrons are 3XX and 4XX. 5XX was used to designate the attack squadrons flying the A-6. The photo-reconnaissance airplanes were usually 6XX while the airborne early warning squadrons use the 7XX series numbers. The system has been modified since the A-6s and F-14s have been retired. Now, the fighter/attack squadrons flying version of the F/A-18 are usually the 1XX through the 4XX series. Normally, the commanding officer's plane (which he or she may or may not fly on a regular basis) is the aircraft with X00 and the executive officer's is X01.

NATOPS: (*the acronym is pronounced Nay-tops*) The Naval Air Training and Operating Procedures Standardization program prescribes general flight and operating instructions and procedures applicable to the operation of all U.S. naval aircraft and related activities. This also includes instrument flying where separate annual check rides are also given to each aviator. In addition, there are check rides for qualifications such as flight leader and helicopter aircraft commander and tactics. Open and closed book as well as oral exams are all part of the NATOPS check. In the '70s, the check rides were given in the aircraft, versus today, where they are often administered in a simulator.

OV-10: The North American Rockwell OV-10 Bronco is a two seat, turboprop light attack and observation aircraft. Besides the U.S. Air Force, Marine Corps and Navy, the airplane is/was flown by six other countries. It was developed in the 1960s as a special aircraft for counter-insurgency (COIN) combat, and one of its primary missions was as a forward air control aircraft. It carried four M-60s mounted in the stub wings beneath the fuselage and a mix of bombs, rockets and/or an external fuel tank on the three ordnance stations beneath the belly. Each wing also had an additional ordnance station. The A model was upgraded to a D which had more power and other modifications. Both airplanes could fly for about three hours.

Parachute Bag: Large olive drab bag originally designed to carry a backpack parachute as well as other gear a pilot carries. The heavy canvas bag is very sturdy and most people can pack it with so much stuff that is very heavy to lift. The author's is now used to carry a family's ski boots and other paraphernalia that one takes on ski trips and it swallows them with ease.

Pad Eyes: Indentations in the deck that were about two inches deep and eight inches across that had welded bars across them that you could easily grab with the hook at the end of the tie-down chain. The bars also prevented one's boot from getting stuck in the pad eye.

Pigeons: Term used by Naval Aviators that refers to the bearing and distance from the airplane's or helicopter's present position to a destination.

Plankowner: Term used by the U.S. Navy to describe a member of a unit when it was first commissioned.

PRC-90: Officially known as the AN/PRC-90, the small hand-held operated on two international distress frequencies, 121.5 in the VHF frequency band, 243.0 in the UHF bad and on the "standard" U.S. search and rescue UHF frequency of 282.8 MHz AM. The PRC-90 also included a beacon mode and a tone generator to allow the sending of Morse Code which could be under ideal conditions picked up 60 nautical miles away by an airplane at 10,000 feet or higher. The tone signal could be picked up at 80 miles at 10,000 feet.

R&R: Rest and recreation. Members of the U.S. Armed Forces in country were authorized a one-week trip to Hawaii or other destinations in the Western Pacific. The U.S. government paid for the flight and hotel expenses. The most popular destinations were Honolulu, Hawaii; Sydney, Australia; Hong Kong and Singapore.

ROE: Rules of engagement

RA-5C Vigilante: The RA-5 was originally designed as a supersonic replacement of the A-3 to deliver nuclear bombs. However, with the increased deployment of submarine ballistic missiles, the mission of the aircraft was changed to photo-reconnaissance. The twin- engine airplane was fast and, for its size, very maneuverable although it was a challenge to get it aboard the carrier. Its design included many firsts such as the first fly-by-wire system, the first head-up display coupled to a navigation and attack system and other innovations. All of which made it a complex aircraft that was difficult to maintain. The RA-5Cs, which were beautiful airplanes, were all retired in 1980, almost a decade before the A-3s were sent to the boneyard in the early 1990s.

Sous-lieutenant: French equivalent to a second lieutenant in the U.S. Air Force, Army or Marines and an ensign in the U.S. Navy.

SPLASH Publication: Stood for Shipboard Platforms for Landing and Servicing Helicopters. The pages of the kneeboard-sized book had depictions of the helo decks of all non-aviation ships, i.e. those that were not a carrier. It contained useful information on the layout of the deck, obstacles, navigation information, lighting and its four letter call sign. The *Sterett*'s page from a 1970 version of the publication is shown earlier in the book.

Spooky: Call sign for an AC-47 gunship that are also known as "Puff, the Magic Dragon." The U.S. Air Force converted 53 C-47Ds, which were originally built during World War II, into a gunship that had three 7.62 millimeter mini-guns firing out the port side of the fuselage. Each weapon could be selected to fire either 50 or 100 rounds-per-second. The aircraft flew in a left-hand orbit at 120 knots air speed at an altitude of 3,000 feet. When it opened fire, the AC-47 could put a bullet into every square yard of a football field-sized target in potentially less than ten seconds. It also carried 45 flares and 24,000 rounds of ammunition and, depending on how far the target was from its base and it ammunition landed, it could stay over the target for a long time. The Colombian Air Force is still using these planes!

SR-71: Known as the blackbird, the SR-71 was a Mach 3+ strategic reconnaissance aircraft developed by the Lockheed "Skunk Works" headed at the time by Kelly Johnson. It officially joined the Air Force in 1964 and continued flying until 1998. Thirty-two were built and 12 lost in accidents but none were ever shot down. It relied on high speed and altitude to out run missiles or airplanes. Its design made it one of the first stealthy airplanes. At high speeds, the airplane literally expanded several inches in length as the titanium skin and structure heated up. Lockheed developed a special few that would not vaporize at high altitudes or temperatures.

Stokes Litter: The Navy's version has a metal wire frame to make it easy to carry through a narrow ship passageway, up and down the ship's ladders or be hoisted up to a hovering helicopter. Some versions can be disassembled to make it easier to transport. The litter gets its name from its designer, Charles Francis Stokes. Stokes litters are notorious for spinning in a helicopter's downdraft so when they are hoisted, the Navy keeps it from spinning by having someone on the ground stabilize it with a rope.

TACAN: Stands for Tactical Air Navigation and provides the pilot both azimuth and distance (in slant range) to a ground station. It can be operated in any one of three modes—T/A provides bearing and distance; REC gives the pilot only bearing information; and A/A provides distance information between aircraft on the same frequency. Post-Vietnam versions provide bearing, distance and closure rates in the A/A mode.

TACAN Approach: These approaches take advantage of the system's ability to provide both distance and bearing to or from a ground station. In the approach, the pilot starts at an initial point and flies an arc at a specified distance from the ground station until he intercepts the final approach radial. At that time, he/she intercepts the radial and descends to designated altitudes at specific distances from the runway until he/she either breaks out beneath the cloud deck and sees the runway or waves off the approach.

TAD: Temporary Additional Duty. Also known as TDY in the Air Force which stands for "Temporary Duty."

Talos: The Talos was one of the earliest long-range naval surface-to-air missiles deployed on U.S. Navy ships. It used radar beam riding for guidance to the vicinity of its target, and semi active radar homing (SARH) for terminal guidance. The four antenna array on the missile's nose are the missile's receivers. Thrust for the missile was provided by a solid rocket booster for initial launch and a ramjet for flight to target with the warhead doubling as the ramjet's compressor. Due to its large size and dual radar antenna system, there were few ships that could accommodate the large, 30-four foot long, three-and-a-half ton missiles and their supporting radars. The *Oklahoma City,* one of the three *Galveston-* class light cruisers to carry the missile, had 14 that could feed the launcher and 30 more un-assembled in a separate magazine. Three MiGs were also shot down by the missile that had an effective range of about 50 nautical miles. Later anti-radar versions were deployed and used to attack North Vietnamese radar sites.

Tactical Pilotage Charts: Known as TPC charts, the scale was 1:500,000 and they had gridlines every 100,000 yards and tic marks every 10,000 yards along with latitude and longitude. The detailed contour lines, outlines of cities, roads, locations of towers and other geographic data made them ideal for planning and plotting low altitude routes. At the time this novel takes place, the government had just begun updating them using satellite imagery which made them even more helpful. They were large, i.e. roughly three feet by four feet and often had to be cut-up and taped together to plot a route that covered more than one chart.

"Toasted O": Nickname for the *U.S.S. Oriskany* after the 1966 fire. Many carriers and other Navy ships have been given nicknames, some complimentary, some not. The nicknames often changed as the ships got older or after some event. Here are some others for carriers known to the author:

U.S.S. Franklin D. Roosevelt (CV-42), a.k.a. the "Foul, Dank and Rusty"

U.S.S. Shangri-La (CV-38), a.k.a. the "Shitty Shang"

U.S.S. Blue Ridge (LCC-18), a.k.a. the "Blue Maru"

U.S.S. Constellation (CV-64), a.k.a. "Constipation"

U.S.S. Kitty Hawk (CV-63), a.k.a. "the Shitty Kitty"

U.S.S. Forrestal (CV-59), a.k.a. the "Forrest Fire"

U.S.S. Independence (CV-62), a.k.a. "Windy Indy"

U.S.S. Intrepid (CV-11), a.k.a. "Decrepit"

U-2: This airplane was the first high altitude reconnaissance aircraft developed by the Lockheed Skunk Works. It flew at 70,000+ feet and began flying missions in 1955. Variants of the original design and the TR-2 are still flying today on both photographic and electronic reconnaissance missions. Essentially, the U-2 and its derivatives is a high altitude, jet powered glider.

UCMJ: The letters stand for the Uniform Code of Military Justice and the code applies to all members of the U.S. Armed Forces who are on active duty and Reservists when they are drilling on weekends or anytime they are on active duty. Members of the Coast Guard when operating in a military capacity as part of the Navy also fall under the UCMJ.

Its beginnings go back to June 30, 1775, when the Second Continental Congress established 69 Articles of War to govern the conduct of the Continental Army and Navy and Article I, Section 8 of the United States Constitution provided that Congress has the power to regulate the land and naval forces. On April 10th, 1806, Congress expanded the original 69 Articles of War to 101. They were revised in 1916 and again after World War I in 1920.

A major reform to the Articles of War came in 1948 which led to the UCMJ as we know it today. The Navy's version was known as Rocks and Shoals and had its own articles that applied just to naval operations and was not substantially updated since its enactment. On May 31, 1951, the UCMJ went into effect for all branches of the U.S. Military and replaced the Articles of War and Rocks and Shoals.

The sections of the UCMJ articles referenced in the book are provided verbatim below:

Article 90—Assaulting or willfully disobeying superior commissioned officer

> (2) willfully disobeys a lawful command of his superior commissioned officer; shall be punished, if the offense is committed in time of war, by death or such other punishment as a court-martial may direct, and if the offense is committed at any other time, by such punishment, other than death, as a

court-martial may direct.

Article 94—Mutiny or Sedition

Any person subject to this chapter who with intent to usurp or override lawful military authority, refuses in concert with any other person, to obey orders or otherwise do his duty or creates any violence or disturbance is guilty of mutiny;

> (1) with intent to cause the overthrow or destruction of lawful civil authority, creates, in concert with any other person, revolt, violence, or other disturbance against that authority is guilty of sedition;

> (2) fails to do his utmost to prevent and suppress a mutiny or sedition being committed in his presence, or fails to take all reasonable means to inform his superior commissioned officer or commanding officer of a mutiny or sedition which he knows or has reason to believe is taking place, is guilty of a failure to suppress or report a mutiny or sedition.

> (3) A person who is found guilty of attempted mutiny, mutiny, sedition, or failure to suppress or report a mutiny or sedition shall be punished by death or such other punishment as a court-martial may direct."

Article 97—Unlawful detention

Any person subject to this chapter who, except as provided by law, apprehends, arrests, or confines any person shall be punished as a court-martial may direct.

> (1)That the accused apprehended, arrested, or confined a certain person; and

> (2)That the accused unlawfully exercised the accused's authority to do so.

Westpac: Slang and acronym for Western Pacific. At the time CHERUBS 2 takes place, it is a general reference to ships and aircraft operating in and around Vietnam and the Philippines.

**For the Finest in
Nautical and Historical
Fiction and Nonfiction**

WWW.FIRESHIPPRESS.COM

All Fireship Press books are now available directly through
www.FireshipPress.com, amazon.com and via leading bookstores and
wholesalers in the United States, Canada and the UK

Interesting • Informative • Authoritative

CPSIA information can be obtained at www.ICGtesting.com
Printed in the USA
BVOW06s1202030116

431634BV00003B/134/P